SHINING CITY

ANNE FOX

Star on the
Mountain
Books

Shining City: Book 16 of The Unit Series
COPYRIGHT © 2020 Anne Fox

First edition 2020
Printed in the United States of America
10 9 8 7 6 5 4 3 2 1

ISBN
978-1-950389-35-3 (ebook)
978-1-950389-36-0 (print)

Cover design by Momir Borocki
Cover images: Sue Critz, Shutterstock
THE UNIT logo by Michael Critz

OTHER BOOKS IN THE UNIT SERIES

ERROR 403 - FORBIDDEN (Book 18 of *The Unit* series) 2021
Hunted (Book 19 of *The Unit* series) 2021
Mirror, Mirror (Book 20 of *The Unit* series) 2021
Gridlocked (Book 21 of *The Unit* series) coming soon

AUTHORS NOTE

Shining City deals with a very controversial topic: extremist groups and their radical beliefs. As such, you will encounter in this book disturbing language that may be seen as racist, sexist, homophobic, and prejudicial in the extreme.

In no way should you construe that this language and the portrayal of the extremist group central to the book's plot reflects my personal feelings and beliefs. In fact, the beliefs portrayed for the extremist group are about as far from my own as they can get. The language used is merely an attempt to be as realistic as possible in showing the extreme concepts which some actual extremist groups embrace.

If you find some areas of the book difficult to read, you may be assured that they were just as difficult for me to write. But they were written to make a point, as all of my writing has attempted to do, and the point is this: these groups exist within our society. Their expression of their beliefs has been ruled in many cases by the Supreme Court of the United States as being protected under the First

Amendment of the Constitution. It is therefore a tightrope walk for those in law enforcement to determine when some expression or action of an extremist group has crossed the line from freedom of expression and into criminal activity.

Congress shall make no law respecting an establishment of religion, or prohibiting the free exercise thereof; or abridging the freedom of speech, or of the press; or the right of the people peaceably to assemble, and to petition the Government for a redress of grievances.

– First Amendment to the Constitution of the United States of America

1

"It's a beautiful day in the neighborhood," Spud quipped as he took his seat in the conference room.

"It *was* ..." came the general grumble from the rest of the team.

"Oh, come now," Spud said. "We all had a *great* breakfast served up by our master chef, Mama Rose, and now the rest of you all get to relax and just listen to my morning intelligence briefing. No effort involved, and I see that Mama Rose has even provided a nice little pastry wrapped around a slice of apple to go with our coffee."

"N if guh, doo," Hank said through a mouthful.

"See? Hank approved."

"Since when is anything edible *not* Hank approved?" Voice asked.

"When it outruns her," Cloud snorted.

Hank raised an eyebrow, then held up her hand palm up, looking at it.

"Looks like one of these fingers is longer than the rest," she observed. "I think it's *this* one," she added, showing Cloud which finger she meant.

"Now that my wife has concluded her salutations to our former Army rotorhead, let me begin. First up, we have a report about how the FBI is apparently botching requests for wiretaps."

Hank was now supporting her head with her thumb under her chin and her fingers resting alongside her cheek. "How many wiretap requests did the inspector general review?"

"Twenty-five."

"And how many of them had problems?"

"Twenty-five."

"The more I keep hearing about my former bosses, the more I appreciate falling from a helicopter and ending up here," Hank moaned.

"And now you know why we watch the alphabet agencies," Spud said, "even the ones we work with."

"Stop to think that maybe they're botching things when they ask for us to come back them up?" Hank asked.

Spud give a thoughtful nod of his head. "Not a bad point, and I think from now on we should take a careful look at the requests and perhaps ask for more background information as well," he agreed.

"We are still seeing fallout from NovoRo. With the elections coming up, the country is collectively sitting on the edge of their seats wondering if the election outcome will result in some positive progress toward economic recovery, no matter who wins. With the collapse of so many small businesses, the job situation is still pretty bad, and lots of people are still out of work."

"Most people don't realize that fifty-five percent of the jobs in the U.S. are provided by small businesses," Cloud said. "And they were the hardest hit by NovoRo."

"Tacked onto that, the environmentalists are up in arms again, given the government's desire to roll back controls aimed at moderating climate change. The government is claiming this is necessary in order to get the economy back in gear," Spud said, reading another of his stories for the team to consider.

"The tea kettles have been simmering away," Crow noted. "It's going to take some very careful watching of the stove to not have one of them pop its lid."

"That's all I've got," Spud said, sitting.

"No You Can't Make This Shit Up?" Cloud asked, hopeful that Spud had simply overlooked his habit of ending the meeting on a more humorous note.

"I don't have one."

"Damn."

The team members began to rise from their seats.

"But I do," Hank said.

Spud smiled at her, knowing Hank had prepared for giving her own YJCMTSU story for the team that moment. The rest of the men grinned and happily regained their seats.

"This one," Hank began, "comes to you from the annals of the Taos, New Mexico PD, where I encountered a number of things that you just can't make up. This one involves a 911 call received one day by Dispatch."

"Hoax?" Edge asked.

"No, very real, and very disconcerting. It seems a little boy was on the line, hysterically screaming that his mommy was in trouble, screaming in her bedroom, and he couldn't get in to help her."

Edge started to snicker.

"What makes you think that's so funny?" Cloud asked indignantly.

"He's just *way, way* ahead of me," Hank interjected for Edge. "So, I'm close by. Hit lights and siren and off I go, hearing other units calling in to say they're responding as well. I get there just as one of the other guys on the shift arrives. The little boy is on the porch, bawling his eyes out. 'Mommy was screaming and screaming, and now she's stopped,' he blubbers out, 'and I can't find Daddy.' I'm thinking, 'Oh, God—someone raped and killed her.' So, I go running up the stairs to where the kid says his mom is locked in the bedroom. As I get to the door, I hear giggling coming from inside the room—"

"Bet you did!" Edge commented.

"So now, I'm not so sure we've got an emergency on our hands. But the other officer doesn't wait for any explanation from me. As he's getting ready to kick in the door, I shout, 'No!' But it's too late. His foot connects and the door goes flying inward."

Edge was now laughing and shaking his head.

"I take it you've already guessed what my jackass coworker got an eyeful of?" Hank asked him.

Still laughing, Edge nodded his head 'yes.'

The rest of the team had now also caught on and were starting to laugh themselves.

"And how profuse were the apologies from your fellow officer when he caught Mom and Dad butt naked making the little boy a brother or sister?" Crow asked.

"He just stood there staring while his face turned the most magnificent shade of magenta I've ever seen," Hank said. "A Taos sunset could not have generated a more glorious color. Then he turned and trotted down the stairs without saying a word. Mom and Dad took a look at me, like, 'Well?' I just averted my eyes, gave them a wave of my hand, and said, 'Carry on.' I also felt it necessary to go back down to the kid and tell him Mom and Dad were just fine— they were both upstairs in their bedroom.

"The kid asks me, 'What are they doing up there?'

"Am I going to explain the birds and the bees to a couple's little kid? *No, I am not!* So, I tell the kid they're playing a game to see how loud Mommy can scream, but I'd be happy to stay with him until they were done with their game. I take the kid to the back yard and swing him on a swing that's back there until Mom comes out all red-faced and thanks me for watching little Bobby while they ... finished playing their game."

The team members were now all laughing with tears running down their faces.

"When you and Spud settle down and have a kid, is that what you're going to tell him when you start getting loud?" Crow asked.

"Oh, shut up."

That got the men laughing even louder.

"That's it. You know the drill," Spud said. "Work on your skill sets, and rendezvous for lunch back in The Restaurant."

HANK AND VOICE decided to try their hands at the climbing wall in the gym as part of their practice of their skill sets. Both being the same height and close in weight to one another, they made a good pair for the exercise, with one climbing, the other on belay.

As they walked into the gym, they both stopped and stared at the wall.

"What the hell?"

"Oh, this is going to be *fun*," Voice asserted.

"Glad *you* think so," Hank said. "I personally think Edge is a fucking sadist."

Gazing up at the wall, Hank realized that Edge had

devised something a little more challenging for the Field Team members to attempt.

"You know, if we had a taller level, he could have really devised something outstanding. But, when you've only got fourteen feet, you just have to be a little more horizontal and a lot more difficult in the types of moves you have to use," Voice beamed. "We should put in a request to have Allen Chelon build us a really tall wall out at Lockridge."

"No we shouldn't."

"Sissy."

"You *like* this stuff?"

"I did quite a bit of indoor wall climbing during the time I worked for Thor. Great exercise, and you can do it year-round."

"So, how do we conquer this thing?"

"It's going to require some different sorts of moves," Voice explained. "Heel holds. Knee bars. Stuff like that."

"Why do I have the impression I'm going to be sore tomorrow?" Hank moaned.

"You've got a lot of leg strength," Voice said. "I don't think you'll have a problem. I might. It's been a while since I've climbed a wall set up like this one."

He stood back and gazed at the placement of holds that Edge had set out, making a mental note of how he wanted to approach the wall. The route seemed clear to him, but not easy.

"Wonder what the little arrow is at the very top," Hank observed, seeing a handhold with an arrow pointing to it at the top of the route.

"The final goal, I'm sure," Voice said.

"He didn't leave a belaying line."

"No need. We have the crash pads."

"What if I fall on my head?"

Voice looked at her. "Maybe you should practice some falls before you go for the entire route," he advised.

"I don't like this. Not at all."

Voice chuckled. "Isn't that supposed to be Spud's line?"

Hank gave him an annoyed look. "Well, I guess I won't conquer this thing by standing here complaining about it."

"Here's what you do, Hank. It'll help you build confidence that you won't die."

The annoyed look she gave him this time was substantially more annoyed-looking.

"Start up." Voice demonstrated by choosing some hand- and footholds, then standing against the wall.

"Now, just let yourself fall to the mats."

He let go and fell, landing on his feet, tucking himself, and allowing himself to roll across his side. "It's like a parachute fall."

"I've never done that either."

"Really? Man, you've lived one sheltered life."

"Yeah, all I ever did was run around trying to capture guys who might be trying to *shoot me*," Hank jabbed.

"Well ... maybe not so sheltered," Voice conceded.

Hank leveled a look at him and mimicked his example. Voice walked over and looked down at her. "Still alive?" he asked, smiling.

"Smart ass."

"Now go a little higher and do it again."

Hank continued to climb a little higher, then fall back to the mats until she got to a point where she was stymied about how to continue up the wall. Reaching, she couldn't grasp the next hold, and she didn't feel stable enough to leap the way Edge had taught her.

"None of this course is dynamic," Voice observed. "It's all static holds. No leaping required."

"How am I supposed to get from *there* to *there*?" Hank asked, emphatically pointing.

"Come on down, and I'll show you."

Hank executed her best fall and got back up on her feet while Voice commenced heading up the wall. When he got to the spot in question, he swung a heel into a depression in a hold to his left and hauled himself up until he could swing his left arm up to another hold while gripping a hold below and to its right with his right hand.

"See? You don't always climb using just your fingers and toes to grip with." He pointed to another spot along the route and added, "Right there, you'll want to wedge your leg into that spot, with your foot against one side and your knee against the other."

"I wouldn't have guessed that you knew so much about climbing," Hank said as she climbed back up the wall herself and attempted the heel hold.

"It was one of the great things about working at Thor. They had all kinds of stuff like this for those of us who programmed to go and do right in the buildings on the campus. Management felt it helped our creativity, so they had a gym, a big climbing area, rollerblading paths where you could rollerblade or skateboard ... Quite an outfit."

"And you gave that up to come here."

Voice shrugged. "Like I've said before, I could program a game or I could do the real thing. Then program a game when I retire that will be unbelievably real. Besides, Thor never let me actually modify their mainframes."

"NOT OFTEN WE get a lesson from the old man," Voice commented as the team made their way back to the conference room after finishing lunch.

Spud resisted the urge to turn and at least give Voice a look. He was, however, considering using Voice as the "practice dummy" for the lesson he was about to give.

"Alright, everyone," he began after ensuring he'd get his share of the cookies Rose had left for the team in the center of the table. He munched on one appreciatively. "Oatmeal raisin."

"You know Mama Rose's secret, too ... right?" Cloud asked

"She's got some secret to oatmeal raisin cookies?"

"Yeah. They're practically fat-free."

Spud took a look at the remainder of the cookie in his hand that he'd bitten. "How does she make a fat-free cookie that tastes as good as this one?"

"Apple sauce. She uses apple sauce instead of shortening or butter. And because of that, she uses a little less sugar, too."

Spud rubbed his stomach. "So, that's how I get to eat all that good cooking and still have a nice six pack. Rose has a bunch of little tricks."

"Got a nice butt, too," Hank remarked, getting the rest of the men chuckling.

"Now that my wife has gone into the 'too much information' department, let's talk about a little different bit of anatomy. Because today, I've decided it might be a good idea for *everyone*—not just myself and our medic—to know how to treat a sucking chest wound in the field."

Edge slowly lowered the cookie he was about to take a bite of to his napkin on the table. "Thanks for the head up."

"You're welcome. Hal, first slide."

The conference room main monitor came to life, showing an anatomical view of a man's chest.

"The areas that we're interested in for today's lesson are these: the lungs and the tissues that enclose them, called the pleura. The pleura consists of two thin layers of connective tissue, with a space between then called the pleural cavity. Each lung and its associated pleura form a pulmonary cavity."

Spud was watching as some of the team members appeared to begin to glaze over.

"Yeah, it's not exciting stuff until you need to know your way around these structures because your buddy is on the ground with a chest wound," he prodded. The comment brought those who had slid into a somnambulant state back to full consciousness.

"Any defect in the lung and/or wall of the chest can lead to air being trapped inside the pleural cavity. This condition is what's called a pneumothorax. Pneumo- from Greek meaning 'lung', and thorax from both Greek and Latin meaning 'breastplate'. Given in anatomy the thorax is roughly the space enclosed by the ribs, sternum, and vertebrae, you can perhaps deduce how the Greeks decided on 'breastplate' to describe it.

"By the way, this is how I died."

The team was now awake, given most of them had never heard of how Spud came to be in the unit.

"Had an accident, broke a rib, punctured a lung, developed a pneumothorax that went on to become a tension pneumothorax, which in turn lead to cardiovascular collapse and my being loaded aboard a G550 for a trip to Quantico. I would not like that to happen to any of you, given you've already had one death to contend with. Unless there's something I don't know, your next death will be a bit more permanent. Which is why I chose to do this lesson."

His statement was met by nervous laughter.

"Where were you that they couldn't get you to a hospital in time?" Cloud asked.

"The middle of Nowhere, Afghanistan."

"I thought you were in PPD."

"I was. The president wanted to visit the troops in Afghanistan, and I was on the advance with a team of CAT guys scoping out the area the president wanted to go."

A sudden recognition of just which president Spud was talking about was evident among the team members, with only Hank not showing any surprise, having heard the whole story.

"But back to this. Today I want to talk about a specific kind of pneumothorax, and that's what I mentioned right at the beginning: sucking chest wounds."

"Seen a few," Edge remarked. "Not pretty."

"No, they're not. A sucking chest wound is where something punctures a large enough hold through the chest wall to allow air to be sucking into the chest when you inhale, and blown out of your chest via the hole in it when you exhale. The hole basically defeats the way you get air into your lungs, and the air within the chest cavity can cause the lung that's affected to collapse. As you might guess, this can result in rapid breathing and heart rate, and for some, pain when trying to breathe. Also, it's not unusual to see blood bubbling around the wound.

"So, why should we worry about this?"

"Got no idea," Hank said, drawing her handgun and placing it on the table.

"Me, neither," Edge added, drawing his knife and doing the same.

"Exactly. Our bad guys out there like knives and guns, and they're not afraid of using them. Even something like an explosion could create a pneumothorax if debris hits you hard enough in the right place. Could have been one of Nordby's bombs, or Kathryn Hamburg's bullets, Joe Cornett's scalpel, Edwards's bullets ... We've been exposed to a number of missions everyone here knows about, as well as quite a few more in the past where the possibility of a chest wound was rather high. It will pay for us if the first person who can get to the one with the chest wound knows how to handle it in this scenario."

Spud looked directly at Voice and beckoned with his finger to get Voice to come to him.

"Whatcha need, Spud?" Voice asked as he came forward.

"I need a dummy to demonstrate on."

The rest of the team tittered.

"Gee, thanks for the compliment," Voice groused. "Why do *I* get to be the dummy?"

"Because only a dummy would call me an old man." Spud leaned forward as if he was leaning on a cane and trembled. Adopting the stereotypical old man voice, he added, "I might be feeble, but I ain't dead yet, and I ain't *deaf*, neither!"

Now the rest of the team was laughing while Voice's face adopted a bit more discomfort.

"You're not going to hurt me, are you?"

"Oh, heck no," Spud assured him. "Everything I do will be to save your life. Hop up here and lie down on the table so everyone can see you."

Voice gave Spud a wary look and complied with the request. Taking up what looked like the sort of refillable ketchup bottle seen in restaurants, Spud squirted something red on Voice's shirt. Voice craned his neck to look and see what it was.

"I'll save you the effort, buddy. It's fake blood," Spud informed him. "At which point, you shout out what?"

"I was peeking in their bedroom window and Spud shot me!" Voice declared.

"Oh. Well, under *that* scenario ..." Spud started to walk off. "You're on your own, asshole."

The rest of the team roared.

Returning, Spud said, "Aw, heck. I guess I'll save you anyway. If I don't, I won't be able to beat the crap out of you later.

"First thing you want to do is the usual preliminary assessments. Which are?"

"ABCDE," Crow recited. "Airway, breathing, circulation, disability, and exposure."

"Give the man a quarter."

"I should get five. I got all of them correct."

"Don't push it, or you'll be the next dummy I use.

"Once you've done your initial assessments, you're going to look for injuries, which is when you're sure to notice, if you haven't already, this nasty gunshot wound," Spud said, giving Voice's stained shirt a poke. "You know about this one —you're looking at it. So, this is what you use."

He grabbed a trauma kit and opened it up, extracting a flat pouch from it and opening it as well.

"One package of wound seals. Each package contains one that completely seals and another which is vented." He tore it open, then looked down at where Voice was lying on the table. Going back into the trauma kit, he came up with a pair of trauma scissors. When Voice saw them, he sat up abruptly.

"I'm not so far gone that I can't take off my shirt," he said, yanking it off and tossing it on the floor.

The others couldn't detect it, but Hank noted the almost imperceptible twinkle in Spud's eye. *Don't mess with the old man,* she thought. *What's that about age and treachery triumphing over youth and vigor?*

Once Voice had lain back down, Spud once again grabbed the squeeze bottle and put a generous squirt of fake blood directly on Voice's chest. The material slowly coursed over to Voice's side and dribbled onto the table.

"Bleeding pretty bad there, son. So, this is what we do next. Take a piece of gauze, clean around the wound," Spud recited as he demonstrated, leaving a small patch of the goo where the fictitious bullet had entered Voice's chest. "Then, take the vented seal and place it over the wound with the hole in the vent aligned with the hole in the wound." Noting that Voice had a patch of chest hair around his nipple, Spud made sure to press the adhesive from the wound seal down well in that area.

"Now, we're going to log roll you and see if there's an exit wound." Doing so, he then gave Voice a manly slap sufficient to leave a red mark on his back. "Lucky you! No exit wound," he declared to Voice's simultaneous exclamation of *"Ow!"*

"This is looking pretty good, and we can think about getting our intrepid programmer back here to HQ where Doc Rich and her merry band of men and women can fish the bullet out of him. Unfortunately for our teammate, though, he's developing a tension pneumothorax."

Spud leaned over and looked Voice directly in the face.

"This one will kill ya, son. Trust me: I know this from first-hand experience."

The rest of the team was grinning, now realizing that not

only was Spud giving a lesson on how to treat sucking chest wounds but was also getting back at Voice for his earlier 'old man' remark.

"So, this is what we use next," Spud declared, taking a pen-like object from the trauma kit. "This little device is for doing a needle decompression of a tension pneumothorax before it results in cardiovascular collapse. This one is a little different than the ones I learned about in the Secret Service, but Doc Frank assures me that these have definite advantages."

He twisted the case open and extracted the device while watching Voice's eyes go wide.

"Is that a needle?" Voice asked, his voice trembling slightly.

"No, this is a ten-gauge cannula."

"Why does it look like it's a needle?"

"It has a needle *in* it, but you don't leave the needle in the patient."

Voice was now looking at Spud with apprehension as Spud continued. The rest of the team was watching with great attention, not only to learn how to use the thing, but also to catch Voice's reactions.

"We're going to take our needle—"

"I thought you said it wasn't a needle," Voice protested.

"We need to create a hole the cannula can pass through into the patient," Spud began, eyeing Voice and trying not to betray his amusement. "That's done with the needle, but the needle gets removed once the cannula is in place. We're going to take our needle," he began again, approaching Voice.

"No, we're not!" Voice practically squealed, jumping from the table. He stood looking wild-eyed at Spud.

"You're right—I need a different dummy."

Spud reached down and took a practice dummy from the floor. Placing it on the table, he proceeded to continue with his demonstration of how to insert the cannula to relieve a tension pneumothorax while Voice took a seat, watching him warily. When he regained confidence that Spud had used him for demonstration purposes as much as he had intended to, he settled in with the rest of the team to watch as Spud continued with his lesson.

As Spud finished up and dismissed everyone, Voice scooped up his shirt from the floor and prepared to leave with the other team members.

"Hold on a second there, Voice," Spud said, getting everyone turning to look in his direction.

Spud walked up and looked at the chest seal that was still glommed to Voice's chest. Reaching out, he grabbed a tab on the thing and gave it a yank.

"*OW!*" Voice looked down at the red welt on his chest, noticing that the area underneath where it had been affixed was now devoid of any chest hair. He looked up at Spud as if to make some remark, but then just turned to leave.

Seeing the bald spot on his chest, Edge quipped, "Looks like Spud got all the new hair you grew after discovering what women are good for."

Voice got an annoyed look and said, "Quit being crude." Yanking his shirt on, he passed through Honor Way on his way back to his residence to clean up the goop on his chest and change into a clean shirt before dinner, trotting down the stairs ahead of the rest of the team. As he stormed off to his residence, the others watched him go, smiles on each and every face.

"That was a really memorable lesson," Hank remarked.

Spud walked into the residence he shared with Hank. Knowing the most probable place he'd find her would be in the reading nook, he peeked around the corner. Sure enough, she was propped up with a book in her lap.

"What are you reading this time?"

"A novel."

Spud felt a wave of exasperation pass over him.

"A crime novel again?"

"Surprise! Answer is no," Hank declared.

"What's it about, then?"

"It's one of these apocalyptic, dystopian things."

Oh, Lord ... "May I ask why you're reading it?"

Hank sat up and set her book down on the coffee table.

"Do you remember when we were discussing what we each were keeping an eye on one day during intel? I've been watching this right-wing religious white supremacist group."

"Shining City."

"That's right—Shining City. You know what the reference is to, right?"

"It's biblical, isn't it? A reference to being a city on a hill."

"Right again. Well, part of the mindset of this group is that they believe the end is near, and that they need to prepare for the Second Coming. And part of that preparation is to establish a pure community—a shining city on a hill, that people will be attracted to."

"And this relates to this book how?"

"This book talks about what happens when the shit hits the fan. I'm hoping it will give me an insight into the kinds of people who would have this mindset."

Spud settled down slowly on the loveseat next to her.

"Is this just routine, or are you concerned about something?"

"I'm concerned that I'm not the only one watching this group. We've seen what happens when some agency gets over-zealous around these kinds of groups. You get a Ruby Ridge or a Waco. I'm not sure what the ATF thought was a realistic threat from the Weavers, but I know what I think about the way the FBI handled the situation at Ruby Ridge once the ATF got done screwing the pooch. And though I think David Koresh should certainly have been brought before the courts on charges of statutory rape, once again the ATF got a bit over-zealous and the FBI stepped in and got more so, resulting in the immolation of men, women, and children. I have to ask myself how we might handle a case similar to Ruby Ridge or Waco. We're not exactly unlike other elite policing units. Two of the Field Team are former military, and with the exception of Voice, the rest are from one federal alphabet agency or another. We practice and utilize tactics that are very similar to military tactics, and I get concerned that we might be getting too much of a military mindset."

"And so?"

"And so I want to know more about the groups we might encounter."

"There's certainly logic to that. But how are you supposed to ascertain that the group isn't truly a threat?" Spud asked.

"Get inside. Infiltrate."

Spud's face went straight to Secret Service neutral. "Been there, done that—more than once. And I'm not terribly anxious for a repeat performance, given how close I came to getting one of my own bullets in my head last time."

"Don't worry—I've got your back," Hank quipped.

"You did, and I'm forever grateful. But can't the danger of a group be determined by less direct means?"

"By?"

"Watching what they're purchasing," Spud proposed.

"Remember Nordby? Remember the book on explosives I read? How would any of the many stores he obtained ammonium nitrate from know that he was making bombs and not fertilizing his lawn? He apparently realized that if he bought a shitload of ammonium nitrate all at once that it would raise suspicions, so he spread out the purchases. The bad thing about that is that *we* might now have a mindset that says, 'That guy just purchased fifty pounds of ammonium nitrate, so he's going to make a bomb.' Maybe. But it's still much more likely that he's using it as fertilizer.

"Then there's the scenario of a group purchasing guns. Are they stockpiling weapons to enact some sort of mass killing? Or do they simply live off the land and everyone has a gun to hunt with? They might also be buying powders for reloading. So, do you say guns plus reloading equals sport shooting or terrorist activity? There also, remember that Kaczynski used reloading propellants to make his bombs. It turns out that for reloading, mixing powders is a bad, bad thing. But for making bombs, it works fabulously."

"You worry me sometimes."

"If you want to stop what a terrorist might do, you need to think about how the terrorist thinks and acts," Hank said in her own defense. "If I want to determine if this group is planning on committing some kind of terrorist act or if they're just a bit out in left field, then I need to research the kinds of mindsets people like them have. This guy," she continued, tapping on her book, "is a prepper. He's concerned about a nuclear war and the collapse of the economy and society. The way he's written the book, he's likely also networked with other preppers who share his concern. This group, Shining City, talks of maintaining autonomy and winning converts. Are they just building their community, or are they building an army to subvert the government? Are they also preppers, thinking the end is near and they have to be a holy community and prepared to survive? Do they see themselves as the meek who will inherit the Earth?"

s the team members started making their way to
The Restaurant for breakfast, they noticed Edge
returning the log for the log carry obstacle back
to its starting station. He was dressed in workout clothing,
and sweat dripped from his hair and streaked down his
shirt.

"I'll just be a few," he remarked before trotting off toward
his residence.

"He gets up early to run the obstacle course?" Cloud
asked incredulously.

"He's been saying he worries that Rose will make him a
chunky monkey," Spud related.

Cloud laughed heartily. "Edge? A chunky monkey? Is
there any portion of that man that's got an ounce of flab on
him?"

"There isn't, but I gather he doesn't want there to be,
either."

"I don't think that's anything he should worry about,"
Crow observed. "Of all of us, I'd wager he's probably the
most physically fit. No offense, brothers. And sister," he
quickly added with a nod to Hank before she could say
anything.

"I won't argue with you," Hank said. "I bet if someone

ever gave him a shot to the gut, he'd just stand there and laugh at the guy before pounding him to a pulp."

"You know, Edge is kind-of like you, Hank. He reserves force for times when it's truly necessary," Cloud said.

"Yeah, for being a big guy, he's pretty mild mannered," Crow agreed.

"It's his faith," Voice noted. "Vengeance is mine, saith the Lord."

"Sometimes God asks someone to enact his vengeance for him," Hank said, remembering what the pastor had told her after she'd shot Nordby.

Cloud looked at her appraisingly. "Didn't take you for being religious."

"I'm not. Just remembering what someone once told me."

The team members all grabbed coffee, Cloud filling both his and Edge's mug and setting Edge's down at an empty chair. Shortly afterward, the man himself strode in, his tall frame allowing him a lengthy stride, and went directly to the coffee pot.

"Where's my mug?" He sounded annoyed.

"All ready for you right here," Cloud replied, tapping the table next to Edge's cup of brew.

"Thanks, bro," Edge said, giving Cloud a clap on the back and prompting Cloud to spill some of his coffee before he sat. "Dang. Sorry," he added, noting the spilled coffee. Getting up, he grabbed a cleaning cloth and wiped the spill from in front of Cloud.

"Want me to top that off for ya, given I made you spill it?" he asked Cloud, holding out his hand for Cloud's mug.

"Nah. Not much spilled. But thanks. What I would like to know is how you got showered so fast."

"Did he shower?" Crow asked.

"Smells like soap and aftershave," Cloud confirmed.

"When you shower aboard ship, it's done quickly and with as little water as possible," Edge explained. "Ships don't carry fresh water, they make it. They can only make it just so fast. You'll actually have a guy outside the shower with a stopwatch to make sure you don't use more than your allotted share."

"What's your allotted share?" Amigo asked.

"Two minutes."

"*Two minutes?* I couldn't get my armpits washed in two minutes."

"I think maybe the lady here doesn't want to hear about your armpits over breakfast," Edge cautioned.

"There's a lady here?" Hank asked.

"I wasn't talking about you—I was talking about Rose," Edge poked, getting the men hooting.

Hank licked a finger and reached up to do an aerial chalking of one point for Edge. You can guess which finger she used.

"You know," Hank began, "I've been reading this book."

"Is there any time you're *not* reading a book?" Crow asked.

"I'm sorry if it bothers you that I like to stay better educated and informed than you do," Hank snipped. She continued with, "It's probably the worst written book I've ever read. I mean, the story is OK, but the author I don't think even bothered to edit the book himself. He's got entire words missing from sentences, and he consistently spells 'where' as 'w-e-r-e'."

"Why are you even still reading it then?" Voice asked.

"Because the guy is a prepper."

With the exception of Spud, who kept his Secret Service face in place, the rest of the team smirked.

"Have we gone from psychics to preppers now?" Crow asked.

Hank scowled. "It's a novel written by a prepper, and I'm reading it because I want to understand the mindset of these people."

"OK, so what's their mindset?" Cloud asked.

"They all see an overwhelming need to be prepared for some cataclysmic event, with most focusing on a single scenario."

"Like?"

"Like nuclear war, or a pandemic—"

"Bet they went nuts during NovoRo," Edge interrupted her, smiling.

"They probably did, though it would have only taken one member of an isolated group to get sick for all of the others to get sick," Hank returned. "I have to observe, though, that in a way, *we're* preppers."

"How do you figure that?" Voice asked, chuckling.

"Look around you, genius. We live in a facility that can be totally isolated from the outside world—even air-tight. We have a silo full of stored food. Not a little silo. A silo that's fifty feet in diameter and a hundred and seventy feet deep, with three levels devoted to a conference room and a huge mainframe computer, two more devoted to water treatment and electrical generation, one devoted to a closed ecological life support system for oxygen generation, and four more that are stocked with hydroponic growth chambers. Then we have an outlying underground facility for treating people with dangerous communicable diseases, another that's an ammunition storage facility, and yet another that's at least partially filled with stored food. Above ground, we're surrounded by a farm that gives us milk, meat, eggs, chicken, fish, and in case you didn't notice them yet, even a few goats and sheep. That's just the protein sources, because we've also got vegetables that get grown when it's not varying between fifty-four and twenty-three degrees at night the way it has been lately. And when the weather is like that, we have *two* two hundred by eight hundred foot walipinis to grow vegetables and fruit in, which doesn't count what we have down here in the residence level. If you ask me, we're the *ultimate* prepper group."

Everyone reflected on this for a beat.

"I guess you're right," Voice admitted.

"Nobody likes me. Everybody hates me. I'm gonna eat some worms," Spud sang.

"Said *what?*" Cloud asked.

"It's an old kid's song," Spud replied. Finishing the ditty, he sang, "Great big fat ones, little scrawny skinny ones, full of yellow goo."

"O—K," Cloud remarked.

"Does this mean no one will grumble about intel?" Spud asked.

"Not a chance," Crow replied, his head bobbing on his hand as he spoke, given he'd already settled in for the long haul.

Spud's eyes narrowed ever so slightly as he looked in Crow's direction.

"First up, we have an interesting reason the environmentalists are currently up in arms. They believe that global warming is responsible for the outbreaks of novel viruses and pandemics."

"Is there *anything* that the environmentalists don't

believe is caused by global warming, climate change, or whatever the heck it's being called these days?" Hank asked.

"You don't believe we should protect the planet?" Cloud asked.

"I believe in protecting the planet, but come on. Not everything is due to climate change. Besides, how many of those who are going nuts over climate change have planted a tree to help soak up all that CO_2 they believe is responsible?"

"Also related to the nation's recovery from NovoRo is continuing anger over the loss of jobs and what many consider to be the poor response by the government to help those who suddenly found themselves unemployed."

"Better unemployed than dead," Crow remarked.

"Dunno about that," Voice said. "Which is worse? Living in your car or dying? That is, if your car didn't get repo'ed because you couldn't make the payments."

"Which is part of the controversy. Many of those who found themselves out of work are now sharing space beneath overpasses with the weather getting colder as we head into winter," Spud said.

"What can the government do, though?" Cloud said. "The country hadn't paid off the debt incurred during the previous pandemic before this one hit. You can't get blood from a stone, as the old saying goes. The country is broke."

"And *also* along with the ongoing news connected with NovoRo, we see growing activity among far-right extremist groups who are pushing their agenda while the country still is distracted by other fallout from the pandemic."

Hank *tap-tap-tapped* her knuckles on the table. "And you wonder why I've been watching this group, Shining City? And reading things to try and understand their mindset?"

Everyone looked at her, not quite sure how to respond.

"What's that quote I heard one time? 'You can watch what happens, you can make things happen, or you can wonder what the hell just happened.' I'm trying to watch what happens in case we need to make things happen, and you guys are all willing to sit around and wonder what the hell is happening."

"That's a little unfair, Hank," Cloud said. "We've all got our pet project that we're watching, along with trying to get some answers with regard to UniPerp. Just because we're not all watching an extremist group doesn't mean we're not keeping our eye on something important."

"You're looking at sexual abuses in the military, right? Isn't that something the military should be taking care of? Why is it important to you?" Hank countered.

Cloud slapped his hand on the table angrily and leapt to his feet. *"Because it happened to a buddy of mine in boot and the Army didn't do a fucking thing!"*

A deathly silence fell over the room.

"I think we can all be a little less judgmental about the cases each one of us is following," Edge said quietly. His deep voice and even tone seemed to smooth the waters considerably.

"Let's move on," Spud said. "Unless you don't want an episode of—"

"You can't make this shit up?" Crow asked.

"That's the one."

The silence in the room was replaced by a vigorous rapping of knuckles on the table.

"This one comes from the police blotter in Richland, Michigan. It seems an officer was sent to check out an alarm at a business that was closed for the evening. When he got there, he found the back door of the business open, so he called for backup.

"When his backup arrived, the fellow was a little leery of going inside to investigate the potential burglary, given the nature of the business."

"Which was?" Amigo asked.

"A funeral parlor."

"No, no, no," Crow said, shaking his head emphatically from side to side. "Not right after the Grand Forks mission."

"I'm sorry, but yes. This one *does not* deal with a fortune teller," Spud assured him.

"The two officers decided that perhaps calling in a dog and handler was the way to go, so they called and had the dog brought out. When the handler arrived with the dog, he informed the officers that he couldn't send the dog in, because the dog can't discriminate between a dead man and one who's holding *very, very* still."

"Maybe the handler should have trained that dog to check for a pulse," Voice cracked.

"Anyhoo, the other two officers get left to investigate, in the dark, through this funeral home. They open every casket, some of which *were* occupied. They touch each of the occupants to determine they're not warm in case it's the burglar hiding in a casket."

"Don't they dress up the dearly departed?" Crow asked. "How many burglars dress up to rob a place?"

"Dunno," Spud said. "But all the occupants of caskets are cold to the touch. So, they look in the last room, which as it turns out is the embalming room. There, they see a body stretched out on the slab, naked, ostensibly waiting to be prepped for embalming. They both agree that neither of them want to touch a naked corpse, so they turn to leave. Which is when they hear, '*Ah-CHOO!*'"

"But he's not dead yet!" Cloud declared through laughter

as the rest of the team likewise broke out in a raucous chorus of their own.

"Maybe not dead, but they did cuff him and haul him off to jail. Butt naked, I'll add."

"At least the desk sergeant didn't have to wonder which lockup to put him in," Hank chuckled.

"That's all I've got. You all know what comes next."

"Work on our skill sets, and reconvene for lunch," the rest of the team chorused.

CLOUD REACHED OVER ONCE the team had made its way through Honor Way and gave Hank a little back-handed slap on her arm.

"Wanna head to the airport?"

Hank tapped a corner of her watch.

"According to Hal, it's twenty-seven knots gusting to thirty-four out there."

"Yeah, I saw that, too. But it's also coming out of one-eight-zero, so practically right down runway 17."

Hank looked at him dubiously.

"I realize you never flew in the military. Nor have you gone through the usual transition of flying some dinky airplane for a regional cargo firm getting 'it was supposed to be there yesterday' cargo to its destination. In either case, you would have been exposed to a lot of 'sure it's nasty out there' weather that you would have flown in anyway because the cargo's gotta go where it's gotta go, or the mission requires it. What are you going to do when the mission requires we take either a Latitude or the helicopter somewhere and it's snotty?"

"Snotty doesn't necessarily blow me off the runway," Hank protested.

"It won't in this case, either. But this will be good for you. It'll grow hair on your chest."

Hank laughed. "Spud will appreciate that, I'm sure."

Cloud smirked. "You know what I mean."

"Do I want to do this?"

"It's not like I'm asking you to fly the helicopter today."

"Good thing. I've never shit myself before, and don't want to start now."

"That's right. You didn't even stink up your pants when Kathryn Hamburg was shooting at you."

"Couldn't. I was scared shitless."

Cloud laughed exuberantly. "Had just a little pucker factor going, eh?"

"She had Amigo and me pinned down pretty well. When I saw her stagger and fall, I thought someone else had managed to get a shot in."

Cloud nodded in appreciation of the event. "Go grab your gear and let's go play."

"OK." *'Play' he calls it. 'Sweat' is more like it.*

As they drove to the York airport, Hank had the definite sense of having been robbed. Instead of a long summer of watching the fields being planted, growing, and being harvested, she was now greeted by stubble that would be turned under in preparation for first winter, then next year's harvest. "Time doesn't stand still," she mused.

"You've got that sense that time somehow got interrupted during NovoRo as well?" Cloud asked her.

"Yeah."

"I thought that was interesting: what you said about us being the ultimate prepper group."

Hank chuckled. "You don't think we are?"

"Oh, I think you're absolutely right. We've probably considered even more scenarios than your most paranoid prepper, with perhaps the exception of a nuclear strike."

"In that case, we just bug out to one of the Atlas F remote bases. They're built like a big Faraday cage, you know."

"Really? I didn't know that."

"Yeah. They weren't ever intended to have offensive capability. The idea was that if someone struck us, we could strike back. So when they built the silos, they were practically solid rebar. Just enough space between the rebar to pour in the concrete. Do a three-foot-thick enclosure like that and an EMP can't get through it.

"Did you know that both the silo we have in Roswell and another one nearby had accidents?"

Cloud twisted his head to look at her, then quickly went back to watching the road. "I didn't know that, either."

"Yup. The nearby one had an accident during a readiness drill. Fortunately, they had removed the warhead. I don't remember if it was while trying to defuel the missile or put fuel back in, but they had fuel spill into the bottom of the silo. Keep in mind that the fuel for those things was kerosene and liquid oxygen. They sent two guys in to see what was going on, and when they saw that, they both high-tailed it back to the command and control room, closing off the blast doors. The whole missile went up—even threw the silo doors off the silo. Threw chunks of the missile a mile away from the silo. The command and control survived, as did the two guys in it. They had to wait it out down there until the all clear was called."

"Holy shit!"

"I think if I'd been in the silo at the time, 'shit' would have been the operative phrase. But there wouldn't have been anything holy about it," Hank said through nervous laughter.

"The silo we have had an accident, too, during construction. A crane operator got his crane too close to the rim of the silo, and the crane dropped all the way to the bottom. Sent up a fireball when it hit and its fuel tank ruptured. Killed four people. Think the place might be haunted?"

"I don't know about ghosts, but I heard there's an alien robot in there," Cloud joked, getting them both laughing. "Seriously, though: the last thought I want to entertain after our last mission is that the Roswell base might be haunted."

They arrived at the airport to find Frank just finishing fueling 101UN. He was bundled in a coat and hunched in an effort to keep the wind from chilling him.

"I have no idea why you guys want to go out on a day like today," he muttered as they walked up.

"If the mission requires it, we have to go," Cloud said.

"If the mission requires it, do you have to die?" Frank asked.

"No. We had to do that to get to do the mission in the first place," Cloud said with a grin. "Besides, it's really not that bad out there for a plane like a Latitude."

"So he says," Hank added, leaning toward Frank.

"Yeah, well ... have fun ... I think," Frank said as the two began their preparations for the flight.

"Where do you want to go?" Cloud asked as the two climbed aboard, Hank making her way to the left seat.

"I dunno."

"How 'bout we zip on down to MCI, then back up to Lincoln, and then back home? That should allow us to get back in time for lunch as well as work in three approaches."

"Sure, why not? Although, you know, when I first joined this outfit, I'd have never imagined I'd even be flying, never mind going out to the airport and deciding where I want to go on a joyride in a jet without even thinking about how much that would cost." She considered a moment. "Do you ever wonder if the controllers who handle us wonder who the hell we are?"

"I'm sure they do."

"Should we be worrying when they see us coming back to York as our base?"

Cloud considered this a moment. "I figure if they make an inquiry about the N-number, OKC might just tell them to mind their own business."

Hank thought about this a bit. Then she intoned, "Hal, run FAA aircraft registry search for November one-zero-one Uniform November."

November one-zero-one Uniform November. Citation Latitude. Registered owner: Hamilton Farms Organics, Incorporated. First placed in service—

"Thank you, Hal."

You're welcome, Hank.

Hank's eyebrows shot up. "That's a first. Voice has evidently programmed in some courtesies for Hal to use."

"Voice considers Hal to be ... almost human, I think," Cloud said as he finished up programming the FMS. He turned to Hank and smiling said, with a point of his finger, "Engage."

Hank chuckled and went through the start-up procedures, then made her radio calls to announce their intention to depart after Cloud had finished getting the clearance.

"What's our clearance, Clarence?" she asked, grinning.

"Here's your vector, Victor," Cloud returned.

They both laughed as Hank taxied out to the runway, for as long ago as *Airplane!* had been around, it was still the favorite movie of all time as far as pilots were concerned.

Most had watched it enough times to be able to recite the dialogue word for word.

"It'll probably be a little bumpy, both as you head uphill and as you head back downhill," Cloud advised her.

Hank resisted the urge to pull her seat restraints so tight that they would cut off circulation to her legs. "I am *not* a fan of turbulence," she admitted.

"No one is. But once you learn to handle it, it's not so freaky. Plus, the Latitude isn't like the Archer or Seneca. Because it's so much heavier, it rides out the bumps a bit better."

"Sort-of like heavier, faster bullets," Hank commented.

"Only you could think of it that way," Cloud observed as Hank commenced the takeoff roll.

As they settled into flight, Hank once again took a few moments to watch the ground below her as well as the sky all around her. The 'ride uphill', as Cloud had called it, really wasn't as bad as she had expected it to be, but she nonetheless gave it her full attention so as not to be overly surprised by anything the weather might want to throw at her. The Latitude's three-axis autopilot performed its job well, seemingly unperturbed by the bumps.

As they passed through a little turbulence, Cloud chuckled.

"You find turbulence funny?" Hank asked.

"I find the announcement we got on an Air Mobility Command flight one time funny," Cloud corrected. "We were coming home from the Middle East and were transferred onto an AMC flight leaving out of Ramstein Air Base. The pilot announced that he was Major Richard Dreyer, and his first officer was Captain Benjamin De A'Morelli. He told us that if we liked the flight, we should be sure to let his CO know, and again repeated that he was Major Dreyer. If we didn't like the flight, we should let his CO know, but also inform him that the pilot flying was Captain De A'Morelli.

"It all went pretty uneventfully until it came time to land at Fort Stewart. The landing was a bit ... *firm*, shall we say. Which is when the Major's voice came back on and said, "That's capital D-e, space, capital A, apostrophe, capital M, o-r-e-l-l-i."

"What's that they say?" Hank queried. "'Any landing you can walk away from is a good landing. If you get to use the plane again, it's a great landing'?"

Cloud chuckled. "Something like that."

They settled into doing their approach into Kansas City's airport, then executed the missed approach, heading to Lincoln. Completing an approach to another missed approach, they headed back to York.

Being only about four miles away from the Lockridge range complex, Hank found herself somewhat distracted by her observation of the ranges from the air. They were clearly visible, even though the airport and range complex had four miles separating them.

Through her headset, she suddenly heard, *November one-zero-one Uniform November, would you like vectors, or can you make a visual approach to York?*

She checked the glass panel in front of her as well as the approach plate displayed on the center panel and realized the autopilot had flown through the approach course. "Shit. How did that happen?"

Cloud was grinning at her. "Caught you daydreaming, didn't I?" She realized with that remark that Cloud had pulled the trick of decoupling the approach while she was preoccupied looking elsewhere.

"One-zero-one Uniform November would like to cancel IFR; airport in sight," Cloud called to the controller.

As the controller acknowledged the request to cancel their IFR flight plan, Cloud turned to Hank.

"H-a-n-k-y, space, S-p-a-n-k-y," he grinned.

Hank rolled her eyes as she maneuvered for a landing. *I guess I deserved that.*

OVER LUNCH, Cloud's postscript of his retelling of Hank's morning flight was, "I think she wanted to go out to Grand Island and shoot another approach, but I figured we'd be late for lunch if I let her do that."

The team members around the table expressed their amusement at how Hank had been caught checking out the firing ranges rather than checking out the progress on her approach into York with chuckles and jostles by the men on either side of her.

"Alright, alright—I blew it," she admitted. "Maybe I can redeem myself this afternoon by doing well on the lesson Spud's intending to give."

"What's it going to be, Spud?" Cloud asked.

"I'm going to teach you all how to start an IV," he said. "This time, no practice dummy. You've be starting IVs on each other."

"Really," Hank said evilly while strumming her tented fingers together. "I'd like to be partnered with Cloud."

HANK SNAPPED her book shut and tossed it on the coffee table.

"The way you tossed that, I gather you didn't find it all that good."

"The story has merit," she told Spud. "But the writing leaves a lot to be desired. I don't think he had this edited. I don't even think he edited it himself. I had to keep filling in the blanks, because he'd omit entire words and phrases."

"Did you get anything out of it?"

"It did give some insights into the mindset of these kinds of individuals. The author's bio says he's a prepper himself. He expresses some strong Christian convictions as well, but in the book he doesn't seem to have qualms about depicting an entire town of people slaughtering a large number of other people who come into the area and proceed to kill off a family in yet another prepper compound."

"I see. A little action not in sync with ordinary Christian beliefs."

"He portrays the main character as not liking the people in this compound to begin with, as they're white supremacists. So, I wonder if in his story having the compound be attacked and nearly everyone killed is his way of showing how he doesn't like white supremacists."

"Who survives?"

Hank wrinkled her nose as if she was smelling something bad. "A few young men who are treated like slaves and some young girls who are beaten and repeatedly raped."

"Does this dovetail with the extremist group you've been studying?" Spud asked.

Hank sighed. "Well, the Shining City group is a mixture of radical right Christianity and white supremacy. *And* they use al Qaeda-like tactics to spread their message and build their community as I've told you before. Once a faction in an area gets large enough, they send off part of the group to another area to start a new community, first settling in and establishing their compound, then recruiting others to join them."

"How is it that anyone knows that they're all part of the same group then?" Spud wondered.

"All they have to do is look for the church," Hank said. "They actually call their church 'The Shining City Brotherhood of Christ'. If you go into a community and you see a church by that name, guess what? Welcome to Shining Cityville."

"Brotherhood? No women allowed?" Spud asked.

"Women are considered second-class citizens as far as Shining City is concerned. You know, that 'women be subject to your husbands' thing the New Testament talks about. 'The woman is the weaker vessel.' 'Obey the way Sarah obeyed Abraham and called him lord.' This is pretty much their guiding principle on women," Hank continued, tapping on her tablet. "'Women are to remain silent in the churches. They are not permitted to speak, but must be in submission, as the law says. If they wish to inquire about something, they are to ask their own husbands at home; for it is dishonorable for a woman to speak in the church.'"

"Where the heck does it say that?" Spud questioned.

"First Corinthians, chapter fourteen," Hank said, passing him her tablet so he could see for himself. "They hold to all the crap the Bible has to say about subjugating women. That women will give birth in pain as a punishment for eating an apple in the Garden of Eden. That women have to keep their hair covered. Et cetera, et cetera."

"The women put up with that?"

"They believe it as well. Why? Because it's right there in the Bible, that's why. Do you see now why I have a hard time with religion?"

"You won't be submissive to me and call me lord?" Spud poked.

"Watch yourself, bud," Hank cautioned.

Spud tapped on his own tablet. "I do not permit a woman to teach or exercise authority over a man; she is to remain quiet," he read.

"Where does it say that?"

"First Timothy."

"You know what bothers me? How quickly you found that," Hank said, her eyes narrowing.

Spud tapped again. "So ought men to love their wives as their own bodies. He that loves his wife loves himself. For no man ever hated his own flesh, but nourishes and cherishes it." Spud looked back at Hank. "Ephesians."

"They probably had to put that in there so that a few women wouldn't kick those men's asses," Hank asserted.

Spud chuckled. "In spite of all those biblical admonitions, the saying still arose that says, 'the hand that rocks the cradle rules the world.'"

"You bet your damned tootin' it does," Hank declared.

"So, if these are such heartfelt Christians, why do they hate blacks?"

"Not just blacks—I've told you that before. Jews, Muslims, Orientals, so-called 'half-breeds' ... They think Hitler had the right idea: establish a genetically pure race. They point at a verse in Leviticus and say that they are all 'marked on their body', either by God Himself or by someone else. The logic is, God marked them so white people would know they're not worthy of inheriting the Earth, which they believe they alone will do."

"I guess they've never heard how scientists say genetically pure animals and plants get wiped out when something like a new disease comes along," Spud remarked.

Hank laughed. "Do you think this group believes in science?" She shook her head 'no' vigorously. "If it isn't in the Bible, as far as they're concerned it's not worth knowing."

"What about what the kids learn in school?"

"They don't send them to public schools. They either home school them, or run their own schools."

"Are they all totally brainwashed, or do some of them decide to leave?"

"That's a really good question," Hank said. "Because it seems some members disappear, and no one outside of the group knows what happens to them. It's possible they just move on to another community run by Shining City, but no one knows for sure."

"That sounds a little suspicious."

"Which is why I'm watching them."

Hank picked up her tablet. "In the meantime, so I don't get soggy with this stuff, it's on to reading more of this novel I've got."

"You read two books at once?"

"When one is written as badly as that one is," she said, casting a look at the book on the coffee table, "I find I need to take a break. So, I'm reading a cozy mystery."

"What's a cozy mystery?"

"It's a mystery where any violence or sex isn't explicitly stated in the book."

"This sounds like some kind of crime fiction," Spud said.

Hank blushed. She knew what was coming next.

"It is," she said quietly. "It's a subgenre."

"Hank, do you *ever* do anything that's not work-related?"

"Well, if you call three witches who are sisters, a fourth witch who is their aunt, a bunch of other weird people and a mysteriously dead body on the floor of a café 'work-related', then I guess the answer is 'no'."

Spud's eyes blinked rapidly. "Did you just say four witches and a dead body?"

"Yeah, pretty sure that's what I said."

"Have you had a chat with Doc Andy lately?"

Hank resisted the urge to smack him with her tablet.

Spud chuckled. "I guess, Love, I would not call that work-related if it hadn't been for all of the odd events during our last mission."

"One of the witches has 'sight', too," Hank practically whispered.

Spud gazed at her steadily for a prolonged moment. Finally he said, "Not even going to go there."

3

"What do ya say, Spud? Want to put in some time in the Latitude today?" Cloud asked as the team made their way to the conference room for morning intel.

Spud tapped a corner of his watch. "It says it's blowing twenty-three knots out there."

Hank smirked, which Cloud noticed.

"Your point is? Hank went out yesterday in twenty-seven gusting to thirty-four."

Spud looked from Cloud to Hank and back.

"Tell him it'll be good for him. Tell him it'll grow hair on his chest," Hank giggled.

Spud returned his gaze to Hank. "Is that what he told you yesterday?"

This time Hank laughed. "Yup!"

Spud looked back at Cloud. "Good thing I didn't notice any, or someone would be getting his jaw busted right about now."

"It'll be good for you. Grow hair on your chest," Cloud repeated.

"Hank likes the amount of hair I've already got."

"Is that right, Hank?"

Hank's face spread into a wide grin. "I do. But as long as

he doesn't start looking like Edge, I'm fine with a little more."

Edge shot her a glance.

"No offense, Edge. I'm sure that pelt keeps you warm at night," Hank poked.

A low rumble emitted from Edge, cut short only by his entry into Honor Way.

"Alright, everyone. Grab your coffee and grab a seat. It's time for intel!" Spud proclaimed.

"Not till you tell me you'll go with me to the airport when intel is over," Cloud said, crossing his arms.

"Sure, why not? Hank and I had a bit of a discussion last night over biblical sayings regarding women's inferiority, so if I want to prove the Bible right or wrong, I'm going to have to fly today."

Cloud gave a satisfied nod before snagging a couple of Rose's goodies from the plate on the table and going to pour himself a mug of coffee as Spud took his usual seat.

"First up ..." Spud set his tablet back down on the table, settled back in his chair, picked up his coffee and the blueberry mini-muffin he'd selected to go with it. He nibbled, then sipped; nibbled, then sipped.

"Ok, whatcha got?" Crow asked.

"Nothing."

Everyone stared at him.

"Nothing?"

"Not a thing."

Everyone grinned, figuring it had to be a joke.

The grins turned to questioning looks as Spud reached out, grabbed another mini-muffin, and continued to nibble and sip.

After a prolonged silence, Hank asked, "For real?"

"Yes."

"This isn't because you two were ... *busy* last night, is it?" Voice questioned, looking from Hank to Spud.

Hank gave him a scowl. "We went to bed and all we did was sleep."

"Why does that sound unlikely?" Cloud wondered, getting the rest of the team chuckling.

"It may be unlikely, but it's the truth," Spud confirmed.

"Then ... what have you got?" Cloud asked.

"I already told you: nothing. I didn't find anything in the news worthy of our attention."

"So, you're saying ..."

"There is no intel."

"How 'bout 'You can't make this stuff up?'" Edge asked.

"Don't have one of those, either."

"I do."

All eyes shifted toward Crow.

"Happened during jury selection for a case where I was the principle witness for the prosecution."

Hands reached out to claim mini-muffins of their own while Crow proceeded to give some background on the case.

"We had grabbed two guys during a raid on a stash house. They had each obtained their own counsel, and the counsel spent quite a bit of time during the jury selection conferring on which prospective jurors they wanted to keep, and which ones they wanted dismissed.

"They got to this one guy, and the prosecutor asked him if he believed in God. 'Yeah, I believe in God,' the guy answers.

"'Do you believe in angels?'

"'Yeah, I believe in angels too.'

"'How about demons? Do you believe in demons?'

"'If you believe there's a heaven, you've gotta believe there's a hell,' the guy says.

"'How about Sasquatch? Do you believe Sasquatch is out there hiding in the forest?'

"'I think it's possible Sasquatch is out there,' the guy says.

"That's when I see the two defense attorneys lean toward each other. I hear one of them say quietly to the other, 'What do you think? Should we keep this guy?'

"The other says, 'Believes in Sasquatch? Sounds high to me. He'll probably want our guys to stay in business.'"

The team laughed.

"Did he get selected for the jury?" Amigo asked.

Crow chuckled. "For some reason, the prosecutor didn't like him."

That made the team laugh harder.

"That's it. You know the drill," Spud said.

"You were really serious that there's nothing in the news we should know about?"

"There's plenty that you personally might find interesting," Spud said. "But for the team to watch? Not ... a single ... thing."

Everyone practically flew from their chairs, still harboring a fear that Spud might be pulling their leg.

Spud stayed seated, as did Hank. She looked at him closely.

"There's really nothing?"

"What can I say? Occasionally, there's a slow news day."

Hank stood. "I guess I'd better head down to the range, then. And you should grab your flight gear and meet up with Cloud."

"Yup. But I'd just like you to notice how easy it is to make the entire team happy."

Hank laughed enthusiastically. "Yes! You should do it more often."

Spud scowled at her. She went and kissed him.

"I love you," she said. "But every so often, I have to give you a hard time."

"THE *MUSLIM* TALKS OF THE *INFIDEL!*"

Robert Benkovic stood at the head of his small congregation in the Shining City Brotherhood of Christ Church in Sharples, West Virginia.

"But who is the real infidel? The hater of truth! The hater of Yeshua HaMashiach, the one and only true Son of Yahweh, our Abba! The ones who will not acknowledge the firm teachings of holy scripture and would corrupt it with modern interpretations and downright lies!"

His congregation, the men sitting in front, the women in the back of the small assembly building behind a wall of wooden slats, sat raptly while he expounded his sermon. The men murmured and nodded their agreement, some of them even exclaiming, "That's right!" or "Tell it, Brother Bob!" The women remained absolutely quiet, neither making a sound nor even nodding their heads.

"The *Muslim* says that their *Mohammed* was taken up and then set back down onto the Earth alive. But we know that only *one* man was ever taken up to heaven and returned to Earth alive, and that is the man who conquered his very death and who we are willing to follow unto *our* death as well.

"The *Muslim* opens his book of blasphemies and reads, 'Make war on the infidels living in your neighborhoods.' But who do they call infidels?"

He stepped down off the small podium he'd been standing on and walked slowly through the seated men.

Leaning down to one, he said in a quieter voice, but loud enough for all to hear, "They call *you* infidel, David." Walking over to another, he added, "And *you,* Stephen." Going to another: "You too, James." He spread his arms wide. "They call *all of you* infidel! And why? Because you *believe.* You *believe* in Yeshua, his Abba, Yahweh, *and no others.* And because you *believe,* they would hunt you, and your wife, and your children in order to cut your head from your body and leave it for the birds to pluck and the animals to gnaw."

The mothers in the back clutched their children to them. The murmuring of the men in the front grew louder, angrier.

"We need not fear, however," Brother Bob said serenely. "We know we are blessed by Yahweh." His voice rose into a new crescendo as he made his way back to the podium, his fisted hand emphasizing his words as he pounded it into the palm of his other hand. "We *know* we are *blessed* because years ago when first Yahweh sent the pale horse and its rider, *not one of our congregation was taken.* And once again, just recently when the pale horse and its rider came, *once again* not one of us fell. We hold to the ancient command to keep the word of Yahweh on the doorposts of our homes, and the blood of a lamb above the door so that we will be recognized and spared the punishment others are given for their disbelief.

"Be not afraid, we are told." He thumped his finger on his Bible and opened it to where he had set a ribbon to mark a passage. "For Scripture says, 'Be strong and of good courage, fear not, nor be afraid of them: for the Lord thy God, he it is that doth go with thee; he will not fail thee, nor forsake thee.' We are warned to prepare, and prepare we have. And when the battle comes, *we* shall be victorious."

HANK GAVE Spud a kiss and sent him on his way with Cloud. "Have fun," she told him.

"Yeah, right."

As he went out the door, she pulled on her shoes and thought of what she might like to practice down in the range as she tied her laces. Walking from the house, she made her way over to the staircase that led to the other levels of the main headquarters complex. Stopping before she exited to head to the range, she read what Luigi had posted on a plaque above the door.

Be strong and courageous. Do not be afraid or terrified because of them, for the Lord your God goes with you, He will never leave you nor forsake you.

"Does He?" she murmured.

As she descended down the stairs, she reflected on the last mission, still wondering about Miss Martha and her visions, Blobel and his obsession with his tarot cards, and wondered again at what made people believe what they believe. She weighed her own doubts about faith in a higher being, one of her voices gnawing at her. *Did Miss Martha convince you of a heaven? Did Blobel convince you of a hell?*

She reflected as well on something Edge had told her since they had arrived back at the headquarters: *I feel sorry for him, Hank. I feel sorry that he killed himself. My faith taught me that suicide is a path straight to hell; that there is no salvation for someone who would take their own life.*

She recalled some of her own former beliefs as well.

*I believe that there's **something** out there, but I'm not sure what it is. But you don't slap that higher power in the face by taking your own life.*

When did I stop believing? she asked herself. In her mind, she saw Blobel step backward when she pulled out her Saint Michael medallion. Saw herself kiss her thumb and press it to the Sword of Saint Michael engraved on the side of her sniper rifle.

Why do I do that? If it's meaningless, why bother?

She shook her head to clear her thoughts as she walked into the range. Luigi was standing there waiting for her, her Savage Stealth Evolution and her SigSauer MK25 laid out on a small equipment table waiting for her as well.

"No SWAT gear today?" Luigi asked, seeing her dressed in her facility casuals.

"I guess you could say I'm goofing off a little," Hank said. "But I'll probably want to run this drill again in SWAT as well. For now, I just want to get the hang of it so I can get the others working on it. You got the rifle mags all set up the way I asked?"

"Ten round magazines, one dummy round in each one," Luigi confirmed.

"Thanks, Papa. This is going to be a stoppage and transition drill. I'm going to start simple: just a typical side-to-side engagement of two assailants with two to the chest for each of them, going back and forth until I encounter the dummy round and then transitioning to my handgun to finish the exercise."

"So, you not goin' to do a double-tap and then go for a head shot?"

"Nope, not this time. I have to get Voice to do a little target work for me before we go there. I'm not happy with a target that just sits out there the way these FBI qualification targets do. You hit a guy with two rounds in the chest, he's going to start to fall. I'm betting Voice can rig up a target that will simulate that and will be a bit more realistic."

"Two center of mass shots don't do the trick?"

"Not right away, which is the whole idea of the follow-up with a head shot. You've got to kill the brain to get a guy to stop shooting before he bleeds out."

When did I start thinking like this? When did this become my normal? Hank thought as she clipped her dropped-and-offset holster onto her duty belt and slung her Savage from its sling around her neck. *Have I become a little less than human?*

As Hank went through the exercise, Luigi could see that she was distracted. Minor fumbles and her exasperated sighs through clamped lips told him she had more on her mind than just working on a training exercise for the team. Hank realized it herself. Calling a halt to the exercise after a few tries, she went over to the table and leaned on it, resting on her forearms while she tried once again to clear her mind of its many questions.

"Whatchu got goin' on in that head of yours?" Luigi asked her.

"It shows, does it?" Hank commented.

"I don't usually see you havin' difficulties gettin' a mag in a well," Luigi pointed out.

"I've got a few things I've been thinking about, Papa."

Luigi chuckled. "Oh, I see. Thinkin' got you all worked up. Maybe you should stop thinkin'."

Hank smiled and shook her head. "Somehow, I don't think that's the best approach."

Luigi placed a hand on the table himself and leaned on it. "Maybe you wanna tell me whatchu thinkin' about?"

Hank pondered a moment. "I'm thinking about God," she finally said.

Luigi gave her a steady look. "Whatchu think God wants from you?"

"That's just it, Papa. I'm not sure God's asking *anything* of me. I'm not even sure there's a god."

"You know, me and Rose are like most Italians: good Catholics. We go to mass every Saturday night. Most times, the boys go with us, but I think maybe Seb and Danilo don't believe the same way we do, even though we brought them up in the Church. Rose always gets dressed up. She says she's gotta look good in front of God. I dress up too, just to keep her happy even though I think God looks harder at the inside than the outside."

"What makes you so certain that there's a god?" Hank asked.

Luigi shrugged. "I guess I count my blessin's and figure with so many more blessin's than hardships, my faith must be doin' somethin'. Look at me: I got the best job a gunsmith can have. I got the kinda shop any gunsmith not workin' as a master gunsmith for a big outfit would ever dream he'd have. Maybe even some of them, too. I work for an outfit I personally think is the most important group a gunsmith could work for, and I feel good that my guns help keep them safe when they do what they have to do.

"And that's just my job. Then I got a beautiful wife who caught my eye and has caught it ever since I first saw her. She's smart, she's feisty, and she gave me two handsome boys. She stands by me all the way. And as you know, she can *cook*—which is perfect, 'cuz I like to eat," he added, smiling and patting his stomach.

"This place gave me a daughter, too," he added, taking her chin in his hand. "She's a pretty good shot when she's not thinkin' too much."

"It's your fault," Hank said.

"Oh? How's it *my* fault?"

"You're the one who put that Bible verse the truck driver told me up over the door on the residence level."

"You don't think maybe God kept you safe when you were out there lettin' those men think you were a little girl peddlin' her wares? I think you got a tooth in that little pouch of yours says otherwise," Luigi said, giving a poke to where Hank's little medicine pouch of teeth hung under her shirt.

"Spud's the one knocked that tooth out of the guy's mouth," she said.

"Well *I* heard that guy had a good hunderd pounds on Spud. And yet, Spud knocked him stone cold before he could do anythin' to you."

Hank chuckled. "Threw him out of his rig like he was a limp rag, too."

"You don't think maybe God helped you make that shot that saved Spud's life?"

Hank thought about that a bit. *I prayed to God I wouldn't hit him ... wouldn't kill my own husband.*

"I guess I need to eat a few more tangerines," she said.

Luigi chuckled. "What's tangerines got to do with it?"

Hank rolled her eyes. "We have a tangerine tree planted in one of those big planter tubs up on the residence level. I'm sure you saw it during the lockdown. It's where Edge goes to do what he calls 'talking to The Man'. Maybe I can't talk to The Man the way he does, but I can still sit there and meditate."

"You know, we Catholics got something we use for that."

Luigi reached into a pocket and pulled out a rosary.

"Isn't saying the rosary just saying a bunch of prayers over and over?" Hank asked, skeptical.

"You know how an AM radio works?" Luigi asked. "You got a carrier wave on a set frequency. Then the wave is amplified up and down to get things transmitted over it. The rosary is kinda like that. Yes, you gotta few prayers you say over and over. But as you do that, your mind starts to wander. You start thinkin' about how you gonna pay the bills, if your son is gettin' some girl pregnant when he stays out late, what special thing you think your wife would like for her birthday ... All kindsa stuff. I used to feel guilty about that, till one day I got to talkin' with one of the nuns we had in our church. I asked her, 'How can I keep my mind on the prayers?' She told me, 'You don't need to. All those things you think about when you're reciting the prayers are the *real* prayer. They're all the things you worry about and want God to help with, all the things you remember that made someone happy that you want to thank God for, all the things you want to be that you want God's guidance for.' I stopped thinkin' about the prayers they tell you to say and started thinkin' about the prayers that came to my mind as I was sayin' them. I gotta thank that nun. She taught me how to actually *pray* the rosary and not just mumble words."

Luigi pressed his rosary into Hank's hand. "Why don'tchu take this and see if it'll work for you? You don't need to know the prayers that go with each of the beads. Maybe just count them. Go round and round countin' them until your mind starts to wander. When it does, then you'll know how to pray. Then maybe while you're sittin' under that tree, God will answer you."

"WHAT'S it going to be today, Spud?" Crow asked.

"Today, you're going to learn how to intubate a patient."

"Wouldn't this be better taught by Doc Frank?" Cloud protested, rubbing the back of his left hand. Crow turned red. It seems that during the prior day's exercise on starting an IV, Cloud had been Crow's "patient" and vice versa. Cloud had done a good job of getting Crow's IV started, but Crow? Not so much—and Cloud still had the bruise to show for it.

"We're not going to be intubating each other," Spud explained. "We'll be using Dummy Dan the Airway Man. Trying to intubate a conscious individual isn't an easy task to start with, and gets harder when he gags and heaves up his lunch."

Spud proceeded to introduce the team to the equipment usually carried along on missions, showing them which pieces of equipment in the kit were his favorites to use and explaining why, but qualifying that with admonitions for each team member to try other things to find what worked best for them. He then showed them how to check the functioning of each piece of equipment.

"Medical checks the kit on a regular basis," he explained, "but you'll want to check before you attempt an intubation as well. As the saying goes?" He invited Hank to express the saying for him with a hand gesture.

"Shit happens."

"Indeed it does."

"He's not making that shit up, either," Hank added to the laughter of the rest of the team members.

"Indeed I am not."

Spud lifted a manikin up onto the table. "Meet Dummy Dan," he said. "Dan, this is the team. Team, Dan."

"Hey, Dan," Cloud called out. "Watch out for Crow."

"This stuff is just a step beyond what we got in the DEA academy," Crow pointed out in his own defense.

"A bit beyond the basic first aid I got in the Army, too,"

Cloud parried. "But you don't have one of *these* to show for it," he added while pointing to the bruise on his hand.

Spud then proceeded to demonstrate the techniques required to correctly intubate a patient. As he demonstrated the proper technique for inserting a Mac blade, Cloud once again voiced his original protest. "Shouldn't Doc Frank be doing this?"

Spud's face betrayed the barest hint of exasperation.

"First, as far as giving the lesson goes, Doc Frank is in the middle of finals, and isn't available. Second, as far as what happens in the field goes, what if someone takes out Doc Frank?"

"Then *you* can do it," Cloud said.

"And if I'm not around either?" He leveled a gaze at Cloud. "Do you have some valid objection to learning this stuff?"

Cloud gave a nervous glance to Edge.

"Don't look at me, fella. I don't have any problem with learning this stuff."

"Well ... uh ..." He lowered his eyes and nearly at a whisper admitted, "Makes me a little queasy."

"Ain't like it's spinach," Edge noted.

"Spinach I can do. Looking at someone's insides? Not so much."

"If Nickell had managed to get Hank in a little different location, you might have been looking at *her* insides," Edge commented.

"I think if that had happened, I'd have been getting a close-up look at the southern New Mexico sand."

The rest of the team members were now paying close attention to Cloud.

"You flew combat missions, right?" Crow asked.

"Yeah."

"And medevaced soldiers?"

"They were in the back, I was in the cockpit paying attention to what was in front of me—not behind me."

"You've got to stop thinking about what you might see and start thinking about what your teammates might need," Voice gently admonished him. "I didn't want to start working on being a physician's assistant, either. Having those skills. But I told myself that one day, one of us might need those skills, and if it wasn't me that needed them, perhaps I should be the one to have them."

"There are a lot of bananas out there that are grateful he stitched them up," Crow quipped to renewed laughter from the group.

"Alright." Cloud stood up, making the rest of the team wonder if he was about to walk out. Instead, he walked up to where Spud stood with the manikin. "Walk me through this stuff."

HANK AND SPUD made their way through the walipini, gathering strawberries that hung below hydroponic trays. The dark of a winter's early nightfall was repelled by the lights hung above the growing plants, though Hank found that the wavelengths used for the walipini made the strawberries glow eerily.

"It's the lutein in them," Spud informed her when she remarked about it.

"Strawberries have lutein?"

"That's what Doc Gillie told me," Spud related. "She says I should get plenty of lutein, given cataracts and macular degeneration run in my family. Supposedly, that will make me more prone to macular degeneration and cataracts later in life as well. She says the lutein can help with that. Prolong the onset. Maybe even keep it from occurring."

"She tells me I should get plenty of lutein too," Hank said. "She's concerned about light-colored eyes, obviously. My dad had the same light blue eye color I do, and he didn't develop any problems—at least not for as long as he lived. But Doc Gillie tells me that spending as much time on the range as I do puts me at risk as well."

"Why don't you wear sunglasses?"

"I can never seem to get the eye relief on the scope adjusted so I see a good field of view wearing glasses of any kind. I'll usually have my goggles on if it's a tactical rifle I'm using, but for the sniper rifles with their scopes, I'll look through with my bare eye. There's a big difference between sighting through an ACOG or a red dot and through a scope." She looked at their gathered bowl of strawberries. "Think we have enough of these?"

"Looks good to me. Are you going to be wanting some chocolate to dip them in?"

"Not tonight. Makes a mess of a print book," she said as they made their way back through the garden shed and down below deck.

"You finished your cozie?"

"Yup. Got something more work-related to read for a bit."

"Should I read the cozie you were reading?"

"Witches and fairies and curses, oh my?" Hank quipped. "You'd go for that?"

Spud grinned. "Not really, I suppose. Did you get anything at all out of it?"

"Just one statement that I liked. Something to the effect of perhaps living under a delusion if you believe that everything you see is all that there is in the world."

As they walked to their house, Spud considered that.

"The number seven figured prominently in it, too. It made me keep thinking about UniPerp and his current MO of seven victims and embedding s-e-v-e-n in his message. Kind-of discouraged me."

"Why?"

"Even a novel portrays the number seven as something mystical. What if UniPerp is fashioning his actions after a book? Do you have any idea how many books are out there?"

"Must be millions."

"Maybe millions of millions if you count books from all over the globe. But certainly millions in the English language. I think I saw some statistic where they said that Amazon alone offered something like fifty million books—and that was years ago."

"Well, which of the fifty million are you reading now?" Spud asked as they made their way back to the reading nook after the strawberries had been rinsed.

She held up a book, not capable of answering after having crammed an entire large berry in her mouth.

"A book on deadly skills?"

"Why not?"

"We don't have enough deadly skills at our disposal? You especially?"

"Never know when you might find something you don't know or need to refresh your memory on." Hank fidgeted in her seat. "This thing is jabbing me," she muttered, withdrawing the rosary Luigi had given to her and dropping it on the coffee table.

Spud eyed it. "Converting?"

Hank looked at it. "It's Luigi's. He insisted I take it and use it to help myself meditate."

"My upbringing didn't look kindly on repetitive prayers," Spud noted.

"Luigi says the stuff you repeat over and over isn't the real prayer." She looked at him. "We've never spoken much about it, but what faith are you?"

"I guess you could say I'm a run-of-the-mill Christian now, but I was raised as a Methodist."

"I know next to nothing about how Methodists are different from any other Protestants," Hank said.

"What were *you* raised as?" Spud asked.

"Muslim."

Spud acted startled.

Hank laughed. "I'm kidding. Mom and Dad never took us to church. I don't even know if they were married in one, to tell you the truth. There was a Bible in the house, complete with New Testament, so I guess they believed in Christ." Hank laughed again. "At least for as many times as I heard Dad call on Him while he was working. You know, as in, 'Jesus Christ, where'd I leave my fucking wrench *this* time?'"

"My parents would have frowned on that."

"Good thing they never met my dad, then," Hank quipped. She reached out and grabbed another strawberry, chewing on it while Spud gazed at her. Their eyes met, serious faces transforming into grins, and then both of them sputtering into laughter.

"Yeah, my parents would have considered your dad a heathen."

"And Dad would have considered your parents tight asses."

4

"Good, Davey. Good," his father encouraged the young man as they practiced on the community's small firing range. "I think it's time we got you your own gun."

The boy beamed. "When I have my own gun, can I go hunting with you?"

"That's the whole plan, son. You and I are the men of the house. It's our place to be the ones who provide."

"Can we go get one today?"

"Sure. We'll drive into Charleston and see what they've got."

As the father and son packed up rifle and ammunition, then went to retrieve their target, one of the other members of the Shining City Brotherhood of Christ Church arrived. Recognizing them, he greeted them, taking a look at the young man's target.

"That your shooting, Davey?"

"Yes, sir!" the boy replied proudly.

"You've got a right to be proud. Those are some good-looking shots right there."

"Dad says I can have my own rifle now," David beamed. "We're going to Charleston to get one."

"Good for you! Then you'll be able to go with your dad

and each of you can get a deer this season. Just a couple more weeks before the season starts. Gonna get yourself a big buck?"

"I sure hope so!"

As they drove to Charleston, Bill Cantor, the boy's father, and David discussed their plans for the upcoming deer harvest. At ten years of age, David already looked more like a twelve-year-old, standing nearly five feet tall and already checking in at ninety-five pounds. But then, other boys his age in the community were much the same, appearing more mature than their age as a result of hard work and a solid diet centered largely around lean meat and fowl they hunted themselves with their fathers.

Walking into the store, they walked up to the gun counter and were greeted by the clerk there.

"How can I help you today?" he asked.

"I'm in the market for a hunting rifle for my boy here," Bill told the man. "Time to get him some hardware of his own."

The clerk walked along the counter to where traditional hunting rifles were displayed in racks. Bill Cantor walked along with him, his son following along as well. Bill stopped and pointed.

"Whatcha got right there?" he asked.

"That's a Ruger American Ranch. Chambered in .223. You might want a little bigger bullet for deer."

"It's legal for deer, though."

"Yeah, it is. But still, you've got to be able to make a good shot with a .223 to get a good kill."

"We already do a lot of reloading of .223, and my boy's been practicing. I don't think it's beyond his capability to get a one-shot kill with a .223. And I like that it has that ten-round magazine."

The clerk ensured the rifle was unloaded, set the safety, and handed it across the counter to Bill, who then passed it to his son. Shouldering the rifle, the boy beamed. "I like it!" he said.

The clerk gave a slight twitch of an eyebrow upward, still convinced a larger caliber would be better. Inwardly, he shrugged. *If that's what the man wants to spend his money on, who am I to argue with him? He's the one going to have to chase down a wounded deer.*

"Will you be wanting a scope for that?" he asked Bill.

"I've got an extra at home I can put on it," he said.

"We've got some nice scopes on sale right now ..." the clerk urged in an attempt to make another sale to his credit.

"Nah. We'll use the one I've got."

"How 'bout ammo?"

"Like I told ya, we reload. I've probably got a couple thousand rounds of .223 sitting in ammo cans at home," Bill said.

As he concluded the sale with the clerk, filling out the Form 4473 and presenting ID, a man dressed in jeans and a flannel shirt had stood looking over items in an aisle nearby, listening to the conversation between the clerk and Bill Cantor. He hovered near where the sales transaction was taking place until the clerk placed the gun back behind the counter and disappeared through a door to make a call for the NCIS check. As soon as the clerk was out of earshot, he walked over to the father and son.

"I couldn't help but overhear. Gonna do some deer hunting this season, are ya?"

"First season for my boy here," Bill said proudly, clapping his hand on David's shoulder.

"Where you thinking about going?"

"We live in Sharples. Lots of woodland around there that's great for hunting all kinds of game."

"Sharples. Must be a little place. I don't think I've ever heard of it."

"Yeah, it's small. Quiet. Good neighbors. A nice place to raise a family."

"Don't say. I'll have to check it out some time. At least check out the hunting."

Bill just looked at him. Like most members of the Shining City church, he was a little leery about strangers taking interest in the community, even though the compound where most of the members lived was secluded well off the beaten path. Still, he gave the man a smile and said, "Just make sure you've got your paperwork in order. The game wardens know it's a good hunting spot, too."

"I'll be sure to do that," the man said.

He continued to poke through the nearby aisles as money changed hands and the rifle, now tucked in its original box, was handed over to Bill, who promptly handed it to his son. As the two of them walked out the door, the man took out a small notebook and pen and scribbled some notes, then turned to walk out himself.

"Can I help you find something?" the clerk called to him.

"Nah. I was just looking to see what you've got," he replied.

He walked out of the store and strode into the parking lot like he was headed to his vehicle. Seeing Bill Cantor pulling out of a parking spot, he got a look at the tag and muttered the number over and over to himself. Once Bill had started out of the parking lot, he pulled out his notebook again and jotted down the tag number, then walked back toward the store a short way and cut over one aisle in the parking lot to get into his own vehicle. Scowling as he started his car and proceeded to drive off, he muttered, "Something's going on in Sharples."

"GOOD MORNING, EVERYONE," Spud greeted the team as they took their seats at the conference room table.

"This is the only good part of intel," Crow moaned, reaching out for one of the goodies Rose had supplied for the meeting. "What is this?" he asked, getting a look at it.

"Wazzbehwies an' yogut in a filo dough cub," Hank said through the one she was chewing.

"Raspberries and yogurt in a filo dough cup," Crow repeated in English. He took a bite and nodded approvingly, unlike Hank, who had simply stuffed the entire thing in her mouth.

"First up, there is continued controversy over how small business loans were handled during the NovoRo pandemic, with minority- and women-owned businesses claiming that they didn't receive their fair share. At least in minority neighborhoods, this has sparked off some anti-government protests."

"Just taking to the streets, or committing acts of violence and vandalism?" Cloud asked.

"So far, the most serious thing happening is blocking traffic, but it's likely only a matter of time before someone gets ticked off because they can't get to work on time," Spud postulated.

"We have oil prices fluctuating again, which is creating a tug-o-war between the environmentalists and the oil exploration companies. The government seems to be leaning on the side of oil, saying that increased domestic oil production can serve to stabilize prices. Naturally, the environmentalists aren't on this particular band wagon.

"One of our big social media platforms is coming under fire for outsourcing jobs to India. Protesters there are saying that with jobs still scarce right here at home, the company should be bringing those outsourced jobs back onshore. So far, in a twist of irony, the major protesting has been done on the company's own site."

"I'm mad, but not so mad that I don't want to post a meme about it on my wall," Crow chuckled.

"You know I've got a fake persona on that site," Voice said.

"I wouldn't be surprised if you had a fake account set up on just about every subscriber site out there," Cloud remarked.

"In this case, it's useful," Voice said. "I can monitor the pages that are devoted to fringe groups."

"Really?" Hank blurted. "Can you set me up with another fake account there like you did for the one I use to watch the sex trafficking groups?"

"You can use the same one, you know."

"I think I'd like to keep the two personas separate," Hank said. "At least I'm hoping the pedophiles and the alt right religious types don't overlap so much."

"Wasn't the case with Waco," Cloud pointed out.

"You've got a point there, but I still think I'd like to keep the personas separate."

"Easy peasy," Voice said.

"And that's all I've got," Spud concluded.

"No You Can't Make This Shit Up?" Hank asked.

"Not from me. Edge will entertain you all this morning."

The team settled in with grins on their faces while Edge took the floor.

"Back when I was in the Marines, my Raider team was all composed of big guys. And I mean, *big guys.* You think I'm big? I was just average in that group.

"During one return from deployment, five of us decided we'd go take in a movie and then grab a beer afterward. When we got to the movie theater, there was a big line.

"We were all standing there patiently waiting, when up comes this little toothpick of a guy and just cuts right in front of us. We're all looking at him like, 'Didn't he see us standing here?' We all turned and looked at the biggest guy in the group: Clark Watson. You remember that actor that played in that old movie, *The Green Mile*?"

"Tom Hanks?" Crow asked.

"No, the black guy. Michael Clarke Duncan. We called Clark 'Coffey' because he looked like that character, John Coffey, in the movie. Biggest dude you ever did see. I think if he ever accidentally walked into one of those big trees you see alongside some streets in New England, the tree would just step out of the way rather than get knocked down.

"Coffey knew what we wanted him to do, so he just wanders up to the guy, grabs him from behind, and picks him up. As he's walking the guy to the end of the line, the guy tells him, "Put me down, you stupid…" Yeah, he tacked on the 'n' word right there. That didn't sit too well with Coffey, so he set him down alright. Then he nailed him with his fist. He must-a used some restraint, because he didn't kill the guy. Didn't even knock him out.

"The guy gets up off his rump, and we see him dialing his phone. Next thing we know, we've got a couple of cops coming along. They get up to where the guy is standing, and he points at Coffey. They take one look at Coffey, then back at this scrawny little puke, then back at Coffey. You could tell they didn't want to tackle Coffey without *a lot* of back-up.

Instead, they stand where they are and ask everyone in line, 'Did anyone see what happened here?'

"A little black gal behind us pipes up and says, 'Yeah. That skinny guy walked up and cut in front of those guys, so the big black brothuh picked him up and got him out of line. Then the skinny little asshole called the big guy a nigger, so the big guy hauled off and let him have it." Everyone in the line heard this gal—she wasn't exactly being quiet while she told the cops this.

"The cops tell the guy, 'It isn't assault if you provoked him,' and they walk off. The guy goes to get back in line *behind* us, and the gal just gives him one of these with her thumb" —Edge gave a jerk of his thumb over his shoulder— "so he goes to get behind her. Next person in line does the same thing, and it keeps going like that until he finds himself at the end of the line. I'm not sure there were even any tickets left for that showing by the time he got to the ticket booth.

"And Coffey? We bought him all the soda and popcorn he wanted during the movie. You don't mess with a marine, you sure don't mess with a Raider, and you definitely didn't mess with Coffey."

The rest of the team all clapped, slapped, and rapped knuckles while laughing in appreciation of Edge's tale.

"That's it. I'm going to suggest we take the rest of the morning off. Then I understand my lovely wife has a drill for us down in the range, so see you all at lunch."

"I SEE you are *not* taking the morning off," Spud observed, seeing Hank studying her latest book.

"There's some interesting stuff in here that I think maybe we could take advantage of," she replied.

"Oh?"

"It's an item-by-item discussion of techniques for covert operators. It's got me curious. I know that the guys in the suits who are guarding the president when he appears in public aren't the only ones watching the crowd. This guy talks about blending in with the people in the area you're in. Those of you in PPD were all trained in that, I assume?"

Spud chuckled. "Perhaps not as well as the unit member who played the part of the ticked off Afghani that ran into us with his car, but yes—we were all trained in how to blend in. And you're right that there are always a lot more Secret Service watching the president than the ones you see in suits."

"I wonder how well we could apply some of this stuff to a covert op where we're infiltrating a group."

"Are you thinking about Shining City again?"

"I think there's only one way you'll ever know if a group is a threat or not, and that's by getting up close and personal to see what they're up to. That will require infiltrating," Hank said.

"Been there, done that."

Hank smiled. "You're trying to discourage me."

"If the mission requires it, then it has to be done," Spud conceded.

"Here's the thing about Shining City," Hank began. "Unlike United Border Militias, we're not talking about individual people getting together to conduct a paramilitary operation. You're talking about *families*, for the most part. This group is a mixture of white supremacy and *very, very* conservative Christianity. For instance, they insist that women have to keep their hair covered in public. One thing

I'm trying to find out, given what this book is saying, is if there's a prescribed method that a woman has to use to cover her hair or if a simple hat would do."

"You're not thinking about infiltrating this group ..."

"I'm playing 'What if.' What if we get called upon to take some action against this group?"

"Then we take the action that's requested of us," Spud said.

"Against our better judgement?" Hank waggled a finger at him. "Don't forget what happened at Waco. Those people considered David Koresh akin to a messiah, if not *the* messiah. Even more extreme, look at Nazi Germany. The government literally handed all authority over to Hitler— and this group idolizes Hitler."

"History tends to lose its objectivity," Spud said. "We look back at Nazi Germany and believe that everyone stood behind Hitler and what he was trying to do. Germans in general were vilified long after the war was over. We don't see a lot of accounts of dissenters. You have to ask yourself, though, if the majority of people really stood behind Hitler or if what happened was that there were a few brave and vocal dissenters who likely paid for their bravery by being sent to concentration camps or executed, and a whole bunch of other dissenters who decided they didn't like dissent as much as they liked staying alive."

"I guess that implies that you believe there are people in the Shining City group that don't exactly adhere to every-thing their doctrine dictates. But it's been my observation, with all apologies, that religious fervor has an odd effect on people."

"Good afternoon, everyone," Hank greeted as the team gathered in the lowest level of the Headquarters complex that housed the indoor range. "Today's exercise is going to be a little stoppage drill. One of my 'oh shit' drills that will hopefully prepare you for the event of your rifle deciding it's had enough of being knocked around by recoil and refuses to run."

She picked up her rifle, double-checking in spite of the installed open chamber indicator and taking a glance at the empty mag well to ensure it was safe to handle in front of the rest of the team. Even so, she instinctively turned so that when she handled it, the muzzle was facing toward the backstop at the far end of the range.

"We all know our rifles don't break—Luigi's too good for that to happen." She glanced up to where the gunsmith himself was manning the rangemaster's booth, noting the grin on his face. "But there's never a guarantee your ammo won't have a problem."

"Especially if *you* made it," Amigo jested.

"Hardy-har-har," Hank poked back. "I can put it all together, but I don't make primers and I don't make powder."

She picked up an empty magazine and inserted it into the well of the rifle.

"So, what do you do? Well ... you can do the usual mantra of tap-rack-bang, which will work just fine *unless* you're either out of ammo or you have something like a stuck case and a double-feed. You can try to deal with that, or you can simply go to this perfectly fine handgun you have either right here in your chest holster or in a dropped leg holster, depending upon the situation you find yourself carrying in."

She smiled at them, which gave the men no comfort

whatsoever. Hank always smiled when she was about to hit them with a new challenge, or renew their acquaintance with an old one. So, their usual response to the smile that would erupt on her face when she was about to describe the drill was to resist the urge to whimper.

"Here's the drill. You each have a ten-round magazine for your rifle. Why only ten? Because we don't need more than ten—we don't spray and pray. Only problem is, one of the ten is a dummy round. When you encounter the dummy round, you'll re-engage the target with your handgun. Got it?"

"Doesn't sound too tough," Cloud said. Looking downrange, he asked, "Where are the targets?"

The rest of the men had also noticed that the only thing downrange was a single barricade.

"Hal's pal is down there," Hank informed them. "Hal, reveal target."

From behind the barricade, one of the unit's robotic targets scooted out, took a shot at the group causing everyone to hit the deck as the sim round sailed overhead, then scooted back behind the barricade. Only Hank remained standing.

"Oh, hell no," Crow uttered.

"Why didn't you duck?" Voice asked as he got back to his feet.

"Rob Ot and I have a deal: I give him a little oil every so often, and he spares me a purple welt somewhere on my body." She grinned again, this time devilishly. "I actually took a gamble that Rob would go for larger targets. That won't be a good tactic when I'm up against Rob all by my lonesome, so I'll have to be more wary. And also realize that he could jump out from either side of the barricade."

"You practiced this ahead of time," Cloud said, his face taking on the countenance of a storm cloud.

"Yeah, I did. But not with the robotic target. I decided to use it at the last minute, figuring it would add some extra spice to the exercise. The element of unpredictability. Basically, all of us are doing this for the first time."

Now the team adopted grins of their own, though they still didn't think it would be possible to exceed Hank's performance. Given her job as the firearms expert and sniper, they all knew that the amount of time she spent either down in the range they currently were in or out at the Lockridge complex far exceeded their own.

"Notice there are two other barricades out there as well: one on the left, one on the right. Should you empty your handgun trying to kill Rob, you're going to have to make a dash to one or the other and get your rifle running again, assuming you still have ammo in it."

"What happens if they're *both* out?" Cloud asked.

Hank laughed and shook her head. "Then you're *screwed*."

"No extra mags? No tactical reloads?" Edge asked.

"Not for this drill. Come on—there's only one guy down there. How many shots do you need to get a kill?"

After each of the team members had run the drill several times, Hank called a halt to the exercise. But before dismissing them to turn in their SWAT gear and shower before dinner, she gave them a bit of information she'd withheld from the group earlier.

"Unknown to you, Hal has been keeping track of how many times each of us was hit."

Groans erupted from the men.

Hank shrugged. "What can I tell you, other than make

sure you don't have some piece of your anatomy exposed when you're pinned down behind cover?"

She extracted something from a pocket.

"Hal, who gets the award?"

Crow was hanging his head. He knew for a fact that he had three purple welts on his left shin, having consistently failed to keep it behind the barricade and out of the view of the robot.

Crow, came Hal's single worded reply.

"Congratulations, Crow. You are now the proud recipient of the Purple Polka Dot award for the most hits taken from Rob." She pinned what look like a small service ribbon to his tactical vest, pink with purple dots on it. "Wear it with … uh … pride?"

The rest of the team laughed, as much out of relief at not having won the ignominious award themselves as anything else.

AFTER HANK HAD HANDED over her SWAT gear to Mike, she remained to talk with him.

"You need something, Hank?" Mike asked.

"You might say that. I'm wondering if you could make a couple of things for me."

"Depends. Whatcha need?"

Hank pulled a small sheet of paper from her shorts pocket. "A special pair of pants."

Mike took the paper and looked at it.

Pointing at it, Hank said, "I'd like a small pocket here in the waistband at the center of the back of the pants, and a special button for the closure at the front of the pants."

"What's the pocket for?"

Hank held up a concealable handcuff key. "One of these."

"And the special button?"

"Just needs to be big enough to put one of these inside it. So, a little over an inch around. You know those brass two-piece buttons you can find just about anywhere? Betting you can pop one apart and put it back together with this key inside of it."

"Planning on joining the CIA?"

Hank laughed. "And take a step down from what I'm doing? Hell no."

Mike gave a little disbelieving shake of his head. "Alright, if you want spy pants, I guess I can make spy pants."

"It's just I'm reading this book ..."

Oh, boy. We all know what happens when Hank starts reading her books ...

Hank gave him a look. "You know that I know what you're thinking."

"Wasn't thinking anything."

"Yeah, right. I'm reading this book on covert methods, and think some of the things might be good to incorporate if I ever find myself tasked with going undercover."

"You've got a bum ticker, a watch, and an earpiece."

"Yes I do. And they'll all work just fine until they take my watch and earpiece and leave me with no method of communicating. Those things also don't help much if you've been put in handcuffs and thrown in the trunk of a car."

"You've got a point there." *Maybe on the top of your head, but you've got a point ...* "I'll order a bunch of these keys and make you several pairs of pants like this."

"Don't tailor the pants, Mike. Just get them off the rack. I need to blend in if I'm sent undercover, and you can't blend in if you're wearing tailored clothes."

Mike looked a bit hurt. "But ..."

"Gotta blend in, Mike."

He sighed. "I should have taken a job with the wardrobe department at Paramount."

It was Hank's turn to sigh, but she resisted, thinking another tactic might appease Mike.

"I haven't had a new dress in a while, either. Think you could whip something up?"

Mike perked up. "You know I work on designs all the time ..."

"No, didn't know that."

He walked off to his cutting room and came back with a sketch book. Flipping it open, he showed Hank a page with a drawing of ... Hank. In a revealing blue gown. A small swatch of royal blue satin was attached to the page, along with a very thin, white material. The gown had a swooping split, jeweled along the edges, and held together by the thin material. The split ended at a spot that pointed directly at her crotch. The bodice hung from short sleeves that ended at the shoulders, leaving her back completely bare down to a low-cut waist that just barely covered her behind. Every edge was decked in jewels and sequins.

"Whoa. Spud will never let me out of the house in that."

Mike grinned. "That's the whole idea. It'll give him inspiration."

Hank chuckled. "He doesn't need a lot of inspiration."

"Well, not having a current lady friend, I could use some. Thinking of him getting you out of that—"

"*Mi-ike!*"

Mike shrugged. "I can't make something for Doc Rich that would give me inspiration."

Hank laughed. "What about Janet, then?"

"The problem with Janet is that she's *always* available. Not exactly my type, so not inspired. I don't think I'm *her* type, either."

Hank ran her hand across the fabric and gazed at the rendering. Then she grinned.

"Spud will love it."

"YOU'VE BURIED yourself in that book," Spud remarked as Hank sat reading in the reading nook.

"There's some good stuff in here. Stuff we night be able to use. We rely a lot on our high-tech items, but I don't think we should *totally* rely on them."

"When have we had a situation when we *haven't* been able to rely on them?" Spud asked.

"Edwards. He was moving, so no ability to use the dragon-fly. Plus, he was an active shooter—no time to use the dragon-fly. I had to rely on Amigo to get me a quick firing solution and wing it from there." She gave him an unemotional look. "If I could entirely rely on the tech, we wouldn't need Amigo. But we can't entirely rely on the tech. I was talking with Mike about this just this afternoon, too. Think about it. What happens if one of us gets captured and the perp takes away our watch and our earpiece? Yes, we've still got the bum ticker, so we can be located—but we can't communicate. Any rescue attempt will be going in blind. We will also be unaware of any attempt at rescue. What do we do, just sit around and wait? Hope? While we're being tortured, or worse?"

"This is why Voice made the watch look like a regular smart watch."

"Yes, but even a smart watch can allow you to communicate through your phone. They'd still take it away."

"I'm a bit puzzled about why you're all of a sudden concerned about this stuff," Spud said.

"I suppose you could say it's all of a sudden. Perhaps the research I'm doing on this group, Shining City, is prompting me to look a bit closer at how extremists prepare. You figure they prepare to not be taken in the first place, but why stop there?" She fidgeted a bit. "It also makes me wonder if this is how Spot managed to give us the slip. Did he have a handcuff key hidden on him when he was put in the van to be transported? Did we maybe miss something? If we know how people evade and escape capture, it will help us to better ensure they don't have the means to do so, don't you think?"

"I tell you what: when you think you've learned everything and can capture-proof yourself, the rest of us can see if you really have."

"You've got a deal."

Spud pulled out his set of handcuffs. "Think you can escape me now?"

Hank's eyes went wide, and she leapt up from the loveseat, taking a position on the other side of the coffee table from him. Grinning, Spud went to try and corral her back in the reading nook, but instead she went the other way, laughing and dashing across the living room and into the bedroom with Spud on her heels. Slamming the door shut and locking it left Spud to do a bit of manipulating with the blade of his knife to open the spring latch.

Once he was successful, he entered the bedroom to find the bedroom window open and Hank nowhere in sight. Checking his watch, he sighed. Hank had invoked Hide mode, her icon not visible on the locator. He walked back out to the living room and opened up the front door.

"Hank? *Hank!*"

"Lose your wife?" Amigo called to him from where he was sitting on his porch next door to Spud's residence.

Spud got an exasperated look. "You didn't see her run by here, did you?"

"Nope."

As Spud went to do a search around the house, inside the bedroom the tanning bed opened just a crack. Seeing the bedroom empty, Hank slipped out and went to first the front door, then the back, securing them and telling Hal not to allow entry to *anyone.* Then she went around and secured all the windows as well. Once that was done, she went back to the reading nook and picked up her book again.

"Hal, show Hank," she intoned as she started to read once again.

Spud did a thorough circumnavigation of the house, then stood by the central walkway next to Unitville, looking up and down through the residence level to see if he could see Hank anywhere. He sighed and looked at his watch. The locator screen was still up, and he stared at Hank's icon that showed she was back in the reading nook.

Walking back to the house, he tried the front door.

"Hal, open door to Residence 2."

Entry restricted to FT7.

"Hal, residence also is used by FT6. Open the door."

Entry restricted to FT7 by order of FT7.

Spud sighed a shoulder-heaving sigh, then went to the window at the reading nook and tapped on it.

Hank kept reading her book.

He tapped louder.

Hank still read, her back to him.

He slapped on the window, trying not to break it in the process.

Hank slowly got up and knelt on the loveseat, looking out at him. She then unlatched the window and lifted it open a crack.

"What's the matter? Did you rely too much on your tech to capture me?" she asked.

Hank could just make out the low grumble Spud uttered.

"Open the door, Hank."

"Nope." She grinned at him.

He grabbed the bottom of the window and slid it open, then climbed in through it, landing next to her on the loveseat head first. She laughed as he struggled to get himself upright, right up until he grabbed a wrist and she felt him close one of the handcuffs over it. Snapping the other one around his own wrist, he stood up, forcing her to stand as well.

"Now, you're coming with me, you little perp!"

5

"**Y**ou, all of you, are called to be a holy priesthood," Pastor Benkovic said calmly as he walked among the men of the congregation. "Not just me. Not just Bob Benkovic. All of you."

He let that idea settle in as he slowly walked among them.

"First, you are to be holy as the head of your family: a pure, white family worthy of being called Yeshua's children. Not a half-breed family. Not a papist family. Not an unholy family with *two* men at its head, doing abominable things before Yahweh and bringing condemnation not only upon yourself, but upon all of humanity." He let his voice rise to a crescendo and said, "For Yahweh so loved the world and sacrificed Himself *not* to see it steeped in sin, but in holiness!" His voice dropping low, he added, "And you are the seeds of that holiness, keeping His covenant by marrying pure, raising children who are pure, and teaching those children the ways of purity so that the city on a hill that Yeshua spoke of will be a shining beacon for all to see."

The men murmured and nodded their agreement.

"But it doesn't end there. Yeshua calls you to go forth and make converts among all others whose skin is not stained and whose heritage is not tainted by Jew or Muslim,

Buddhist or homosexual, black man or yellow man or red man. He calls you to go forth and spread His message of purity, and to shake the dust off your feet if you are not accepted in a place, just as it says *right here in the Bible!*" he said, punctuating his words with jabs of a forefinger onto his holy book.

The murmurs of agreement rose in volume, with some of the men lifting a hand in a straight-armed salute.

"He did not come for the lesser races nor the errant religions that some might teach. He did not come so the idolaters, fornicators, and murderers of children in the womb might have solace. He came to separate the *sheep*" —he emphasized with a swipe of his right hand to his right— "from the *goats*" —he asserted with a slash of his left hand to his left— "that the sheep might gain peace and protection by his guiding staff."

"Amen!" someone shouted from within the group of men.

"And how does he console us? By telling us the truth." He broke open his Bible and read from it. "'Blessed are ye, when men shall revile you, and persecute you, and shall say all manner of evil against you falsely, for my sake.' That's what he tells you here in Matthew. *Blessed are ye!* And how true it is. We have seen it ourselves, when the Muslim calls us infidel and the Jew tells us that the Great Extermination was wrong.

"Some will claim that the Great Extermination never happened." He laughed. "They want to deny that it was the *right thing to do*, to purge the Earth of the Jew! Without it, we would be overrun by the Jew! There would be no hope of seeing a shining city on a hill. No hope."

He shook his head sadly, quietly repeating, "No hope, no hope."

He lifted his head back up slowly, his face transforming from sadness to pride. "But here there is hope. There is hope because you, all of you, have taken up the standard and are willing to be a holy warrior for our Abba. To increase His faithful through planting the seed of the true faith in those who have not yet heard of it and by planting the seed of your loins in the wombs of your wives to bring forth a new generation: pure, clean, unblemished before Yahweh."

"GOOD MORNING, everyone. And with apologies, you know what time it is," Spud said as he sat at the conference room table.

"No, no. You have it all wrong. We *love* intel. We wish it could go on all day and half the night. Just can't get enough of it!" Cloud bubbled, getting the rest of the team murmuring their agreement and rapping their knuckles on the table.

The slight undertone of sarcasm wasn't lost on Spud.

"We have some concerns regarding a growing number of parents deciding to home school their children in the wake of NovoRo," Spud said. "The fear is that the kids won't get a well-balanced education, and that some fundamentalist religious ideas will get taught as science."

"NovoRo essentially trash-canned any qualifications for anyone wanting to teach," Voice complained. "We'll end up with a generation of dummies."

"Which is exactly the concern." He consulted his tablet again, then set it down on the table.

"You're kidding," Cloud said.

"Nope."

"Just one?"

"Yup."

"I've heard of slow news days, but this is turning into a slow news *week*," Edge said.

"To make up for that, Hank tells me Amigo has an amusing tale—"

"*You can't make this shit up!*" the rest of the team exclaimed.

"Smothered burrito style," Crow added, getting Amigo smiling.

"Once upon a time on the southern border of the United States ..." Amigo began.

"Oh. It's going to be a fairy tale. We like the real deal there, compadre," Crow said.

"This is el trato real," Amigo said. "I and a fellow agent were patrolling the fence when we get a notice of a sensor going off. So, we take off down along the fence to where the sensor is, and we find a group forming up after going through a breach in the wall. Naturally, they take off. Scatter. A bunch light out in one direction, another bunch lights out in another direction, and the ones right by the wall just go back through to the other side.

"I take off after one group, and my partner, who was driving, takes off after the other. We're both on foot, chasing these ilegales, when we notice all this dust being kicked up back where the hole in the wall is. Which is when I thought, 'Oh, shit. He didn't.'"

Hank started laughing. She'd heard the story before, but still found it hilarious the second time around. "I never did anything this stupid," she said.

"Yeah, he did. My partner left the keys in the ignition of our patrol vehicle, and a bunch of the group that had gone back through the hole in the wall came back and stole it."

Eyes went wide among the other team members while Hank nearly fell out of her chair laughing.

"I start walking back to where the patrol vehicle was, and here's my partner coming the other way toward me. I'm telling you, I was so *enfurecido* I charged him and started smacking him in the head with my cap. '*¡Idiota! How could you do this **again**?*'"

Eyes went wide once more.

"You're kidding," Voice said. "This wasn't the first time he'd let the patrol vehicle get stolen?"

"By a group of *illegals*, no less," Amigo said. "Do you know how embarrassing it is to call in and say, 'Be on the lookout for a group of illegals in an SUV, description: white with a diagonal green stripe and a Homeland Security logo on the door'? When they recovered it, there were *fifteen* illegals in it. Of course, we can't transport them all crammed in like sardines, so they had to call additional vehicles in to transport all those illegals, which didn't leave anyone to transport *us* for a while. I didn't just ask for a different partner—I *begged* for one."

"That guy still in the Border Patrol?" Crow asked.

"I don't know, and I don't care. My supervisor never had me partnered with him again, and then I applied and was accepted for BORTAC."

"And then you disappeared into the desert after your vehicle broke down. They figured you tried to walk out in the southern Arizona heat and didn't make it, though your body has never been found," Voice said, smiling.

"It's a big, lonely desert out there," Amigo said.

"That's it. You all know the drill. Work on your skill sets and see you at lunchtime."

As she emerged from Honor Way, Hank heard in her earpiece, "Hank to Quartermaster."

"Got my pants, Mike?" Hank asked over the comm link as she made her way to the staircase.

"Yes, ma'am. And I'd like to do a fitting."

"Catch up with you later," Hank told Spud, her face beaming as she skipped down the stairs to the fourth level. Swinging into the quartermaster area, she heard Mike call out, "Come on back to the cutting room."

Walking in, she saw two things: a pile of ordinary off-the-rack women's pants and jeans, and a blue satin dress, minus jewels and sequins, draped on Mike's manikin.

"I take it these are the pants with the hidden handcuff keys?" Hank asked, looking first at them.

"I'm a bit miffed that you asked about those ... *things* first," Mike said with a twinge of annoyance.

"You know why you eat your vegetables first and your dessert last?" Hank asked. "Because just about everybody likes saving the best for last."

Appeased, Mike picked up one of the pairs of pants. "I put a little blind stitching here to close the pocket the key is in," he explained, turning the waistband at the center back of the pair he was showing her. "That will keep the key from falling out. If you look closely, you'll see there's a little knot right there. Grasp it with your fingernails and you can pull the thread that keeps the pocket closed."

Hank looked closely, noting the little knot poking out but no other evidence that there was anything unusual about the waistband of the pants. Feeling, she could detect the flat, round key itself hidden in the waistband.

"Very cool."

"Here in the front is your requested special button," Mike said. "These buttons generally snap together. To get it to snap apart, just press on the center of the button. The top of the button will pop off, and the key will drop out, so you want to make sure you're prepared to catch it."

Hank played with the button, pressing it and getting the button to pop apart and drop the key in her hand.

"You can put it back together again as well," Mike conveyed. "Just put your key back inside the cap, put the cap up against the base of the button, press like you're opening the button back up, and gently release the pressure. The cap will snap back onto the base, and you're set to go again."

Hank tried that as well, easily getting the button with its hidden key back together. She chuckled. "I love it."

"I added a little something extra as well." Mike pulled out what looked like an ordinary web belt with a buckle closure that pressed together. "I found these on the Internet and thought the belt buckle would make a good addition to go with the pants."

He disconnected the buckle as one would do ordinarily and showed the inside to Hank.

"Right here is yet another handcuff key, stowed in the center of the buckle between the two clasps. And if you look at the groove on each side where the clasp attaches to the body of the buckle, you'll see that there's a small razor blade embedded in the plastic, so if your bad guy ties you up or uses duct tape, you can cut your way out."

"Oh—that is *very* cool," Hank said, admiring the buckle with its hidden escape items. "The book I'm reading doesn't mention these buckles at all."

"And now for the good stuff," Mike said. "You know what I need you to do."

"Before I do, Hal, isolate quartermaster stores."

Mike raised an eyebrow.

"Two reasons: Spud has been acting a bit jealous lately,

and I don't want him to see the dress until I model it for him."

"Ah. Well, now that you've blinded Hal, strip down to your panties, please, back toward me."

Hank dropped her shorts and shirt on the floor and lifted her hands, waiting for Mike to slip the dress over her head so the fit could be checked.

"You've still got nice legs," he said.

"You're not supposed to be admiring any aspect of my anatomy," Hank warned him.

"Purely a remark made to assure myself I was correct in making another dress that will show them off. When a woman has a beautiful attribute, a good tailor will emphasize that attribute with the dress he makes for her."

He dropped the dress over her raised arms and smoothed it down over her hips, giving it a little tug to get the bodice to fall into place. Then he first walked slowly around her, coming to stand back facing her, admiring his work.

"I know you run up and down the silo staircase, but how you do it and don't have your measurements change one iota is beyond me. I used the same measurements I used for both the red dress and the purple gown, and this dress fits perfectly."

"It's called trading fat for muscle," Hank commented.

"Whatever it's called, I think Spud will approve of the new dress." He pulled his full-length mirror out from where he kept it tucked between two shelving units with bolts of cloth and let her get a look.

Hank swooped and turned in the dress, imagining it decked out with the sequins and jewels Mike's drawing showed.

"I think Spud's going to have a hard-on the size of the

Washington Monument when he sees this. The only problem I see is that my panties show."

"They won't when you wear this," Mike said, bringing forth a skimpy thong made of matching blue satin.

Hank took the thong and suspended it from her fingers. "You know, Spud hates the epilator. He thinks it's barbaric. He'd probably *really* think it barbaric if he saw me using it ... to keep southern regions tidy. But something tells me this won't hide much, and having a hairy blond fringe showing would definitely not be very romantic."

"See, this is why I'm hesitant to get permanently involved with a woman," Mike said. "You gals are definitely high maintenance." He pulled the dress off her and hung it back on the manikin. "You can get dressed. Me? I've gotta figure out how to find enough time to sew on about a bazillion sequins and jewels."

"Sure you don't want to try the helicopter?" Crow asked as he and Spud made their way to the airport.

"Positive."

"That's what Hank said, you know."

"I realize that."

"You're willing to be beat by a girl?" Crow chided.

"First off, Hank is not a 'girl.' She's a woman in every sense of the word, believe me. Furthermore, there are many things she beats me at—and I'm fine with that. We all cross-train and try to acquire as many skills as we can, as well as duplicate the skills of others. That doesn't mean we all have the same skills, nor the same level of skill at the skills we share. I'm fine with *that*, too. I think she's fine with the fact that there are things I do better than she does as well."

Crow felt a bit disappointed. He had been looking forward to bringing yet another pilot into the fold occupied by the rotary wing group.

"You're sure."

"Positive."

Damn.

"Alright. We'll take the RG and do a little surveillance along the highway. See if we can spot any more sex trafficking going on."

Arriving at the airport, they did their usual routine of inspecting and readying the small, high-winged Cessna for flight, culminating in Spud taking the left seat and getting the aircraft airborne. He swung out so that his track to intersect I-80 would take them above the Lockridge range complex. Looking down, he noted that the weekend warriors were out in force, with quite a few vehicles parked at the ranges in use. Off to the western-most area of the range complex, he noted a single vehicle: a black SUV, with two people prone at the firing line of the extreme long-distance range. As they passed overhead, the two people occupying the range rolled on their sides and waved.

"Speaking of my lovely wife, there she is now."

"Lying down with another man," Crow poked.

"With a gun in her hands. I think she can fend him off," Spud said.

Crow chuckled.

Spud banked and headed directly south along Road H to intercept the interstate, then turned west. Flying above the interstate, they checked out the rest stops near Grand Island, as well as the truck stops and intersections along the way for any sign of illicit activity. Continuing on, they proceeded to check out every rest stop and truck stop all the way to the state line.

"Starting to get a little bumpy," Spud commented.

"Yeah, the weather report said wind was supposed to pick up. Probably a good idea to head on back," Crow said.

Spud performed a neat tear-drop and resumed his overflight of the interstate.

"IFR flight plan," Crow said.

"You want me to ask for a pop-up?" Spud asked.

"No. You're *on* an IFR flight plan. 'I Follow Roads.'"

Spud laughed. "Never heard that one before."

"Oh, aviation is full of abbreviations," Crow told him. "ILS. 'I'm Lost Severely'. NDB. 'Nasty Damned Beacon'. VOR. 'Very Odd Radio'. VFR. 'Very Few Restrictions'. You get the idea."

Spud laughed. "I'm going to have to write those down. I apparently was told incorrectly, for instance, that 'ILS' stood for 'Instrument Landing System'."

"It pays to not do all your flying with Cloud," Crow quipped. "He'll lie to you every time."

Spud continued eastbound over top of the interstate, continuing slightly past where he'd intercepted it on the way westbound.

"I'd like to get a look at the two nearby rest areas," he said. "Closely. It gives Hank some peace of mind when I report back that I didn't see anything."

As he overflew the eastbound rest area, he reported, "Just one lone tractor trailer rig down there."

"Is it rocking?" Crow asked.

"Negatory, good buddy." As the plane took a jolt, he added, "But if it was, I might think it was due to the wind. Time to head back to the airport."

"Agreed," Crow said. "It's about to become a little less fun up here. The TAF said it was supposed to have built to twenty-four gusting to forty-three a couple of hours ago. I thought maybe it wouldn't materialize, but I think the wind was just taking its time getting here."

"Funny we didn't hit it west of here," Spud said as he turned toward the airport.

"This front is sliding down from the north," Crow said. "Gonna be a cold one tonight for all the above deck folks down there."

Spud took a few minutes to swing out one more time above the Lockridge complex.

"Looks like Hank and Amigo packed up. It must be getting interesting on the ground."

Crow split the radios so that Spud could use one while he listened to the Automated Weather Observation System.

"You've got the twenty-four knots, but not the gusts," he told Spud. "It's coming right down the runway, though. Land on runway 35 and you'll be fine."

IN THE EASTBOUND rest area along I-80 near York, Nebraska, a lone truck driver sat in the cab of his rig and drank coffee from a thermos. He watched in his side view mirror as a small aircraft droned above the interstate, making its way eastward. Leaning over and looking up, he watched as it approached and flew directly overhead, then turned and headed to the north.

"Damned bear in the air," he muttered. "Gonna have to watch my step, keep it nice and legal. Where there's an eye in the sky, there's usually a bear on the ground somewhere as well." He snickered. "They can't hand me a ticket for drinking coffee, though. As long as nobody runs my CDL, I'll be fine."

"I WAS a little worried about you when the wind started picking up," Hank remarked to Spud as they sat drinking coffee while waiting for Rose to finish making dinner.

Edge made his presence known in The Restaurant as well, first making a stop at the coffee pot, then heading into the kitchen.

"What are you making for tonight?" he asked Rose.

"Barbecue spare ribs."

Edge nodded approval. "Sounds good. What kind of vegetable?"

"Mashed sweet potatoes."

He nodded again. "That sounds good, too." He looked around on the cooktop. "Nothing else?"

"Got another vegetable in the oven."

"What is it?"

"Roasted garlic Parmesan cauliflower."

"I don't like cauliflower."

"You'll like this cauliflower," Rose asserted.

"I don't like cauliflower, *period*," Edge complained.

Rose took a look at the potato masher in her hand, shifted it to the other hand, then reached up and smacked Edge in the back of the head with the now-empty hand. Sternly, she said, "You're gonna *eat* this cauliflower, you're gonna *like* this cauliflower, and right now, you're gonna get outta my kitchen and go sit down like a good boy."

Edge stared at her for a moment, then turned and walked out of the kitchen, picking up his mug of coffee that he'd placed on the prep table as he went. When he sat down at the team's table, he noticed they were all grinning at him.

"Ain't funny," he said.

"Says *you*," Voice chortled.

Edge glared at him. "Where does she get off smacking me like that?"

"Be lucky she's not Mexican," Amigo piped up.

"Why? What do Mexican women do?"

"You know those plastic flip-flops you get for the beach? They'll smack you in the head with one of *those*."

The low growl Edge uttered indicated he wasn't keen on the idea of getting smacked in the head at all.

"Maybe you should just realize that badgering Mama Rose is a bad idea," Cloud told him.

Rose came back out to the table, setting bowls of potatoes and roasted cauliflower down. Taking up the serving spoon that was in the bowl of cauliflower, she served some onto Edge's plate.

"Eat your cauliflower," she ordered him.

Edge's countenance showed borderline anger. The rest of the team watched him, expecting him to explode. Not even turning to face her, he growled, "Mama Rose, I don't appreciate being treated like a baby."

"Then quit actin' like one. Eat your cauliflower—it's good for you."

Edge turned red, whether from anger or embarrassment was hard to tell. Rose disappeared back into the kitchen, coming back out with a platter of barbecued ribs and a loaf of bread on a board. She stood next to Edge with a hand on her hip. The team watched to see who would win the contest of wills.

Rose, of course.

Edge reached out with his fork and stabbed a piece of the offending vegetable as if it was a venomous snake. Then he put it grudgingly in his mouth. His eyes opened wide with surprise. Chewing and swallowing, he declared, "That's really good!"

"Told you." With that, Rose disappeared back into the kitchen.

"Rose is going to get you eating vegetables besides corn and green beans in no time," Cloud said with a chuckle.

"You know, as long as we're in such a dry spell as far as news goes, we should sit down at intel tomorrow and go back over everything we know about the UniPerp case," Edge said.

The team members nodded, no one caring to add anything while they were devouring the ribs Rose had made —not even Hank.

Edge speared more of the cauliflower, which was disappearing off his plate faster than the remaining team members ever thought any vegetable would.

"It seems that you've taken a keener interest in the UniPerp case after the last event," Crow noted.

"The bastard takes out seven marines, I take it a little personally," Edge said, his cauliflower consumed and reaching for ribs and potatoes. He hesitated briefly and took some more cauliflower as well, to the astonishment of his teammates. Amigo resisted the urge to notify Medical that there was nothing wrong with anyone's heart, feeling Edge would be sure to get back at him somehow ... perhaps in a way none too pleasant. As it was, Crow beat him to it.

"Don't look now, but Edgie Wedgie likes his veggies."

Edge stood up in a way calculated to display his full six-foot-six-inch, two-hundred-and-sixty-pound frame.

"Edgie's gonna give *you* a wedgie if you're not careful. I'll yank your balls all the way up to your *chin*."

"Not dinnertime conversation," Voice chided.

Edge cut him a look that indicated he might just be second in line.

"Alright, alright—leave the big guy alone," Spud said. "Or he'll kill you."

"You know, we don't have 'pick on Edge day' too often, but it's fun when we do," Crow said.

Edge growled.

"As long as we don't take it too far," Crow added.

"Like I said, we should spend a little time on UniPerp," Edge reiterated.

"We should spend some time on Spot, too," Hank said.

"Now, there's a name I haven't heard in a while," Crow remarked.

"I think I know how he might have escaped," Hank said. "I'm even in a position to demonstrate it for you."

"How are you intending to do that?" Cloud asked.

"By having one of you handcuff me to my chair."

Edge chuckled. "Anyone have any experience handcuffing Hank to a chair?"

Spud scowled briefly, then wiped the scowl clean and replaced it with a Secret Service face as he got up, pulling handcuffs from his back pocket. Going over to where Hank was sitting, he took her wrist and handcuffed her to her chair, then went back and sat down while the other men grinned at him.

Hank grinned as well. She was already dangling the handcuffs from her previously bound wrist.

"Only one way you did that," Voice said. "You've got a key."

Hank showed her empty hands, then stood and pulled her pockets inside out, laying everything out on the table in front of her. Voice pawed through what had been the contents of her pockets, not finding a key anywhere among them.

"It's an old covert ops trick," Edge said. Getting up and going behind her, he looked at Spud and asked, "May I?"

Spud gave his permission with a palm-up motion of his hand.

Edge took his forefinger and thumb and slid along the waistband of Hank's pants. He smiled. Working it loose with his fingers, he removed the hidden key from the small pocket sewn in the waistband of Hank's pants.

"Got me," Hank said. "Go ahead—cuff me again."

Edge took the handcuffs and cuffed Hank's two hands in front of her.

The men watched her closely as she appeared to sit upright and still. When Edge had sat back down, she looked over at him and smiled. Then she extracted her hands from beneath the table and dropped the open handcuffs in front of her.

"You've got another key."

She stood. "You're welcome to try and find one," she offered.

Edge ran his fingers around her waistband again, following it all the way from the button in the front on one side to the other. He patted her down and checked the hem of her shirt.

Nothing.

"Can't be in the hem of your pants," he reasoned. "You never bent down. It has to be somewhere around your waist."

"She's got to have another key, though," Voice said.

"How many keys do you have, Love?" Spud asked.

"Three. There are two left."

He got up and went over to her. "I know that no one else would dare do this just because they'd be afraid I'd break their fingers." He reached down her pants and ran his fingers around the elastic of her panties, then patted her down a bit more thoroughly than Edge had dared: everything from her waistband to her knees that she could have possibly been able to reach.

He looked at her steadily. "I'm stumped."

Hank undid her belt buckle and withdrew the key it held.

"There's one."

She then popped open the button on her pants.

"There's the other one."

"Where'd you learn this?" Crow asked.

"You guys always smirk and chuckle every time I say I've been reading a book. Well, I read a book, and now I'm applying some of the things I've learned." She winked at them all. "Stay tuned. There's more to come."

HANK SAT READING from her tablet, every so often letting out a chuckle or a little laugh. Spud smiled approvingly. *It's about time she read something other than a crime novel.*

Hank finally set her tablet down, chuckling and shaking her head.

"A comedy this time?" Spud asked.

Hank laughed. "You'd probably think so."

"Then what is it?"

"A crime novel."

"Does this mean you're laughing because you know the reaction I'm going to have to realizing you're reading another crime novel?"

"No, I'm laughing because this author is ludicrously funny."

"A *funny* crime novel?"

"Not intentionally funny," Hank said. "But this author is very lacking in a true understanding of both police procedures and forensics. And firearms? This guy knows nothing about guns."

"Did you just decide to quit reading it?"

"No, I read it. It's just nearly totally unbelievable. A sergeant doing detective work? No. Walking around in the crime scene? No. Even doing *anything* at a crime scene without cordoning it off first? Absolutely not. It might make a good episode in one of those stupid cable programs that's just designed to satisfy people's thirst for gore, but otherwise it's terrible. Anyone who believes this is how cops operate would be either sorely disappointed or, if they're a bit more intelligent, totally unimpressed."

She reached over to her bookshelf and slid out a print book.

"More research?"

"Nope. Entertainment."

"Spicy romance?"

"I keep telling you, I don't need a spicy romance. I've got a spicy romance in the flesh. He's handsome, fit, likes to caress, is a helluva kisser, and is great in the sack. Why do I need a spicy romance?"

"The good scenes might make you want to do a comparison."

Hank slapped him with the book while he leaned away and chuckled.

"You're a sex maniac," Hank said.

"I wasn't before I met you. It's your fault." Spud watched her for a beat. "Are you complaining?"

"I don't think you'll find many women out there complaining about getting too much totally satisfying sex," Hank proposed as she cracked open her book.

"What's this one?"

Hank raised her eyes and stared ahead of herself for a moment. *Should I tell him?*

"It's a collection of horror stories."

Spud studied her. "You're beginning to truly worry me."

"Think. Someone conceived of these horror stories *in their head.* In their head is just one step away from actually pulling off what they've conceived. This is getting into the mind of a criminal who has actually taken that step."

"I thought you said it was entertainment."

Hank sputtered and said, "It is. But also research."

Spud sighed. *My wife ...*

6

Spud sat down with his tablet and nested his hands together in front of him. The rest of the team eyed him, wondering why he hadn't given his usual pre-intel briefing greeting.

"Not even going to say it," he finally declared. "Every time I do, the next thing I hear is a bunch of whining and crying about how boring intel is, how all I do is read the news and I have no other talents, et cetera, et cetera, et cetera."

"We appreciate you. We really do," Voice said. "It's intel briefings we don't appreciate."

"And we all know they're—"

"—What keep the unit in business," the rest of the team joined in unison with Cloud.

"I should have stayed in bed," Spud muttered.

The rest of the team could see the slight twinkle in Spud's eye that he let escape through his Secret Service façade, though. He'd simply decided to beat the crew to the usual pre-briefing ribbing.

"First up, we have continuing stories about seizures of drugs coming into the country. It seems that in spite of the border wall, the amounts of drugs seized haven't shown any decline."

"That's because ninety percent of drug smuggling occurs through the ports of entry," Cloud observed. He turned to Amigo. "Am I right?"

"Absolutely," Amigo confirmed.

"How do we stop the drugs from coming through the ports of entry?" Edge asked.

"You won't ever stop it as long as the cartels can buy off our agents to look the other way," Amigo said. "There's a lot of money a dirty agent can get."

"You would think, though, that the interdictions would drive up the cost of the product," Voice figured.

"An addict like my brother was doesn't look at cost. They just look at how they can get their hands on a fix," Hank said. "As far as the cartels are concerned, the interdictions are the cost of doing business."

"We have controversy regarding surveillance being conducted via people's cell phones."

"It's been a hack that's been around for a long time," Voice said. "People think that cell phone security has gone up, but the basic way a cell phone interacts with a cell tower hasn't changed at all."

"How can people avoid being tracked through their phones, then?" Crow asked.

"Stick them in a Faraday bag."

"Then you don't get your calls."

"You'll get your messages," Voice said. "Just don't take the phone out of the bag until you're somewhere you don't mind someone knowing about."

"The technology to stop having a cell phone hacked hasn't been developed?" Amigo asked.

"The problem with any cybertechnology is that as quickly as it's developed, someone figures out how to exploit it. I'm not the only one around who knows how to do this stuff."

"That's comforting to know," Crow said, his voice dripping with sarcasm.

"That's it for the serious stuff," Spud said.

"Again? It seems like there isn't any news out there these days," Hank remarked.

"I think what we're seeing is people's reactions to the election being over, NovoRo being a thing of the past, and just wanting to make a collective sigh of relief," Spud said. "Which isn't such a bad thing."

"Why aren't we planning a ski vacation, then?" Crow asked.

"Because the minute we do, we know the other shoe will drop," Cloud replied.

"I think we're missing something in this briefing," Edge said. "Where's our daily edition of You Can't Make This Stuff Up?"

"Seems like there are more of those kinds of stories than ever," Spud said. "And indeed, you can't make this one up."

The team settled in, each one grabbing another of the snacks Rose had made and left on the table for them, to hear the latest in odd news from Spud.

"It seems we have a black who shares Doc Sue's tastes in candy bars."

A collective raised eyebrow went up among the other members of the team.

"This black comes into a neighborhood market every day and swipes a Snickers bar."

"Why don't they just arrest him?" Crow asked.

"No one wants to do that. This is a big black."

"Call for backup. Anyone think of that?"

"Over a candy bar?" Amigo asked.

Crow shrugged. "Keep letting it happen, and pretty soon all his buddies are going to be in there swiping a candy bar too."

"They eventually did call for backup," Spud said. "Seems this black was intimidating the other customers. Even the management was afraid of him. They didn't want this black getting his paws on them."

"Big guy."

"Yup."

"What happened when backup arrived?" Amigo asked.

"They shot him with a tranquilizer gun, stuffed him in a cage, and let him go far away in the woods."

"That sounds a bit extreme."

Hank started chuckling.

"You think it's funny that they shot the guy with a tranquilizer gun and left him out in the woods?" Amigo asked.

"It's what I'd do if my candy crook was a black—"

"I had no idea you held those kinds of views," Amigo protested, cutting her off.

"—bear," Hank finished.

Spud laughed. "For a second there, I thought Amigo was going to demand someone else spot for you, Love. She's right, this was a big black bear. The local game warden felt it best if the bear reacquainted himself with roots and berries, so the bear was relocated out in the woods, far from any groceries, convenience stores, neighborhood markets, etc."

Amigo had turned a pretty good shade of crimson when the explanation was given.

"That's it, and you all know the drill," Spud said. "See you at lunch."

"We have learned that we are to be holy warriors," Pastor Benkovic said serenely as he walked among the men of the congregation. "We are to take up arms and be prepared to fight against the evil one. Should we tremble? Should we avoid the fight that is to come? What does our Abba say to this? What did the followers of Yeshua, who knew Him when He walked the Earth, say?"

He broke open his Bible and began to read.

"This is from Ephesians. Finally, my brethren, be *strong* in the Lord, and in the *power* of His might. Put on the whole armor of God, that ye may be able to stand against the wiles of the devil."

He bent down to look into the eyes of one of the seated men. "Have you put on the whole armor of God, Leon? Because if you fear what may come, I tell you right now: you have not."

He stood up and addressed all of the men collectively. "*Anyone* who fears what may come has *not* put on the whole armor of God! Yahweh warns us! He tells us who our foes are, even though their faces might be hidden."

He took up his Bible and read further.

"For we wrestle *not* against flesh and blood, but against principalities, against powers, against the rulers of the darkness of this world, against spiritual wickedness in high places!

"So, are we afraid? If you are, then read on.

"Wherefore take unto you the whole armor of God, that ye may be able to withstand in the evil day, and having done all, to stand. Stand therefore, having your loins girt about with truth, and having on the breastplate of righteousness."

He looked into the face of one of the young men in the congregation.

"We know what that breastplate is made of, don't we, Robert?"

He stood upright again and bellowed to the men. *"It is forged from the truth that this nation was founded by Christian men as a Christian nation, with its principles rooted in the Holy Bible that we hold as our guiding beacon."* His voice growing quieter, he added, "For there can be no better, no purer law than the law set forth in this book."

From behind the screen at the back of the assembly room, he heard a young woman say, "Love one another as I have loved you." His head whipping in that direction, Pastor Benkovic demanded, "Who spoke?"

As he strode down the aisle between the chairs the men occupied, he repeated his demand.

"Who spoke?"

Seeing other women distancing themselves from the one who had, he stood in front of her and yelled, *"Was it you? Stand up!"*

The young woman, a mere teenager, stood.

Leaning toward her, Pastor Benkovic asked, "What did you say?"

"I said—"

Her words were cut short by the full-force slap of his hand against her face.

"Women ... are to remain ... SILENT in the church!" he roared.

As the congregation dispersed, the young woman walked with her parents toward their home. When she felt certain only her parents would hear her, she said, "I want to leave this place." She turned to her mother, tears in her eyes, and said, "I want to go home."

The mother's face reflected the conflict she felt as she quietly said, "That will be up to your father."

She turned to look at her father. He looked back at her, and noting the swollen red handprint on her face, ground his teeth. His distaste for the teachings of this church had been growing for some time, and seeing the result of the pastor striking his daughter set his resolve. As the family entered the house they lived in, he turned to his wife and daughter and said, "Pack just what you need to travel. We're leaving tonight."

"READY TO DO A LITTLE FLYING TODAY?" Cloud asked Edge after they'd passed through Honor Way.

"I noticed the wind had calmed down. Finally," Edge said. "Can we get a little time in 100UN?"

"You're a man I can admire," Cloud said, smiling. He, too, had been wanting to get in a little helicopter time, especially after the little competition between him and Crow over which of the two new helicopter pilot candidates would finish first. He felt a need to get Edge along the way to his commercial and instrument rating in the helicopter to make up for tricking Crow into the belief that he would only train Hank to the private pilot level.

Edge figured as much, even though Cloud hadn't said a word about it. "You know, it's fine by me that Hank made it all the way to commercial before I did," he said.

"Well … I figure I owe ya," Cloud admitted.

"I figure I'll be better at the helicopter than Hank is when it's all said and done," Edge said. Though the statement might have sounded like something born of ego, his tone sounded apologetic. "Hank works hard at flying, but I think she doesn't ever feel quite at one with even an airplane. It's her competitiveness that makes her succeed."

"Yeah, she *is* a little pistol, isn't she?"

"I think maybe she feels like she's a little inferior because she's a woman. Being competitive is the way she makes up for it."

Cloud laughed. "You're probably right. Plus, she gives off a little sign of that every once in a while."

"The cussing," Edge said with a grin.

Cloud laughed. "You've noticed that, have you?"

Edge smiled. "I've noticed she's toned down quite a bit since she first arrived. I figure the degree of cussing is directly proportional to her discomfort with a situation."

"I think you're right. Go grab your gear while I head down to Mike and get the key for the SUV."

As Edge gathered up his flight gear, his mind wandered to all of the encounters he'd had with Hank since she arrived. They all seemed to fall into focus on one night under the tangerine tree. *I never told anyone about any of the crap in Afghanistan,* he thought. *Maybe that's why I reacted the way I did.* He felt instantly ashamed. *Spud's my best friend,* he reminded himself, feeling more in control when considering that the need to concentrate on his flying would soon erase all of the present thoughts he was having.

CROW, Amigo, and Voice had opted to join Hank in the gym.

"We'll start with some simple tai chi moves that are designed to loosen up every muscle and joint," Hank said. She was looking forward to the session, having had what she considered to be an overly-long hiatus from doing tai chi herself. "Tai chi is kind-of like the old joke about the person who goes to his doctor and says, 'Doc, it hurts when I do this,'" she continued, holding an arm up. "The doctor says, 'Then don't do that.' As you do the tai chi exercises, don't do them to the point of pain. Once you feel resistance, you've gone far enough. These preliminary exercises start at the head and move down to the legs and feet. First up: loosening the neck."

She rotated her head around slowly, letting it fall as if her neck was like the spring on a bobblehead doll. "Nice and slow. Six turns to the right, then six to the left."

Her three proteges imitated the move.

"This is supposed to prepare us to do a martial art?" Crow asked.

"Tai chi isn't really a martial art," Hank said. "It's a method of conditioning the body. It can *help* with doing a martial art, but it really isn't one." She finished the exercise and then announced, "Next move is lowering the shoulders. Hunch your shoulders up," she continued, demonstrating, "press your shoulders down by extending your arms straight down your sides as far as it's comfortable for you. Six times."

She found herself a little distracted as she watched Spud pad his way barefooted across to the pool, a towel draped across his shoulders and wearing a pair of Speedos. She smiled and reflected that she could see how he got his code name. *And you call **him** oversexed,* one of her little voices chided. *He at least had the wisdom to choose black,* another one observed. *Still, nice butt.*

She was shaken from her reverie by Voice telling the others, "You know what Spud said to her on the way to Quantico on the plane? 'If you like what you see, you can see more of it.'"

"You're kidding," Amigo said.

"No, he's not. I heard it on the comm as well," Crow said.

Hank rolled her eyes. "Third exercise is shaking the

hands. This is an especially useful exercise if you find your-self with the urge to slap someone."

SPUD DROPPED his towel by the edge of the pool and dove in, slicing smoothly into the water and back to the surface in an easy freestyle stroke. He enjoyed his workouts, no matter what he chose to do on a particular day. Something about the repetitive motion allowed him to let his mind drift to other things: things he found more interesting or pressing. Today was no exception.

It wasn't long before he found himself thinking of the few times when Hank had bolted upright in bed, awakened by another nightmare. *Always Spot. Out, out, damned Spot.* He questioned whether it was really wrong of him to have wished NovoRo would claim him. *Maybe it did. But then, wouldn't we have gotten word that his body had been recovered? Maybe not if he's squirreled himself away the way Unabomber did. Hiding in the woods somewhere, living off the land as best he can. If I could give one gift to Hank, it would be Hunt's death certificate. This afternoon, we pull out everything we have on him, too.*

"WELCOME BACK. I trust everyone got in a good workout this morning—including our aviators," Spud began as the team settled back down in the conference room.

"We want to take a look at what's happening with two of our long-standing cases: Daniel Hunt, aka Spot; and UniPerp. I thought we'd start with Hunt, given he's still giving Hank nightmares."

"His is probably the easiest one to get out of the way as well, given we really don't have a lot on him," Crow pointed out.

The team took note as Doc Andy walked into the room, followed by Rose.

"I hope you don't mind if I sit in on this one," Doc Andy said as he took an offered seat and Rose placed a plate of fresh fruit, cut up in easy-to-handle pieces, on the table.

"Mama Rose, have you been talking a bit too much with Doc Rich?" Amigo questioned, eliciting a raised eyebrow from Doc Andy.

"You need things that are *good* for you," Rose practically ordered before making her way back out through Honor Way.

Doc Andy chuckled.

"Don' miy you sidding in ad all," Hank said through a mouthful of strawberry. She swallowed and added, "It was an oversight to not inform you of this afternoon's exercise, given you're our profiler."

Doc Andy broke a rare smile. Hank didn't know whether it was because he was pleased to be included in the discussion or amused at her attempt to talk with her mouth full ... *again*.

"We know that Hunt managed to get over or through the fence at Quantico without being seen during his escape," Crow began. "We also know that he used an assumed identity to get a job at an animal shelter doing euthanasias. It's probably safe to assume he's taken yet another identity, as Hal's searches of people matching the name of the identity he took hasn't come up with anyone matching his description."

"We also know that he has apparently not gotten his teeth fixed," Voice said. "I had Hal do a search of dentist's records and didn't find anyone with a fake ID that matched the kind of bridge he would have had to have made. Plenty with fake IDs, plenty with that kind of bridge, and even a number who had implants done. None of the fake IDs matched up with the dental work he'd have wanted."

"You got into people's dental records?" Crow asked.

Voice grinned. "It's not that hard."

"It doesn't mean he didn't get the teeth replaced with either a bridge or implants," Hank said. "If he's managed to get down to the border, he could have crossed into Mexico and had the work done there."

"He'd have been flagged as a wanted fugitive the minute he tried to come back," Crow said. "They use face recognition at the ports of entry, and you have to have at least a border crossing card. You need a valid ID to get that."

"It all depends on how he might have crossed," Cloud pointed out. "He could have got in and out the same way illegals do. Just hop a barricade or go through a breach in the wall. We just heard Amigo tell us a little story about illegals going through a breach in the wall and swiping a Border Patrol vehicle."

The rest of the team chuckled, recalling the tale.

"Whatever the circumstances there, we haven't heard or seen any news of Hunt since finding his face for the issuance of the ID he had at the animal control facility. And we're further hampered by the fact that we aren't officially on Hunt's case," Edge reminded them. "Unless and until the U.S. Marshals Service decides they need our help, we won't have access to much of what *they* have, either."

"Sure we do," Voice asserted.

Spud reacted with an 'of course' gesture of his hand toward Voice. "Hal. What has Hal gathered from the Marshals Service?"

"They don't have anything we don't on Hunt," Voice said, sounding dejected. "It's like he fell off the planet. It also appears that they've more or less given up on getting him. It's currently filed as a cold case."

"It may be cold for them, but there's no reason it should be cold for us," Spud said. "It's become a little personal for me. He assaulted and tried to rape my wife, which is bad enough. Now Hank has nightmares about him, and the only way they're going to stop is if he's either put behind bars or his body is found. If you ask me, preferably the latter."

Doc Andy noted some of the team member's eyes glancing at him covertly.

"It's not unusual for a woman who has either been sexually assaulted or come close to it to have recurring thoughts or dreams about the event. It is also not unusual for the spouse of that woman to wish harm to come to the assailant. Both reactions are not only natural, but to be expected. It would be more troubling if I *didn't* see such reactions," he said. "They fade with time, but I agree with Spud. They will fade faster when the wrong that was done to Hank is balanced with bringing Daniel Hunt to justice."

"What's your take on it, Doc Andy? What do you think happened to Spot?" Crow asked.

"Daniel Hunt is both narcissistic and predatory—not the best combination of dangerous traits, and something he was clever enough to keep hidden during his intake examination for acceptance into the unit. His narcissism allows him to talk a good talk, which he might use to satisfy his predatory nature as well. He may still be raping women, but also be able to manipulate them into believing they initiated the event. They might come away feeling used rather than feeling raped."

"Hank believes he may have prepared for potentially

having to make an escape by hiding a handcuff key in his clothing," Spud put forth. "His shackles were found on the floor of the transport van."

"He could also have taken a key off the marshal he killed," Cloud said.

Doc Andy pondered this a bit. "He is certainly narcissistic in my professional opinion, and the attempted rape also speaks to him being predatory. Taking a job at an animal shelter as the one doing the euthanasias speaks also to his predatory nature. He exhibits two of the four dangerous personality types already. If he had indeed sequestered a handcuff key on his person in order to prepare for a potential desire to escape, that may indicate he incorporates yet a third of the four traits: paranoia."

Hank looked at Doc Andy steadily. "Do you think it's paranoia that *I* have not one but three handcuff keys currently sequestered on my person?"

Doc Andy gave her an unemotional look. "May I ask why you have three handcuff keys hidden on your person?"

"Not just three handcuff keys. Two razor blades as well."

"Again, may I ask why?"

Hank smiled. "It's preparation for any future mission that might require that I go undercover. The purpose of the handcuff keys is intuitive. The next most common method of binding someone is with duct tape, and that's what the razor blades are for."

"She's been challenging us to keep her from escaping," Edge explained. "She's using some tried-and-true covert ops methods."

"Very interesting," Doc Andy said. "Given that, I'd say no, you aren't displaying paranoia, Hank."

"It's good to see *someone* believes I'm sane."

"I am also the one who counts. But back to Spot, I hardly

believe *he* is sane. It's even potentially correct to say he is not just insane but unstable. If those last two hold true, then he would possess all four of the dangerous personality types: narcissistic, predatory, paranoid, and unstable. The quadfecta, if you will, of dangerous personality traits. This would make him a very dangerous man indeed—one who might do anything simply to make a point, under the belief that he is superior to everyone around him and therefor invincible. If this is the case, then finding Daniel Hunt should not be a case that ever goes cold. Not until he is found, dead or alive."

"I'll keep Hal on it," Voice said. "I've kept Hal on it all along. If anyone can think of any other factor that I can use as part of the search criteria, let me know."

"Let's move on to UniPerp," Spud said, setting aside his tablet's display of information on the Daniel Hunt case with a swipe of his finger to bring up the UniPerp information.

"A little recap," Edge began. "So far, we know of eleven different incidents with a total of one hundred and ninety-two victims. The first six incidents seem to not have any pattern to them. Since those first six, he has fallen into the pattern of choosing seven victims with some identical trait. For each of the events, he leaves a message either in the Lincoln newspaper or on a billboard nearby along I-80. His first ten events featured having one letter in the message capitalized, which if put together spell out 'UNIT WILL DIE.' The last event had five letters capitalized sequentially that spell out 'SEVEN.'

"He's so obsessed with the number seven that Voice has Hal programmed to alert when an event with anything to do with the number seven comes up. It's what got us involved in the Grand Forks case: there were seven victims. In that case, though, there was no message in the Lincoln paper nor on the usual billboard, so we don't believe the case was related to UniPerp."

"I might not be so quick to dismiss the Grand Forks case as being unrelated to UniPerp," Doc Andy said. "He may simply have not had the time to post a message, or had decided he'd given you enough clues. There hasn't been another incident that Hal has alerted you about since your return from Grand Forks, has there?"

"It's a little early to make that call," Cloud said. "UniPerp doesn't hit back to back. In almost two years, he's struck eleven times, and the intervals between events aren't regular."

"I still believe that there had to be another event early on that we missed," Hank said. "If he's so obsessed with the number seven, then why were there only six initial events? I think if we could identify that initial event, we'd know what sparked him off. That in turn might give us a valuable clue as to his identity."

"That seems reasonable," Doc Andy said. "I agree that he seems obsessed with the number seven. But then, the number seven has been thought for centuries to have mystical or magical properties associated with it. It was the seventh day on which the Bible says God rested from creating, making the seventh day a holy day to be specially observed. The New Testament talks of seven archangels, seven seals, and seven trumpets."

"Blobel, the perpetrator in Grand Forks, was a fortune teller. He used tarot cards. The woman we met in the diner, Martha, said he saw me as having a crown on my head with seven stars at the top. One of the tarot cards has a blond-haired woman with a crown on her head that has seven stars on top," Hank remarked.

"More than one religion talks of seven heavens," Edge

said, "and some even talk of seven hells or seven underworlds."

"In the Cherokee belief, there are seven clans," Crow said. "The animals and plants got their characteristics when they were all told to stay awake for seven nights. The first woman would give birth every seven days until there were too many; then she could only give birth once a year."

"Surprising how people from different locations that couldn't communicate with each other all see the number seven as something mystical," Doc Andy remarked. "But this points to why UniPerp may also hold the number seven as special. He uses the number seven as a talisman to keep him from being captured. I think Hank may be correct in concluding that there must have been an initial event to the ones before he started actually using the number seven for his kill number. It would reinforce the number seven as something magical to him. In which case, I would expect that he might change tactics after the fourteenth event to maintain the pattern of seven."

"Then we might lose what we've been able to use to identify the events," Voice said. "Unless he continues to post a message as well. Right now, I have Hal identify seven victims with a common factor. Even though we don't think it's a UniPerp event, the Grand Forks case was seven victims with thallium poisoning as the manner of death, which caused Hal to flag the event and send an alert."

"What's your take on him, Doc Andy? What makes him tick?" Edge asked.

"I still feel that we're looking at someone with a military background and most likely one of the special forces. He would have perhaps been given a reprimand, lost a coveted position, or been court marshaled as a result of some transgression. He's seeking revenge against the authorities he sees as having caused his downfall. It seems clear that he's taunting someone in an attempt, perhaps, to show his superiority. With one hundred and ninety-two victims, he is by far the most prolific killer this nation has ever seen."

"Do you still think he's posting the messages here because he lives nearby?" Cloud asked.

"Do all of you still believe he may be a truck driver?"

"It's *my* best guess," Hank said. "The events occur all around the country, and whoever this is has to have both the income and the means to do that. It makes sense that he's a truck driver, but thus far we haven't been able to track a driver that could have been in all of the areas we know the killings occurred. We have Jack Blue keeping an eye out for someone who might be picking up loads from other drivers, and who then wouldn't show up on any computer records used by trucking companies or even the independents. Jack thinks he could be taking loads for drivers who have had breakdowns and need to get their loads to their destinations without undue delay. Jack's only one trucker, though, so who knows when he might stumble on enough guys doing this for us to try and take a whack at determining which one is UniPerp?"

"Well," Doc Andy said with a note of finality. "We can only hope that UniPerp trips and gives some advance notice of some event he's planning. Until then, it will remain to analyze what has already occurred and hope some clue will reveal itself that way."

"STILL READING YOUR HORROR STORIES?" Spud asked, finding Hank in the reading nook after dinner.

"I did that before dinner. Now I'm reading more of this book."

"You read another book before dinner?"

"No, I went back over all the UniPerp stuff. Thought maybe something might bring another idea to mind about the guy."

If Spud hadn't agreed with the sentiment that the UniPerp case was indeed a horror story, he would have chuckled. As it was, he merely asked, "You can read horror stories after studying the UniPerp case?"

Hank shrugged. "This book isn't really what I'd call all that horrific. I've seen a lot worse happen in real life than what's in this book."

"I guess I can count my blessings that we never had a serious event while I was in PPD."

"You've never seen horror until you have to deal with a bad accident or a house fire where people can't escape in time."

Hank said this with such a lack of emotion that it frightened Spud.

"You can just say that? Just like that?"

"If I let myself dwell on those scenes, I'd be a mess, and off the team in a flash. The only way to deal with it is to not let it rip you up too badly," she said, tapping a temple with a forefinger.

"How *did* you deal with it?" Spud asked.

"Not the way lots of cops do. Not by drinking, or drugs, or being slutty. I cussed. Slapped the cruiser around a bit while I was in the Taos PD. Never took it out on a person. Then I'd head to the range. I found that concentrating on making a perfect shot didn't allow me to think about other things. Accomplishing a good shot assured me that I was still in control and could be a professional. That extended into my FBI days as well."

"Does it bother you now that making the perfect shot entails having a human being as a target?"

"I'd say yes if I knew I didn't use that as a last resort, and that the vast majority of the shots I take are still at nonliving targets. Except during a hunt, and even there I don't like to see the animal suffer. I like a clean kill, and I only kill what I'll eat. The humans? I only kill to lessen the count of innocent lives that are certain to be lost. I've been involved in, what now? Fifteen major missions? And I've killed four people. Not that I've wanted to, but I had to in order to protect the innocent. If anything, the practice still assures me that I'm in control—perhaps more so now that the target might be a living human being. If I can't feel good about killing a deer without its death being swift, then I certainly don't feel good about even having an active shooter like Edwards not die immediately. His is one death I truly regret, because even after hitting him twice, he still lingered. But I had to stop him, and he was moving around which made the shot a tough one. I just tell myself that, and think of ways I might be able to track and lead a moving target better."

"I don't think I could do your job," Spud remarked.

"You have to get yourself into a mindset," Hank said. "You have to remind yourself of the innocent people every single time. If I didn't do that, I couldn't be the team's sniper."

Spud moved over and drew Hank into him, cradling her against his chest. "I'll let you read your horror book in peace."

"Like I said: not really very horrible. Real life horror is

worse, and lacks the paranormal element as well. Real life horror is just plain horrible with no real rhyme or reason."

THE MAN USHERED his wife and children into his truck. He had earlier loaded everything they planned to take with them into the bed of the truck and secured the tonneau cover. It was now around two in the morning. With the compound quiet and only a single gate sentry to deal with, he and his wife had sworn the children to silence and discussed the story they would use to make their escape.

Driving to the gate, he leaned out his open window and shouted for the sentry to let them through.

"Where are you going?" the sentry demanded.

"We've got to get to the hospital in Charleston," he called out, throwing as much anxiety in his voice as he could. His wife sat next to him, groaning and acting as if she was in agony. "My wife ... I think my wife is having a miscarriage! Please! Let us out!"

"Why are you taking the children?" the sentry asked, looking inside at the children who now looked genuinely frightened.

"Please!" the man cried. "Please, we need to be together. We need to pray for the baby! We need to pray for my wife! Please!" Next to him, his wife wailed, forcing tears down her cheeks.

Convinced, the sentry opened the gate and let the truck through. It was well known among the congregation that the wife had miscarried before, accounting for the age difference between the two children they had.

Once through the gate, the man sped off as fast as he dared on the winding roads that led from the compound in

Sharples. Once he felt certain he was out of sight and hearing of the sentry at the gate, he slowed down to a safer pace. Taking a quick glance in the rearview mirror, he caught the gaze of his teenage daughter looking back at his reflection.

"He's never going to slap you again," he told her as his eyes went back to the road. "He's never going to touch *any of us* again."

7

"**W**here is Brother Larry?" Pastor Benkovic asked as he looked around at the men in the congregation.

"He might be still at the hospital in Charleston," one of the men replied. "He left early this morning. A little after midnight, I think. Brother James was standing sentry last night, and told me his wife was having a miscarriage. The entire family went so they could pray while she was being seen by the doctor."

"Let us devote this time this morning, then, to fervent prayer for our brother and his family, that he may increase his number, if that is Yahweh's will."

The men settled into prayer, their hands upraised, some quoting verses from the Bible. The women, too, behind their screen prayed, but silently, to themselves, not wishing to bring upon themselves the punishment they had seen the other day when one had dared to murmur a Bible verse.

"EVERYONE READY FOR THIS?" Spud asked.

"Ready as I'll ever be," Amigo grumbled, taking up the

standard of being the lead complainer regarding the morning intel briefing.

"Cross your fingers," Crow said. "We've had two slow news days; maybe we'll get lucky again today."

Knuckle taps on the table indicated agreement from the others.

"You guys always give me a hard time. Even my own wife gives me a hard time," Spud countered with a complaint of his own.

"Let's get to it. We have continuing angst over the persistent unemployment in the wake of NovoRo. This is the root of some protesting across the country right now that the government isn't doing enough either to get the economy back in shape or provide relief for those who haven't yet been able to find a job. Some of those protests are being aired by extremist groups, who as usual are chanting the 'America first' mantra."

"*White* America, they mean," Voice pointed out.

"And we have a very interesting group of protesters now making their voices heard as well," Spud said. "It seems that with the elderly being hit especially hard by NovoRo, *they* are now protesting that the country was willing to sacrifice them during the pandemic."

"Are you heading to Washington D.C. with a sign, old man?" Crow asked.

"It's *Grand* Old Man, and stay off my lawn," Spud responded.

"Yet more protests. Native Americans are also upset about the hit tribes took during the pandemic, citing poor health care facilities and inadequate numbers of health care workers."

"Is anyone *not* protesting?" Hank asked.

Crow shrugged. "I'm happy."

"One. Do I hear two?" Hank asked.

"The rest of us are listening to an intelligence briefing," Cloud said, getting the team laughing.

"Environmentalists are now taking on the oceans—again. And once again, it's over plastics that are floating around out there. They would like to see better methods for keeping plastics from washing down storm drains and eventually ending up in the oceans."

"Are they protesting?" Edge asked.

"Do you have to ask that question?" Spud replied rhetorically to renewed laughter from the team.

"That does it for the serious stuff. Time for—"

"*You can't make this shit up!*" the rest of the team chorused. "And you won't find us protesting," Voice added.

"We have a tale of a community that has gone to the dogs," Spud began.

"Like crazy cat ladies, but dogs?" Crow asked.

"Oh, they took it a step further. They elected a dog as mayor of the town."

Eyebrows went up.

"Where is this place?" Cloud asked.

"In Kentucky. It's called Rabbit Hash."

Chuckles erupted around the table. "I wonder who named that place," Edge said.

"Maybe one of the mayors. This isn't the first time Rabbit Hash has elected a dog as mayor."

"What did he run on? Infrastructure improvements? More fire hydrants?" Cloud asked.

More laughter.

"Seriously, though, the town does it as a fundraiser. They've been doing it since the 1990s. Electing a canine mayor, that is—not improving access to fire hydrants."

"You've got to appreciate a place with a sense of humor," Hank said, smiling.

"With a name like Rabbit Hash, you've got to *have* a sense of humor," Crow attested.

"That's it, and you know the drill."

Spud found Hank back in their quarters. She appeared to be muttering to herself and patting herself down.

"May I ask what you're doing, Love?"

"Taking inventory."

Spud grinned. "I took inventory last night. You have all your parts."

Hank gave him a look. She began patting herself down again while giving him 'the eye'.

"Cuff key number one, number two, number three," she said, patting the locations on her person where she had sequestered covert handcuff keys.

"Razor blade number one, number two, and number three," she continued with a pat to the small of her back, her shoe, and her belt buckle.

"You have three razor blades on you? How do you keep from getting cut?"

"I've put a bead of silicon sealant on the edge. It can just be stripped off before use." She exposed a small bar near her hip.

"Diamond saw."

"You've got a saw blade in your waistband?"

"One of those cable saws. Compass," she added, tapping her other shoe.

"Where?"

"Under the tongue."

"Why do I get the impression we might be doing another hound and hare sometime soon?" Spud wondered.

"Now, there's a thought. They're saying by the weekend it will get down to freezing overnight. Maybe we could go to Yuma again."

"We should head to The Hole," Spud said.

"Oh, no, no. Buried underground in earthquake country? In an old missile silo? Which, from the description, sounds like it might be marginally better accommodations than the Taj Mahal *before* Allen renovated?"

"You've never been there. It won't kill you to be familiar with the place."

"Says you! What happens if an earthquake hits?"

"We apologize to the guys for getting too vigorous in the sack," Spud poked.

"You're incorrigible."

"That's what you tell me. Seriously, though, we haven't been to The Hole in a while."

"How does this one work? Is there a caretaker there?"

"We have a contact on the Air Force base, but maintenance of the facility is our responsibility."

"Wonderful. Bet it's crawling with creepies and full of dust bunnies."

"I love your enthusiasm," Spud said sarcastically.

"Can't we go somewhere else? The base near Tucson should be warm."

"I detect an ulterior motive," Spud said.

"Like what?"

"Like a rockhounding trip."

"We do have to replace all the specimens that we collected for Doc Sue that got contaminated by the ants ..." Hank said, hoping to manipulate a trip to any place *other than* The Hole.

Spud began to feel like he was dealing with someone considerably younger than Hank's actual age. Perhaps five years old. Maybe even two. "Do you like the base near Tucson?"

"Yeah. It's set up pretty nicely."

"Then aside from clearing out some dust, you should like The Hole. It's a Titan II silo complex as well."

"Oh." Hank's arguments against a trip to The Hole suddenly hit a snag with that news.

Spud gave her a look and started consulting his tablet, giving her an occasional additional look meant just to keep her in line until he was done. When he was finished, he turned his tablet for her to see.

"It looks as if there are some interesting things to find on this beach."

Hank took a look at his tablet. *"Fossils!"*

Now she's happy.

He showed another image on his tablet. "Supposedly you can find this on a nearby beach as well."

Hank leaned in for a closer look. "Gem rhyolite. *So pretty!"*

"What do you think? Should we check in on The Hole?"

Hank smiled. She had to appreciate that Spud, who she knew hated her rockhounding hobby, had talked her into going to a location she considered questionable by dangling a rockhounding trip in front of her.

"Tell me what the wind is doing," Amigo requested of Hank as they practiced on the Hamilton Sportsman's Haven's extreme long-distance firing range.

"It's freezing my tits off," Hank complained, trying to be

the kind of spotter that Amigo was and voicing at least one complaint so he'd know what it was like to be on the receiving end.

"That'll bug the crap out of Spud," Amigo said, nonplused. "What's it going to do to my bullet?"

"Here by the firing line, I'd say by the feel of it against my face that it's maybe five miles per hour. At the tree tops midway, more like ten. At the target, from the little bit of grass down there, maybe back to five."

"Got a firing solution for me?"

Hank showed him her tablet, her figures for all of the ballistic elements having been punched in for Hal to compute.

"OK, let's see if you're right. Send the dragonfly."

Hank set the small drone on the end of his barrel and commanded Hal to send it to the target and retrieve it while computing the actual wind in both directions.

"And the winner is ..." Amigo compared the two solutions. "Hal. But then, Hal always wins. You're pretty close, though."

"Could you make the shot with my solution?" Hank asked, gazing through the spotting scope down to where the target sat a thousand yards away, a dark circle six inches in diameter demarcating Amigo's hit zone.

"Probably. Unless I blow it."

Hank nestled on the ground, her eye peering through the scope.

"Shooter ready," Amigo announced.

"Send it," Hank advised.

Watching, she confirmed, "Hit. On the left side of the mark. Was that with my solution?"

"Yes, ma'am."

Amigo was busy counting clicks to adjust his scope to Hal's dragonfly-assisted solution.

"Shooter ready."

"Send it."

Hank lifted her eye from the scope. "Still a couple inches to the left, but closer to a center hit."

"Just shows you're getting better and I'm ... still doing something wrong."

"Try adjusting your trigger finger placement."

"Which way?"

"More. Slide your finger to the left."

Amigo adjusted his finger placement on the trigger and tried again.

"Not bad. About an inch off, which for the wind isn't a bad result."

"So, I get to shoot for the next mission that requires it?"

"No."

"Are you saying I can't shoot well enough?"

"No, I'm saying I can't spot well enough. But maybe you'll get to do some sim round stuff on the training mission Spud and I have been discussing."

"What's it going to be this time?"

"Another hound and hare."

"I take it if I'm shooting, then you are the hare."

"I've been learning covert ops. Not only will I be the hare, I'll be the little rabbit that got away. I have to escape before I run."

Amigo grinned. "Sounds like fun. What if you can't escape?"

"Then as a hostage, I'm screwed." She grinned back. "I don't intend to stay captive, though. Spud has given me a little incentive. If I can regain and maintain my freedom, then he has to be Sherpa while I go rockhounding." She sat up. "I don't know about you, but I think I've had enough."

"Yeah, I've put quite a few rounds downrange," Amigo admitted. "Time to head back to the HQ."

"Hɪ, Jᴀɴᴇᴛ."

"Hi, Edge. What brings you up to Medical?"

"Not sick or anything. Just need a haircut."

Edge sat in Janet's beautician's chair while Janet gathered up her clippers and draped him with a cape to keep the cut hairs off his clothes. Setting about clipping his hair to the high-and-tight cut she knew he liked, she didn't expect much conversation from Edge. When she'd first been introduced to him, she thought his personality would be totally different than what she soon discovered it to be. She thought he'd be boisterous, but he turned out to be completely the opposite: typically quiet and reserved. So, she was used to having him sit in the chair and not say a word other than 'thanks, Janet' when she was done. So, it surprised her when he began to strike up a conversation.

"Say, Janet, do you think I'd look better if I was waxed?"

Janet was feeling glad of the fact that she was behind Edge when he asked this question. It took her so completely by surprise that she almost croaked out her answer.

"Um, well, I don't know. I guess I've never thought about you without—"

"My pelt?" Edge finished for her.

"I don't think of you as having a pelt," Janet lied.

"Someone made a remark about my pelt."

Janet now realized that Edge's pride had been wounded. *Just a big, soft puppy,* she thought.

"I guess you could give it a try," she said. "If you don't like it, just let your hair grow back."

"I take a lot of pride in my body," Edge said, exhibiting a candor rare for him when talking about himself. "Try to keep a good set of muscles on this frame. I'm thinking maybe if I was waxed, it would show off the definition a bit better."

"Could. Just how much were you thinking about having waxed off?"

"Everything. Well, almost everything. Keep the hair on my head, and the hair ... you know."

Thank goodness for small blessings, Janet thought. Though her usual observations of the men around her had her a little curious.

"When do you want this done?"

"Do you have time to do it now?"

"Uh ... yeah," she drawled out tentatively. "You want it *all* done now?"

"I'll look kind-of funny if I don't," Edge said.

Janet's mind went wickedly to imaginings of what it might look like if she sculpted the hair on Edge's body, patterning it as if a little man had gone over his chest, arms, and legs with a little lawnmower. She tried not to laugh.

"Well? Can you do it all at once?"

Janet cocked her head questioningly. "As long as you realize we're talking about pulling out all of your body hair. Except what's on your head and ... you know," she tacked on, imitating his modesty. "It's going to sting."

"I can take it," Edge said confidently.

OK, she thought. *I guess we get to see how tough the big guy really is.*

She briefly considered whether she even had enough hot wax to do an entire man Edge's size. Doing a mental shrug, she went into her stores of beauty aids and considered that she had enough to do his whole body.

Spreading a sheet on her massage table, she invited Edge to lie down as she heated the wax. *As hairy as he is, this is going to smart,* she thought.

THE TEAM HAD all gathered in The Restaurant and were eagerly awaiting Rose's reveal of what would be for dinner. She had already placed a big salad on the table, as well as a platter of raw vegetables with a bean dip. Still, the smells emanating from the kitchen were making their mouths water.

She soon came out with a tray. "Careful—it's hot," she warned, setting a ceramic dish in front of each. It was obvious from the appearance that the evening's offering had been baked in individual dishes.

As it was placed in front of him, Edge asked the usual question: "What is this?"

"Shepherd's pie," Rose told him.

"What's in it?"

"All kinds-a things."

"What's the yellow stuff on the top?"

"Mashed potatoes with curry."

"That sounds good. What's under the mashed potatoes?"

Rose was looking at him, obviously annoyed.

"Stuff that's *good for you.*"

"Is any of it green?"

"Peas," Rose drew out.

"That's OK. I like peas," Edge said.

He spooned out a bit of the potatoes and looked at what was underneath.

"What are these little round things?"

"Lentils."

He fished around in the dish.

"There's no meat in this."

"What makes you think there gotta be meat in every single thing you eat?" Then she reached out and smacked him across the back of his head. "And why you gotta ask twenty questions every time I put something in front of you to eat? Huh? You afraid I'm gonna *poison you* or somethin'? Quit asking questions and eat your dinner before it gets cold!"

Edge glared at her. The rest of the team tried to hide their amusement.

"An' don'tchu look at me like that, or I'm gonna smack you again."

"What are you, Rose? Five foot two, maybe a hundred and forty pounds, and about fifty-five years old? Am I close?" Amigo asked.

"Pretty close. Why?"

"Because Edge is six foot six, two hundred and sixty pounds, and forty-one years old—and he's scared to death of you."

At that, the rest of the team—minus Edge— laughed out loud.

Edge reached out for some of the raw vegetables and dip, then some salad. As he did, Voice took note of his arm.

"Wait a minute ..." Voice said, grabbing his wrist.

"Better let go before I punch you," Edge snarled.

"Aw, quit acting sore. I just want to know ... What happened to the hair on your arms?"

That question got everyone's attention. They all now took note of the fact that Edge's arms were completely barren of hair, as well as Edge's face now being covered by a glowing blush.

"If you must know," Edge began, having not figured out any way to avoid the topic, "I had Janet give me a body wax."

"For real?" Crow asked. "That must have smarted like a sonuvabitch."

"It wasn't so bad."

"You didn't do that because of what I said," Hank ventured.

"No, I've been thinking about having it done for a while now," Edge lied while simultaneously in his mind asking forgiveness from God for the fib. "I was just a little chicken, because I figured it would hurt more than it did."

"Did she wax you everywhere?" Crow asked.

Edge threw a look filled with daggers at Crow. "Obviously, I didn't have her wax my head. As for anything else, that's not dinnertime conversation."

Much as he may have wanted to simply divert the question, Edge could see that all it had done was instill *a lot* of curiosity in the minds of his teammates. Hank was looking at him wide-eyed, with some of the men's faces mirroring hers and others expressing empathetic pain.

He decided to end the speculation. "I was still *a little* chicken," he said.

The pained expressions transformed to relief, while the astonished ones fell into little smiles.

"Well? Let's see it," Cloud said.

"You want me to take off my shirt at the dinner table?" Edge asked, incredulous.

"Yeah—let's see it."

"I don't think that's appropriate. There are women present."

"Like I haven't seen you bare-chested before?" Hank asked. "Well ... maybe not *bare* bare-chested ..."

Even Rose had been attracted by the conversation and had come to stand behind Edge. Once again, she smacked him in the back of the head. "Take off your shirt," she demanded.

"Mama Rose ..." he protested.

"You want me to smack you again?"

This is gonna be good ... Voice thought.

Edge sighed and stood up. Then he pulled off his shirt. The team chuckled. Rose had won. But they stopped chuckling when they got a look at Edge.

I'd go see Janet myself if it wouldn't be so embarrassing standing next to the guy ... Spud thought. Hank turned and looked at him, giving him a raised eyebrow and a subtle shake 'no' of her head. *I like your man patch,* she mouthed. *That seals it, I guess,* he concluded.

"I think you just put Amigo and Hank out of business," Crow said. "First bad guy gets a look at that chest of yours is going to just whimper, sit down, and put his hands behind his back so you can cuff 'im."

Rose was hardly swayed by any sense of modesty. She reached out and ran her hand down his chest, making Edge step back in surprise.

"I gotta get you to tell Luigi your secret."

HANK HAD her tablet out again.

"Reading another novel?" Spud asked.

"Not this time. Looking over one of the past missions and trying to see what I learned from it."

"Which mission?"

"The Nickell gun-running case."

In his mind, Spud saw the scar that still coursed its way across Hank's hip where Nickell had managed to connect with a swing of his knife.

"I never thought to pat him down for hidden weapons," Hank said. "It's not like we carried knives in the Bureau. The circumstances weren't the same, though. He was clearly involved in criminal activity and knew it, so I should have expected him to perhaps employ some of the tactics of the criminal element. But I can tell you that after reading the book on what covert operatives do and might have hidden on their person, I'll be a lot more careful next time I have to take someone into custody."

"What have you managed to hide on yourself at this point?"

"Three handcuff keys, three razor blades, a diamond cable saw, a small compass, the means to make another compass, a small LED light with a red lens, some cash, a pen, and something to draw a map on."

Spud looked at her, not quite believing the grocery list of items she'd just rattled off.

"You have all of that on you?"

"Yes," Hank confirmed.

"That does it, then."

Spud stood up and grabbed her, throwing her over his shoulder.

"What do you think you're doing?"

"Taking you into the bedroom to strip search you."

Hank had her various means of escape, but this time opted not to use them.

8

"Where is Brother Howell?" Pastor Benkovic asked as he scanned the congregation.

"He hasn't returned from Charleston yet," one of the men answered.

"Sad. His wife must have given up the contents of her womb again," the pastor remarked. "I'll have to check in on them after this morning's service. This must be a time of great sorrow for Brother Larry and his family. They will all need spiritual uplifting and the strength of prayer."

"First up, you might remember the news of additional videos of unidentified flying objects by our military," Spud said.

"It's not Oscar," Crow quipped to the chuckles of the team.

"Apparently, in at least one case, it's not a UFO, either," Spud said. "It turned out to be a weather balloon."

"Wait. Didn't Oscar use old weather balloons to construct some of his UFOs?" Voice recalled.

"Maybe it is Oscar," Crow said.

"They've been seeing these things over the ocean," Hank

said. "Oscar is currently back in Massachusetts pursuing his degree."

"He's one smart lad," Crow observed. "I wonder if he's controlling them through Hal?"

Cloud laughed. "Wouldn't that be something!"

"If the kid is *that* good, maybe Voice should retire and we should bring Oscar on board," Edge said.

"It's not Oscar," Voice said emphatically.

"I think suddenly Voice isn't feeling like he has job security," Spud said. "Don't worry, buddy. We've only got room for one fucking genius on this team."

"That's what's got me worried," Voice mumbled.

"Moving on, we have environmentalists pointing at the growing average intensity of hurricanes as proof of climate change," Spud said.

"So, what can you do about a hurricane?" Crow asked.

"Not a thing," Cloud said. "You have to stop it at its source, meaning you have to go to Africa and have a chat with the butterflies."

Crow gave him a skeptical look. "What do butterflies have to do with hurricanes?"

"Chaos theory," Edge said. "It's usually stated that if a butterfly flaps its wings in Africa, it can start a disturbance in the atmosphere that eventually ends up as a hurricane in Florida."

"I'm surprised you know that," Cloud said.

Edge gave him a hard look. "I *am* literate, Cloud."

Cloud held up his hands in surrender. "Not arguing with you." *Wouldn't dare argue with you, now that I've seen what your muscles look like under all that hair you had.*

Spud took the opportunity to nip a potential interpersonal discussion of intellect in the bud by saying, "There's continued worries over the slow pace of economic recovery in the wake of NovoRo that is increasing tensions in a lot of quarters."

"How do we actually gauge the angst over certain topics?" Hank asked.

"A number of things," Voice said. "Hal monitors crime, posting on social media, government actions, employment figures ... Anything that might lead to unrest. Environmental issues are hot right now. Racial tensions are high right now. Dissatisfaction with Congress is at an all-time high, meaning people are more likely to take matters into their own hands than expect the government to resolve any problems. They revert to religion and past prejudices and base their actions on those things."

"Good grief—those are the sorts of things I see this extremist group I've been watching clinging to."

"Are you thinking they might be preparing to have a holy war or something?" Crow asked.

"I don't get a sense of what is happening *within* the group—only what organizations such as the Southern Poverty Law Center has to say about them. Those things might not be based on any insider observations, either."

"This might be a lot like United Border Militias," Spud said. "Homeland Security was concerned about them detaining illegals, but didn't realize they were murdering them." He hung his head, recalling the things he had had to say in order to not blow his cover when embedded with the group and the things he had not wanted to see but did as well.

"In a more focused case, we have a woman who was beaten to death. Investigators thought they had identified the perpetrator, but their suspect has also now turned up dead. That leaves the police investigating the case literally clueless. On top of that, with now a double-homicide on their hands."

"Do you think we might get a call on that one?" Amigo asked.

"If it remains unsolved and the FBI gets involved, there's a possibility," Spud replied. "And speaking of the FBI ..."

"Is this one of those You Can't Make This Stuff Up stories?" Amigo asked.

"This could very well have come from the You Can't Make This Stuff Up file," Spud acknowledged.

Everyone shifted a little forward onto their chair and rested their chins on their hands in anticipation of another odd but true story stripped straight from the headlines.

"We have a woman who apparently wanted very badly to be a Special Agent," Spud said.

"To the extent that she impersonated one?" Hank asked.

"Indeed, that's what she did."

"What clued someone into the fact that she wasn't?"

"Her love of chicken."

"OK. Now I've gotta know what loving chicken has to do with impersonating a federal officer," Amigo declared.

"She would show up at a local fast food restaurant and demand a free chicken dinner, telling the person at the counter that she was FBI and would arrest him or her if she wasn't given one."

"Him or her? She tried this more than once?" Hank asked.

"She tried it every day over the course of a week," Spud related.

Hank did a blink of her eyes that clearly displayed her disbelief. "Did they ever, at any point, give her a chicken dinner?"

"Not once."

"The very apex of the stupidity pyramid," Hank declared. "Not only impersonating a federal officer, but trying it seven days in a row after being refused the first time, the second time, the third time ..."

The rest of the team members were chuckling and shaking their heads.

"You ever ask for a free chicken dinner?" Crow asked Hank.

"I never asked for a free *anything*," Hank asserted. "I never even took something for free when it was offered, and occasionally it was. Just never wanted to get into trouble with the Colonel, Popeye, or even Ronald McDonald for that matter. Besides, I made a lot better pay than anyone working at a fast food restaurant."

"I didn't think you even patronized the places," Crow said.

"Sometimes, you just don't have time for anything else. Other times, I'd just get an irresistible urge for some fast food, American style."

"That's all I have," Spud concluded. "You all know the drill."

ROBERT BENKOVIC PARKED his truck and walked into the hospital. Looking around, he spotted a reception desk and went over.

"I'm looking for Zena Howell's room. I'm her pastor," he told the woman at the desk.

The woman set about typing some information into her computer. Looking puzzled, she looked back up at Benkovic.

"Could you spell her last name for me, please?" she asked.

"Howell. H-o-w-e-l-l."

"I'm sorry, sir, but I'm not seeing a patient here with the last name of Howell," the receptionist said.

"Perhaps she was recently released?"

The receptionist typed a bit more.

"I'm sorry, Mister?"

"Benkovic. *Pastor* Benkovic."

"Pastor Benkovic. I don't see that we have recently had a patient with the last name of Howell."

A puzzled furrow set between Benkovic's eyebrows. "I must be mistaken," he apologized. "I assumed she would have headed for the nearest emergency room, given she thought she was having a miscarriage."

"No, I'm not seeing a record for her from the emergency department, either," the receptionist said.

"Thank you, anyway," Benkovic said with a forced smile. "Have a wonderful rest of your day."

He walked back out to where he had parked his truck and got in, sitting for a few moments.

"An apostate," he muttered. "Larry Howell was always a good parishioner and a strong head of his family. He must have for some reason convinced Zena and the children to leave the fold."

He mused as he drove back to the Shining City compound in Sharples. He had not had many fall away from his teachings, but when one did it always troubled him. *Why did they leave? What lies could they be spreading? What damage might they do? Could they bring the government down on our heads?*

He gripped the steering wheel tighter, a mixture of fear and anger coursing through his thoughts. *We could end up like the Weavers. Like the Hataree. Like the Davidians. We are the few who are chosen, but the world is a vast cesspool of unbe-*

lievers. They will hate us for our faith and for the truths we proclaim. They will come to destroy us.

Resolve set into him as he was readmitted to the compound in Sharples. Parking his truck by the assembly building, he got out and rubbed his arms, warming them as the chill breeze wending through the hills and gaps swirled around him. Looking around, he set off for one of the houses that lined the narrow canyon in which the compound was located. Walking up to the door, he knocked and waited patiently.

A woman opened the door, and seeing who it was, immediately bowed her head. The simple tichel she wore covered every hair. A little girl peeked from behind her, and her pregnant belly told of another child yet to come. She kept her eyes lowered as the pastor spoke to her.

"Good afternoon, sister," he greeted her. "Is Brother William at home?"

"He's in the back," she said almost at a whisper. "With David."

"Thank you. I'll see myself there."

He walked around the side of the house, finding William Cantor with his son. William was splitting firewood with an axe, pausing only momentarily when his son would dart in to grab correctly-sized logs to stack against a nearby tree. He stopped when he saw the pastor place a hand on the shoulder of the boy, resting the head of the axe on the stump he was chopping wood on.

"You're a fine lad," Benkovic told the boy. "Learning the ways of providing for the family you will have one day by helping your father with providing for you, your sister, and your mother. That's a fine tribute. A fitting way to honor your father and mother as the Commandments order."

"I like helping with the wood," David said. "Dad has

promised me when we're done that he'll take me on my first hunt!"

"That's right—you got your first gun the other day. Won't it be an exciting day when you come home with a fine deer?"

He tousled the boy's hair, then went to speak with his father.

"How may I help you today, Pastor?" William Castor asked as the pastor approached him.

"I have disturbing news," Benkovic said. "It seems that Larry Howell and his family *did not* go to the hospital the other night. The hospital has no record of them."

William looked at him steadily, assessing the emotion he saw drawn on the pastor's face.

"Do you believe he has renounced the faith?" he asked Benkovic.

"I believe he may have. Help me alert the others. I'll also alert the other communities. If they return on their own, then we'll welcome them with gladness as returning prodigals. If not and they should be encountered, they should be brought back to undergo correction rather than be allowed to be lost."

"W HAT IS THIS, M AMA R OSE?" Edge asked as the team sat down to lunch.

"What's it look like?" Rose asked. "You got salad, fruit—"

"I'm talking about *this*," Edge said, indicating what looked like a folded-over pastry.

Rose gave him the infamous 'look' that women throughout history have perfected.

"You been livin' a sheltered life, ain'chu? That's calzone."

"You're kidding me," Voice told him. "You've never seen a calzone?"

"I smelled pizza cooking, but I don't see any pizza," Edge said.

"It's like pizza, but the crust is folded over. Think of it like an Italian turnover," Crow said. "You just eat it with your hands." He grabbed one and proceeded to eat one himself.

"What's it got in it?" Edge asked after Crow had taken a huge bite.

"Afk Wose," Crow said through a mouthful, getting the others grinning as his own rendition of Mouthful Hank triggered Hal to give a translation.

Rose gave Edge a stern look.

"I take it things that are good for me," he said meekly.

Rose gave a curt nod and headed back to the kitchen.

"You might as well stop asking and just eat what she puts in front of you," Hank advised him.

"If he doesn't want his, I'll take it," Crow said.

"Does it have spinach in it?" Edge asked him.

"Not that I can detect," Crow said.

Edge took that as an endorsement and grabbed one for himself.

"You know," Hank began after taking a bite of her own calzone. She scowled and casually reached up to wipe sauce from next to her mouth with a finger. Staring at it for a beat, she then licked the sauce from her finger and took another bite. In a rare show of dining discipline, she chewed and swallowed before continuing.

"I got to thinking that maybe instead of going to someplace warm, we should go to Pennsylvania for a training exercise.

"You want to go to Mars Hill?" Crow asked, surprised.

"Not the Taj—the house in Alba. We've never been there for a mission training exercise, and we've not done a cold weather exercise since I've been in the unit."

"Got a point there," Cloud acknowledged.

"I need to be used to that," Hank said. "I still have too much desert dweller in me. I need to learn how to ski."

"How is it you don't know how to ski?" Edge asked. "Living right next to Taos and going to school in Angel Fire and you didn't learn how to ski?"

Hank shrugged. "It was ski or hunt. *You* guess which one I chose."

"Do we have skis?" Voice asked.

"Cross country skis," Spud confirmed. "It was considered that alpine skis wouldn't be appropriate for the kinds of missions we might encounter."

"Yeah, I've never done that, either. I'd go to Tahoe for alpine skiing, but have never done any cross country skiing."

"We could do cross country skiing here if there was some snow on the ground," Spud said.

Crow chuckled. "Just a little warm here still for that. I think it's over seventy degrees outside right at the moment."

"We might not have the right length of skis for Hank," Spud said. "I'm sure Mike can get them in for us, though. Probably take a couple of days for them to get here."

"That sounds like a good excuse for some crash time," Cloud said. "Get all the gear we intend to take with us squared away, and then rest up. It takes a lot of energy to do cross country skiing."

"WHAT ARE YOU PLANNING ON TAKING?" Spud asked as he saw Hank checking off mission items on her tablet.

"Pretty much everything, with the exception of black and desert cammies," she said. "I figure we'll either be in trees, or snow or both." She looked at another item in the list and checked it off with a tap of her finger. "Temperature controller. Definitely have to have the temperature controller. My nipples will freeze off without it."

"Which vehicle are we taking?" Spud asked with a grin.

"Time en route in a Latitude is two hours and about twenty minutes, depending on winds. In the H155, it's over five hours. Cloud and Crow would like to have the helicopter there, but I've got 'short legs', as they say. I'll have to pee way before five hours are up. So we're thinking about getting the Air Force to airlift 100UN to Wilkes-Barre Scranton International for us, land the Latitude there as well, and then fly 100UN to Alba and land right next to the house. You remember that it's pretty rural there, so it shouldn't raise too many eyebrows. At least, we hope not. The alternative is to just plan a fuel stop halfway through the trip so we can all empty our tanks while 100UN is getting its tanks filled. Then any ol' airport that has Jet-A will do once we're near Alba."

Spud got a haptic tap from his watch. Looking at it, he noted Crow's face and Field Team ID standing outside on the porch.

"Hal, allow access," he said, then followed that with, "We're back in the bedroom, Crow."

Crow made his way through the house and peeked tentatively around the open bedroom door.

"What's got you so shy?" Hank asked as she packed personal items in a small duffle.

"Just didn't want to interrupt anything," Crow said.

Hank chuckled. "I hardly think we'd have let you past

the front door if there was anything going on we wouldn't have liked you to interrupt."

"You're the one I need to see," Crow told her. "I wanted to give you a head up that we're not going to take a Latitude. Just 100UN. One stop south of Chicago, then on to Elmira Corning Regional in New York. It's just north of the Pennsylvania-New York state line."

"OK. This is important to me because?"

"You and I are flying."

Hank blinked and stared at him. "Say again?"

Crow gave her an intense look and repeated, slowly for her benefit, "*You* and *I* are flying."

"That's like ... what? Five hours?"

"Five and a half."

"I'm gonna have helo butt after five and a half hours," Hank protested.

"You would if you sat in the back, too. Suck it up, Sweetheart—you're flying."

"Who gets the right seat?"

Crow extracted a quarter from his pocket. "Heads or tails? Call it." He flipped the quarter in the air and slapped it on the back of his hand, holding his hand on it until Hank made the call.

"Heads."

Withdrawing his hand, Hank slumped, looking at him pleadingly.

"Don't look at me—you called it. Heads it is, and PIC you shall be."

Hank sighed. Looking back at her tablet, she intoned, "Coverall, comma, flight, comma, Nomex, comma, one each." She then scowled at Crow and added, "Because it looks cool."

SPUD MADE his way down to the gym with Hank.

"Just what do you want to do for this workout?" he asked.

"A little exercise I saw in the book on covert ops."

"And you need my help for it?"

"Yeah. I'm going to need you to take the heavy bag down for me and put it back up."

Entering the gym, she turned to him and said, "Here's the drill. First thing I do is work out on the heavy bag for a minute. Then I sprint around the perimeter of the gym five times. While I'm doing that, you lay the heavy bag down on the floor. I'll work out on it for a minute while it's laying on the floor, then sprint five times around the gym again. Then I pick it up and carry it for a minute, then five times around the gym while you hang the bag back up. We'll see how long I can last."

"You're not going to be so worn out that you won't be able to fly, are you?"

"I am *not* trying to get out of flying," Hank asserted. "This is going to be like tai chi: if I start getting tired, I'm throwing in the towel. I can always put this in my exercise routine and build up my endurance over time. But one thing the book impressed on me is that I perhaps rely a little too much on my aikido to get me out of a scrape. Edge works with me to throw in Krav Maga tactics, but I typically resort to ... I've gotta face it: fighting like a girl."

"You probably should be wearing boxing gloves for this," Spud remarked, seeing that all she wore on her hands were her shooting gloves.

"I don't intend to hit so hard that it hurts, either," Hank said. "I can build that up as well. Get so I can do harder hits without hurting my hands in the process. I don't think I'll have the benefit of boxing gloves should I be taking on a bad guy, do you? Unless I'm trying to take him down while he's at the gym, that is."

"You've got a point." Going to the bag, he asked, "Do you want me to hold it for you?"

"Let it swing. My observation has been that unpredictability is a common criminal trait."

"You've got a point there, too."

Spud stood and watched while Hank attacked the bag, not connecting with it too hard for fear of hurting her hands at first, then upping the strength of her strikes a bit.

"One minute," he informed her after she'd been at it for that long.

She took off at a sprint while he removed the bag from where it was suspended and placed it down on the floor. He gazed at it for a moment, reflecting that using the bag as if it was a downed opponent had not occurred to him before. He considered the timing and decided that after Hank had completed her next round of boxing that he'd do a bit of his own. He went and retrieved sports tape while Hank completed her sprint around the gym, continuing to think of a good as well as realistic routine to do with the bag.

Stopping Hank as she came back to where the bag was, he said, "I think I have a good routine we can both do together."

"OK," she said through slightly winded breath. "What did you have in mind?"

"Instead of punching the bag while it's hung, why don't we stand the bag up on its end? Then you start out by punching the bag and knocking it over. Do your workout on the floor, then do your sprint. I'll set the bag back up and do the same thing, then do the same five-circuit sprint around the gym. You pick up the bag and carry it for a minute and drop the bag on the floor, and I'll do the same while you're doing your sprint. Then we do it all over again. Set the bag up, knock it down and punch it on the floor, pick it up and carry it."

"What happens if you catch up to me in the sprint?" Hank asked. "It's a given you'll catch up to me. I don't think I run as fast as you do."

"I'll do an extra circuit or two. I can use the exercise."

"You don't need extra exercise," Hank scoffed.

"Needed or not, it doesn't hurt," he began, putting a hand to her cheek. "I have a young wife who I have to keep up with." He hunched over, acting like he was leaning on a cane, and added in a wavering voice, "I'm an *oooold* man." Shaking his fist, he punctuated his remarks with, "Get off my lawn!"

"OK, old man." Hank stood the bag up on one end and punched it with a right and left blow, then pounced on it, straddling it and pummeling the bag with her fists. After a minute, she got up and commenced sprinting around the gym. As she ran, she thought, *We've never worked out together before.* The idea gave her a feeling of contentment as she added it to her visions of what life would be like for the two of them after leaving the unit.

9

P astor Benkovic stood in front of the congregation. He walked solemnly to the church's flag: a curious mix of the Gadsden flag's familiar coiled snake and the Washington's Cruisers' flag with its triangular pine tree, the snake coiled around the tree. At the top of the flag was the Washington's Cruisers' motto of 'Appeal to Heaven'; below that, the Gadsden flag's 'Don't Tread on Me.' The green tree with its black rattlesnake twisted around it stood out on a background of red, as did the black lettering of the two mottos. Stretching out the flag from its pole so its details could be seen by all, he began to speak.

"There is a reason we chose this flag as our emblem. For it signifies the wishes of our Christian founding fathers that this nation we are citizens of remain a nation with its eyes fixed upon our Abba, Yahweh, and His Son, Yeshua. It further signifies our willingness to stand firm in the face of the heathen nation that has arisen as a result of the corruption of the Founders' message.

"The Bible tells us that faith is like a mustard seed. Yeshua Himself spoke it. 'If ye have faith as a grain of mustard seed, ye shall say unto this mountain, Remove hence to yonder place; and it shall remove; and nothing shall be impossible unto you.'

"And Yeshua again tells us, 'They on the rock are they, which, when they hear, receive the word with joy; and these have no root, which for a while believe, and in time of temptation fall away.'

"You may know by now that one has fallen away. Brother Howell and his family have left us, for what reason I cannot contemplate. His faith was like a mustard seed, but it fell upon rock and only flourished while it could grasp a bit of rain. But when drought entered his soul, his faith dried up and took his family with it. Perhaps it was the loss he and his wife had endured when she conceived and then lost the child in her womb. Perhaps that was also a sign of their faltering faith, that Yahweh chose not to bring another child to them.

"We must pray for our brother that he finds his faith once again. We must watch for him wherever we travel, so that we might bring him back and plant his faith firmly in good soil, both for his good and that of his family. For if he is not corrected, his soul and the souls of his wife and children shall be cast into Gehenna. Again, Yeshua teaches us: 'And if thy right eye offend thee, pluck it out, and cast it from thee: for it is profitable for thee that one of thy members should perish, and not that the whole body should be cast into hell.' And in Hebrews it is taught, 'For whom the Lord loveth he chasteneth, and scourgeth every son whom he receiveth.'

"So, let us seek out Brother Howell that we might bring him back and save his soul and the souls of his family. Our love for him demands that he not be cast out, but brought back to true faith in Yahweh. Better he feel the stripes than the flames of hell."

HANK SETTLED 100UN down in a hover over a T-marking on the ramp at Elmira Corning Regional Airport. "I guess they don't get a lot of helicopter traffic," she commented. "No helipad. I also wish this lineman would either move away from us or hunker down a little before he loses his head."

"Just hover here a bit," Crow said, and tuned one of the radios to the FBO's frequency to ask that *someone* please inform their lineman that where he had positioned himself was *b-a-d* and that he needed to move before they could safely land. Before he could make the call, though, the lineman's hat blew off, and he turned to retrieve it, leaving Hank to land the helicopter on her own—for which she was grateful.

"That solves that problem," Crow said. Turning to the team and the medical personnel in the back, he informed them, "Last stop for fuel, so if everyone can just deboard and stand by on the ramp while they get us fueled, we'll hopefully be on our way in a jiffy. Might want to grab your jacket—it's only forty-seven degrees out there at the moment."

As the rest of the team chatted, Hank and Crow watched while the linemen serviced the helicopter, not having gained a lot of confidence that they had much experience, given how the guy who'd parked them had stood so close.

"We probably wouldn't have whacked his head off, given he was standing right off the nose," Hank commented.

"Yeah, but it might have gotten messy if he'd decided to move away before the rotor stopped turning," Crow said.

"Where are we going to park the bird when we get to the house in Alba?" Hank asked.

"You remember the concrete area Joe Cornett had right outside the garage?"

"Yeah, but that's going to be pretty tight."

"Don't you have a commercial ticket in this thing? It won't be too tight."

"What about the power line that goes right over it?"

"I checked with Dave Ambrose. He had the utility company come out and bury it."

"Did he also have them cut down the tree that's right off the corner of the garage?"

"Hey—that's a nice tree. You won't hit it."

"You *hope* I won't hit it. Last question: How do we get the SUV that's in the garage out of there if the helicopter is parked in front of the garage?"

"You'll set down on the far side of the concrete from the garage. You only need to get the helicopter's gear on the concrete. The rest can hang over the edge."

"Isn't that going to be a bit tight for getting the SUV in and out?"

"Don't worry—no one will hit 100UN when they're driving."

"What makes you so sure?"

"I'll kill them if they do."

With the helicopter refueled and everyone back aboard, Hank took off once more and headed on a direct route to the house that would serve as their base for this training exercise. As they approached, Hank began to feel like the cockpit suddenly got a bit warmer. She could feel the sweat form in her armpits.

"Crow, that's *tight*."

"Take a look," Crow said. "See the flag on the flagpole? You don't have much wind, and what you do have is coming so you can just come right in and land where I told you to. Once you get down a few feet from the ground, swing your tail so it overhangs the edge. That'll leave enough room for getting the SUV in and out."

Hank could also see Dave Ambrose standing by the front door. Unlike their lineman back at the airport, he was hunched down and had turned his face away from the helicopter while holding onto his hat.

"You can tell the guys who've been here, done this," Crow commented.

Hank maneuvered the helicopter as Crow had instructed her, with him keeping an eye on the rear gear to insure the tires would still be a few feet from the edge of the concrete while still leaving the Fenestron overhanging the grass. When she'd finished settling in, he smiled and complimented her on a job well done.

"Just don't ask me to do it again," Hank said. "Next time, I might not be so lucky."

"You never want to think of it as luck," Crow admonished her. "Think of it as skill, and consider that with each skillful accomplishment, your ability takes a step forward."

She looked at him. "I think I'm going to steal that. It seems I hear a lot of 'dumb luck' remarks on firearms abilities as well."

"It's all yours," Crow said, smiling as he opened his door and dropped out of the helicopter.

As Hank followed suit, she observed that the rest of the team had already joined up with Dave Ambrose for handshakes and hearty pats on the back as she and Crow went about securing the helicopter with tie-downs for the blades, covers for the turbine inlets, and chocks for the gear. Crow came over and handed her a couple of tie downs to complete the job of securing things.

"Just how are we ..."

Her objection was stifled by Crow's grin and a point of his hand. Embedded at just the right distances, she noted something new about the concrete platform on which

100UN was perched: tie down rings embedded into the concrete, flush set so they could be driven over.

She raised an eyebrow. "I gather you and/or Cloud asked for those?"

Crow shrugged. "Seemed like a good idea. This base is just like our others: somewhat remote. Doc Frank over there thought it would be a good idea to be able to get a helicopter in and out in case someone needed to be medevaced."

"Does this mean that all the bases are getting what is essentially a helipad?"

"Let me just put it to you this way," Crow said. "You remember the small concrete platform that was off the northeast corner of the Roswell complex? It's bigger now."

"At Roswell, we could just land right on the silo lid," Hank said.

"Yeah, but a helicopter is a bit visible there. Although Dick has planted a few Italian cypress trees out there."

Hank just gave him a bit of a skeptical glance, realizing she was likely going to be called upon to do a bit more helicopter flying than she thought she might when she first got convinced to learn to fly the thing. *Conned into it is more like it*, she thought.

As the two of them walked up to join the rest of the team, she heard Dave remark to Spud, "I wondered why I hadn't seen your little lady yet." He walked over and gave Crow a vigorous handshake and slap on the back, then proceeded to give Hank a hug.

"How's the sniper business?" he asked.

"Great. How 'bout for you? Do you manage to get in a little trigger time?"

"Not so much sniping anymore," Dave admitted. "I was just telling the guys, though, that I hoped the unit didn't mind that I've spent a bit of time here. Lots of woodland. Good deer hunting. Just walk out the back door."

"I didn't even think about that," Hank lamented. "We could have gotten in a hunt while we're here."

"Still can. A .308 can take down a deer easily."

Hank laughed. "That would be some kind of different hunt. Me all done up in my tactical gear with a tactical .308, taking down the dangerous deer element."

Dave steered the team members and their Support personnel into the house. "There are four rooms here on the main level, and six more upstairs," he explained. "That's enough for everyone, plus me if you don't mind me hanging around while you're here."

"Missing the unit?" Crow asked.

"I didn't think I would. When I retired, I found a nice place up north of here, complete with a fishing pond. Figured that's how I'd spend the rest of my days on this Earth. You can only do so much fishing, though. Only so much hunting as well. And I do a little woodworking as a hobby, sometimes selling some of it at a farmer's market. Beyond that, if you're not into watching television, there's not a lot to do. It's a big switch from constantly either working a mission or preparing for one. I still like to keep myself in shape, but sometimes I wonder why I do it.

"For you and Hank, Spud, I might suggest one of the bedrooms here on the ground floor. They're a little better isolated than the ones upstairs."

The team members all chuckled.

"You guys think it's funny. I never did find myself a woman to settle down with, not that I wouldn't have liked to. But there's a certain fear in thinking that you might talk in your sleep."

That silenced the chuckles, especially given everyone

except Spud and Voice had harbored the idea of retiring, finding a suitable mate, and living happily ever after.

"Didn't mean to put a wet towel on things," Dave apologized.

After organizing all of their gear and settling into a room, Hank stripped off her flight suit and changed into the more casual facility uniform. Sitting on the edge of the bed, she turned to Spud and asked, "Is that what it's going to be like for us, Spud? Retire to boredom?"

Spud had been silently considering the same thing. "I hope not," he said. But Dave's mention of his apparent lack luster life now that he was retired gnawed at Spud.

"I'm thinking maybe we should plan on some kind of business that would keep us occupied," Hank said. "Maybe a training outfit, or a firing range." She grinned. "Or a training outfit with a firing range."

"I see you're not planning on giving up shooting," Spud said.

"Not unless I somehow lose both arms," Hank asserted. "Even then, I'd be pushing for prosthetics that would allow me to keep doing it, even if just so I could have a fun day at the range. I've thought of doing competitions when I get out. I figure my not-so-little nest egg will allow me to do that."

Spud smiled. "Will you need a spotter?"

"Maybe. You want to learn how?"

"Sure, why not? I'm always up for learning another skill."

"Don't look at me to do it," Hank said. "I struggle with spotting. Amigo's the real expert. His ability as a spotter will always trump mine."

"I think I'll ask him to show me all his tricks," Spud said. "Who knows? I might want to get into competitive shooting as well. We might make a good team."

10

"We have to stop. We have to rest," Zena pleaded with her husband, Larry. "The children need rest."

"If they catch us, you know what they'll do to us," Larry said. "What they'll do to me, especially. We can't stop. We can't until we know we're safe."

He glanced over at her. "Take off your tichel," he said.

"Larry?"

"Take off your tichel. Anyone who is a member of a Shining City church will see your tichel and know we're from a Shining City community. The same for you, Lois," he added with a glance in his rearview mirror.

Zena reluctantly pulled the tichel from her head. Lois yanked hers off and threw it out the window, watching it flutter and tumble to the pavement at the side of the road. Seeing it in his side view mirror, Larry grabbed the tichel from his wife's hands and did the same with it.

Zena had started to quietly sob, tears running down her face. "We're apostates," she said through her tears. "Abandoners of the faith, destined to hell."

"We have *not* abandoned our faith," Larry objected. "What we've abandoned is the violence of a man consumed by the power he holds over others. I will not have him silence my wife simply because she is a woman. Being subject to me doesn't mean you're my slave. And I will not have a man strike my children as if he knows what's best for them. I'm their father. You are their mother. It didn't anger you to see how he hit Lois?"

Zena lowered her head. She still strongly felt her requirement to be subject to her husband, and voiced no objection to his argument. But she also felt conflicted by his voicing ideas that ran contrary to what she'd heard Pastor Benkovic teach in his sermons to the Shining City congregation.

"You may speak, Zena," Larry said quietly. "When we joined in marriage, we became one flesh, just as the Bible says. If we are one flesh, then we are equals—not a master and his servant, but a couple joined in a single enterprise: the forming of a holy family. The raising of children who will understand their place as white and therefor superior people. Children who can openly declare their obedience not to a tyrant who preaches but the God of the Bible whose word we follow without exception."

"But Pastor Bob preached the truth of the Bible," Zena objected.

"Did he? You know that I've made a regular study of the Bible, Zena. It is always in my hand, but not closed up; open, its words not just going into my eyes, but making their way into my soul. One night, my eyes fell on this passage from Second Corinthians: 'And no marvel; for Satan himself is transformed into an angel of light. Therefore, it is no great thing if his ministers also be transformed as the ministers of righteousness.' I believe that God Himself brought my hand to this page, so that I might see the real truth. Satan is a deceiver, and he uses people to help him deceive. *I* was deceived. *All of us* were deceived into believing that everything Pastor Bob said was somehow inspired by God speaking to him. But how much of what he said was just Bob Benkovic speaking? Why else would he rule by fear rather than by the love Yeshua commanded us to have? He rules with a fist—a literal fist. A fist and a whip, and he takes pleasure in it. He steps into places where he doesn't belong, even into our bedroom, commanding us to bear child after child. But we have lost as many as we have brought into the world. If Yahweh wanted this, would that have happened? Or is this just Pastor Bob wanting every woman to be a factory for children so that he can increase his followers that way?"

Zena sobbed, her face in her hands. "How has it come to this?" she whimpered.

"It has come to this because I dared to read my Bible," Larry said. "I dared to read passages you *never* heard Pastor Benkovic read."

Larry pulled over to the side of the road and took Zena's chin in his hand.

"Does the Bible not say that a man should love his wife the same as he loves his own body? Doesn't this make sense, given the Bible also says a man leaves his father and mother and becomes one flesh with his wife? Why, then, did Pastor Benkovic command us to beat our wives if they should disobey us? And for what? The things he called 'disobedience' were hardly challenges to a man's authority. Saying 'I cannot make bread because I have no yeast' is not disobedience—it's merely a statement of fact." He smiled at her. "I love you, Zena. And I love the children you have given to me. I want them to grow up being obedient because they love me, not because I take a whip to them for every tiny indiscretion they may commit. I want them to honor us because they see how righteous we are, not because they're afraid of us.

"What Pastor Benkovic is doing is wrong, and he knows it. Why else is he afraid of the authorities? Is it really because he believes they are poised to destroy Shining City the way they destroyed the Branch Davidians? Or is it that he feels his authority over us is threatened and that he will no longer hold power over us through fear and intimidation and the threat of the whip?

"I believe that it's time the authorities know what's happening in Shining City."

"No!" Zena cried. "What if he's right? What if they go to all the communities and slaughter them all? We're supposed to be the remnant—the few that will remain to inherit the Earth."

"Think, Zena. If Yahweh has ordained that there be a remnant to inherit the Earth, do you think mere men will stop Him?"

HANK AND SPUD made their way back out to the living room of the house where the rest of the team and Dave Ambrose had all gathered. A few of the guys were discussing whether a poker game was in order. Dave was settled in a chair reading a book, which piqued Hank's curiosity. She went to sit near him and cocked her head to get a look at the title.

"W. Edwards Deming? Wasn't he an economist?"

"Statistician, actually," Dave replied.

"You're interested in statistics?" Hank asked.

"Actually, I'm interested in his economic insights."

"You have to be careful reading around these guys," Hank said with a jerk of her head toward the men, who were now making their way to the dining room table with a deck of cards.

"I always had to be careful around the ones who were in the Field Team the same time I was as well. They seemed to think that reading a book was some sort of alien endeavor."

Hank chuckled. "We are more alike than just in the shooting department. I'm constantly seeing eyes roll every time I say, 'I've been reading a book ...'"

Dave gave a nod toward the men as well. "Do they ever let you play poker with them?"

"Never."

"A little sexist, are they?"

"It's not that. It's because I beat them."

Dave looked at her, an amused smile on his face. "I've not met many women who are into poker, so I find it refreshing to encounter one who not only plays, but regularly takes the pot. What's your secret?"

"One of my areas of expertise is reading body language, including microexpressions."

"Ah. They haven't learned to wear sunglasses when you play?"

"They have, but it doesn't help them," Hank acknowledged with a smile. "Did you know that when someone gets excited that their ear might twitch? Or a muscle in their face can either relax or tighten? They'll even move their feet, shift their body, and do subtle little things with their fingers. If they're really good at controlling all of that, then what they often *can't* control is the blood flow to places like their ears or cheeks." She turned and looked at the men seated around the table in the dining room. "For instance, right now Crow has a really good hand."

Heads jerked up around the poker table, and faces

swung in her direction. Five men folded their cards and set them on the table. Crow practically threw his down.

"*Hank ...*"

"Sorry, Crow." She decided to switch topics back to the book Dave was reading.

"What's your interest in his economic theories?"

"It's more of an interest in seeing what it takes to be a good manager."

"Oh. Are you thinking of starting a company?"

"Actually, I'm thinking of running for office. In Wellsburg, of course, where I live."

Hank expressed amazement. "Are you going to be able to do that and stay as caretaker for us here in Alba?"

Dave laughed. "Wellsburg doesn't even have a thousand citizens. The mayor and two trustees are a considerable portion of the population. Somehow, I don't think I'll be all that busy if I win, but if I do win, I want to make a good go of it. I figure understanding economics and learning how to motivate people to do the best job will be assets."

"Well, I guess we have things that make us different as well," Hank observed. "Although motivating people to perform well is part of what I do when I'm training the others, I don't think I could ever see myself running for mayor of anywhere. When I feel frustrated, my fuse gets short."

"IF EVERYONE IS DONE PLAYING poker, I'd kind-a like to talk about the hound and hare we're starting tomorrow," Hank said as she stood next to the poker players around the dining room table.

"Can we at least play this hand?" Crow asked. The cards had just been dealt, and everyone was looking over them.

Hank examined the faces of all the men. "Cloud hasn't got squat, Edge thinks he's got a good hand, so does Voice, Spud's wondering if he can pull off something that's not statistically likely like an inside straight, Doc Frank over there doesn't have squat, either. And neither do you, but you think you can bluff the others."

All of the men tossed their cards to the center of the table in disgust.

"Dammit, Hank ..."

"Mission first."

From over in the living room, Dave Ambrose could be heard chuckling.

"Alright. Seeing as you've blown this hand for us, you might as well sit your ass so we can get this over with. I need to win a few quarters back. Which I *wouldn't have to do* if someone hadn't screwed me on my first hand," Crow added, glaring at her.

"Just how good was it?" Cloud asked.

"Full house, aces and sevens."

The rest of the men groaned.

"Anyone wants to play poker with Hank better be wearing a ski mask and sunglasses," Edge remarked.

She grinned. "You can try it."

The men all studied her for a moment or two, looked at each other, and shook their heads 'no'.

"Where's Doc Rich hiding?" Hank asked.

"She said something about taking a nap," Doc Frank said. "She said spending that much time in a helicopter takes something out of her."

"Understandable. You know that's how she died, right?" Hank passed along.

"I thought Support personnel didn't get new identities," Doc Frank said.

"She's the only one who has. It's a long story best told by her, but she had requested assignment to Afghanistan and was involved in a helicopter crash. She was the only survivor, and for reasons best left to her to relate, asked to have her death faked and be given a new identity when she was approached for duty in the unit. Just the same, I think it might be a good idea for someone to go wake her for this."

All eyes looked expectantly at each other with the hope that someone else would do the honors. Each considered Doc Rich to be a force to be reckoned with under ordinary circumstances, and no one wanted to discover just how much of a force she'd become when awakened from a nap.

"You guys are fucking sissies," Hank said, getting up to go find the doctor.

"I would like to point out," Crow called after her, "that we could have played that last hand while Doc Rich was dressing you down for waking her up …"

Hank sighed. *Men.*

She made her way down the hall to the room across from her and Spud's. Giving the door a gentle tap, she then cracked it open a hair and said, "Doc Rich? You among the living?"

She heard a grumble come from the other side of the door.

"What do you need, Hank?"

Hank opened the door a bit wider to find Doc Rich stretched out atop the blankets on the bed, still in her facility uniform. Considering that other circumstances might have made it an unsurvivable event should one of the men had gone to make the wake-up call, Hank considered that it was probably best that the task had fallen to her.

"I'd like to do a briefing on tomorrow's training exercise."

"Mmf," Doc Rich mumbled, sitting up and rubbing her neck. "Give me a few minutes. I'll be right there."

Hank made her way back down the hall to the dining room.

"You're still alive," Voice remarked.

"She really wasn't as grumpy as I thought she'd be," Hank said.

It wasn't but a couple of minutes before the doctor herself arrived in the dining room. Even though she wore the same uniform she'd been wearing while napping, it looked as though she'd just pressed it. Her hair, likewise, didn't look like she'd spent a moment in bed, either. Hank wondered to herself how the woman could pull herself together so quickly. *Probably got lots of practice in the military.*

"Now that everyone is here, let's go over what we're going to be doing," Hank said. "Here's the scenario: You guys in the team have taken me hostage. You're not law enforcement, so you're not going to search me the way you might if you *were* law enforcement. You'll secure me as best you can, using anything you can find in the house. I took the opportunity to see just what's here while everyone was getting settled in. I'll give you a hint: there are lots of goodies down in the basement.

"My job is going to be to escape and evade recapture. If you *do* manage to capture me, you'll bring me back here and try to secure me even better. Second time around, you get to search me. Then my job is to try and escape again.

"Everyone understand what we're doing?"

Heads nodded all around.

"OK." She grinned at them. "I'll let you use handcuffs."

The team members all laughed, already knowing she'd be out of them in a flash.

"I'll let you guys plan how you intend to secure me while I go get a good night's sleep. I anticipate doing a bit of running tomorrow." She grinned at them again. As she went to leave the dining room, she turned and said, "Oh, and if I *do* manage to escape, please leave the gun you'll find during a cursory pat-down on me. I don't want any surprises of a real nature while I'm running through the woods, either animal or human. I intend to be armed out there."

Spud hadn't considered that scenario, but when Hank mentioned it, was glad she had. Especially as it wouldn't be the first time a bad guy had been encountered in the woods on a training mission.

After she was out of earshot, Spud said, "Let's give her a little twist."

"What do you have in mind?" Crow asked.

"Handcuffs."

The men all sounded their protests.

"Hold on—not secured the usual way."

"OK. How, then?" Cloud asked.

"We sit her on the floor and handcuff her hands under her knees. She won't be able to reach any of the handcuff keys she has on her ... at least, I don't think so. She also won't be able to get up on her feet to run while still cuffed." He grinned. "She thinks she can escape handcuffs, but maybe she's thinking a bit too traditionally when it comes to how they're applied."

LARRY HOWELL DROVE through the streets of Charleston, West Virginia, looking in earnest for a federal law enforcement office. His family huddled in his truck, their fear of being in a city with its many "heathen" inhabitants at night evident. Larry had passed by the local police offices and the county sheriff's offices as well, not trusting that they wouldn't encounter a Shining City adherent within their ranks.

Stopping at a gas station, he went inside, bringing his family with him. He handed the clerk forty dollars in cash, given Pastor Benkovic forbade the use of credit cards, citing the ability of the government to track people's movements when they used them.

"Regular unleaded on pump three," Larry told the clerk at the counter. He turned to go back out to his truck, then turned back. "Could you tell me where the FBI office is?"

The clerk looked at him with a raised eyebrow. "No FBI office in Charleston," he said. "Closest thing we have is the ATF office."

"Can you tell me where that is?"

"Not right off the top of my head. You can probably look it up on your cell phone."

"I don't have a cell phone," Larry revealed. "Do you have a phone book?"

The clerk looked at him as if he must be from another planet, or had just been dropped off by a time traveler returning from the past. He took out his own cell phone and did a search.

"It's at 300 Summers Street."

"Do you have a map I could buy?" Larry asked.

The clerk shook his head in disbelief. "Don't you have a GPS?"

"No."

The clerk sighed, reached for something to write on, and

wrote down a series of directions for streets to take to the location. He handed it to Larry.

"Thank you, and God bless you," Larry told him.

"Good luck," the clerk said, still not quite believing the encounter with the odd man and his family, who stayed huddled behind him the entire time, not saying a word.

"What's the ATF?" Larry Junior asked as they left the convenience store and Larry went to fill up the truck.

"The Bureau of Alcohol, Tobacco and Firearms," Larry said.

"Will they help us get away?" Lois asked.

"I don't know," Larry admitted. "But if they can't help us, they at least should know what's happening in Shining City. They need to know what Pastor Benkovic is doing."

11

"Good morning, my little bunny," Spud said, rolling to face her.

"Good morning, my big, brave K9," Hank replied. "Think you can catch me today?"

Spud chuckled. "This all greatly depends on whether you can escape."

"True," Hank said, her demeanor exhibiting confidence that she would have no problem with that. "I at least will get a good breakfast before being held hostage, won't I?"

"Of course. We wouldn't want your stomach grumbling while you sit here wondering how to get out of the predicament we've planned for you."

As they joined the others for breakfast, Hank noticed that they were all smirking. *Obviously, they think they've figured out some way of keeping me incarcerated.* She commenced doing a mental inventory of everything she had on her person. *A roll of duct tape and a wire coat hanger is all I need to be called MacGyver.*

Hank drank coffee and ate her bacon and eggs, her face never exhibiting anything other than serenity. The men's faces all exhibited their confidence that she would never make it out of the house. As she popped the last piece of her toast in her mouth, she saw Crow and Cloud both give a subtle nod, realizing too late that Edge was right behind her.

Damn, he's sneaky, she thought, remembering the times in the past when she had observed Edge move both swiftly and silently to apprehend someone. He grabbed her in a come-along hold and steered her toward the living room, then forced her to sit on the floor.

Spud came over and pulled his handcuffs from a back pocket. "Sorry, Love," he said as he grabbed a wrist and cuffed it, then reached below her knees and pulled the loose cuff through, cuffing her other wrist such that the handcuffs and her two hands were under her knees.

"Pat her down," Edge ordered.

Everyone looked at Spud, who then took it upon himself to relieve her of her knife. Noting that indeed she was wearing her gun, he left that in her charge in the event she should encounter some unsavory person or hungry beast during her escape. *Assuming she escapes*, he thought.

"What now?" Voice asked.

Crow went over and opened the door to the coat closet by the front door. "This should do nicely," he said. Picking her up, the men placed her inside the closet and closed the door.

"Let us know if you need anything, Love," Spud called through the door. "We wouldn't want you to wet your pants in there."

The rest of the team chuckled. Crow pulled a deck of cards from his pocket and said, "I think we can finally get some poker in without having our body language expert give away what we're all holding this time." With a wave of his arm, he indicated they should adjourn to the dining room. Taking up seats around the table, he took up the deck and started shuffling.

Hank didn't spend much time thinking about her escape. *Tai chi is great flexibility exercise,* she thought as she straightened her legs while working her hands up and over her behind. *I guess I should stop complaining about my skinny butt,* she thought as she slipped her hands up behind her waist and felt for the handcuff key she had hidden in her waistband. Considering that the men likely believed she would never have been able to reach any of the keys given the manner she'd been handcuffed, she smirked to herself as she manipulated the key so she could get it into the lock. Fumbling, she dropped it on the floor, silently mouthing *shit!*

Dropping over on her side, she felt around with her fingers, shuffling on the floor until she felt the key, then made another attempt at unlocking the handcuffs—this time with success. She carefully laid them on the floor, then just as carefully felt for her camouflage coat among those hung in the entryway closet. Slipping into it, she felt through her pockets, smiling at finding the second knife she'd sequestered there, as well as a few other items she felt might come in useful.

Opening the closet door the barest bit of a crack, she peered out, noting that she couldn't see the men from where she was. Considering that if she couldn't see them, they couldn't see her, she slowly continued opening the door until she felt she could soundlessly make her escape. First she considered that perhaps escaping through the adjoining garage might be the best way to go, but her reevaluation of that plan told her it would expose her to a greater chance of being seen by the men, who were now happily engrossed in their game of poker. She settled on the simple plan of just exiting out the front door.

Once outside, she first got her bearings, taking note of

the still-healing scar on the ground where Robin Cornett's she shed had been first burned, then bulldozed of what wouldn't burn and removed according to Joe's wishes. The small stand of trees behind where the she shed had stood she identified as her planned point to make her escape into the woods, which would require her to make a mere three-hundred-foot sprint across the open grass to where the trees stood. Once within the trees, she could then follow the edge of the forest around until heading southwest, where she could hide herself among the thickening forest, being as cautious as possible to leave no sign of her movements. *I was the one who taught them how to track people*, she mused. Taking off at as fast a sprint as she could manage up the slight slope to the trees, she grinned gleefully.

Out of the corner of his eye, Spud saw a flash of light brighten the area toward the front of the house momentarily. He went back to his poker hand, not thinking much of it for a couple of beats. Sudden realization hitting him, his head jerked up and he leapt to his feet.

"What?" Cloud asked.

"The front door just opened," he said, striding quickly in that direction.

The rest of the men followed him as he glanced through the open closet door, seeing his handcuffs sitting on the floor, then out the front door. He got an eyeball on Hank just as she disappeared into the trees near where the she shed had stood.

"*Damn it!* How did she get loose?" Cloud cursed.

"Tai chi," Edge said, his perturbed tone reflecting that he had neglected Hank's martial arts accomplishments. "It's designed to develop strength and flexibility. I'm betting she just slipped her hands up behind her back and had a hand-cuff key hidden in her waistband."

The other men all turned and glowered at Spud.

"I had no idea she was that flexible," he explained as he grabbed his own coat and prepared to follow her.

"Yeah, then how'd she hurt her back that time?" Cloud asked accusingly.

"Like I said, I had no idea she was that flexible. How else would she have hurt her back?" He dashed out of the house and up the slope to where he'd seen Hank disappear into the woods, the men on his heels. Stopping abruptly at the edge of the trees, he squatted down and looked across the surface of the leaves. The minute he did, memories of past tracking exercises that Hank had conducted came to them. The men spread out in a line and each examined the area in front of them.

"Got her. On on," Crow chirped, pointing in front of him.

The others all looked, noting the barely perceptible trail of disturbed leaves stretching farther into the trees from where Crow stood. Falling in behind him, the others let him lead the way as he knelt, studied Hank's path, then trotted ahead, repeating the process to keep the group in trail of her while the ones behind him scanned the area for any sign of their escapee.

Larry Howell and his family woke from an uncomfortable sleep in his truck. Having parked next to a gas station and convenience store, the family first trooped in to use the restrooms and do a cursory wash of themselves. Then Larry picked up four bottles of orange juice and paid for them with the cashier, wishing him God's blessings as he did so.

He didn't really need to buy the juice; it was done more as a courtesy for the use of the restrooms.

Looking at his written directions that had been given to him the night before, he made his way to the ATF office. Parking and having his family members accompany him inside, he walked up to a reception desk.

"I'd like to talk with someone about something that's happening in Sharples," he said.

An agent who was walking by stopped and came back to where Larry and his family were standing.

"Sharples?"

"Yes, sir. We just came from there."

"I'll handle it, Teresa," the agent said to the receptionist. Indicating that the Howells should follow him, he led them down a corridor to an empty conference room.

"I'm Oliver Gavin," the agent said, introducing himself. "May I ask who you are?"

"I'm Larry Howell. This is my wife, Zena and my two children, Lois and Larry Junior."

"Very nice to meet you, Larry," Gavin said. "Can I get you all something? Some coffee for the adults? Maybe a soda pop for the kids?"

"You're very kind. Perhaps just water for all of us," Larry said. He didn't want to sound impolite by informing the agent that he and his family drank neither coffee nor soft drinks.

Gavin went over to a small fridge at the side of the room and came back with four bottles of water. The children took theirs and looked at them strangely, having never seen water in anything other than a glass before. Larry opened their bottles and smiled at them, opening his own and drinking from it so the children would know it was OK to do so.

Gavin had noticed that both Zena and Lois held their

eyes lowered. "You aren't perhaps from the Shining City community, are you?"

"As a matter of fact, we are," Larry said. "That's what we wanted to talk with someone about."

"I'm here to listen to what you have to say," Oliver Gavin said pleasantly. "I've been very interested in the Shining City community for some time now." *Ever since I started noticing how many of them show up here buying guns.*

"They're holding people prisoner there," Larry said. "The pastor there uses intimidation, threats, and even physical violence to keep people from leaving. If you leave, he has his converts hunt you down and drag you back. Then he has you beaten into submission."

Not exactly what I wanted to hear about, Gavin thought.

"Did you leave because you felt your family was in danger?"

"Take a look at my daughter!" Larry exclaimed. "Do you see the bruise on the side of her face? That's where the man *hit her.*"

Gavin looked at Lois, noting that she actually did have a large, purplish bruise on one side of her face. "Did you get that from the pastor hitting you?" he asked her.

Lois shrunk down farther in her seat, keeping her eyes on the floor.

Gavin looked questioningly at Larry. "Can she speak?"

"Yes. Yes, of course. It's just that she's grown up in the community, and women are commanded not to speak unless given permission by their fathers or husbands."

Oliver Gavin's eyebrows shot up. *Yeah, my wife would go for that ... not!*

"It's alright, Lois. You can answer the man's questions," Larry said.

Lois Howell took the opportunity to not just speak, but to speak forcefully for the first time in her life.

"He *hit* me and he *screamed at* me because I spoke in the assembly. All I did was say a Bible verse."

Wondering which verse of the Bible could possibly have enraged the pastor so much that he'd left a black and blue mark the size of his hand on the teenager's face, he asked, "What verse was that?"

"The one where Yeshua says, 'Love one another as I have loved you.'"

*Well, **that's** a bit ironic.*

"He hit you because of that verse?"

"He hit me because I spoke."

Gavin turned back to Larry. "Is there any other reason you have for fearing this community? Do they have weapons? Guns? Explosives?"

"Everyone has a gun, mostly for hunting. But the pastor has preached that we ... the community has to be able to protect themselves from invasion by mud people and extermination by the ZOG. We ... they are to be the remnant that inherits the Earth when Yeshua comes to judge the heathen."

"The ZOG? Who are the ZOG?"

"The Zionist-Occupied Government."

Oliver Gavin sat back. *If they're afraid of the so-called Zionist-Occupied Government, why are they here talking to the ATF?*

He decided on an indirect route to the answer for his question. "Have you talked with the local law enforcement people in Sharples?"

"Sharples doesn't have a police department," Larry said. "And I was afraid the county sheriff's department might have Shining City members within it. Same for the state police.

They have communities everywhere—all over the country." Gavin noticed Larry's eyes get glassy as he concluded, "I don't know if there's any place safe for me and my family." His face got angry. "It's not that I'm in love with the niggers and the kikes—I'm not. But that's not enough for Shining City. The leaders require strict obedience. If you don't agree with everything they teach, then they say you have to be corrected."

"Just how do they correct you?" Gavin inquired.

"They tie your arms around a tree, tear the shirt off your back, and give you thirty-nine lashes with a whip. They say if thirty-nine lashes were given to Yeshua for our atonement, then thirty-nine lashes is appropriate for correction."

I know next to nothing about this place, but this sounds really whack to me, Gavin thought. "Do you know if they ever killed anyone?"

"I don't know. I really can't be sure. A couple of other people disappeared before I left, and no one seems to know what happened to them, so I guess it's possible."

"You say everyone has a gun. What about explosives? Do they have explosives?"

"They make some out of fertilizer," Larry said. "Fertilizer and some other stuff they get from hardware stores. Fireworks. Fuel oil. They use it to blow stumps when clearing land for another house or for a garden. Everyone grows a garden, and everyone stores up what they grow by canning it or dehydrating it. The pastor tells everyone what to grow, and the food is shared and distributed. Everyone is required to have a year's worth of food stored in their house, and every house has a basement for that."

"Where do they get their ammunition for their guns?" Gavin asked, recalling that when he saw a Shining City member and his son buy a gun, they hadn't bought any ammunition.

"They make it. Most people have something like an AR, so they make a lot of .223."

"Do you have an AR?" Gavin asked him.

"I did. I left it behind. I didn't see it as essential to us getting away. I couldn't have shot my way out of the community—they have guards, and they're armed. I couldn't risk my wife or children being shot."

"How did you get here, Mr. Howell?" Gavin asked.

"I drove my truck. We left very early in the morning. The guard let us out when I told him my wife was having a miscarriage and we needed to come here to the hospital."

Zena whimpered, tears starting to roll down her cheeks. "He told an untruth," she said quietly. "He bore false witness. He sinned."

"He's trying to protect you and the children," Gavin said reassuringly. "I'm sure that God will forgive him for a fib if it means saving his family."

Zena was shaking her head. "Yahweh's law is absolute. Yahweh commands us not to bear false witness. He doesn't say *except* afterward."

Gavin thought for a beat on how to respond to her. Then he said, "Jesus came to forgive all sins, Mrs. Howell. He will forgive your husband for that one."

She thought about that. "There is truth in what you say," she agreed.

Gavin stood up. "I hope you all can excuse me for a few minutes. I need to talk with my supervisor to see how we can help you. Is there anything I can get for you for while I'm gone? More water? Something to eat?"

"What we have is fine," Larry said, fingering his bottle of water, still half full.

Gavin got up and walked to his supervisor's office. Giving a knock on the door, he was invited inside.

"Kind-of unusual for you to still be here at this hour," the man said after glancing at his watch. "Aren't you usually out checking up on our FFLs by this time?"

"I have an unusual situation," Gavin said. "I have a man, his wife, and his two kids in the conference room. You remember me telling you about all the guns being purchased by this small group over in Sharples? This family just came from there. The way they put it, it's more like they had to escape in the middle of the night."

His supervisor sat back in his chair and looked at Oliver in a way that invited him to go on.

"He says they're some sort of apocalyptic extremist group. White separatists or something like that, practicing a bizarre Christian-based religion. He says they all have guns, and that they make explosives. He says the guns are for hunting and the explosives for blowing stumps, but he also says their leader claims that the group will have to defend themselves from invasion by minorities and against the government." He paused. "You should see these folks, Howard. The kids act like they've never seen anything in the modern world. The wife and daughter wouldn't even speak until the husband gave them his permission. The entire left side of the daughter's face has a bruise on it where supposedly the pastor hit her for speaking in church."

"Maybe it's time you decided to pay them a visit."

"That's easier said than done. They're a pretty secretive group. They all live up in a canyon, and the road in has a guard post and a gate. Plus, I'm not sure I'd like to be walking around in a community where everyone has a gun and doesn't trust the government."

The supervisor considered this. "You're right—this one might be beyond our resources to handle. Write me up a report, and I'll send it up the line and see what kind of response we get."

"In the meantime, we've got to figure out how to handle this family," Oliver said. "The husband acts like he's scared for his life and that of his family. The wife keeps talking about how he sinned by tricking the guard to let them out with a lie. She's acting like they're all going to hell. He's afraid that someone from the community is going to find them and drag them back to the place. He says if that happens, they'll tie him up against a tree and scourge him like Jesus was. Says the pastor calls it 'correction'."

Howard considered this. "I can use some emergency authority here. We'll get them situated in a hotel room on an upper floor so we can safeguard them with a single agent while we're waiting for some word on how to handle the rest of the situation. It sounds like something for the Special Response Team, given how little we know about this group."

As the sun started getting low in the sky, Hank decided to call it quits for the night. She was betting the rest of the team hadn't wagered on being out this long, but she had prepared for the event herself. Having doubled back and created a false trail, she no longer heard the men behind her. Deciding that her escape would likely be considered assured, she then made her way back around to the house and went inside, finding Dave Ambrose still reading through his book.

"Where are the guys?" he asked.

"Good question," she replied, grinning. "Last I heard, they were barking up the wrong tree in their attempt to track me through the woods. I set them up on a pretty good false trail. It seems there's some decent deer activity out back of here. I think they might be tracking deer right now, whether they realize it or not."

Dave chuckled. "I think I would have liked serving with you."

"In a way, you still do." Hank tapped her watch to see just where the men actually were. Seeing them moving in an area she knew she had not traversed, she commanded Hal to take her out of Hide mode.

"Team," she called over the comm link, "dinner should be ready by the time you get back here."

In the expanse of forest that stretched southwest of the house, the six men all stopped in their tracks. Crow pulled out his tablet and commanded Hal to show Hank's location overlaid on the area map.

"Sonuvabitch."

"Where is she?" Cloud asked.

"Back at the friggin' house."

The men all let Crow lead the way as he monitored their progress on the map, allowing Hal to direct them over the fastest route back to the remote base.

"Now you have to tell me how you got back here without them detecting you," Dave said as Hank monitored the team's position on her own tablet.

"While they were hiding in the trees chasing deer, I was walking across the open field south of the house to get back here."

Dave laughed. "I definitely would have loved serving with you. Though I might not have liked being outsmarted by a girl, as they say."

"Awwww ... Poor little men," Hank chided.

Dave got up. "They're likely going to be cold and hungry

when they get back. What say we really have dinner ready for them?"

"Sure, why not? What do we have in stock that's good?"

"I've got all the makings here for beef stew and biscuits."

"Sounds like a plan," Hank said.

She and Dave were just finishing up the meal when the men made their way back into the house.

"OK, how'd you manage to escape?" Edge asked.

Hank shook a finger at him. "You of all people should know that anyone who does martial arts is flexible enough to pass their joined hands from in front of their body to behind. From there, it was an easy grab for a hidden key to the cuffs. You guys stashed me right by the front door, so how could I resist? Then it was just a matter of getting from the house to the trees without getting noticed. I gather I failed at that one."

"Spud somehow knew the door had opened," Voice said. She turned to him. "How?"

"I saw the light from outside shining down the hallway."

"Gotta remember that for tomorrow," she said with a grin. "Mental note to self: don't open the door so wide."

"Mental note to self," Crow began, "post someone outside the closet."

That got the rest of the men laughing.

"Better yet, tie her up in the basement," Spud suggested.

"We're doing this again tomorrow?" Cloud asked.

"Might as well. There's no snow on the ground for doing any cross-country skiing, in spite of being as far north as we are," Edge said. "It should be more interesting, too. They're calling for rain tomorrow." He grinned at Hank. "I say, make sure she can't get to any rain gear."

"This doesn't sound like a good plan," Doc Rich said, having overheard the discussion. "Highs have only been in the mid-forties during the day, and are forecast to stay that way. It's a setup for a case of hypothermia."

"We'll give you the kill switch," Cloud remarked. "You can monitor everyone's biometrics and if it looks like anyone's parameters are starting to slide, we can call the exercise off."

"Will that work when I'm in Hide mode?" Hank asked, understanding that there was a good reason for the precaution.

"Hal's got a failsafe, remember?" Crow said. "If Hal sees your biometrics slide too far away from normal, it breaks Hide and sounds a medical alert."

"That's right," Hank recalled. "Again tomorrow, then. Who wants beef stew?"

12

"Good morning, everyone. So far, so good—no rain. And they're calling for only a fifteen percent chance for the rest of the day," Hank chirped as she arrived for breakfast.

"Yeah, but it's cloudy and thirty-seven degrees as well. Some little bunny is gonna freeze her titties off," Cloud smirked.

"Unless you never get out of the basement," Voice said.

"We'll see," Hank said, smiling confidently. "Eggs, pancakes, and bacon. Plenty of fuel for a cold day," she added as she grabbed coffee and sat down.

"I hope you guys aren't going to use handcuffs again. It's not very challenging to escape them."

"We've got our plan," Spud said, sounding as confident as Hank.

As she finished up her breakfast, Hank kept a wary eye on the six men who would pursue her. She had considered that perhaps the best tactic for the day, given her teammates were likely to be a lot more cautious in restraining her, would be to simply not allow herself to be taken in the first place. *Doorway ... windows ... No, not a window. Not sure I could crash through and not get cut up, which even in a real scenario might produce life-threatening injuries. Window is a last resort. Go for the door.*

She popped another forkful of pancakes in her mouth. *They're expecting you to finish. Time this right, and you might be able to get through the door and out through the kitchen before anyone can grab you. Then run, rabbit, run!*

Seeing the men all somewhat distracted by finishing up and getting dishes into the sink, she decided it was the right time to try to make a break for it. Leaping up, she made a dash for the door. Crow bolted after her, and with a swing of his hand managed to get a handful of her shirt, yanking her to the floor.

"We figured you might try to make a break for it before you were even done with breakfast," he told her, a grin spreading across his face.

She struggled with him, considering if it would be against the rules to give him a jab in the crotch with her foot. Deciding that might make for bad team relations later if she did, she decided she'd save that tactic for a real situation.

Spud came walking over, a grin on his face and a roll of duct tape in his hand. "I'm betting you don't have a key for this," he said. "But just in case ..." He looked at the other men. "Get her up against the wall."

From his vantage point in the living room, Dave Ambrose had leaned over and was amusedly watching the proceedings. *If I was a betting man, my money would still be on Hank*, he thought.

Spud proceeded to pat her down thoroughly. He extracted a handcuff key from the waistband at the small of her back, as well as a razor blade. He found the flexible diamond saw hidden in the waistband at her side. He relieved her of her knife, took a small compass from her shoe, found a map and some cash in her other shoe, and even cleared the granola bars out of her pockets. He stripped her of her belt, grinning when he noticed an additional handcuff key sequestered in the buckle and the small razor blade embedded in the plastic on one side. Feeling down the flap that covered the zipper in her pants, he found a couple of lockpicking tools, and located another handcuff key and razor blade when he ran his fingers around the hems of her pants.

"Pretty impressive," he said as he noted the small pile of items he'd retrieved. Then he went over her once again to assure himself that he'd found everything. He took a hand and wrapped her wrist with duct tape, placed her other hand so it overlapped the first with fingers pointed in the opposite direction and continued to wrap the duct tape around both wrists, binding them in front of her in an involuntary self-hug.

The men then marched her over to the door to the basement and took her down the stairs, where Spud then bound her ankles in duct tape as well.

"In case you manage to get loose from the duct tape, be aware the Edge will be sitting in a chair in front of the cellar door, too," Spud said. He leaned and gave her a kiss. "Have a nice day, Love."

She stayed silent, but extended him a finger he'd neglected to immobilize.

"Tsk, tsk," Cloud said, chuckling. "Not very lady-like."

She twisted her wrists slightly so Cloud could see that neither of the two fingers had been immobilized.

The men all chuckled as they went back up the stairs. "Poker, anyone?" she heard Cloud remark as the door closed. Then someone turned off the lights so she was surrounded by darkness, which was followed by a *clunk!*

sounding from the area of the door above her. She surmised that Edge was now stationed at the door.

She waited for some minutes, letting her eyes adjust to the darkness. Then she raised her bound wrists to her mouth and proceeded to gnaw at the duct tape. After what seemed an interminable time, she managed to get a split in one edge and, working her wrists, was able to get the tape to tear along the split, freeing her wrists. Her ankles she then simply unwound. She decided to keep the tape, figuring it might come in handy later.

Going to her pants, she removed the pull from her zipper. Pressing in the sides of the pull activated a small, red LED light which she used to scout what was available in the basement. Finding a treasure trove of items on the workbench and in cabinets, she filled her pockets with a flathead and Phillips screwdriver, a utility knife, a hacksaw blade, a roll of electrical tape, a couple of fifty-five-gallon trash bags, a lighter, and a handful of nails. Scouting further, she also took an old blanket and a knit cap. Then she dropped her pants and lowered her panties.

She chuckled. "You, for one, should have known that there's plenty of room here, Spud," she murmured as she extracted a carefully-wrapped package of materials from her vagina that replaced everything Spud had taken off her person—right down to a multitool. She then shoved it in a cargo pocket.

Now to deal with the issue of the Incredible Hulk guarding the door.

She considered first taking him hostage, but figured his size and training would make it unlikely that she would succeed. *That, and the fact that the door opens outward.* Then she thought, *KISS. Would this place have been built to code if there wasn't another way out of here? Someone could be trapped down here in a fire ...*

Figuring the most likely place for a second exit would be opposite the door leading down from the kitchen, she walked around the basement, her tiny light illuminating where she was stepping so she wouldn't inadvertently make some noise while occasionally stopping to scan the ceiling above her. When she got to the northeast corner of the basement, she noticed a rectangle of faint light on the ceiling above her, and shining her light upward noticed a pull-down ladder of the type often used to access an attic nestled between the rafters. Searching her memory for what might be above, she grinned. *It goes into the garage.*

She took a deep breath and pulled on the rope that would bring the ladder down, being careful not to let it fall and thump an alert to her quest for freedom that the men above might hear. Getting it fully extended, she took a first tentative step on the bottom step, cringing when it creaked under her weight. She froze, listening intently for any sound that might indicate anyone had heard. Hearing nothing, she took another step. The ladder creaked again. Sighing, she resigned herself to the fact that there would be no silence as she ascended the steps to the opening above, which she had noted had flooring above it. She prayed that Joe Corbett hadn't bought the house from someone else and decided to nail the flooring over the ladder.

When she got up to it, she noticed that it was simply a covering to the ladder. Pushing on it, it rose up from where it was seated, having been just loosely set over the opening to the cellar. She carefully slid it to one side and crawled out into the garage.

Not through the garage door, she thought. *It will make too much noise when it opens.* Looking around, she saw another door that she recognized led into the kitchen, a regular door that opened to the outside, and a single window. Going over to the side door that led outward, she tried the knob. *Locked.* She examined the lock as well. *Deadbolt. This one will be beyond my capabilities. Memo to self: get Voice to teach you lock picking.* She then went to the window. Grinning, she flipped the simple locking mechanism and quietly lifted the window open. Slipping out, she dropped behind the bushes that had been planted at the side of the garage, made an assessment of where she was, and headed northeast into a thin stand of trees that she knew could be used to sneak back around to where she had escaped into the woods the day before or alternatively would allow her to head due north through more woodland. She opted for the latter. Recalling Doc Sue's typical exits, she attempted her own rendition of *Sentimental Journey.* She got as far as a very off-key rendition of the first line of the song and decided she couldn't do it justice.

A brief sprint later and she was in the thin stand of trees. Walking further, she occasionally peered back at the house. When the number of trees had nearly obstructed her view of the house, she gave one more look, noted that no one was outside the house, and simply walked off, using the second compass from her intimately-sequestered set of escape tools to keep her on a northward track by picking out the farthest thing she could see and guiding off of it while she walked.

Back at the house, Edge had leaned his chair up against the door, satisfied that he could doze if he wanted to and still not have Hank shove her way past him. The four other men were happily engaged in yet another game of five-card draw until Voice at one point took a look at his watch.

"Incoming," he said while pulling out his tablet. He and Amigo both looked at the coded message that had come in.

"It's from Steve Katz," he announced. "ATF has a mission for us. HQ told him we were here. He'll be coming in around noon, so we've got a couple of hours before he arrives."

"Maybe we should get Hank out of the basement," Amigo suggested. "No telling how quickly we might have to bug out."

"Eh! Leave her down there," Crow said. "If nothing else, it will give Steve something to talk about when he gets back to his office."

The others considered this for a moment.

"Nah, we need to get her up here. Let her know the training exercise is called off due to having a mission forthcoming," Amigo said.

Edge leaned back forward in his chair with a thump. Opening the door to the basement, he called down, "Hank!"

Silence.

"*Hank!*"

Still silence.

"What the? Come on, Hank—we need you up here. We've got a gunny coming."

When he was still greeted by silence, Edge turned on the light and trotted down the stairs.

"*Stink rot, hogwash! She's gone!*"

Standing at the top of the stairs, Cloud laughed and asked, "What did you just say?"

Emerging from the basement, Edge repeated, "Stink rot, hogwash."

"Where the hell did *that* expression come from?"

"Dunno. I've said it ever since I was a kid."

"Stink rot and hogwash aside, we now have a problem," Crow said. "Hank is in Hide mode, and we've got no idea where she is and a gunny arriving in two hours." He turned to Voice. "Can Hide mode be broken?"

"Hal breaks it automatically in a medical emergency situation."

"Hank may *never* develop a medical situation in the next two hours," Crow said. "She might not develop a medical situation until she decides to mosey on back here at night-fall. Any way you can command Hal to break Hide so we can call her in?"

"I buried that code really deep and made it pretty iron-clad, but I can see what I can do. It might be as simple as getting Hal to recognize me and stop execution of the protocol temporarily. As long as Hal also takes Hank out of Hide ..." He trailed off.

"I'm taking it this can be complicated," Spud said.

"Could be," Voice admitted.

Spud turned to Cloud and Crow. "Would it be faster to just take the helicopter and hope she recognizes that it isn't part of the scenario? We're supposed to be tracking her on foot."

"One way to find out," Crow said. He motioned to Cloud, and the two pulled on coats and headed for 100UN, removing tiedowns and chocks and quickly completing a preflight inspection before starting the helicopter up and lifting off into flight.

Flying up in the direction Hank had escaped through the woods the previous day, Crow maneuvered the helo in a search pattern while Cloud kept a careful eye on the ground, trying to spot Hank. Hearing the helicopter above her, Hank hunkered down in the underbrush. "Cheaters," she mumbled. "You're supposed to be on foot, guys."

Cloud smacked his forehead. "FLIR," he said, getting the

system up and running. "It's friggin' cold out there. She'll show up like a lighthouse on a clear night."

Noticing the helicopter swing with its nose facing in her direction, Hank likewise remembered the FLIR equipment 100UN sported.

"Shit!"

She bolted, trying to get herself into the thickest area of trees she could find in an attempt to make any rappel down to capture her impossible without risk of serious injury to the rappelers.

"She's running," Cloud said. "She doesn't realize this isn't part of the exercise."

"I'll get over her, you call her on the loudspeaker," Crow said.

As Crow continued to fly to be over top of Hank, she continued to dodge and run in an attempt to evade them. "Damn, she's squirrelly," Crow complained.

Finally, Cloud decided it wouldn't matter who else heard his call over the loudspeaker.

"Hank, hold up!" he broadcast.

Yeah, right, she thought as she dodged off in a different direction.

"Hank!" he broadcast again. "Hank, *scramble!*"

Scramble? Hank stopped in her tracks. Moving to where she could look up at 100UN, she shielded her eyes and lifted her face up to where the helicopter hovered above her. Watching it pivot in the air and move off a couple hundred feet to the northeast, she headed in that direction herself. As she approached, she saw the trees give way to a clearing, where Crow was settling 100UN onto the ground. The door sliding open, she saw Cloud then wave her in.

Hunched low, she dashed over and stepped up via the

TSOP attachment rail and grabbed Cloud's hand as he pulled her inside.

"What's going on?" she shouted over the rotor noise as Cloud pulled the door shut and she took a seat. She reached up and put one of the headsets located in the back on as Cloud came to sit across from her.

"ATF gunny is coming in. He'll be here in an hour and a half. We have a mission."

"THAT WAS A PRETTY GOOD ESCAPE," Edge remarked to Hank as the team took an early lunch while waiting for the arrival of Stephen Katz, the ATF gunny. "I had no idea there was a second entrance to the basement."

"Neither did I," Hank admitted. "I just went looking for it figuring the house wouldn't have met code without a second way out of the basement in the event of a fire."

Voice tapped his temple. "This is all making me believe that in this kind of scenario, what you've got up here is as valuable as any toys you might have hidden on your person."

"If you think about it, the toys we have are pretty good," Spud said. "But a captor might take both our watch and our earpiece. We'd still have the bum ticker, but no way to use it."

"Sure we would," Crow said. "Maybe not for outbound communications, but we could communicate with the captured team member."

"How?" Spud asked skeptically.

"Morse code through the bum ticker's haptic."

"Admittedly, I didn't consider that," Spud said. "But you've just pointed out that I don't know Morse code."

"I'm rusty on mine, I'm betting," Cloud said. "Another skill to learn or relearn, as the case may be."

Hearing the doorbell, Dave Ambrose got up to answer it.

"Hello," they heard a man's voice say.

"Hello. How can I help you?" Dave said in reply.

After a pause, he then said, "Come this way."

Walking into the dining room, they noticed that Dave was leading Katz in. He left the gunny with the group and wandered off to be out of sight and hearing of the team and their ATF contact.

"What have you got for us to consider?" Spud asked.

"We have a somewhat touchy situation in West Virginia. Ordinarily, we'd call in the regional SRT, but as you can imagine, the post-pandemic situation has been keeping all of our Special Response Teams pretty busy. Hard times tend to bring out the worst in people."

"Tell us about it," Edge said. "We had a mission in the middle of all of that."

"Really? Any of you get sick?"

"Every single one of us, beginning with me," Edge revealed. "I've got some advice for you: don't hold the end of a bandage in your mouth if you find yourself having to patch up a gunshot wound during a pandemic."

"You got *shot?*" Katz asked.

"Just grazed me. Nothing to get my mom excited if she were still around."

"Hopefully, this mission won't add to your battle scars," Katz said, dropping a file in the middle of the table.

Spud slid it over to himself. Looking through the initial pages, he muttered, "Extremist group."

"Which one? Cloud asked. "They're a dime a dozen these days."

Spud looked over at Hank. "Shining City."

"Really? Shining City?" she repeated.

"My wife has taken an interest in this group as part of our monitoring of potential situations we might become involved in," Spud explained. He slid the file to Hank.

As she opened it up, she told the others, "Shining City is a ... how can I put this? A merry mix of far-right ideologies. They preach an extremely conservative Christian religion that requires women to speak only when spoken to and given permission to do so. Their hair must be entirely covered. They wear a tichel, which is a head covering usually seen among orthodox Jewish women, in obedience to Old Testament teachings about a woman's requirement to keep her hair covered. Women aren't allowed in positions of authority, nor to speak during church services. They are required to remain behind a screen and stay silent. Men have absolute authority over the women.

"They are anti *everything*. Everything except white, male faces. Like a lot of white supremacist groups, they'll call Hispanics, African-Americans, Orientals, and Native Americans 'mud people'. They idolize Adolph Hitler, because of his eugenics policies in his misguided attempt to breed a 'master race' of Aryans.

"They are also anti any religious belief other than their own. They refer to God as 'Yahweh', which isn't too unusual among fundamentalist Christians. They refer to Jesus as 'Yeshua HaMashiach': 'Yeshua the Annointed.' Everyone who believes something other than what they do are 'errant', 'Papists' if Catholic, 'Satan's children', or if they've fallen away from the Shining City faith, 'apostates'. Apostates, if they return to a Shining City community, are treated extremely harshly. There are also rumors that the leaders of a Shining City community will put out the equivalent of an APB on apostates so they can be returned and face punishment as part of a kind of purification so they can re-enter the community. There are questions as to whether apostates are treated so harshly that they are even killed, though there has been no proof of that.

"And to ice the cake, they're apocalyptic. They believe that the end of the world is coming very soon, and that they alone will be the inheritors of the Earth. They see their mission as being to recruit as many followers as they can into their faith and way of thinking as possible before the end time comes. They see the government as being an agent of Satan, so I hope you haven't tried to send any of your agents into their compounds."

"You know quite a bit about this group," Katz acknowledged. "If you look through our file, you'll notice that one of our agents in Charleston, West Virginia had the same caution regarding sending someone in to snoop and ask questions. You'll also see that we have in protective custody a family that recently left the compound in Sharples."

"Sharples, West Virginia is not Shining City's only community," Hank said. "They use al Qaeda-like tactics to recruit followers. They'll go into a rural area and convert over as many people as they can, gain enough following to take over the local government, then send a splinter group to another rural area and repeat the process. You might say that they metastasize like a cancer: a cell here, a cell somewhere else. Then grow a community like a tumor. When it gets large enough, send out more cells to start more communities."

"Regardless, the word we have from the head of this family is that everyone is armed, and that they make explosives as well. The explosives we didn't know about until this man contacted us. One of our agents has been covertly monitoring gun sales at stores in Charleston and noted that a lot of members of this group have purchased firearms there. Most of the time, these are AR-style rifles. This former member of the community says they're making their own ammunition as well. So, we naturally have concerns that they may be planning on increasing their influence through violence."

Hank took a breath. "If you're not careful, you might just provoke them into violence."

"We need to know what's going on there," Katz said.

"I'm glad you put it that way. But if you're ultimate desire is to provoke these people into a confrontation by sending us in to get one of us killed as justification, then I'm all for telling you to shove it."

Katz gave her a hard look. "I know you don't like me very much ..."

"It's nothing personal. I just think there have been plenty of examples of the ATF having their heads up their asses and creating a totally fucked up situation," Hank responded, the edge of anger evident in her voice.

"That's enough, Hank," Spud warned.

"I tell you what," Hank began, addressing both Katz and Spud. "If we can agree that the first thing we do is infiltrate the community in order to gather information, then I'll go for it. No ATF presence until we make our report on what's happening, or if they really are intent on violence, one of us buys it. You have a statement here by a single individual. Do you know for certain that what he's telling you is the truth? Or is he exaggerating things a bit? Perhaps even has some sort of vendetta against the head of this community, espe-cially given what the report says about the girl who was ostensibly struck by the pastor. If we can get into this community and corroborate what this man says, then perhaps the evidence we gather will allow you to bring charges against the leader and any other involved individuals. It looks like they leave the community from time to time to get supplies they can't produce themselves—the most notable being diesel fuel for their vehicles. That would give you an opportunity to make an arrest."

"You know, you talk like we're storm troopers and haven't learned anything since the '90's," Katz said. "I can assure you that our tactics have become much more refined. As I told you in the beginning, we'd use our own SRT if they weren't already tied up and we didn't consider this case to be important enough to warrant immediate attention. And infiltrating the community is exactly what we need, so if that's your first plan of action, have at it."

Katz and Hank leveled looks at each other for a bit. Relenting, Hank said, "I apologize for any insinuation that ATF might not be prepared to face this situation other than in a reserved and professional manner. You know there's a history here, and I'm aware of how it affects the culture between your agency and my former one. If it's any consolation to you, I've come to question some of *their* tactics as well. It's easier to do when they're no longer the ones who provide your paycheck."

"And I'll concede that we haven't handled things well in the past, and will probably have a day when we screw the pooch again. But that's not what we're aiming for here. We just want to know if these people are so far out in the field ideologically that they're a threat to national security or if we should just not poke the tiger."

Hank sighed. "I guess that's what I'd like to know as well," she conceded.

"Then we're on the same page. How soon can you guys get started?"

"We're going to need to plan out our approach to this

group," Crow said. "We have just about everything we need to go straight to the mission area. What we *will* need and don't have is our ATF credentials. We were here for a training exercise, and didn't think any LEO creds would be necessary. We don't have one of our jets with us—just the helicopter, and it's five and a half hours back to our head-quarters. West Virginia isn't such a big hop in the H155, so we could leave here and go directly there, but we're going to need someone back home to gather up the credentials and bring them back for us."

"Probably the nearest airport to the HQ that you could get into would be Lincoln," Hank said. "I'm assuming that you brought in a G550?"

"Yes. York won't have enough runway for us. Getting in isn't a problem—it's getting back out. At least that's what the pilots tell me. They say it's going to be a squeaker just getting out of Charleston when we drop you off there."

"Then our man Voice will get in touch with our HQ to gather up the team's credentials and meet us in Lincoln. I'll go along for the ride to take possession of them." She smiled at him. "Will there be a bagel with cream cheese and straw-berry jam for me on the plane?"

"Bagel with cream cheese and strawberry jam?" Katz asked, puzzled.

"The last time I flew on a DoJ G550, I was served a bagel with cream cheese and strawberry jam along with my coffee. It was much appreciated. So much so that I married the guy who ordered it for me."

Spud grinned. "I caught her looking me over and told her if she liked what she saw, she could see more of me. I guess she took it somewhat literally."

Hank blushed, then got serious. "Only one more thing I

have to do before we go, though. I need to plant some flowers."

"Excuse me?" Katz queried. "You want a delay so you can *plant flowers?*"

Hank cut him a hard look. "You probably don't know how we got this base. This house belonged to the perpetrator in a case we were called in on. His motivation for doing what he did was that his wife had a botched operation that left her disfigured, and which ultimately caused her to commit suicide. You may have noticed the area on the hill up in the far corner of the property that doesn't quite have grass growing in it yet. She had a little cabin up there—a she shed. Her husband pled guilty and asked for the death penalty and for it to be administered immediately because he believed he would be reunited with his wife that way. When the court denied the request, he was so distraught he had a heart attack right there in court and died. I found out later that he left this house to me. He and his wife are buried up in the farthest corner of the property, cremated and placed in a single urn as he requested.

"I don't anticipate getting here that often. In fact, this is the first time since their burial. So, I brought some flower bulbs to plant at the gravesite. It won't take me long, and I owe it to both of them."

Katz felt a bit ashamed. He had no idea how the unit had acquired this particular base.

Hank didn't wait for his approval. She went and grabbed her coat, a trowel, and the bag of flower bulbs. Heading out with the men trudging behind her, she made her way up to the simple granite stone that marked the Cornett's grave and commenced spading up soil and shaking the earth out of the clods of grass. Then she pressed the bulbs into the ground in groups.

"The crocuses will come up and bloom first," she explained to the others. "Then the daffodils, then the tulips and irises, then the gladioluses and lilies. There will be flowers here from the spring and through into the summer."

She stood back up. "Joe, I hope if you and Robin are back together and happy that you'll give me a sign. Make these flowers grow and multiply, and let them cover this entire corner of the property. If love lasts forever, show me that it's so."

13

Hank had boarded the G550 in Elmira, New York, and hadn't spoken a word to Stephen Katz since sitting down. She read through the transcript of Larry Howell's interview by Oliver Gavin again, comparing what Larry had told the agent with what she knew of Shining City from her own research.

She scowled. "I'm going to need a Bible," she muttered. "A King James, and not one that's brand new. A used one."

Katz looked at her. "What did you say?"

"I need a King James Bible. Not a *New* King James—a plain old King James. One written in the English of the 1600's. Every biblical quote I see on their website is from the original King James translation. The one with all the 'thees' and 'thous'. And it has to be used."

"Why used?"

She looked up at him. "The King James Bible is these people's guidepost. It's a given that they read it all the time and have it in their possession when they meet for church services. They will have opened it dozens of times weekly, if not daily. It will be well-worn as a result." She grumbled and added, "And I'm going to need a tichel and learn how to wear it." With a grin, she said, "YouTube U. You can find how to do most things on YouTube. I'd even be surprised if you can't find how to do open heart surgery there."

Katz chuckled in agreement.

Hank grumbled again, this time in a tone that conveyed true annoyance.

"I'm going to have to wear a dress. Trust me, none of the dresses I own would meet this group's approval."

A sudden realization hit Katz. "You're planning on being the infiltrator."

"Not just me. I think both me and Spud. There's a big emphasis on families in this group."

"Are you going to hire some kids?" Katz asked somewhat sarcastically.

"Just tell 'em the truth," Hank murmured as she continued to look over the file. "Spud and I can't have kids."

"Forbidden while you're serving in the unit, I take it," Katz remarked.

"Not just forbidden. Gotta agree to surgical sterilization."

"So ... you and Spud never intend to have any kids? Even after you retire?"

"Didn't say that. Just won't happen the old-fashioned way," Hank mumbled as she read. "Might not happen at all."

"At the risk of continuing to ask personal questions, why not?" Katz asked.

Hank closed the file she'd been studying. "Biological clock. Tick, tick, ticking away," she said. "How 'bout you? Got any kids?"

"Two boys and a girl. Seventeen, fifteen, and twelve. The two youngest are the boys. All my gray hair is from worrying about the girl every time she's a little late getting home. I'll give you a some fair warning: When you have a boy, you worry about what he's going to do with his one penis. When you have a girl? You worry about what every boy in town is going to do with *his* one penis."

Hank shook her head and laughed. "I'll keep that in mind."

"Back to your Bible issue, why not just check one out of a library?" Katz asked.

Hank couldn't help a smile this time. "In a remarkable bit of irony, the book that has the admonishment in it to not steal is the book most often stolen from public libraries."

"Take them two new ones and ask if you can have an old one."

"That's a thought, but I think it will be quicker just to go to a used book store." Calling over the comm link, she said, "Voice?"

"What do you need, Hank?"

"Can you have Hal find me a used book store in Lincoln that has preferably two copies of the King James Bible? Not the new version—the original."

"Did you get religion?" Voice asked. Hank could practically see him smirking over the comm link.

"They're needed for the mission," Hank said, with Voice likely able to hear her scowl over the comm link as well.

Hank started making notes on her tablet. "Probably the best thing to do here will be to visit some second-hand stores," she said. "I'm thinking the way to get into this community will be to literally drive in hauling a trailer of used household stuff. Just a husband and his wife looking for a new place to call home, far from the cities and their quote-end-quote mud people and Jews and Muslims and women wearing pants," she added derisively. "You know, some backward little place where closed minds can flourish."

"If you feel that way, are you sure you want to be an infiltrator?" Katz asked.

"It's not what I believe but what I can make them believe I believe. In this case, it will likely be easy, as I won't be allowed to speak. I can just keep my mouth shut and make observations. Just stay two steps behind Spud and let him to all the talking."

"You're the team's sniper, though, aren't you? Have you done an undercover operation before?"

"This will be my first," Hank admitted. "I've been involved in some stings, but never embedded. Spud has, though."

She continued to make notes on her tablet. "Going to need a gun, too." She looked at Katz. "Wouldn't know where a dead person can get a gun, do you? Preferably used as well?"

Katz laughed. "I'm betting we could scare one up. What are you thinking you might need?"

"A BUG for both Spud and me. A revolver for Spud, .357 magnum. A lever rifle for me, also .357 magnum. The BUGs will stay hidden, and are for just in case. Spud will want a Glock, but I'm not a fan. Just don't like how they feel in my hand. If you could provide us a Glock 26 for Spud and a Sig P365 for me, that would be great. I figure we can pick up an AR for Spud when we get to West Virginia, but I'd like to have something like a Marlin 1894 for the lever gun. Again, used. Preferably one with an octagonal barrel that I could say has been in the family a while."

"How are you going to explain a woman having a gun to this group?" Katz asked.

"My husband has a heart condition."

"Really? Spud has a heart condition?"

Hank laughed. "He will once someone in Shining City asks why I have a gun."

Noting that the G550 had entered a descent, Hank made a call over the comm link regarding the arrival of the credentials. Page answered that she not only had the documents and badges that were needed, but also a list of used book stores. Hank intended to visit them before leaving with Katz for Charleston, West Virginia.

As they deplaned in Lincoln at the Air Force base, Hank noticed that Page was already parked on the ramp in one of the unit's SUVs. Turning to Katz, she asked, "Care to tag along?"

"It's do that, or cool my heels in the plane for however long it might take," Katz replied. "Browsing used book stores might only be marginally better, but I think I might like that. Sometimes, you can find a nice old edition in one of those places."

"You read?"

"Voraciously."

Hank's face expressed surprise. "Then you and I have something in common. Do your coworkers roll their eyes when you mention having read something in a book?"

"All the time."

Hank laughed. "Then we have more than one thing in common."

Getting into the SUV, Page handed Hank a zippered pouch containing all of the team members' credentials as well as those for Doc Rich and Doc Frank. She then drove off, leaving the Air Force base and heading into Lincoln.

"Do you know where you're going?" Katz asked.

Page tapped on the multimedia display in the SUV. "Voice has Hal programmed to go to a list of addresses by the most efficient route. I just need to listen for the directions being given."

"The tech you guys have is amazing."

"You should get it sometime," Hank said. "Perhaps in ten years or so," she added, getting Page chuckling.

Page parked in front of a small storefront that declared itself a used bookseller. Getting out with Katz, Hank went inside and approached the clerk, noticing that Katz headed directly for the bookshelves.

"Could you tell me where to find the used Bibles?"

The clerk pointed down an aisle. "You find them in the Religion section, right at the beginning."

"In the beginning ..." Hank chuckled.

Walking down the aisle, she found what she was looking for. There was an amazing number of used Bibles of various translations. Looking through, she discovered a number of them that were the King James version she was seeking. She pulled out each of them, one by one, examining the edges of the pages and the covers for wear. She selected two with somewhat tattered covers and a good degree of staining on the edges of the pages where the oils from the previous owners' fingers had deposited. Walking back up to the counter, she set them down for the clerk to ring up.

"I think we have some back there that are in a bit better condition," the clerk remarked.

"I actually wanted ones that looked like they had been lovingly read," Hank said, trying to make it sound like she actually had an interest in them. "These are still in good condition. They just look like they've been read often."

The clerk shrugged. "I'm glad you were able to find what you were looking for."

Hank looked around, trying to find where Katz had gone

off to. "Did you happen to notice where the man I came in with went?"

The clerk pointed again. "The last time I saw him, he was headed down the aisle to the Classics section."

Hank cradled her two purchases in her left arm and turned down the aisle, seeing Katz engrossed at the end of it. As she walked up, he said, "Look at these. I can't believe anyone sold them to a used book store."

Hank took a look at the books he was talking about. They appeared to be an older set of classics: a collection of Shakespeare's works, a copy of *Moby Dick*, Charles Dickens's *A Tale of Two Cities*, and several others. They were all bound in slightly-worn tooled leather. Katz was removing them and setting them in a stack to carry up to the counter.

"You're taking all of those?" Hank asked.

"You bet."

She raised an eyebrow. "Weren't you sort-of forced to read most of those in high school?"

"I wouldn't say 'forced'. I loved them all. Still do."

"Why buy books you've already read?"

Katz looked at her like she'd just arrived from Pluto. "These are leather-bound books printed on rag paper. The price they have on these? Whoever owns this store doesn't know what he has. These nine books are going to cost me ninety dollars. But for books like these, even used it should be more like four- to five-hundred dollars. These are going to look great in my library, and I can read them again and again without much fear of damaging either the bindings or the pages."

"You even have a library," Hank commented.

"Of course! Don't you? I used to have books scattered all around the house. Then I brought in a contractor to build me a library case along one wall in my great room. It's twenty feet long and ten feet high. I've got a step stool so I can get to the upper shelves. It's my pride and joy."

Whatever floats your boat, Hank thought, making a note to herself that Spud should consider himself lucky. Also thinking that perhaps she should suggest that their house have a library in it, too.

"UNTO *THEE* LIFT I up mine eyes, O Thou that dwellest in the heavens. Behold, as the eyes of servants look upon the hand of their masters, and as the eyes of a maiden unto the hand of her mistress; so our eyes wait upon the Lord our God, until that He have mercy upon us.

"Have mercy upon us, O Lord, have mercy upon us: for we are exceedingly filled with contempt. Our soul is exceedingly filled with the scorning of those that are at ease, and with the contempt of the proud."

Robert Benkovic snapped his Bible shut, hung his head for a few beats, then began to pace through the assembled men, addressing them.

"Are we not surrounded by the heathen? By those who refuse to believe that there is but *one* chosen people Yahweh intends to lift up? What did He demand be brought to Him? Leviticus says an offering without blemish. If *we* are to be that offering, then we, too, must be without blemish. Not an offering with a spot on its head, or black skin, or with tattoos. A *pure* offering. When Yahweh sends down a pure snow from the sky, is it not white? Have you ever seen a black snow, or a brown snow? A red one or a yellow one? No! It is a *white* snow!"

The men murmured and nodded their agreement.

"This nation was built on Christian principles,"

Benkovic continued. "But the *government*," he added, emphasizing the word, "says we must accept the heathen Muslim and Papist, Buddhist and Jew, and worse—the atheist who believes that man is the highest being in heaven and on Earth. Is this truly what our forefathers intended? If they did, why did they keep black men as slaves and not allow them to be free? It is because our forefathers recognized that the black man is not an acceptable offering. Why did they drive out the savages? Because they recognized that the red man is not an acceptable offering. But our current heathen-loving government accepts all of this, because just as the psalm says, they are the wealthy and the proud who hold all that Yahweh commands in contempt."

He walked around and stood behind the men. As he glanced at the women behind the screen, they all lowered their eyes. He then turned and addressed the men to their backs.

"We know that same government would like to see us vanquished before Yahweh can show us His mercy and raise us up as His remnant. It is all part of the great battle to come, when the heathen will take arms against the righteous so that Satan may inherit the Earth instead.

"*IS THAT NOT SO?*" he bellowed.

"Yes!" the men returned their acclamation.

"Which is why we prepare," Benkovic said calmly. "Which is why we have no dependence upon the heathen. Not for food, not for water, not for shelter nor heat in the winter. The meat we eat is what we hunt, and the vegetables what we grow, and the bread what we make from the grain sent to us by those of our number living in places where grain flourishes, just as we send fruit and lumber to them for their needs. I think many of the heathen would be surprised by how well we live and how we have avoided the pale horse, not only because we have set ourselves apart, but also because Yahweh's protective hand hovers over us.

"Given all of that, can you believe that we had a man turn apostate and leave like a thief in the middle of the night under a false pretense, taking his entire family with him? He went back to the heathen world, where they worship neither Yahweh nor Yeshua, but the almighty dollar, admitting their love for money over Yahweh."

He had walked back to the front of the assembly and turned once again to face the men.

"We know better, don't we? You cannot eat dollar bills, nor can you eat coins. They are but tools we use in the heathen world to get what we need and cannot produce ourselves. As we grow, though," he added with a hint of coyness in his voice, "we will gradually be able to produce everything we need. We will gradually instill in the communities that adjoin us the true law we already follow. For the Lord gives to those who follow Him authority over the heathen."

"Amen!" the assembled men shouted.

"READING SOMETHING?" Spud asked as she and Spud relaxed for the night in the hotel rooms that the team had taken while in Charleston.

"Watching a YouTube video."

"OK. Recreational or research?"

"Research."

"About?"

"How to wear a tichel."

"You were serious earlier about you and I being the infiltration team."

"Dead serious."

"I'm curious about why you think we'd be best for this."

"This group puts a lot of emphasis on families," Hank said. "They'll be less suspicious of a man and his wife than they would be of a single man."

"How do we explain the lack of children?" Spud asked.

Hank scrunched up her face. "I'm having a sense of déjà vu," she said. "I had this same conversation with Steve Katz on the plane." She shrugged. "We tell them the truth. We're both sterile, but we're hoping God will bless us with children one day," she said, her tone flowery. "Besides," she added, "you have a bum ticker. Can't over-stress your heart," she concluded with a tap to where his bum ticker was hidden beneath his skin.

"Does this mean you're going to give me the 'mission first' celibacy routine the entire time we're embedded?"

Hank acted startled. "I hope not! We just can't be doing anything while hanging from a chandelier."

Spud laughed out loud. "I can see that's going to be the standard joke from now on."

Changing the topic, Hank said, "I think the first thing I want to do is interview the Howells. See if I can read them well enough to know if they're telling the truth or exaggerating."

"That should be fairly straightforward," Spud said. "They're right here in the same hotel we're in."

"Great! Let's see if we can't have Steve make the introductions to the agents here in Charleston tomorrow, and then see if we can't interview the Howells. We've got to start gathering up a few things, too. Stuff that makes it look like we're just a nice conservative Christian couple looking for a new place to call home."

14

Spud and Hank got dressed in their unit formal wear.

"I always feel like a cast member in *Men in Black* in this outfit," Spud related. "I look in the mirror and say, 'this screams fed.'"

"True," Hank admitted. "But in this case, we want it to scream fed."

"I'm not so sure about that. If this group is as fearful of people in government, it stands to reason they'll be even more fearful of people in federal law enforcement. We're going to be telling them we're ATF agents."

"Hopefully, the shock will be lessened by the fact that they've already been talking with ATF agents."

A knock on the door alerted them to the arrival of the ATF agent they had been told to expect. "Team comm," Spud said, alerting Hal to activate communications so that the entire team could hear what was said during the interview.

Hank opened the door to find a man unfamiliar to them standing there. He didn't look any bit the part of an ATF Special Agent.

"Can I help you?" Hank asked.

He withdrew credentials from his pocket. As he did so,

Hank noticed the badge on his belt that had been hidden by his jacket.

"Special Agent Oliver Gavin," he said.

Hank took out her own unit-issued ATF credentials. "Katie Hank," she said. Giving a nod over her shoulder, she added, "My partner, Spencer Banyon. Special Operations."

Gavin gave them both a look. Realizing what he was thinking, Hank said, "No, we're not bunkies. He just came to hang out here while we were waiting for you." *You liar!* one of her voices chided.

Gavin stood up a little straighter. "It would have surprised me if you were," he admitted. "I'm the agent who has been handling the Howell case. If you'd like to come with me, I can take you to the room we have them in."

"Before we do that, I'd like to talk with you first," Hank said. She indicated that Gavin should come into the room, directing him to the table that straddled the kitchen and living areas.

"Nice accommodations," Gavin remarked.

"There aren't a lot of choices in Charleston," Hank said. "At least, not a lot that are worth staying in."

Gavin gave a glance into the bedroom area. "Just one bed?"

"Just one woman in the team," Hank said, her little voices echoing, *That, at least, is true. If you don't count Doc Rich …* "The men all share. Two to a room."

"I see. The advantage of being a woman."

"I suppose you could say that." *Not sexist, are you?*

"What's your role in the team, Agent Hank?"

"You can call me Katie, and I'm the sniper."

She watched Gavin's surprised reaction.

"She's very good. I can attest to that—she saved my life

once. Head shot to a guy with a gun to my head from about eight hundred meters away."

"Eight hundred and fifty," Hank corrected. "I wouldn't be in this team if I wasn't good." She was unsure if any of this information bolstered Gavin's opinion of her or not.

"OK. I can hopefully answer any questions you have," Gavin said.

"First up, how did you get involved in this case, Agent Gavin?"

"The guys all call me Ollie," he said. "I prefer Oliver, but you know how it goes."

"I guess I do. The guys all call me Hank," she said. "Doesn't bother me." She wondered if they called him 'Ollie' because they equated him with Oliver Hardy of Laurel and Hardy fame.

"I do a bit of surveillance in the local gun stores. The owners know I'm ATF, but the customers don't. I like to keep an eye on who's buying guns—the regulars especially. I've been noticing that the people who live over in Sharples in the Shining City compound are buying a lot of guns.

"One day as I was getting ready to head out from the office, I overheard the Howells talking with our reception-ist. Because I've been watching this group, I was anxious to get a little better feel for what's going on over there. You know, to see if they're amassing guns, have explosives ... that kind of thing. So, I took the Howells in to interview them. They have quite a story to tell about the situation, saying everyone has a gun and that the group makes explo-sives. I'm assuming when they say 'everyone', that they mean at least all the men and the male children. Just the other day, a man came in with his kid to buy a rifle. The kid must have been all of ten years old, and Dad was buying him an AR."

"Did you happen to catch why Dad was getting his son an AR?"

"He said for hunting. But who buys an AR for hunting?"

Hank gave him an incredulous look and said, "If it's a kid that it's for, because it has a fairly low recoil and the stock can be adjusted to fit him, don't you think? And as the kid gets bigger, the stock can be adjusted to fit again. No need to buy him another rifle."

Gavin just stared at her.

"You shouldn't assume that just because someone buys an AR that it means they're some kind of potential mass murderer or insurrectionist," Hank counseled him. "Jumping to conclusions without doing a thorough investigation is how things go south in a hurry. This isn't the outcome we want, no matter what the situation turns out to be over in Sharples."

"I've been watching this group for some time," Gavin protested.

"So have I," Hank informed him. "I've read your report, and I can tell you that I probably know as much if not more about this group than you do. I'll need to know even more if we're to infiltrate this compound, which is why I want to talk with the Howells. Hopefully, they can give us the kind of information that will allow an infiltration team to go in, gain the confidence of the group, and thus be able to gather the kind of information that will tell us if they're a threat, and if they are, what the appropriate action to take will be. We're not going to just go in guns blazing, Oliver. Not if we don't have to. I think you can agree that the last thing ATF needs is another Waco under our belt."

Hank could see that Gavin wasn't happy with her analysis. *He's convinced he's right. Worse, he sees this situation as a big case that can further his career. What he doesn't see is that if he's wrong, it could be the end of his career.* She contemplated whether she could convince him of that. She decided that diversion would be a better tactic.

"Our team consists of seven people, plus our medic and a doctor. Two of the team will be infiltrating, which might go well, or might not. If it doesn't go well, then the other five members of the team will attempt extraction, which again might go well or might not. In a worst case scenario, it will fall to the local agents to fight it out and round up the members of this group. You see, we do consider worst case scenarios, Mr. Gavin.

"In a best case scenario, we'll find out that the group has rifles to hunt with and explosives to blow stumps with. The manufacture of explosives, if we find that to be the case, is an actionable matter that we can bring charges against the responsible members of the group for. The purchase of firearms is not illegal, and neither is reloading ammunition. The threat or planning of terrorist activity *is* actionable, assuming the information is credible. My team's job in a best case scenario is to gather enough evidence that will stand up in a court of law to bring any justified charges against responsible individuals. Our first and foremost objective is to determine if any charges are justified, and bring the matter before the courts. Don't you agree?"

Gavin gave her a grudging look.

"If the matter can be resolved without bloodshed, it will be a major accomplishment—one that will demonstrate that the agents involved did a careful and thorough investigation and demonstrated sound leadership skills as well as skill in dealing with those who hold extremist ideologies. That latter is vitally important, given First Amendment protections and Supreme Court rulings with regard to those protections. We may not agree with what a group believes and says. We may completely disagree and dislike what they believe and say. But we have to acknowledge their First Amendment rights to believe and say what they will, as long as there isn't violence involved. You know what they say about that: we can disagree, and it's just a disagreement until your fist hits my face. Then it's assault and battery. We don't want to be the first ones to give a bloody nose. The public won't care what this group believes if we are. They'll simply see us as another bully agency of the government. It will be a smear on the ATF's record, and we have enough of those."

Hank could see that her point was being made with Gavin. "Do you think you can formulate a worst case scenario plan and perhaps have materiel staged in case it's necessary? Keep in mind that what we're talking about here is the deliberate injury or death of one or more of the members of my team."

Gavin's demeanor now indicated that he had more enthusiasm for what was being proposed. *He sees his opportunity to strut his stuff,* Hank thought. *Good. This will keep him busy and prevent him from convincing his SAIC that they need to go in there with armored vehicles.*

"If we're done here, I think that Agent Banyon and I would like to talk to the Howells. Unless you have something to add, Spence?"

Spud was wearing his Secret Service face. "I think you pretty well covered it, Katie." Hank picked up a hint of disapproval in his expression.

"Let me take you to their room," Gavin said.

He led the way to the elevator. Hank considered pointing out that they had at most one floor either up or down and could take the stairs given the team's rooms were all on the second floor, but decided instead to simply take the elevator and not make a fuss. Arriving on the third floor, he led them to a room midway between the elevator and the staircase at the end of the hallway. Knocking on the door, he announced, "It's Gavin."

As the door opened for them, Hank took in the scene: the agent standing guard looking stern, the four members of the Howell family huddled on one of the two beds in the room.

Addressing the agent in the room, Hank queried, "Agent?"

"Schneiderman," he replied.

"Nice to meet you. Katie Hank; my partner, Spencer Banyon. Special Operations. If we could ask you and Agent Gavin to step out for a while? Maybe head to the lobby and grab some coffee."

"I thought—" Gavin began.

"We'd like to interview them without either of you present," Hank said. "I'm sure having a room full of federal agents would be very intimidating." In fact, what Hank hoped to avoid were any interruptions of the 'that's not what you told me yesterday' variety.

After the two local agents had left, Hank settled down in a chair, Spud preferring to remain standing, leaning against the desk built in to the wall in the room. She sat silently, assessing the ATF's four charges.

Finally, Larry Howell spoke. "You are both federal agents?"

Hank looked over to Spud, her eyes telling him to answer the man.

"Yes," Spud said.

"Are you married?"

Spud looked at Hank, and she gave him a little nod.

"Yes, we are. But that isn't something we would like the other two agents to know," Spud replied.

"Why was she the one to speak to the other two agents?" Larry asked.

"I love my wife very much," Spud explained. "We're partners and equals."

Hank was watching all of the Howells very closely. *He more or less accepts that. She? Not so much. The children are very puzzled by it.*

"I believe you love your wife very much as well, Mr. Howell," Spud ventured.

"I do. She is a wonderful helpmate, and has given me two wonderful children. There's not much more a man can ask for."

"I agree. Perhaps we can allow our wives to be a part of this discussion?"

Larry looked from Hank to his wife.

"Zena is free to speak her mind," he said.

Hank reached out and squeezed Spud's hand, reflecting that he had handled the introductions perfectly.

"Do you have children?" Larry asked.

Hank noticed that Zena was watching her expectantly.

"We've both been told that we can't have children," Hank said truthfully. "The doctors tell us that we are both sterile."

"It's your punishment," Zena blurted out. "It's your punishment for working with the ZOG."

"Zena," Larry said sternly, silencing her.

Zena's disapproving glare was obvious. Hank met her gaze and said, "We're hoping for children someday. We're hoping Yahweh will grant us a miracle." *Get her thinking. Get her wondering.* She could see the look of surprise flit across Zena's face, then be replaced once again by hardness.

"Yahweh will not grant you such a favor unless you renounce the ZOG and all its ways."

"Is it that the ZOG must be renounced, or that it must be converted?" Hank asked. "Did Yeshua HaMashiach come to cleanse the sins from all, or only from a few? Is the goodness of Yahweh limited?"

Hank already was getting the impression that Zena Howell had been brainwashed. Larry, she felt, had more of a questioning nature and still retained his own concepts of right and wrong, though his concepts might match those of the Shining City group fairly closely. The children's minds weren't set, but it was obvious they had never heard arguments that ran contrary to the teachings they had been exposed to.

In their earpieces, Spud and Hank both heard Edge say, "He hath not dealt with us after our sins; nor rewarded us according to our iniquities. It's from a psalm."

Hank looked at Spud and gave him a blink of her eyes.

"He hath not dealt with us after our sins; nor rewarded us according to our iniquities, says the psalm," Spud repeated. "I believe this. I believe that Yahweh will even deliver the ZOG."

Larry scoffed at him. "Do you think you can change the minds of the ZOG while you act as their agent?"

"Vengeance is mine, says the Lord. But sometimes, the Lord asks men to enact His vengeance for him," Hank recalled the pastor of the church whose carillon tower she had used as a sniper's nest telling her. "Sometimes the Lord asks men to teach His mercies as well. Isn't this what Shining City is doing? Going out, spreading Yahweh's truth and making converts to it? How can you convert anyone if you don't go among them?"

The looks that both Larry and Zena Howell were now

giving Hank and Spud showed that they were both weighing what had been said to them. Hank continued to watch their faces closely. Larry had begun staring at Spud, surprise crossing his face the moment Spud had quoted scripture. Zena continued to gaze at Hank, but her face now expressed puzzlement as she considered what Hank had just said. Finally, Zena's face became resolute.

"There is truth in what you say," Zena conceded. "Though we increase our number through our children, it would be a sin to not make converts of those that would change their ways if only they heard Yahweh's true message. We would be condemning to hell those that Yahweh wishes to be among His remnant."

"That is what we believe the Lord is asking us to do," Spud said, seeing how the exchange they were engaged in with the Howells was leading to opening an avenue of trust between the two Field Team members and the two adults from the Shining City compound.

"You see," Hank began to venture, "we have a fear. We fear that the other agents will search for an excuse to go to Sharples and exterminate the Shining City group there. We're trying to keep them from doing that, but we need your help. We need to be able to go to the Shining City community in order to gather evidence of the truth so the other agents will have no excuse to go there—none whatsoever. We need to prove to them that they should leave Shining City to live in peace and according to their own beliefs. We know that you can't go back there without fear of punishment, because the pastor there believes you to be apostates. So, you will have to continue in the faith on your own, as we do. They don't know that we are working to convert the ZOG. Neither does the ZOG, and we have to keep it that way. I hope you will help us."

The looks on the faces of the Howell adults showed that they were now convinced. "We'll help you in any way we can," Larry Howell said to the accompanying nods of his wife.

"Spencer, why don't you go downstairs and let the other agents know that they can return now?" Hank said.

Spud got up, the barest hint of an amused expression on his face, and left to go get Gavin and Schneiderman.

Hank and the Howells sat looking at each other for a while. Zena then said, "Your husband has a great deal of faith."

"Which gives me great joy," Hank said. *Boy, you're laying it on thick,* one of her voices chided. *Pretty much have to,* another conceded.

"I see he has taught you well," Zena added.

Hank blushed and smiled, not so much because of what Zena had said, but what she had just heard in her earpiece: Edge's voice saying, "Yeah, after *I* told *him* what to say ..."

When the two ATF agents had arrived back at the room, Hank and Spud went out into the hallway, closing the door so they could pass along their observations.

"They are both very sincere individuals," Hank told them. "They strongly believe—especially the wife—that the Shining City teachings are close to, if not *the* truth. You may want to pass along that anyone charged with guarding them not use a heavy hand with them. They'll find that very threatening, given they believe we're all agents of the Zionist Occupied Government," Hank said with a sneer. "We're going to want to talk with them again, so we can get an idea of how we should dress and behave while trying to infiltrate the group. In the meantime, can I ask how they got here?"

"They drove in," Gavin said. "The guy has a truck. Older model."

"Has it been searched?"

"Yeah, we got a warrant. Pretty much all he has in it is clothing, some nonperishable food, water … He said he left in the middle of the night, and from what it looks like, he fled with little more than the shirt on his back."

"Did you find a Bible in it?"

"Two."

"Do me a favor, then, and bring them their Bibles. Check first for anything that might be stuck in the pages or binding. They might have some escape tools hidden in them that we might not want them to have. If they're clean, let them have their Bibles, and tell them that we asked that they be given to them."

Gavin was smirking. "Are you expecting a hollowed-out book?"

Hank turned around and put her hands behind her back.

"Cuff me."

"Say again?"

"Cuff me," Hank repeated.

Gavin shrugged and took out handcuffs, securing them on Hank's wrists. She turned around to face him, paused slightly, then handed him his cuffs back.

"I'm envisioning that they might have the kind of tools that I just used. Check the Bibles over, then let them have them if they're clean. We'll stop back in tomorrow to talk with them again."

As Hank and Spud made their way back downstairs to where the rest of the team had sat listening in on the conversation, they heard Voice say over the comm link, "Boy, what a bunch of bullshit!" followed by laughter from the rest of the men.

"Yeah, and I did most of the shoveling," Hank admitted, grinning at Spud as they went to rejoin the group.

"THE TIME WILL COME when we will face adversity," Pastor Benkovic said. "The Bible says that Yeshua will come like a thief in the night to claim those who are his, and that we won't know the time nor the place. But we know that it will be soon. We see the signs all around us. The four horsemen come riding, bringing famine, war, pestilence, and in the end, death. Twice now we have seen the pestilence come to the heathen, with many of them falling and dying as a result. But we were spared. War has raged unabated across the Earth, and though it hasn't come to us, we cannot believe that it won't. Perhaps it is already here, and we fail to see it. After all, over three thousand of the heathen died when the planes hit the towers as the Muslim struck here on our soil. Perhaps the Zionists who control our government are plotting to come to this very spot, intent on our destruction. Droughts continue to threaten the land and keep it from producing food, yet again we are spared. Our fields and trees in our communities across this nation continue to yield enough plenty to keep all of the Shining City faithful fed and with enough left over to store for any lean time that may come.

"In the end, there will surely be death—but not a death of the body. A death of the soul. Who is this reserved for? Why, the heathen. The unbelievers. The ones who taint their blood by crossbreeding and do things Yahweh finds despicable. They mark their skin with ink, eat that which is unclean, and fail to keep Yahweh's day holy. For them, the shield of righteousness is too heavy. They would rather abide by the desires of the flesh: eating to excess, drinking, escaping with drugs, engaging in sexual acts whenever and with whomever they desire. Only a pure body can contain the pure spirit Yahweh desires to bring back to Himself. Only a holy union of a holy man and a holy woman can bring forth children who can grow in righteousness and themselves become holy. Am I right?"

"Amen!" the men of the congregation shouted.

"This is why we are the chosen ones, the remnant. Because we keep ourselves clean: body and soul. Because we read this great book," he added, holding his Bible aloft, "and understand its words, taking them into our hearts and applying them to our lives. This is why Yahweh spares us from the punishments he gives to the heathen: because we have made ourselves worthy of better things."

HANK SAT ENGROSSED with her tablet.

"What are you reading?" Spud asked her.

"Not reading anything. Watching a video I found earlier."

Spud waited for an explanation.

"Trying to learn how to wear this thing." She held up a long scarf.

"It's a scarf. You just drape it around your neck, don't you?"

"It's a tichel. It goes on your head and has to cover all your hair."

Spud smiled. "You don't have a lot of hair to cover, so it should be easy."

"This could be useful in the future. Beyond this mission, I mean. When my mom was going through chemo with her breast cancer, wearing something like this could have made it less obvious that she had lost all her hair. She found that particularly demoralizing." Hank struggled with the tichel, tying and retying it to get it the way she wanted it.

Spud reacted with shock. "You don't think you could develop breast cancer, do you?"

"You never know," Hank commented as she tried to tie the tichel another way. "I had the DNA test to see if I had breast cancer genes, and the results came back negative for mutations in both the BRCA1 and BRCA2 gene, but there are over a hundred genes that have been shown to be associated with breast cancer. I also have a double-whammy, because my dad also died of cancer, even though his was in his brain."

"You say that so matter-of-factly," Spud said.

Hank shrugged as she pulled the tichel off her head to try again. "There's not much I can do about it if I have the genetics for it except try not to do anything that might trigger it. It's part of why I've always avoided eating anything that has artificial flavors or colors in it. Same goes for farm chemicals. I've always tried to eat as much in the way of organic foods that I can. I think you have to do that if you know you might be at risk. I'm human, and I'll grab something every so often that I know isn't organic just because I have a craving, but I try to not do that very often."

"Is this why I catch you sometimes feeling your breasts?"

"Breast self-examination. It's still the most common way a woman discovers she's got a lump in her breast that might be cancerous," Hank said. "You know, sometimes a lump will be discovered by her husband as well."

"Is that so?" Spud said, smiling. "I guess I'm going to need to pay more attention." He walked over and slid behind the chair she was sitting in, reaching down through the neck of her polo shirt. "You're always saying that your breasts are too small, but I just discovered by doing a more careful analysis that I can do an exam of one of your breasts with a single hand."

"You're not making me feel better about how lacking in feminine attributes I am," Hank cautioned.

"I love your 'feminine attributes', as you put it, just the way they are," Spud said, snuggling his head against her neck.

"Maybe it's just nature's way of averaging things out," Hank mused. "You're really well-endowed. Me? Not so much."

"As long as neither of us is complaining, I don't think size matters."

"We're going to need a lot of stuff," Hank said, changing the subject. "I figure the best way to get into the Shining City compound is going to be to just drive in."

Spud moved back a bit and looked at her skeptically. "Gee, why don't we just land the helicopter there?"

"Smartass. No. We get ourselves a used truck, a used trailer of some kind that we can load household goods in, and we just go around to garage sales to get stuff. Make it look like we're house-hunting. It would look suspicious if we showed up with everything new: new clothes, new dishes, new furniture. A couple that's moving to a new place will take their old stuff with them. Everything from couches to clothing." She looked up at Spud with a questioning gaze. "Have you ever hauled a trailer?"

"Uh ... no."

"Hoo boy. Because hauling one isn't so hard, but backing one up is a bitch—especially if it's a small trailer with a single axle."

"I take it you've done this?"

"Yeah. Sometimes Dad and I would have to go load up an engine for a plane he was working on. Once we had to even load up a plane. The guy had a connecting bolt break and ended up putting 'er down on a dirt road in the middle of nowhere. Dad and I and the guys in the shop all went to recover it. And we'd take some time once or twice a year to gather up all the junk from inside and outside of the hangar to take to a recycler or to the dump."

"Then why don't *you* drive the truck?"

Hank put down her tablet and twisted around to look at him more directly. "These people are conservative fundamentalist Christians," she said. "Men do the hard labor, drive the vehicles, etc. Women cook, clean, do laundry, and spread their legs about once every year to pop out another baby. That old saying of 'keep them barefoot and pregnant'? This group takes that as a commandment."

15

"Hearken; Behold, there went out a sower to sow: And it came to pass, as he sowed, some fell by the way side, and the fowls of the air came and devoured it up. And some fell on stony ground, where it had not much earth; and immediately it sprang up, because it had no depth of earth: But when the sun was up, it was scorched; and because it had no root, it withered away. And some fell among thorns, and the thorns grew up, and choked it, and it yielded no fruit. And other fell on good ground, and did yield fruit that sprang up and increased; and brought forth, some thirty, and some sixty, and some an hundred."

Benkovic marked the place in his Bible with a finger as he held it in one hand and began his circumnavigation of the meeting hall.

"Do you know what's important about this teaching of Yeshua's? What's important is what happened next. He had to *explain* it to His disciples. *To His very own chosen twelve, He had to explain the meaning of what He had just said.* The very ones who were closest to Him!

"This is why there is someone put to be your pastor within your ranks. For you know what the word 'pastor' means, do you not? It comes from the Latin: one who leads the flock to pasture, sets them to grazing, and causes them to eat. Will a good pastor lead his flock to where Satan can grab them up? Put Yahweh's word in their hearts and do nothing to help it to abide there? Leave them adrift in the heathen world so that the word is choked out of them by worldly cares?"

The men murmured among themselves.

"Of course not," Benkovic said, answering his own question. "A good pastor leads his flock to where they can find nourishment for their souls and instills a true understanding of the word so that they can be strengthened by it. He teaches them so that they can take it back first to their wives and children, so the whole family can increase in holiness and become pleasing to our Lord.

"This is why we must sometimes grieve. Because some *do* fall by the wayside, and Satan snatches them up. Some *do* first take in the word with gladness, like our own Brother Howell, whose roots never were firm enough to keep his faith from withering. And we know what happens when a crop withers and dies: it gets gathered up and the torch is set to it. It is *burned in the fires of hell!* It is cast out to find itself among the heathen thorns, where what little green of true faith remains is choked away.

"But we know that if there is the barest bit of root left, the barest hint of green, with suitable treatment even a man such as Howell, turned apostate, can be brought back to life and once again can bear good fruit. Yes, the withered and dead portions must be stripped away, cut back so that the bit of remaining life can once again come forth. It will not happen while he and his family sit by the wayside, nor on stony ground, nor among thorns. They must be brought back here, to fertile ground.

"So it is that I tell you to be watchful whenever you

travel into the heathen world, and if you should encounter our brother who is now fallen away, bring him back. Bring him home for the sake of his soul and his family."

"WE ALREADY HAVE A COUPLE OF BIBLES," Hank said. "I had Voice do a little Internet searching for us here in Charleston. He made us a list of people selling things that we need. I asked him to give me a list of people selling old pickups first. He has that arranged so that we can drive the most efficient way through it until we find a suitable truck. He has a second list for trailers being sold, and he says that all I need to do is ask Hal to optimize the travel route until we find a suitable trailer. Last is a list of garage sales he found on Craigslist and Facebook. We do the same thing: have Hal draw us up an efficient route for getting to them. I figure we can take the rest of today and tomorrow getting the stuff we need."

"You know, I've never been to a garage sale," Spud said. Thinking a moment, he added, "I've never bought a used vehicle, either."

Hank's face expressed disbelief. "You have led *one sheltered life*," she said. "Was your family independently wealthy?"

"I wouldn't say *wealthy*," Spud said, taking exception. "We were comfortable."

"Did Dad buy you a new car?"

"No, he bought me a decent used one. But *he* bought it—I didn't."

"What about when you got your own place?"

"My bachelor pad? I was in the Secret Service by then."

"Meaning?"

"I bought new stuff. Including a Mustang."

"Hot shot."

"Not really. I just thought the car would be good for picking up chicks."

"Really?"

"Yeah. Just cruise around the loop. The hot spot in D.C. The business girls there are really something."

Hank slapped him playfully while he laughed. Getting serious, he said, "I just thought the car looked slick, that's all. You know I never had to cruise for girls."

"Yeah, I know."

"They'd cruise for me."

Hank slapped him again.

Getting serious, she said, "Then here's the thing you need to know when going after used stuff and shopping garage sales. Never pay the asking price. Always do some horse-trading."

"Why not just pay what they're asking?"

"They're trying to get rid of the stuff, silly," Hank pointed out. "If they want to get rid of it badly enough, they'll let you dicker with them. Besides, they always set the price higher than they expect to sell for, because they expect you to try and talk them down. They'll ask for five dollars for something. You offer half that."

"Good grief, Hank—the committee gives us a blank check on everything and you think we should squabble over two and a half bucks?"

"Unless you want yourself branded as some kind of patsy, offer them half. If they go for half, see if they'll go even lower."

"This is a game to you."

"Hell yeah—and it's a fun game, too."

"I'll let you do the talking, then. Is someone driving us to where we can find a truck, or will we be in two vehicles after getting one?"

Hank considered this. "I hadn't even thought of that, but I suppose it would be better to have one of the other guys drive us, then let whoever is driving take the SUV back to the hotel while we continue on with the truck."

"Then I think we're going to need a credit card and take one of our tablets so we can get the routes from Hal," Spud said.

"And a shitload of cash," Hank added.

"Why cash?"

Hank looked at him wide-eyed. "How many people who are selling stuff at garage sales do you think take credit cards?"

"Ummm ..."

"It's *zero*, Spud. "None. Da nada. Strictly cash. No checks, no credit cards."

"What happens if we have a problem with something?"

"No returns, no refunds. All sales are final."

"So, if the truck turns out to be a lemon?"

"We fix it or we just junk it and get another one."

"That doesn't give me a lot of confidence."

"Aren't you the guy who just asked why we should squabble over a couple of bucks? Besides, at least *one* of us helped her dad fix cars and trucks as well as airplanes. We never took a vehicle into an auto shop for work." Hank began to mutter to herself. "You can't fix anything, you've never bought anything that was used, and you can't even hang a picture on a wall and get it straight."

"You deprived every person who makes their living by fixing things, making new things, and doing interior decorating of an income," Spud countered.

Hank gazed at him. She didn't have an answer for that one.

"Let's grab Voice and get this show on the road," she said, avoiding Spud's observation entirely.

"Why Voice?"

"It's *his program*," Hank said. "If he ends up driving all over Charleston, it'll be his fault."

Spud rolled his eyes. "Voice, grab the keys to the SUV and meet me and Hank downstairs," he called over the comm link.

When the trio had gathered, Hank outlined to Voice what the game plan was for getting everything she considered would be needed to make her and Spud look like a couple traveling with their household goods.

"The big thing we're going to need is a bunch of cash. Like, maybe ten K in mostly small bills."

"Really? You need ten thousand dollars?" Voice asked.

"Might even need more than that," Hank said. "We've got two big items on the list: a truck and a trailer. Even used, we can expect to pay decent money for each of those if we want something that's in good shape."

"We're going to have to split up where we get the cash from," Voice said. "Unless the local ATF office has that kind of cash on hand—and I'm betting not only that they don't, but it would take a bit for them to request it. We can use our credit cards at ATMs and get fifteen hundred dollars at a time, given the usual withdrawal limit is five hundred and there are three of us. It will all be in twenty-dollar bills unless you ask for lower denominations. I noticed an ATM in the hotel lobby, so we can start right here and then just pull into any convenience stores we might pass along the route while we're looking for a truck."

"You can't just get Hal to spit us ten K out of an ATM?

They're linked to computers, aren't they?" Hank asked with a clandestine note to her voice.

"We could do that, but it will get us a lot of stares as we stand there grabbing money while the ATM doles out ten K in twenties," Voice said. He pulled a quarter from his pocket. "Bets on how long it would take someone to call the cops."

"Put your quarter back in your pocket. You're right. But won't it also look funny if we all go into some convenience store at the same time and stand in line to get money?"

"Here's how we do it," Spud said. "Either Voice or I will go to the ATM; you and the other one of us will go to the restroom. When Voice is done at the ATM, he walks out and lets the next one go to the ATM. Repeat for the last person."

"Why don't I go to the ATM first?" Hank asked.

"One of us guys can go to the men's, and you go to the women's. It'll look funny if two guys are standing at the urinal doing nothing as well, don't you think?"

"One of you could go into a stall. You guys always take forever taking a dump," Hank said.

They both looked at her. "What? Do you time men's bathroom time versus women's?" Voice asked. "Because you women take *forever*, no matter *what* you have to do."

"Let me clue you in on something," Hank said, leveling him a look. "You guys don't have to half-undress every time you go into a restroom. Add to that the fact that I have a gun and handcuffs and other stuff that now have to be not only kept from falling into the toilet but also have to be concealed ..." She stewed a moment and added, "It's a lot easier when all you have to do is unzip a zipper and fish through your boxers for the slit, I'm betting."

"Don't you have a prosthesis for that?" Spud remarked.

Voice busted out laughing, both because of the remark

and the mental image of Hank wearing her artificial member so as to look more "manly."

"Oh, shut up," Hank groused. "With all the ribbing I've gotten about that ..."

"Hey—it wasn't *my* idea," Spud noted. "In fact, I recall emphatically telling you *not* to show the thing off."

The three made their way out to the ATM, each one using their unit credit card to withdraw five hundred dollars, then made their way to the SUV they'd borrowed from the local ATF office.

"Hal, find locations of ATMs; seven required. Plan route to meet truck route at stop number one," Voice commanded. He took a quick peek at his tablet and said, "Thank you, Hal."

You're welcome, Voice. Let me know if you need further assistance, the three heard in their earpieces.

"You and Hal are way too chummy," Spud said.

Voice shrugged. "Hal might be a bit jealous."

"Said what?"

"Page," Voice explained.

"I don't want to know this," Hank declared. "Just *don't want to know.*" She gave a point forward and said, "Let's get going so I can let the scenery distract me from the mental picture I just got."

Voice drove around to the seven ATM locations Hal had found. With an additional fifteen hundred dollars being withdrawn by the three collectively, he then drove to the first of the locations where Hal said someone had a truck for sale.

Hank got out and walked up to the door, ringing the bell and getting a man coming to it.

"I'm interested in the truck you have for sale," she announced.

"Yeah—got it right over here," the guy said, coming out and leading the way around to the side of the house. He was somewhat surprised when, instead of Spud walking forward to look the vehicle over, Hank did.

Walking around the truck, Hank noted a few things that made her cautious about putting any money at all on a purchase.

"Crank it up for me," she requested of the seller.

The truck started well, but Hank noted that it blew some blue smoke when it did, and continued to cough forth more smoke than she'd like.

"Needs four new tires," she said to the man.

"Can't have everything on a used truck," the guy said.

"It's got bad rings and needs a valve job, too."

"Nah. Just needs a tune-up."

"Nope. It's blowing oil past the rings, and I can hear the valves are sticking."

"I can knock a thousand off the price if that'll help ya ..."

She gave him a pat on the shoulder. "A thousand dollars won't come close to what it will take to get this thing in shape, and I pretty much need a truck right now—not in two weeks. Sorry."

She turned and walked with Spud back to where Voice waited in the SUV.

"You didn't want to horse-trade with him?" Spud asked when they got back inside and Voice started off for the next stop.

"Not for that piece of shit," Hank said.

Arriving at the next address, they were greeted by a modest house. Two kids played in the front yard, their father sitting on the porch steps with a cup of coffee watching over them. Walking up, Hank said, "I understand you have a truck for sale."

"That's it right there," the man said, pointing at what appeared to be a well-maintained truck in the driveway. "Only about three years old, and I really only drove it to work and back."

"What are you asking for it?"

"Seventy-five hundred."

Hank was taken aback. "What's wrong with it?"

"Not a damned thing," the guy said. "I'll be happy to go with you so you can test drive it if you want."

Hank was still a bit disbelieving. "Go grab the keys."

While the man went inside, Hank leaned to Spud and asked, "You can drive a stick, can't you? I notice it's got a manual tranny."

"My Mustang was a manual. So was the car my dad got me when I was in high school. He swore that people who didn't drive manual transmission cars didn't know how to drive at all."

"Great! Because if this truck checks out, we're done truck-hunting."

The man came back and handed Hank the keys, then went around to the passenger side and got in while Hank climbed into the driver's seat and Spud took up residence in the back seat of the double cab.

"Your kids going to be OK?" Hank asked.

The man merely pointed. Looking, Hank saw that now their mother was sitting on the porch keeping an eye on the kids.

Starting the truck, she noted that the engine ran smoothly at idle in spite of the chill weather. She also noticed that it shifted cleanly, accelerated smoothly, and handled nicely. Her curiosity was piqued by the very low asking price.

"I have to ask: why only seventy-five hundred? I mean,

this is a nice truck, and I know it should blue book for four times that."

The man smiled weakly. "You know your trucks," he said, sadness in his voice. "I really don't want to give this guy up, but NovoRo got my boss and the business went under. I haven't been able to find a job—not that I haven't been trying. You saw my kids and my wife. My unemployment is running out, and what I had saved in the bank is pretty much gone. I've even had to dip into my retirement account, and I'm getting penalized for doing it. There aren't a lot of people out there these days who can drive a manual transmission, so it's been hard finding a buyer. Lots of the people who are looking aren't doing much better than I am, either. They're just looking for a cheap jalopy to get them around while job hunting and to the unemployment office. I already sold one of those. Really wanted to keep my truck." A quick glance had Hank notice the glassiness in his eyes. "But it's sell the truck or have the bank foreclose on the house, which they're saying they're going to do. I figure I can use a bicycle until I can get back on my feet."

"If it's any consolation to you, this is exactly what I've been looking for, and at a steal of a price. Don't let me get lost getting back to your place," Hank said.

When they arrived back at the man's house, Hank got out and went to the bag of cash in the SUV. Motioning to the other two, she said, "Each of you grab some and count out twenty-five hundred." She added theirs to three thousand she had counted out herself. Going back to the man, she said, "I'm sorry that it's all in twenties. There's eight thousand there, if you want to count it out."

His eyes flashed both sadness and gratitude. "I trust you," he said.

"Count it out, just the same," Hank said. "You won't offend me. And I'll need the title, of course."

"Yeah. Of course," the man said, inviting them inside.

They sat at his dining room table and counted out piles of five twenties each, laying them crisscrossed to make eight piles of a thousand dollars each. Seeing that all eight thousand dollars was there, Hank took the title from the man after he'd signed it as the seller and signed it with "Katie Hank" as the buyer. Then she and Spud shook hands with the man.

"I'm sorry you had to sell," she said. "That's a nice little Tacoma, and it's just what I need. I'll take care of getting the tags back to the DMV and get a temp tag."

"I've got to thank you for the extra five," the man said. "Every bit helps."

"I hope things start looking up for you soon," Hank said.

Arriving back at the SUV, Hank told Voice he could return to the hotel while she and Spud grabbed the cash and continued to make the rounds, looking for a trailer and household items to fill out their requirements for their attempt to infiltrate the Shining City compound in Sharples. As she and Spud drove off in the truck, Spud turned to her and said, "I thought you said to horse-trade. Talk the guy down." He wasn't being critical; he'd seen the look on Hank's face when she gave the man his money. It was a look of remorse. He knew she had wished she could have given him even more, but wouldn't have to spare him his pride.

"You heard the guy. He's trying to keep a roof over the heads of his family."

"I know. I would have done the same thing. I guess one thing bad about living in the Mole Hole is that we haven't been able to see just what all of the effects of the pandemic have been. I won't tell anyone that you got generous with unit funds, either," Spud said, his tone conciliatory.

"Just don't expect it to end there," Hank said. "Because I've got a plan."

Spud knew that tone, too. It was the tone of voice Hank used when she'd decided there was a right thing to do and that she intended to do it, regardless of potential repercussions.

"Just what do you have up your sleeve?" he asked.

"When we're done with this mission, this truck's going to get stolen."

Spud gave her the kind of look an older person does when looking over his glasses at an errant child. "Am I guessing correctly that whoever steals it is going to, by some odd coincidence, park it back in that guy's driveway?"

Hank turned and smiled at him. "With the keys in the mailbox that's on his porch and the title signed back over to him in the glovebox."

THE UNIT MEMBERS all stood looking at what Spud and Hank had returned with. The bed of the truck was now filled with everything from boxes of kitchen items to plastic bags filled with clothing, while an old former U-Haul trailer sat on the hitch, filled with old furniture, mattresses, and appliances. Spud and Hank tied a tarp back down over the bed of the truck. Then Hank returned to the truck, taking a paper-wrapped item about a foot square from the back seat.

"I hope none of that furniture has bedbugs," Doc Rich was commenting.

"I did just what you said and checked over every place a bedbug could hide with a UV light," Hank assured her. "No evidence of bedbugs. Trust me, I don't want them in my house back in the Mole Hole."

"What have you got there?" Crow asked Hank, eyeing the wrapped item.

Spud rolled his eyes. "You'll never guess."

Spud's reaction got Crow smiling. "In the game of animal, vegetable, or mineral, I'm going to make a guess of mineral."

"Just look at this," Hank cooed as she carefully revealed the contents of the paper.

Everyone bent in to see what she had.

"You know that West Virginia is coal country, right? This is a slab of fossilized fern fronds in coal. Probably some miner managed to unearth it. The people who had it at their garage sale had *no idea* of its value." She grinned with satisfaction. "I got it for a hundred bucks."

"She got a lump of coal for a hundred bucks. Should have waited a month. I'd have put a lump in her stocking for free," Spud poked.

Watching Hank turn and glare at Spud, Cloud said, "I think you'd better watch your step, or Bambi ain't gonna let you back in her chimney."

"You realize Bambi was a buck ..." Hank pointed out, glaring at Cloud as well. She looked back at her find appreciatively. "This could easily have been sold to a museum for ten times what I paid. This specimen is absolutely gorgeous."

"Did you use unit money for that?" Doc Rich asked, her tone a bit accusing.

"Nope. This one was on me, because this one is *mine* and is going to stay mine long after I leave the unit. I might just ask to be buried with it."

"We all get cremated," Edge pointed out.

"That's OK—coal burns," Cloud said, ducking—wisely —for incoming, but realizing after Hank just renewed her glare at him that she wasn't about to throw the slab of coal with its fossil ferns at him. Instead, she just rolled her eyes and grabbed a couple of clothing items she had set aside, walking with them into the hotel.

"She seems a bit touchy," Spud remarked. "I don't think she's looking forward to embedding with a group of far-right extremists."

"Who can blame her?" Crow returned as the group followed her inside. "A closed mind is a terribly wasted thing," he added, putting a twist on an old slogan.

Hank went immediately up to their room with Spud following on her heels. Once the door was closed, she stripped off what she was wearing, then donned a simple gray dress over a dark leotard. Slipping on a pair of similarly simple flat shoes, she then set about taking a scarf and tying it around her head in a wrap, ensuring that not a single hair showed. She finished off by wrapping herself in a thick shawl.

"Time to go see the Howells and see if I pass muster," she declared.

Making her way up the stairs with Spud accompanying her, she walked down the hallway until getting to the room where the Howells had been sequestered. Knocking on the door, she showed her credentials to the agent posted there. He stared at her for a moment, then admitted her to the room. She indicated he should wait outside the door.

To her surprise, she found the Howell children watching television, their mother and father watching along with them and making comments about what they were seeing. It impressed Hank that, although she didn't agree with some of the ideas expressed by the parents, they were taking an interest in what the children saw and were guiding them by comparing that with their own beliefs. *More parents should monitor what their children are exposed to,* she thought.

Zena Howell looked up at her. Rising from where she had been sitting on the end of one of the beds, she looked Hank over. She then turned to her husband, who nodded to her.

"I see you are truly not one of the ZOG," Zena said quietly. "No heathen would dress with such modesty."

Hank likewise turned to Spud, who imitated Larry Howell's nod. "It's difficult behaving like one of the heathen when your heart isn't there," she said. "But it must be done to get them to accept you as one of them. Only when they accept you will they hear what you have to say."

Zena looked at the silver chain that hung around Hank's neck, her Saint Michael medallion hanging beneath the neckline of the dress. She reached out and pulled the medallion out where she could see it.

"This is a Papist object," she said, her eyes growing hard.

"It isn't," Hank said. "There are no Papist symbols on it. The same battle we fight now was fought before in heaven, before Satan was cast out. The archangel Michael led the forces that aligned with Yahweh. It's how he got his name. 'Michael' is a battle cry. It means, 'Who is like God?' He was calling the forces of good to join with him to vanquish Satan from heaven, and in the end the angelic warriors with him prevailed. This is my reminder that I must prevail against the forces of evil here while I move among the heathen who are still in evil's grasp."

She must have considered this might happen—that someone would question her medallion, Spud thought. He considered how he might have to explain his own Sword of Saint Michael, especially given its inscription was in Latin and his team designation and code name were engraved on the back. *That sword nearly got me killed once before ...*

"Pastor Benkovic exhorted us to be warriors of Yahweh," Larry said.

"And you must," Spud returned, pulling out his own sword. "There are some who have pledged themselves to be just that, battling against evil wherever it might be found." He decided there was a seed to be planted at that moment. "You are here because you dared to read this book," he continued, pointing at the Bible Larry held clutched in his hand. "You dared to read it for yourself, and let Yahweh write its words in your heart and soul. When you compared them, you found that some of Pastor Benkovic's words matched the truth that Yahweh had written inside you, and some of them did not. Am I right?"

Larry hung his head. "I am an apostate," he murmured.

"Are you? Or is Pastor Benkovic the apostate? That is what we are here to find out," Spud said. "That is our calling. If he's leading this group astray, then Yahweh will give him a just punishment. If everything he has preached is in accordance with this word, then all is well. If not, then *he* must be corrected. Better that he face correction than be thrown into the fire."

"Will you make him submit to the whip?" Larry asked.

"We will let Yahweh choose his punishment," Spud said.

"You are agents of the ZOG," Zena declared, untrusting.

"Would agents of the ZOG wear next to their hearts a sign that they wish to wage war against Satan?" Hank asked.

Zena considered this for a time. She turned to look at her husband.

"I believe they are telling us the truth," Larry told her. "Just as it's possible for people to find faith, it is also possible for them to lose it. Pastor Benkovic taught us many truths that are found in Scripture, but didn't balance them with other truths also found in Scripture. He chose those passages that support his own views and not necessarily the views Yahweh holds. He has in some ways corrupted the word to support his own ends. You've watched him scourge men. It doesn't pain him—he enjoys it. Do you think Yahweh finds enjoyment from suffering? From losing one of His flock? Because that isn't what the Bible says."

Zena hung her head. "There is truth in what you say."

Hank put her hand on Zena's. "Read together and learn together. There's much you can teach to others."

Getting up, Hank and Spud turned the family back over to the care of the agent who had been posted at the door and made their way back down to their own room. Before Hank could get a chance to change out of the clothes she'd put on, they heard Crow announce that the team was gathering for dinner in the room he and Cloud were sharing.

Hank looked down at the dress she was wearing as she tossed the shawl on the bed. "Ah, fuck it," she said. "I'll change later. I'm hungry!"

Turning back and heading out the door, the two walked down to Crow and Cloud's room. As they walked in, the other members of the team and the medical away team were all talking animatedly among themselves as they grabbed food and found a place to sit and eat. As Cloud raised his head to greet them, he instead fell into an awed silence.

"Hank?" he finally eased out.

"Shut up and let me get something to eat," Hank said. "The only reason I'm still wearing this is because I'm hungry and didn't feel like changing first."

The others had similarly fallen into a stunned silence. Everyone except Doc Rich, who was obviously trying not to chuckle, given how out of character the outfit was for the person wearing it.

"I thought maybe you were getting ready to join an Amish commune or something," Edge said after getting over the initial shock of seeing Hank in a—gasp!—dress.

"What part of 'shut the fuck up' did you miss?" Hank asked him. "And Amish women don't dress like this. They have this little bonnet thingie they wear on their heads, not a tichel. This group is even more conservative than the Amish when it comes to a woman letting her hair show."

"Gonna wear an apron with that, too?" Cloud asked. "Because I think Edge left his in Nebraska."

That got the entire mission contingent laughing out loud.

Hank decided it was time to divert attention away from what she was wearing.

"If you think what *I'm* wearing is something, wait until you see Spud in work boots, jeans, a flannel shirt, and a fleece-lined denim jacket."

All eyes now swayed to look at Spud.

"Don't look at me like that," he admonished them. "I wasn't about to model that getup for anyone before I absolutely have to."

"Oh, how the mighty have fallen," Crow crooned. "From formal suits, ties, and cufflinks while guarding presidents to flannel and denim."

"Oh, shut up."

"You're starting to sound a lot like Hank."

"Hopefully, this will be a quick mission and we won't have to be embedded for six weeks like I was with UBM," Spud hoped.

"All depends. You might want to stay longer if Hank learns how to be submissive," Amigo remarked.

Hank nearly choked on her food. "Fat chance of that!"

"She's submissive when I want her to be," Spud suggested.

"That's not being submissive. That's being a willing participant."

"Kin you guyv knog id off?" Hank asked through her food.

"You can change her clothes, but you can't change the woman in them," Crow observed. She acknowledged the truth of his observation by giving him a one-fingered salute.

"When's the big move?" Crow asked.

"We're going to drive the truck up to Sharples tomorrow," Spud said. "See if we can't talk to the locals and see if there's a house to rent. I'm hoping we'll get lucky. The place is tiny."

"By tiny you mean?"

"Population: seventy-five. Thirty-two of them are in the Shining City compound from what we can gather. The typical household there has four people in it, so half of the Shining City community is kids. This is a big part of why we don't want the ATF going in there like storm troopers, shooting everything in sight," Hank said. She made like she was punching herself in the face. "Huge black eye for the government, and likely would just encourage more like-minded people to join the group. Especially given Sharples is one hundred percent white folk."

"You guys are bugging out of Charleston, too," Spud said. "Logan is close by, so if we need the rest of you to extract us, we'll have you staged there. It will also be convenient for us when it comes to making exchanges of money and intel reports."

"If Sharples has a whole seventy-five people, just how many does Logan have?" Edge wondered, thinking the accommodations might not be much better than Hank's beloved 'Taj Mahal.'

"You'll find it's a decent-size town," Spud said. "The hotel will seem very, very familiar. It's the same brand we're staying in now, so you'll have a kitchen and all the amenities."

Edge looked relieved to hear that, a fact Hank noticed.

"You don't like shabby hotels?" Hank asked.

"Not a fan."

"But the Taj is OK?"

"I don't worry about bedbugs and lice at the Taj," Edge revealed.

"You're just all kinds of squeamish, aren't you?" Hank noted.

"I had enough experience with sand fleas in Afghanistan to not want to add to my experience with lice and bedbugs," Edge asserted.

"The big guy doesn't like the idea of little guys invading his guys," Amigo chuckled, pointing downward.

"Is this dinnertime conversation?" Edge complained.

Amigo held his hands up in surrender.

"You're going in all dressed up like that?" Crow asked Hank.

"At the risk of having everyone roll their eyes again," Hank began, "one of the things the book I read on covert operations said was that you need to blend in with the group that you're infiltrating."

"That's true," Spud declared. "I had to do a lot of front work for the UBM case, starting with simply observing their online rhetoric to actually joining in online and eventually leading to making the trip down to the border and joining up in person. About the only thing you *can't* do is engage in any of the illegal activity they might be engaged in. For instance, if the Shining City group is actually making explosives, whether it's for blowing stumps or not, we can't help them nor make explosives ourselves."

"What about the undercover narcotics officers who make drug buys?" Cloud asked.

"That's gathering evidence," Crow said. "Unless you determine it's the real deal by sucking it up your nose or injecting it, that is."

"The idea," Hank said, getting back to the topic, "is that if we look the part, the Shining City group might decide to at least let us hang out with them to get a feel if we're Shining City material or not." She smiled a bit. "It reminds me of something one of our officers did while I was in the Taos PD. He was doing a theft prevention assessment for a local department store. He noticed that lots of high-ticket items were stacked up right by the doors. So, he had the manager with him help him get a bunch of stuff in his cruiser. 'Can you help me with this flat screen? Can you help me with this printer? Can you help me with this game console?' The manager helpfully assisted him with loading up his cruiser with a few thousand dollars' worth of stuff. Then our officer thanked him for helping him rob the store." Hank chuckled. "He did it by acting like he'd just bought the stuff—which is how he told the manager that someone who wasn't a police officer would probably rob the place. Just act like a legit customer. Crooks do it, too—even carry old receipts so they don't get questioned. Make it look like you belong, and you can probably get away with just about anything."

16

Spud guided the Tacoma with its load of goods and hauling its trailer of household items onto the edge of the road where Hank had pointed out a good spot.

"We're going to get stuck," he declared once the wheels on the passenger side of both truck and trailer had cleared the pavement.

Hank had been at her wits end the entire trip from Charleston. Spud's inexperience with hauling a trailer had put her on edge, which mostly she had been able to hide from him, especially as he'd generally kept his eyes riveted on the road in front of him while gripping the steering wheel with a white-knuckled grasp.

"For the thousandth time, we're not going to get stuck," she assured him. She considered that it could be worse. She could be trying to get him to back the trailer up, which thus far they had avoided having to do. She just hoped that would continue to be the case, as it was now necessary for her to play the part of the silent, submissive wife. That didn't dovetail well with her also being the one driving the truck and backing up the trailer.

Spud sighed in a way that Hank recognized as a sigh of relief. She was tempted to utter something about it not being *that* bad, but her examination of her own feelings during the trip got one of her little voices saying, *Yes, it was.*

"We've got the fire department and the post office. Which one do you think we should hit up for some information?" Hank asked.

"The post office clerk might be a woman, in which case I doubt she'd be a member of a cult that keeps their women barefoot and pregnant," Spud remarked.

"It's a cult now?"

"Feels like one to me."

"OK. Should I go with, or just stay here with the truck?"

"Come with me, wife. But keep a respectful two paces behind me, and keep thy mouth shut. And grab thy cloak—it beith cold."

"It's going to be a long mission, I see," Hank grumbled. "But I believeth I can remain chaste until the Lord doth come again."

"Why is it that angry wives always threaten withholding sex?" Spud asked.

"Because we know men can't live without it, and can't live with it if they go looking for it elsewhere to try and fill the gap."

"But if we're Shining City types, we're supposed to be popping out a baby every year," Spud noted.

"Babies? We cain't be birthin' no babies," Hank said.

"Welcome to the Sharples Volunteer Fire Department," Spud said quietly as Hank fell silent behind him. "Looks like this is where the good ol' boys hang out."

"Does it look like there's anything else to do in Sharples?" Hank whispered.

Spud walked up to where the fire station door in front of one of the station's fire trucks stood open. Glancing inside, he noticed another door leading into a different area of the fire station. Going over, he knocked on the door while Hank stood quietly behind him.

A man opened the door and looked him over. "Some way I can help you?" he asked.

"Yes, thank you," Spud said, trying to sound both humble and polite. "My name is Spencer Banyon. My wife and I have been traveling, hoping to find a place where we can set down roots. You wouldn't know if there's a house we could rent in this town? It seems like a nice, quiet place."

The man looked behind Spud to where Hank stood.

"Your wife, I gather?"

"Yes, sir."

"She's pretty quiet." He leaned and looked at Hank again. "What's your name?"

Hank retreated behind Spud, saying nothing.

"Come forward and tell the man your name," Spud said to her.

Hank stepped to the side so she could be more easily seen. "I'm Katie Banyon," she said quietly.

The man at first raised an eyebrow, then smiled at Spud. "She is submissive to you."

"As the Bible says she must be," Spud remarked.

"She covers her hair."

"Again, the Bible says she must."

"The Bible does say that. I see you know yours."

"I study it always," Spud said. "But it's hard to be a believer when in the cities and large towns you are constantly surrounded by heathens. You find them even in the churches."

The man now seemed a bit more relaxed. Studying Spud and then Hank up and down, he said, "I think there's a house that might suit you. It's in an area off Sodom Road. You'll see a gate with a man guarding it."

"Does the road in have a name?" Spud asked.

"No name. As I said, you can't miss the gate, though. It's a well-traveled dirt road."

"I have a truck and am hauling our household goods in a trailer behind it. Can I get up the road with that?"

Figures he'd ask that question, Hank thought.

"You'll have no trouble," the man said. "When you get to the gate, tell the man there that Robert Benkovic says he should let you inside. I'll call ahead for you so they can show you the house there."

Spud had suppressed his surprise at hearing the man give his name. "Thank you, and may Yahweh show you seven times the kindness you have shown us."

Throw out a mystical number—that's doing your homework, Spud, Hank thought.

As they got back into the truck, Hank remarked, "We've just met the man himself."

"Yeah, I had to try not to react to the news when he told us his name," Spud agreed.

"There is one good thing, though," Hank said. "Unlike David Koresh, he's not hiding inside the compound. I'm almost betting, though, that the guys with him are also part of the Shining City group. Maybe his lieutenants. I wonder if they use the firehouse to monitor who comes and goes through Sharples?"

"Could be."

"Did you notice something else?" Hank asked. "Even though we haven't seen a lot of faces here, everyone we *have* seen has been white." She intoned, "Hal, find demographics, race, Sharples, West Virginia."

Sharples, West Virginia. Population: seventy-five. Population by race: white: seventy-five. No other races recorded.

"That clinches it. This place is as lily-white as they come," Hank said.

"It's probably why the Shining City group set up a compound here," Spud said. "They may have figured it would be relatively easy to convert the entire town. You'd think the jump in population would make someone in government curious about what's going on, though."

"Sharples is unincorporated," Hank said. "When they do census counts, they're just rolled into the rest of the county, so an increase of two or three dozen people isn't going to register with anyone. We have lots of places like that in New Mexico. In Nebraska, too, for that matter."

Spud had been guiding the Tacoma with its load of goods and trailer up a narrow dirt road once they had departed from the paved road they'd been on. Hank could see his grip get tighter on the steering wheel. To distract him, she commented, "Did you find it ironic that there's a religious compound built in an area off of a road called 'Sodom Road'?"

Spud chuckled but kept his eyes riveted on the road ahead of him. As they rounded a slight bend, they could see a closed gate with two men standing to one side. Spud drove up and stopped far enough from the gate to not have the truck in the way of it opening should it swing outward as the two men approached them. He rolled the window down so they could talk to each other.

"Hi, there," one of them greeted. "My name's Joe. So's his, so it'll be easy for you to remember us. I take it that you're Spencer Banyon?"

Hank noticed that the two men were pretty much ignoring her.

"That I am," Spud replied.

"Pastor Benkovic told us to expect you."

"Pastor? I had no idea I was talking to a preacher. Good thing I'm not a cursing man," Spud said. "He did tell us to mention his name."

The men gave him an approving look. "He said to show you to ... a vacant house we have here in our community. Joe's going to go in with you to get you to it. It'll be easy for you. The way the houses are laid out, you can just drive the circle and pull your trailer right up almost to the front door."

Phew! Spud thought. "I thank you."

The second of the Joes gave a look through the window. Hank lowered her face, then opened the door and got out, leaving the door open for the man and going to the passenger seat behind him in the double cab. Opening the passenger door, she noted that the seat was already jammed with clothing they'd purchased during their garage sale shopping. Picking up a large plastic bag stuffed with clothes, she wedged herself in, finding a place for her feet as best she could, and set the bag of clothes she'd removed in her lap. *I hope the drive in isn't very long ...*

To her relief, it was only a short distance further before the truck came out into an opening. Straight ahead, she could see a larger building in the center at the lowest point of a terraced oval area. About a dozen smaller houses were built on the first terrace from the floor of the area, a compacted dirt road granting access to them. The road they were on sloped upward to meet the road the circle of houses was built beside. Joe pointed the way around, guiding Spud and having him stop by the last house they encountered. She looked over at it, noting that it was a modestly-sized cabin nestled among trees, a garden space between it and the next house over.

Stopping in front of it, Spud turned back to her and said,

"I think this is going to be quite nice. What do you think, Love?"

"Such a blessing," she said quietly.

As they all got out of the truck, Hank couldn't help but notice the solitude of the place. Except for the sounds of children playing, it was uncannily free of human noise, making the sound of the idling truck seem unnaturally loud. Once Spud had killed the engine, the sounds of birds filtered through, punctuated occasionally by the chatter of a squirrel scolding the new arrivals. A slight breeze sighed through the trees, rustling the few leaves that hadn't already made their way to the ground and swaying the branches of the pines ever so slightly. She began to think that, aside from being on a mission, perhaps she should also consider it a bit of a vacation from the sameness of the Mole Hole.

She got out and hauled the huge bag of clothing to the front door. Joe came up with a key and proceeded to unlock it. She noticed that the door wasn't your typical urban one, but was a robust wooden door with sturdy locks. Joe stood aside and let her pass, half-dragging the bag of clothes with her. Depositing the bag in the first room she encountered, Spud came alongside her.

"Let's see where everything will go," he said.

She followed behind him through the house. It was simply constructed in a way to be functional rather than showy. With the exception of the bedrooms and bath, the rooms were more defined by their contents rather than walls, with the kitchen serving also as the dining area, which in turn melted into the living area. The entire house seemed to be heated from a wood-burning stove set into a hearth in one of the interior walls. She silently hoped that the builder had employed a sense of what might constitute a fire hazard by offsetting the stove's flue from the wooden structural elements of the cabin.

She was also somewhat surprised to find that the house had both electricity and water, the water apparently being provided by a water tank she had seen located on the upper rim of the terraced area. Peering out the back window, she noticed that there was both a propane tank and a fuel oil tank, so she assumed that closer inspection of the house would reveal a fuel oil burning furnace. Although different in style, it wasn't that different from some rural homes she was aware of when still a resident of New Mexico. She doubted, however, that Spud would know much about how to run the house.

The most shocking thing she noticed, though, was that the house was completely furnished. There was even a large amount of food stored within it, as well as a considerable amount of ammunition, though there were no guns. About the only thing missing was clothing. The closets were stripped bare, leaving only empty hangers on the closet rods.

She looked questioningly at Spud, who in turn looked at Joe.

"No one lives here?" Spud asked him.

"Not anymore. There was a family here. Husband, wife, and two children. They left in the middle of the night. No one knows why."

Hank had wandered back to the living room, considering it might be a good plan to start a fire and get the house warmed up. With the temperatures hovering at fifty-five degrees Fahrenheit at midday, she calculated it might get down into the low forties that night. She made her way to the wood stove and proceeded to stoke it with kindling from a bin that stood on the hearth nearby. As she removed some of the kindling and transferred it to the stove, she noticed something underneath. Taking it out, she realized it was a small wooden sign, hand-carved.

It read, "The Howells."

Hank's hand shook as she picked it up, and a tear made its way down her cheek. Tucking it back down under some of the logs in the bin, she wiped the tear away and continued to build a fire.

"Your wife seems like a fitting helpmate for you," Joe remarked, seeing her building the fire. "She takes on even a man's task."

"It's necessary, I'm afraid," Spud said. He unbuttoned the top of his flannel shirt and indicated the spot where the outline of his bum ticker could be seen under his skin. "I have a heart condition and need a pacemaker. She assists me with everything. You shouldn't be surprised if you see her chopping wood or with me while I hunt."

Hank was glad her back was to the men, because it took all her inner strength to keep from laughing. *Because you've seldom hunted, and never chopped wood in your life, I bet!*

"They're calling for rain later today," Joe remarked. "Perhaps you and I should move what you think you'll need into the house while your wife gets things put away."

Spud and Joe went back outside and began unloading the truck first, then the trailer, bringing everything inside and stacking things in the living room while Hank finished starting the fire and started hanging clothes in the closet. During one of her trips, noticing that both men were outside and struggling with a piece of furniture, she grabbed the sign from out of the wood bin and took it with her into the master bedroom, hiding it in the bottom of a dresser drawer and then stacking clothing on top of it. She then continued to put items in their places, in spite of not really needing much above clothing. The Howells had left everything except their clothing, towels, bed linens, and toiletries. As Hank continued to get things they had brought into their proper places, she continued as well to find tears coursing down her cheeks. *These people were so afraid at what might befall them, they left with practically nothing. With the economy still struggling and jobs scarce, they would have ended up on the street, living out of their truck.*

At one point, Joe noticed that she had been crying. "What has you crying, woman?" he asked her.

He and Spud put down the old couch they had just brought inside. Spud looked at her, wondering the same thing. "Tell the man," he ordered her.

Hank looked up and said, "Tears of gladness. I can't believe our good fortune at finding such a nice home in such a quiet place. Yahweh has surely blessed us beyond our fair measure."

Joe put a hand lightly on her arm. "You will find that Yahweh has blessed this entire place."

Hank smiled weakly. *Like hell.*

ROBERT BENKOVIC SAT in his living room. His house stood across from the one the Howells had once lived in, and which was now occupied by Spud and Hank. With him were the two men who had been at the firehouse when Spud and Hank arrived, asking about a place to live. The two Joes were also there. They had watched as Hank had come back out of the house with a broom and swept the porch, then carried in an armload of firewood from an open shed that stood to one side of the house. The Banyons's immediate neighbors had brought over dinner to welcome the couple, and Hank had sent them away with some canned goods she had found in the pantry, insisting they accept them as a showing of gratitude.

"What do you think?" Benkovic asked the others.

"They seem like good, righteous people," one of the Joes said. "The wife won't speak unless the husband allows it. She also does much of the labor, as he has some kind of heart condition. He showed me that he has a pacemaker."

"They came in with a couple of guns as well," the other Joe said. "We won't have to worry about any objections to ours. They had several ammo cans of ammunition, too. Seems like they made some good choices. He's got an AR and a .357 magnum revolver. A decent Smith and Wesson that looks like it's seen some use but is still in good condition. She's got a Marlin 1894 that's chambered for the same round: .357 magnum, so they both have a gun that fires the same ammo. I noticed a reloading press and dies as well. I don't think we're going to have to worry about objections to guns."

"What else did they come in with?" Benkovic asked.

"Your typical load of household goods. Bed, couch, a couple of upholstered chairs, a small dinette set, pots, pans, clothes—the usual stuff you see when folks are on the move. I don't think they were expecting to find a house full of stuff already. Also, a pretty good stock of nonperishable foods. I'd say they're of the same mindset as us with regard to being prepared for things to go south."

"Either of 'em have a Bible?"

"They both do. Looks like they read 'em as well. Both the covers and the pages are pretty well worn."

"Not a couple of those heathen *modern* Bibles, are they?"

"No, sir. The Lord's own King James version."

Benkovic smiled. "It's not often someone who's figured

out the writing on the wall just falls into your lap. I'd say that if they aren't already with us, it won't take much to get them there."

SPUD AND HANK sat in the living room, enjoying the warmth of the wood stove before calling it a night.

"What do you think?" Spud asked her.

"Not sure," Hank said. "They're not showing a lot of—how can I put it?—*reservations* about our being here, though they don't entirely trust us yet. I think we'll know more once we've been here a little while. If we notice that everyone seems to be shunning us, then I think it will be a long time before we're accepted as part of this little community."

"It looks like they expect it to grow quite a bit more," Spud said. "They've got the entire location terraced out for additional houses."

Hank grinned at him and shook her head. "This is coal country. This is an old surface-mined coal pit that's been rehabilitated. They'd take off the overburden, then start stripping out the layers of coal, starting from the surface. Mining laws dictate how broad the tiers have to be, and as they go down further, they have to have a ramp for the heavy equipment to access the lower levels. This one just conveniently has tiers that are the right width to allow a house to be built and still have a road in front of it. This house must be on one edge of the pit where they didn't have to strip off what was to one side of the house for there to be as many mature trees as there are here. You may have noticed that the other houses don't have a lot of mature trees near them, as well as few pines. What's on most of the tiers is new growth.

"Where did the trailer end up?" she asked him.

"I've got it parked down next to the church. Or rather, the assembly building is what I guess they call it. Good thing, because I was trying to figure out how I'd pull off backing the thing up next to the house. We've been invited to morning services, by the way."

"Tomorrow's Monday," Hank said. "They have services on Monday?"

"They apparently have services every day of the week, and a Bible study on Wednesday evenings for the men, Thursdays for the women, and Saturdays for the children."

"I take it we're not just invited, but expected to attend," Hank said, her tone indicating that she wasn't certain she could tolerate that much religion.

"I take it attending will be a good course of action."

She sighed. "I guess that means I get religion."

"Right now, I think I'd like to get to bed," Spud said. "There's just something about hauling an entire household of stuff and then unloading it all that puts the ache in a man's shoulders. And arms, and legs, and back ..."

"Are you telling me you're too tired to even make love?" Hank asked.

"Not tonight, dear—I've got a headache," Spud quipped.

"Now you really sound like you're getting old on me."

"You really want a little sex to round out the evening?"

Hank laughed. "Hell no. Not after sweeping the floors and porch, cleaning up the kitchen, getting everything put away, hauling in firewood ... I think the minute my head hits the pillow, I'll be out."

"I hope we'll be warm enough tonight," Spud reflected with a look at the wood stove.

"The house has a back-up furnace that runs on fuel oil," Hank said. "I got it set up. The pilot's lit, and I made sure the thermostat is working. So, when the fire dies down in the wood stove, the furnace will kick in."

"Sounds good. And I guess I'm going to have to learn how to do all this stuff, or I'll be a worthless husband when we decide it's time to set up a place of our own."

"Then this mission will be a good learning experience for you," Hank said, getting up. "I'm off to bed. You coming?"

"Only in the sense that I'm following you to the bedroom," Spud said. "Too tired for any other meaning of the word."

17

Hank got up and tried to rub the lingering fatigue out of her eyes. The bed next to her was empty, Spud having risen before she had and already completed his usual morning routine in the bathroom. Figuring it was her turn to occupy the small bath, she trudged off after pulling on her robe to try and wash yet more fatigue away. Feeling a bit achy, she hoped she could be successful at that.

Her shower finished and now dressed in everything but her tichel, she shuffled off to the kitchen, finding Spud already seated with a mug of some sort of hot beverage in front of him. She searched the counters, and not finding what she was looking for, began a search of the cabinets and cupboards as well.

"Where the hell is it?" she grumbled.

"What are you looking for?"

"The coffee and a coffee maker."

Spud grinned, realizing he wasn't the only one who was going to have to make some adjustments during their mission.

"You know, Love, I did a little research on this group as well. One thing I discovered was that they don't consume anything that isn't native to North America."

"What?"

"If it's not grown in North America, they don't eat it or drink it. They also avoid alcohol and tobacco."

"That's not going to be difficult."

"No coffee, either. Doesn't grow here."

Hank's eyes flew open at that news. *"What?! No, no, no, and **hell no!** This mission is over!"*

"Glad to see you're awake now," Spud said, amused.

Hank had begun an agitated pacing of the floor while grumbling obscenities and shaking her head. Turning and looking at him, she strode up and looked in the mug in front of him.

"What's that you've got?"

"Herb tea."

Hank slumped. "That's not going to wake me up."

Spud slid an empty mug in front of her and poured tea into it from a teapot wrapped in a cozy. "Try it. I think you'll find it's a pretty good pick me up."

"What is it?" Hank asked, lifting the mug and giving it a sniff.

"Peppermint ginger tea."

Hank gave it a sip. "Tastes OK." She took another drink.

"It's surprisingly effective at getting the sleep out of your system," Spud said. "It even seems like it helps get rid of some of the morning stiffness."

"That'll be a nice side effect," Hank admitted. "But ginger doesn't grow here either, does it?"

"Apparently it can, and that's good enough for Shining City."

"Then why can't they grow coffee here?" Hank complained.

She got up and looked through the refrigerator for eggs.

"You're going to find them on the counter," Spud said.

"One of the neighbors left some. Apparently, one of the things they do here is that everyone raises something and then it's shared throughout the community. You may have noticed that there are some greens growing in the garden next to the house."

Hank yawned. "Yeah. Looks like swiss chard. Some cabbages, too. And what looks like a late crop of peas. Cold weather plants. The peas might not survive the cold." She picked out four eggs from a bowl on the counter. "How would you like your eggs?"

"Scrambled," Spud replied. "And I have some other bad news for you: they don't eat pork. No ham or bacon to go with the eggs."

Hank yawned again. "This is bullshit."

"No, this is Shining City. Bullshit is a bit farther down the road," Spud quipped. "But I think you'll find some venison in the fridge if you want to cook up some meat to go with the eggs."

"I notice you conveniently left breakfast for me to do," Hank groused.

"And for good reason. If one of the neighbors passes by and sees me doing the cooking, they're going to wonder if I have a submissive wife or if my wife has a submissive husband."

The growl that emanated from Hank's throat rivaled any Spud had ever heard Edge come forth with. He smiled as Hank cooked, all the while grumbling about the lack of coffee, at least there being some venison to go with the eggs, and a postscript of 'just wait until we get back—see if I'm your slave then.'

"Undercover work is fun, isn't it?" he poked.

Hank threw a dishtowel at him.

"Guess not," he remarked to no one in particular.

"Just keep rubbing it in," she said. "I can always cut off your extracurricular activities."

Spud reflected on the terms Hank had just used—especially as she was now brandishing a butcher knife while cutting some venison to go with the eggs. *Better not push it,* he wisely decided.

Placing eggs and venison in front of him, Hank likewise sat to eat. "When's this morning service we're expected to attend?" she asked.

"Nine AM."

She glanced at her watch. "I guess it's good I didn't decide on any extra sack time. I'd seriously considered it."

"I would have told them you weren't feeling well this morning."

"Better to just fall in step with the place," Hank admitted. "The sooner we get them to trust us, the sooner we can determine just what's going on here and report back to the ATF. I'm a little concerned about this guy Gavin."

"Oh? Why?" Spud asked.

"He seems a bit too anxious to storm in here with a bunch of other agents. If I've read this group right from what I've gathered, the biggest thing they share is a distrust of the government. The Howells spoke consistently about their fears of the 'ZOG'. If Gavin decides he has to sweep into this community in bullet-proof vests and guns in hand, it's almost a certainty that someone will fire a shot. Then the whole place will blow up, but it won't be because there are any explosives here. It will be because Gavin incited a shootout. It'll be worse than Waco. Have you seen how many kids there are here?"

"Yes. It looks like over half the camp are children, and most of them are very young."

"Think of the shit storm, then, if reports get out about

kids being shot. Every anti-government extremist group out there will take up arms. No one who wears a badge or occupies a government office will be safe."

"Agreed. This mission goes far beyond just seeing what a single extremist group is up to. We saw what happened in the aftermath of Waco: one hundred and sixty-eight dead, nineteen of which were children when the Murrah Building was bombed. I've never been convinced that McVeigh didn't know about the kids, either. To me, it seems more likely that he felt it was suitable payback for the children that died in the Branch Davidian fire."

"Maybe," Hank said. "He claimed he didn't know about the child care there, though."

"You'd think that if he scoped the place out, that he'd have known, even if he never went inside the building. He was a sick bastard intent on making a point. I don't think he cared if kids died in the process."

"All that aside, I think our primary mission *here* has to be to ensure that we don't have a repeat performance of past events," Hank said. She got up and gathered their dirty dishes, placing them in the sink to be washed after returning from the morning services. Going back to the bedroom, she grabbed one of the head wraps she had Mike purchase and wrapped her head in a traditional tichel style, ensuring all of her hair was covered.

The two bundled up against the chill morning air and grabbing their Bibles walked the short distance to the assembly hall. Overnight, the rain had been replaced by snow, and Hank wrapped her heavy shawl around herself in her attempts to stay warm as the flakes continued to sift down from the sky. Taking her place among the women behind the screen, she sat and remained silent. Spud walked

forward and took a place among the men, exchanging greet-
ings with them.

Pastor Benkovic walked in and made his way to the front
of the gathered men.

"What a grand morning we have," Benkovic began. "Our
first snow is falling, showing the Earth the meaning of
purity. White, white purity born of crystal water—not a
muddy slough as some would believe is acceptable."

Hank nodded, though she found the inference repulsive.
She thought of James back at the headquarters complex.
*These people would have us reject the finest lab tech and pharma-
cist I've ever known.* She smiled. *I wonder if he still wears his
'FTBG' shirt?* she thought, smiling even broader as she
recalled his asking, "What does this stand for? Field Team
Black Guy?" and the team's explanation, given his role in a
training exercise, "We were thinking 'Field Team Bad Guy,'
but that works, too." She also reflected that the team's one
blond-haired, blue-eyed man wouldn't let anyone else touch
him with a needle. *If these people only knew ...*

She continued to think of her teammates, her face
aimed at the floor as she saw all of their faces: Amigo's
Hispanic one, Voicc's half-Japanese one, Crow's quarter-
Cherokee one ... Then on to the Support personnel: Luigi
and Rose, both descendants of Italian immigrants; Doc
Andy and his partner, Nate; Doc Rich, probably the most
authoritarian woman Hank had ever encountered; Gil's total
acceptance of Chandra as his daughter and Mike's adoration
of her as the perfect model with her short-cropped hair and
deep maple syrup skin. *How could anyone condemn these
people?* she wondered. She frowned, then thought, *Mission
First.*

Her reverie was interrupted by Benkovic saying, "I'm
sure all of you have noticed that we have a new person

among us. Stand up, Brother Banyon. Come forward so everyone can meet you."

Spud stood from his chair and walked forward to where Benkovic was standing, then turned and faced the congregation.

"Brother Banyon came into Sharples yesterday, looking for a quiet home where he and his wife could set down their roots. I noticed something different about them right away." He looked back to where the women were partly hidden behind the slats of the screen that separated them from the men. "Stand up, Mrs. Banyon," he said.

Hank looked at Spud and remained seated. The slight curl of his lips told Hank he was amused enough to not be able to hide it. The slight twitch of her eyebrow told him he'd better watch his step. With his hand palm up, Spud indicated to her that she should stand. Gripping her newly-acquired but well-worn Bible, she did so, keeping her eyes averted to the floor.

Benkovic smiled. "See how obedient to her husband she is? She will not even stand when a man of God tells her to."

Pfft! If you're a man of God, then I'm the Virgin Mary!

"She did not put on the tichel in deference to us, either. She arrived wearing it."

What about I shave my head? she thought as she watched Spud's eyes dance with amusement, the movement so slight that only she could have caught it.

"Tell us what brought you here," Benkovic continued, turning to Spud.

Spud indicated that Hank should sit, then said, "My wife Katie and I were sick of the corruption we saw around us in the cities and towns. The more I prayed, the more I believed that Yahweh was calling us to be apart from the heathen world."

Benkovic nodded his approval.

"I note that you have no children," Benkovic observed. "Is it that you didn't want to bring children into a heathen world?"

Spud hung his head a bit. "The doctors have told us that neither of us can bring forth children. That I am sterile, and Katie is barren. Still, we hope for a miracle. We believe that by being apart from that world, we might be blessed with a child."

"Ah!" Benkovic exclaimed. "What faith! To believe that Yahweh will grant a pure child to come into a pure place rather than a heathen one! Do you see?" he went on to the other men. "When we set ourselves apart and quit believing the lies of the heathen world and the ZOG, then Yahweh will bring others to us who have likewise come to realize the truth. This is why the ZOG fear us. They know that Yahweh will increase our number, and that one day the great war that was fought once in heaven will be fought also on Earth. Once again, Yahweh's chosen shall prevail and the rest be consigned to Gehenna, where they will feel the torment of the fires they brought upon themselves by their beliefs in the false gods of their world: power, money, influence, and possessions beyond those they need to survive."

Hank had to give him that last. If nothing else, it seemed to her that greed for one commodity or another was often behind the crimes she saw being committed. *But then, isn't it his desire for power over these people that's driving him?*

"How's our embedded couple doing?" Doc Rich asked as she joined the team members who were gathered and monitoring the exchanges between Spud, Hank, and the members of the Shining City community.

"It seems like the people in the compound are already starting to take to them," Cloud said. "It's gotta be tough on them, though. This Benkovic guy is a real whackjob. What are their biometrics like?"

"So far, so good. They seemed very fatigued last night, though."

Edge laughed. "They moved all that stuff they'd picked up at garage sales into the house they're in yesterday before it started raining. I'm surprised they're not freezing their butts off right now with it snowing."

Doc Rich gazed out the window of the hotel room a moment, then said, "I hope they're well enough prepared for this kind of weather. Supposedly, we're in for a major winter storm."

Crow was chuckling. "You'd better hope there's nothing to this group, Doc Rich. Spud just told them that he and Hank were hoping for a miracle."

"Oh?"

"Yeah. He said they were hoping *Yahweh*," he drew out, "would bless them with a child."

Doc Rich snorted. "Not if my knots and cauterizations have anything to say about it."

"I guess when they're done with Shining City, they'll just have to move on to somewhere else where they can find that kind of miracle," Amigo said.

"Like a clinic that does in vitro fertilization," Doc Rich said. "I trust they'll hold on from doing that until after Hank at least retires."

The team members chuckled. Crow raised the volume on the communication they were hearing over team comm as Hank and Spud made their way back to their house in the compound.

"We're going to need to find excuses for making intel drops in town," Hank said. "We can't send everything over the comm link."

"Like what?" Crow asked her.

"Like a map of the layout of this place," Hank said in reply. "We can get you photos, but not a bird's eye view."

"Gotcha. We can get aerials, though. Just do an overflight."

"Don't want to do that," Spud said. "I already have the impression that these people hold most of their distrust for the government. If they see a helicopter go overhead, they're likely to believe it's government spying. It'll put them on edge—maybe to the point that someone takes a potshot at you. If ATF gets news of that, the fight will be on. Hank's a little worried about one of the local agents as well. She thinks he'd really like to come in ASAP with guns blazing, and frankly I don't want that happening while we're decked out like members of the group. So Voice, if you could get word to our ATF gunny that they need to emphasize to the local office that no action be initiated while there are agents embedded in the group? It's bad enough worrying if someone will decide we should be eliminated from within the group without also worrying if the ATF will come in and shoot us as well."

"Gotcha," Voice said.

"Here's our excuse," Hank said, pointing into the trees as they arrived back at their house.

"What are you looking at?" Spud asked.

"That pine tree up there with the yellow needles. That's pine wilt disease. That tree should really come down before the pine trees around it get infected. It might be why we're not seeing a lot of pines around us where the forest is more mature. They might be harvesting them out."

"In that case, don't you think someone has a chainsaw?" Spud asked.

Hank held up a finger. "Ah—but we don't want to use a chainsaw. A chainsaw is something that will make us dependent upon the ZOG, you see. They wear out. The chains get dull. They need gasoline. What we need," she continued as they went inside, "is a five-foot, two-man crosscut saw."

"A five-foot, two-man crosscut saw?" Spud asked.

"That and a three-foot one for cutting the limbs off the log. Maybe a four-foot one as well. You want the blade to be the right length for the task."

"Where do we get the money for that?"

"Hey, guys," Hank chimed. "Anyone there in Logan still have their unit credit card?"

At the hotel, five sets of eyes looked around at each other.

"You want us to buy you a set of saws?" Amigo asked.

"Gee, how'd you guess? I figure there must be a mercantile or a lumber yard somewhere there in Logan. See if they'll order a set of saws for you. Grab cash to pay for them, and have Voice set up a number they can call when they arrive. Then we'll drive into town and pick them up. Arrange a drop for us so we can get what intel we can't get over the comm link to you, and you can get some additional cash to us."

"What's your explanation for all the cash?" Crow asked.

"We sold our house," Spud said. "Cleaned out our bank account and took everything in cash. We'd just need to have enough on hand to make it appear that we have a lot of dough with us."

"What if they demand to see it?"

"I do not want to tempt my brothers into sin," Spud said. "But if they have a need, we can go into Logan for them and make purchases."

"What if they feel their need is for a new Mercedes?"

"Didn't you just hear Benkovic talk about 'possessions beyond the need to survive'?" Spud asked.

"Oh yeah. That."

"This can be our regular excuse for making contact with the rest of you. Put down things we might not want to be saying aloud over the comm link. We never know who might overhear. They seem to be accepting us, but they also seem a bit wary," Hank said. "We're still strangers as far as they're concerned."

SPUD RETURNED from having gone outside to gather some firewood for the stove. While there, he had stood gazing up at the tree than Hank said should be harvested, given it was diseased. *This should be an adventure, given I have no idea how to cut down a tree.*

He found Hank still engrossed in finding places for things inside the house. On the kitchen stove a pot of stew simmered and on the counter a sheet pan dotted with raw biscuits awaited being put into the oven. Hank strode from one room to another, taking items from what she supposed had been the two children's rooms and which had been temporarily used to store the things they had brought and putting them where they belonged. It saddened her every time she noticed how little the Howells had escaped with. *This pastor rules with a sword,* she thought. Reconsidering, she muttered, "No—with a whip."

As sparsely furnished as the house had been when they

arrived, Hank still found that many items would simply have to remain stored in the children's rooms. This saddened her as well. *These rooms should have children in them—not unused beds and chairs.* An undercurrent of anger coursed through her veins, fed by the knowledge that Benkovic had so terrorized the Howells that they had given up nearly every possession they had owned in order to get away from him.

Spud waylaid her on yet another trip with an armload of items to be put in their proper places. Putting his arms around her waist, he said, "I think it's time to slow down a bit and have something to eat."

Hank pulled up her sleeve and glanced at her watch. "The time completely got away from me," she grumbled. "I hope I didn't cook that stew to mush." She rushed into the kitchen and turned on the stove. "Once the oven heats up, the biscuits will only take about fifteen minutes," she said. She gave the pot of stew a stir and proclaimed it done, turning off the heat from cooking it further.

"What were you doing out there?" she asked Spud.

"I moved some of the firewood to the porch so we wouldn't have to go tramping through the snow after it. Also grabbed some pictures of the compound, met some people in the community, and started gathering some data for drawing up a map as well as identifying who lives where. I got a look at that tree you say should come down, too. You know I've never cut a tree, right?"

Hank chuckled. "A handy man you are not," she said.

"I freely admit it."

"It's not all that hard. You already see that trees grow in alignment with gravity, unless they've been affected by strong winds or shifting earth. That guy is growing straight up, so what you'll want to do is cut a notch at the base in the direction you want it to fall and then cut from the other side to get it to do so. You drive in wedges so it goes where you want it to go. And watch the tree, just in case it decides it's going to split or spiral off its trunk and fall in another direction. If it shows signs of doing that, you run like hell."

"This doesn't sound like the world's safest activity."

"Says the man who was willing to step in front of a bullet so the president wouldn't take one," Hank said, grinning. "Remember that the Howells said they were using explosives here to blow stumps. It's obvious, then, that the men here have some experience when it comes to felling a tree. You're the new guy who just stepped away from the heathen world—the world where all the houses have been built on lots that were cleared by guys with chain saws and bulldozers. The men here will give you a hand with it, I'm sure."

"I'm going to feel like an idiot with all these guys knowing how to do this already."

Hank elbowed him gently in the ribs. Leaning toward him, she gave him a little kiss. "Male bonding," she said. "Gotta get all of your penises in a row."

"You have a way with words ..." Spud reflected.

"And as long as I can remember to not use the kinds I usually do around anyone in this community, we should be able to maintain our cover."

She served Spud some of the stew, then went and retrieved the biscuits from the oven, setting them on a plate and taking her own seat. Grabbing up her spoon, she stopped. Noticing that Spud hadn't eaten anything yet, she asked, "Everything OK? I didn't cook the life out of anything, did I?"

Spud looked at her, grinned, and folded his hands in front of himself. Bowing his head, he intoned, "We thank you, O Lord, for this food you give for the nourishment of our bodies. We thank you for your word, which you give for the nourishment of our souls. And we thank you for this new fellowship we find ourselves a part of. Amen."

Hank eyed him. "Amen," she echoed, then added, "Oh, brother."

"Which of my brother's do you refer to?" Spud asked. "I'd like to know so I can ensure my penis is aligned with his."

"Oh, shut up."

Spud took up his spoon and examined the contents of his bowl of stew. Fishing out a chunk of something yellow, he asked, "What is this?"

Hank at first looked at him wide-eyed, then looked around in mock surprise. "Did Edge follow us here?"

"I'll eat it—I just want to know what this mystery vegetable is," Spud insisted.

"It's rutabaga."

"It's *what?*"

"Rutabaga. Sort of a giant yellow turnip. I found some growing in the garden. Along with the carrots and the potatoes, which all will need to come up before the ground gets frozen."

Spud slurped the contents of the spoon, rutabaga and all. He gave a nod of approval. "I think I like rutabaga better than turnips."

"Good thing. I didn't see any turnips out there." Hank spooned out some of the stew herself. "Not bad for just throwing in a little of this and a little of that."

"What's the meat?"

Hank raised an eyebrow. "You really miss Edge, don't you?"

"He's my best friend. And I think that under the circumstances it's not such a bad thing to ask what the meat is."

"First, let me ask if you like it."

"It's different. Not objectionable."

"Glad you think so. It's squirrel."

Spud stopped eating and looked at her. "Squirrel?"

"What? You don't think it tastes like chicken?" she asked, trying not to laugh.

"When are we going to eat the moose?"

"Huh?"

"The moose. If we're having Rocky tonight, I'm wondering when we'll eat Bullwinkle."

Hank shook her head. "For Bullwinkle, I think we'd have to be embedded with a Shining City compound in Alaska."

"Do they have one there?"

"Dunno. I think they might have one in Maine, though, so we could make that our next stop. Then we can hunt us up a Bullwinkle."

"And here I thought it was odd enough to eat buffalo and feral hog."

"Bison."

"I stand corrected."

"I HOPE these things they're eating have been properly processed," Doc Rich grumbled as the unit members at the hotel listened in to the conversation over the comm link.

"You might remember that we did a survival exercise where we ate everything from acorns to rabbits," Edge said. "And that we've done more than one hunt, bringing back wild game and fish each time."

"Granted, but each time there was a medical detachment right there in case there were any problems. It's not like we can go rushing into an undercover operation to take care of a sick team member."

"Don't fret it, Doc Rich. From the sound of it, this isn't Hank's first rodeo when it comes to eating things like squirrel."

Crow was chuckling. "I pity Spud. Hank will eat anything, but I doubt Spud has ever eaten a squirrel before."

"Didn't he get some of the chipmunk during the survival exercise?" Amigo asked. "Or was he spared that, given he was the first one to die?"

"Don't recall," Crow said. "All I remember is that it tasted better than roots and acorns."

"Well, I think one thing I'm going to want to do is make sure either I or Doc Frank is there to do a medical assessment when they arrive here in Logan to do their intel drop."

"How do you intend to be able to do that?" Edge asked.

Doc Rich thought a bit. "Doc Frank and I will alternate. We can do it in a restroom."

"I have a better idea," they heard Spud say over the comm link. "See if Gavin can rent us an RV."

"The man can still think, in spite of having to eat squirrel," Amigo quipped.

HANK AND SPUD retired to the bedroom after Spud stoked the wood stove one last time and Hank washed and dried the dishes, then put them away. Slipping into bed together, they nestled in each other's arms as much as a means of staying warm as enjoying the physical togetherness. Being a bit distant from the wood stove, the bedroom was several degrees cooler than the living area of the house. Each finding that they were once again too tired to think of anything other than sleep, they lay together and went over plans for further infiltration of the group, as well as how they might get into town for their first intel drop.

"The windows in this part of the house could use some weatherstripping," Hank said. "That could give us an excuse to get our preliminary report into the hands of the team."

"Mmhm," Spud mumbled.

"Being a man in this group wearing you out?" Hank asked, realizing Spud was just about to drop off to sleep.

"It's a different kind of physical activity than we do in the team," he muttered.

"Yeah, gotta admit," Hank agreed. "These folks aren't living an easy life by any means."

It was the last thing she remembered before falling asleep herself.

18

"Brother Banyon," one of the men called as Spud and Hank made their way back to their house from the morning service.

Spud looked around to see one of the men he and Hank had been referring to as "the Joes" striding to catch up with him. Hank dutifully moved behind the men as he caught up and walked alongside Spud.

"Good morning, Brother," Spud greeted him. "I know your given name is Joe; what's your family name?"

"Frisch," Joe replied.

"Brother Frisch. A fine German name."

"That it is. And where do Banyons find their origins?" Joe asked.

"It's a Welsh name."

"Another fine blood line," Joe said.

Are these people into eugenics? Hank wondered.

"What about your wife?" Joe asked.

"She was Hank before we married," Spud said.

Back at the hotel, Voice was making an inquiry of Hal for the most common origin of 'Hank' as a surname. "Tell him it's Saxon," he told Spud over the comm link, given Spud had said 'Hank' rather than 'Hanko'.

"A Saxon name," Spud added.

Hank raised an eyebrow, unseen given she was walking behind the men.

"Wonderful. How are the two of you making do? Do you have everything you need?"

"More than enough," Spud said. "Katie tells me we need to harvest some of the vegetables from the garden next to the house. We have carrots, potatoes, and some peas that have already been bitten by the cold, I'm afraid, but still have some tasty pods. She says the rutabagas and Swiss chard will continue to survive the cold, but that there is plenty there as well. Are you married? Could your family use some?"

Joe Frisch put a hand on Spud's shoulder. "Already you've discovered one of the secrets of our community. We share among ourselves so there is not just plenty for the present, but enough to store for the future as well. We never know when the walls of the heathen nation our country has become will come tumbling down. As the remnant, we are always preparing for that day so that we can come into the inheritance that is ours."

The remnant. I thought the meek were supposed to inherit the Earth, not the arrogant, Hank thought.

"One thing we could use is some weatherstripping for our windows," Spud said. "The area of the house furthest from the wood stove gets chilly at night. You don't know if anyone has some, do you?"

Frisch shook his head. "That's not a commodity that I think anyone keeps in store."

"What about a crosscut saw? I notice there's a diseased pine behind my house, and think it will be best to get it down before it falls on its own, both to avoid it spreading wilt disease to the other pines in that stand and to keep it from perhaps falling on the house."

"A crosscut saw? We have chainsaws ..."

"A chainsaw will be of little use when there's no more gasoline," Spud pointed out.

Frisch considered this. "You have a point, Brother."

"We should have a set of crosscut saws. Perhaps when I go into Logan to find weather stripping, I can get the hardware store to order them."

Frisch looked at him, a hint of suspicion in his eyes. "You want to leave the community so soon?"

Spud looked at him as if he was surprised. "Only to get things that are needed and not here," he said. He smiled. "Besides, I wouldn't leave my wife behind. She needs a man to help and protect her. At the moment, she's still getting the house in order, so I'd be making this trip on my own."

Because I certainly can't hold my own, Hank thought with a scowl, *being a helpless little housewife.*

"Our wives have their responsibilities, and we have ours," Frisch conceded.

Responsibilities? As in, may I kiss your ass? Why, certainly, dear, Hank's inner voices grumbled.

Spud reflected a moment, then asked, "Do you have a wife, Brother Frisch? I never see her at the morning services."

Frisch smiled expansively. "Yes, I have a wife. The reason you don't see her is that she's pregnant with our first child and very near to her due date. She complains that her back hurts." He grinned. "She's about to pop, as they say!"

"I would think you would want to be ready to go to Logan. They have a hospital there, don't they?" Spud asked.

"Have our child among the heathen?" Frisch said. "We discussed this. Our child will be born here."

Hank began to listen intently. *Risky,* she thought. She could see by the way Spud looked at Frisch that he felt the same way.

"I would be concerned," Spud said. "But perhaps my concerns are more born of the fact that Katie and I have been told we can't have children. I have some training ... I have certification as an EMT. But that training might not be good enough if there is a problem with the pregnancy. The baby could be breech, for instance. In that case, the baby could die without a surgeon to intervene."

"We will accept whatever Yahweh's will turns out to be," Frisch said. "Ellen and I trust Him completely."

Saying their goodbyes, Spud and Hank headed to their house. Once inside the door, Hank remarked, "I think I'd have a little faith that Yahweh would put me in the hands of a good obstetrician."

"This whole community is a testament to how faith can go astray," Spud said. "I couldn't find, for instance, where Jesus added 'unless he's black' to his dictum to 'love thy neighbor'." He put his Bible down on the dinette table at his place, Hank doing the same.

"I have an errand to run today," Spud told her. "I'm going to take the truck into town and see if I can't get some weather stripping and order the crosscut saws. Team, did you get that?" he added for the unit members in Logan.

Cloud was currently in charge of monitoring what was happening with Spud and Hank in the Shining City compound. "Gotcha," he replied. "Where were you thinking of going?"

Spud wished they could see him grinning over the comm link, and reflected that maybe he should have been using the video link. "I think there's a whole of one hardware store in Logan," he returned. "Brainiac should be able to fish it out."

Voice scowled and had Hal do a search. "Yeah," he drew out. "Exactly one. You need anything?"

"Some cash. For you guys, I've been able to upload everything to Hal. So far, things have been pretty uneventful."

"It's true. You're boring us silly," Cloud remarked.

"As long as it doesn't develop into the kind of exciting undercover op we had down on the border, I'm happy," Spud said. "Especially given our sniper is presently sitting across the table from me."

"Amigo can take care of any required sniper activity," Hank said. "I'm not terribly concerned."

"You don't have to be concerned at all," Amigo said.

"*Now* I'm concerned," Hank said with a chuckle.

"Perra."

"Pendejo."

"Glad to see the sniper team is still well-practiced," Crow wisecracked.

"OK. If that's all that's needed for now, then I'll see you guys in a bit. Who's going to be dropping me the cash?"

"We'll flip a few quarters and figure that out. Whoever loses will meet you in the area where weather stripping can be found," Cloud said.

"Whoever loses?" Spud asked.

"Yeah. We figure whoever has to go might have to listen to a morning intel briefing."

"Ah, the warm glow one gets knowing his coworkers appreciate him," Spud said, sarcasm oozing out of every word.

He got up. "What's on your agenda this morning?" he asked Hank.

"I'm going to see about digging the carrots and potatoes, and maybe go around the neighborhood to see if I can touch bases with any of the women. I'm gathering we can talk among ourselves as long as there aren't any men around."

"Dress warmly, Love. It's still barely above freezing out there."

"You drive carefully," Hank admonished in return. "It's supposed to warm up a little, and that will likely make the winding roads here treacherous."

"Don't even want to tell you two how incredibly domesticated you both sound right now," Cloud said.

Hank silently raised a middle finger in his honor.

"I heard that, Hank" Cloud replied, certain of what her unseen response had been.

SPUD DROVE INTO LOGAN, following the directions Hal was giving him to find the hardware store. The entire route had been twists and turns on the roads that basically followed the valleys between the low-lying foothills of the Apalacians, generally paralleling the rail lines that served the numerous hilltop mining areas still active between Charleston and Logan. It was a rugged and rustic area that Spud had never seen and which caused him to marvel both at the relatively untouched areas and at the incredible destruction caused by present and past mining activities.

Logan, likewise, wound through the low-lying areas, seeming like a mere strip of inhabitation snaking between the tree-covered hills. Even though one of the larger area towns, its population had begun to make a slow decline with the likewise decline of coal mining and now stood at a mere fifteen hundred souls. *Not exactly the kind of population that supports a robust economy*, Spud thought.

Finding the store, he noted the black SUV parked away from the door in the parking lot. Knowing that whoever would be meeting him was probably already inside, he parked near the door and made his way in.

Looking down the rows of aisles with their overhead signs indicating what could be found in each, he headed for the location where insulation could be found. At first, he thought he must be in the wrong place, given rolls of pink fiberglass batting and sheets of fire-resistant foam filled the shelves near the end of the aisle he'd entered. But a look farther down the aisle revealed Crow, apparently studying packages of something. Walking down, he noticed that Crow was looking somewhat puzzled as he read over the application information on the back of two different packages.

"Looks like you're after the same stuff I'm after," Spud said to him.

"Yeah, trying to decide which one of these will work better for me," Crow said.

"I need something good for sealing the bottoms of my doors," Spud said.

"I hear this stuff works well," Crow remarked, picking up a roll of flexible material marketing itself as door sill sealant. He handed it to Spud, along with a business-size envelope tucked hidden under the package.

"Thanks. Now let me see what they have here for weather stripping windows."

"What kind of windows you got?" Crow asked.

"Your typical casement windows that slide up and down."

"You'll want this stuff," Crow said, taking a package

containing a roll of material off a hanging display and handing it to him with another envelope. "Brush strip. If you've got any sliding doors, this stuff works for those as well. Very simple to use—just peel the adhesive off and stick it in place. They say the adhesive is all you need for that door sill seal as well, but if I were you, I'd staple it in place with heavy-duty staples."

Spud did what he had with the first exchange: examined the package while slipping the envelope into an inner jacket pocket.

"Anything else I can help you with?" Crow asked, a twinkle in his eye.

Spud looked around, then quietly asked, "Got a strip of bacon on you? Turns out the Shining City folk don't eat pork."

Crow just smiled and shook his head.

"Don't drink coffee, either," Spud added quietly. "Hank is having a hard time getting kick-started in the morning."

Crow chuckled. "Bet that's the truth!"

"Thanks for the info," Spud said aloud. "You've been a great help. Now I'd better go find a heavy-duty stapler and some staples as well before my wife complains of being cold at night again."

"Aren't keeping her warm enough under the covers?" Crow whispered.

"Shut up," Spud hissed in return.

Crow smiled. "Glad to have helped," he said aloud.

"Aren't you going to buy anything?" Spud asked him.

"Nah. I just come in and check prices. Usually I find the same thing cheaper on Amazon. You can find both of those things you've got cheaper there."

"I don't use credit cards, and Amazon doesn't take good ol' American cash," Spud said.

Crow walked out of the aisle, heading for the door. Spud likewise walked out of the aisle, checking to see which of the other aisles would have a heavy-duty stapler. Then he went to the customer service desk.

"This store wouldn't have manual two-man crosscut saws for sale, would it?" he asked.

"We don't carry those in stock, but we could order one in for you," the clerk said.

"I'd actually like three of them," Spud said. "A three-foot, a four-foot, and a five-foot."

The clerk eyed him. "You can probably get them on Amazon as well."

"Really? You'll turn away business and let Amazon have it? Besides, Amazon doesn't take cash," Spud added.

"OK. For two-man saws, I see three-and-a-half foot, four-foot, five-foot, and six-foot lengths."

Spud was considering this when he heard Hank through the comm link. "Get the four, the five, and the six."

"I'd like a four-, a five-, and a six-foot one, then," Spud said.

"The total will be seven hundred and forty-two dollars even," the clerk said. "Including tax. We need fifty percent down to put in the order for you."

"That would be three hundred and seventy-one dollars," Spud said, doing the math. The young clerk had just finished computing it on the cash register.

"Yeah, that's right." He looked at Spud as if Spud had just transported down from the *Starship Enterprise*.

No one does math without a calculator anymore, Spud reflected. *I guess if we actually lose Hal at some point, I'll still be able to buy things.*

Spud took out one of the envelopes and counted out

three hundred and eighty dollars in twenty-dollar bills. Again, the clerk looked at him oddly.

"No, I don't have a credit card," Spud said.

"OK."

"You owe me nine dollars in change," Spud advised him, making the clerk lose his own count of the bills.

The clerk sighed and went to start over. Spud likewise sighed and took the bills from him.

"One, two, three, four, five ... that's one hundred," he began, then counted out two more piles of five twenty-dollar bills, finally spreading out the last four. With a tap of a finger on each of the piles, he said, "One hundred, two hundred, three hundred, and eighty. Eighty minus seventy-one is nine. You owe me nine dollars."

The clerk still used the cash register to confirm it.

"Right again," he said.

Twenty-somethings, Spud mused.

BACK IN THE COMPOUND, Hank bundled up in a bulky sweater and headed out the back door to the shed that stood there. Checking out the tools stored in the shed, she grabbed a heavy spading fork and made her way to the garden, taking the large wicker basket she'd brought from the house with her. Starting at one end of the row of carrots, she thrust the spading fork alongside the row with a stomp of her foot and turned the earth up, loosening the carrots. She continued down the row until the entire row had been spaded up, leaving the spading fork stuck upright in the soil with a thrust of the tines downward.

Going back to where she'd left the basket, she proceeded to grab the tops of the carrots, shaking the soil loose and dropping them into the basket. Going down the row, she continued to harvest the carrots until the entire row was completely shaken loose of soil and ready to be taken inside. Balancing the basket on one hip and retrieving the spading fork, she returned the tool to the shed and then took the carrots inside.

Standing at the sink and washing the carrots, she noticed one of the men from the compound walking down the hill and across the yard between the house and the shed. Noticing her, he gave a little nod as she averted her eyes downward. Giving a covert glance, she noted that he carried a Ruger 10/22 in one hand and a dead rabbit in the other. *Someone got his dinner.* She reflected, also, that it appeared the people living in the compound didn't have a sense of private property. *Then again, the place is like a commune. Maybe there is no private property.* She considered that this might be something she'd like to find out about, especially given that she and Spud had simply been given the house the Howells had lived in prior to their arrival.

With the carrots washed and trimmed of their cold-snapped tops, Hank scooped some out for herself and Spud, removed all of the smallest ones also for their use as well, and then bundled back up to go visiting the neighbors, to allow them to take what they could use. Her survey of the house and property had already revealed a basement full of supplies: everything from a root cellar to shelves of home-canned goods in jars, to nonperishable foods and repurposed two-liter bottles filled with beans, rice, and other dry grains stored along three sides; and on a forth side, ammo cans filled with reloaded ammunition, boxes of bullets, powders, primers, and cases in various stages of preparation to be reloaded. If she stood in front of these shelves, she only needed to turn around to be standing at a reloading bench set up with all of the sorts of equipment needed for the remanufacture of ammunition. What she hadn't seen in either the house nor any of the areas associated with it was anything that could be used to make explosives, with the exception of the powders used to reload ammunition. She knew, though, that it was an easy enough process to produce a powerful explosive with the powders available. She recalled her father's admonition to never mix the powders when reloading as well as her research into Ted Kaczynski's bomb-making methods. Still, she saw nothing else that indicated Larry Howell had made explosives in his basement.

She headed out the door, making her way quickly along the dirt road to the house next door. Going up, she at first considered knocking on the front door, then reconsidered. *I want to talk to the wife, if there is one here. She will most likely be in the kitchen.*

Walking around the back, she tapped on the back door. Seeing a woman take a quick glance out from the kitchen window, she waited and was rewarded with the back door being opened to her.

"Sister Banyon, isn't it?" the woman greeted her.

"Yes, sister," Hank replied. "I noticed that there are some things still remaining in the garden between your house and ours, and felt that these carrots should come out of the ground before the ground freezes."

"Come inside," the woman said, holding the door open for her and then closing it behind her. She came from behind Hank and examined the contents of the basket. "That's a fine crop of carrots. I'm sure everyone will appreciate them."

"I didn't know if this was how it's done here," Hank said. "I didn't know if the entire crop should be taken down to the assembly hall so they could be divided and distributed to everyone."

"You've done no wrong," her neighbor said. "This is exactly how we do it: harvest, and then go to all of the neighbors, letting them take what they anticipate they will need. Any left over is taken home to be canned or stored there. If anyone finds they need more later, we know who has it." She indicated Hank should sit at the kitchen table while she removed some of the carrots from the basket. Hank noticed that she didn't select the best ones, but did just as Hank had done, scooping out a generous amount and placing them on the table.

"I see you removed all of the smallest ones," the woman said.

"I didn't think anyone else would want such tiny ones," Hank admitted. "I can use them, so they won't go to waste and it leaves the better ones for the rest of our neighbors."

"I'm Katherine Coffin," the woman said by way of introduction. "My husband is Ralph. I'm sure your husband and mine will find themselves working together on some project soon enough."

Hank smiled. "I'm Katie Banyon. Spencer is already full of projects he wants to complete. He headed to Logan today to buy some weather stripping for the windows and doors. The house is a little drafty. He also wanted to order some two-man saws. It seems we have a tree behind the house on the hill that he believes is diseased and should be removed to spare the trees around it."

"He could have borrowed a chainsaw," Katherine remarked.

"He believes it's an error to have any dependence on the heathen world. He was surprised that no one here had manual saws." Hank feigned a chuckle. "He says manual saws never run out of gas."

"He has a point," Katherine said. "It's true that when the world beyond our communities collapses, it won't be long before everything they call a 'modern convenience' will become inconveniently absent."

Preppers. Survivalists. But then, our headquarters complex and all of our remote bases are likewise stocked for the long-term, Hank thought.

"How many Shining City communities are there?" Hank asked. *After all, I'm supposed to be gathering intel …*

Katherine thought for a few beats. "I'm not sure. At least twenty, if I recall correctly."

Hank held her surprise in check. Her research hadn't revealed that many Shining City compounds in existence. "Are they all the size of this one?"

"I think we're still the largest," Katherine said. "All of the others were founded from pilgrims who travelled from here. Pastor Benkovic decides when a location is large enough to send pilgrims to found a new community."

He's the Grand Poobah, Hank thought. *Chief Cheese, Head Honcho. We're in the right place. Cut off this self-righteous head and the rest of the snake might just die. Or at least become a little less radical.*

Deciding on a change of topic, Hank hung her head and said, "It makes me feel a little unfortunate to be living in the house next door. I've heard rumors that the ones who lived there before turned apostate."

"Yes, that was sad. They were a lovely family, and the husband took such pride in building the home. I think it's one of the nicest ones here. Then all of a sudden, they snuck off in the middle of the night."

"What makes a good family turn away from the light?"

Hank wondered in an effort to pry a bit more information from her neighbor.

"I think that the husband took offense that his daughter was disciplined for speaking in the assembly."

"Didn't the mother teach her that her place is to remain silent?"

"I think she perhaps forgot in her zeal to quote Scripture," Katherine said.

"How harsh could his discipline have been?" Hank wondered aloud.

Katherine weighed this quietly for a moment. "He slapped her across the face hard enough to bruise her," she finally said.

Would you be willing to testify to that in a court of law? Hank thought. She scowled. *Of course not. No one here would take the side of the ZOG over this overbearing narcissist.*

∙ ∙ ∙

"Do we have a place to hide this?" Spud asked, taking the two envelopes of money from the inner pocket of his denim jacket.

Hank thought for a few moments. "I'm sure I can find someplace. The traditional places probably won't do, though."

"There are traditional places for hiding money?"

"Between the mattresses, under the clothes in a dresser drawer, box on the top shelf of the closet, cookie jar," Hank listed. "Somewhat less traditional, but still often utilized: loose board in the floor; toilet tank, though there is usually reserved for guns and drugs sealed tightly in zip-lock bags; space behind a painting; buried in a can in the back yard."

Spud was grinning. "Which was it? The Taos PD or the FBI that put you onto all these hiding spots?"

Hank was still considering what might be a good spot. Getting an idea, she took the two envelopes of money from Spud and went into one of the spare bedrooms where items they had brought in were being stored. Opening a box of pots and pans, she lifted two large pots apart and put the envelopes into the bottom one, then nested the other back on top of it.

Spud watched her, amused. "In case we need to cook up a little cash later," he snickered.

"My dad always had a little cash taped in an envelope under one of the drawers in his tool chest. It probably wouldn't be a bad idea to spread some of the cash around the house, just in case someone discovers a stash. Right now, if they go through that box of pots and pans, they'll find the whole thing."

"Do you think there's a chance someone will break in and steal it?" Spud asked.

"Think, husband," Hank said, sounding like one of the other wives she had talked with while distributing carrots. "Someone other than Larry Howell had keys to this house. How else were they able to provide us with one?"

"It just impresses me that if someone were to be caught stealing, they'd find themselves bound to a tree and getting thirty-nine lashes."

"They get thirty-nine lashes for doing a lot less than steal," Hank said with a scowl. "At least that's what a couple of the other wives told me today."

"Did they happen to tell you who's been whipped?" Spud asked.

"The guy five houses down, for one," Hank said. "Apparently, he made a comment that the Grand Poobah felt was heresy, so he got 'corrected'."

"Am I correct in guessing that the person you're calling the Grand Poobah is our dear pastor?"

"One and the same. And not just Grand Poobah of this camp—Grand Poobah of all of them. I suspect that a certain pastor may not like reliance on heathens, but is fine with using the heathen Internet."

"Shining City does have a website."

"Yes, it does. But he's got to be communicating with the other Shining City compounds as well. Our neighbor tells me that there are at least twenty of them."

Spud expressed amazement. "Twenty? That's a lot more than I gave them credit for."

"I had no idea there were that many, either," Hank said. "And I've been watching this group for a while now. Voice," she called over the comm link, "Can you get Hal to do a search nationwide for any buildings owned by Shining City, or alternatively Robert Benkovic? See if Hal can detect any communications from Benkovic to other people as well."

"I'll get Hal on it right away," Voice returned.

"One of the things I found out today is that Larry Howell built this house," Hank told Spud.

"He's a man with some talent, then," Spud said. "This place is deceptive. It looks rather simple on the outside, but the inside ... I'm surprised that it's not as simple as some of the other homes I've been invited into."

"The women I've talked with have expressed a bit of jealousy," Hank related.

"The men as well. I'm wondering if that's what made Benkovic go so hard on Howell's daughter."

"If Benkovic was jealous of Howell's house, why didn't

he just take it as his own after Larry took his family and fled the compound?"

Spud shrugged and shook his head. "Who knows? Maybe he felt the appearances wouldn't look right. He seems like the most important thing to him is that others look up to him."

"Medical 3," Hank intoned.

"Hank, what can I do for you?" Doc Andy answered.

"See if you can find some background on our guy Benkovic. Robert Benkovic, Sharples, West Virginia. I'd like to know what makes this guy tick."

19

Hank and Spud had fallen into a regular routine, beginning with rising, showering, and eating breakfast in preparation for attending the morning service. This was followed by Spud performing minor repairs on the house, or spading over the soil in the garden in preparation for the next year's planting or harvesting some of the vegetables that still remained in the ground, with Hank following after him to get the produce out of the soil and into a basket, then taking them inside to wash and prepare for distribution around the camp. The other women had taken her under their wing, informing her of some of the cultural mores of the Shining City compound and of which houses the single men lived in and therefore whose doors she shouldn't knock on for more than an alert that she had left some of the produce for the occupants. She wondered with a smirk about how those single men reconciled their need to do the "women's work" of cooking and cleaning with the dictum that it was "unseemly" for a woman not married to him to enter his house for any reason whatsoever unless she was also accompanied by her husband, in which case it was the woman's role to sit quietly when not actually waiting on the men.

For his part, Spud had welcomed the discovery that

acceptance into the group didn't also entail the sharing of his wife with other men. He had been concerned that Robert Benkovic might be another David Koresh, and had even made contingency plans to get himself and Hank out of the compound should that be discovered to be the case.

Nothing either of them had observed led them to believe, however, that this group of people were anything other than extremists. In fact, they'd been more convinced of the extremist nature of the group the more they listened to Benkovic's sermons and attended the Bible study groups, which Hank had begun to call "the indoctrination sessions". The lessons seemed more to serve the purpose of using biblical passages to support various prejudices than try to cast any clarity on what the Bible, overall, had to say.

Spud had made a trip the day before to Logan's sole hardware store to pick up the crosscut saws he'd ordered while making an additional drop of information to the team in exchange for two slices of cooked bacon. For his trouble, he had endured an icy glare from Hank when he admitted he'd eaten both slices himself once he'd returned home.

On this day, he stood outside with his neighbor, Ralph, and pointed up the hill behind his house at the diseased tree Hank had noticed when they first arrived. "That's the one," he told Ralph. "We could cut lumber from it or split it for firewood, though I think using it for firewood would be a waste. It's got a fine big trunk."

"A white pine. I agree: it would be a waste to burn it, though the slash would make good kindling once it's seasoned. You intend to take it down with that?" Ralph asked, noting the six-foot two-man crosscut saw Spud balanced on top of his foot while draping his wrist over the other end.

"A man needs his exercise," Spud said, reflecting that

wasn't such a bad observation, given he currently didn't have a nicely-appointed gym to work out in as he usually would do in Nebraska.

Ralph patted his stomach. "Kathy feeds me well enough. I guess the exercise won't hurt me either."

The two men made their way up the hill, Spud carrying the saw over one shoulder and an axe in the other, Ralph with a sledge and a couple of wedges. Spud was interested in seeing if his research on cutting trees would work as well in practice as in theory.

Standing on the uphill side of the tree, Spud took a look around to determine the best place for the tree to land. Having made his decision, he and Ralph started a cut on the downhill side of the tree with the two-man saw. Using the handle of the saw as a gauge, he determined that they had cut properly for the tree to fall there he wanted it to.

Now for the axe, he thought. *Let's hope I don't cut off my leg.* Swinging it, he began to cut down to the horizontal cut he and Ralph had made with the saw. They spelled each other until he felt the wedge-shaped cut was adequate, then used the handle of the axe as a gauge, wedging it into the cut and sighting along it.

"Still looks good," he announced to Ralph. Noticing Hank standing on the back porch, he added, "It looks like Katie has lunch ready for us."

The two men left the tools up next to the tree and came down, pulling off their boots and sitting at the kitchen table. Hank dished up a hot soup and sandwiches for the men, along with hot herb tea and turnovers. Then she retreated to let the men eat in peace, as a good Shining City wife was expected to do, knowing that once they ventured back up the hill to complete the cutting of the tree she could feed herself.

Making her way to the living room, she sat at an old treadle sewing machine and worked at sewing an apron. She'd suggested picking the machine up when she and Spud had been cruising garage sales, considering that if the Shining City compound really was into survivalism it would be an appropriate thing for another survivalist to own. The other women seemed impressed that she had one and even knew how to use it, and occasionally one would come to visit to make some small item or repair a piece of clothing. For her part, Hank found it gave her time to evaluate what she was seeing inside the compound.

I'm not quite sure what Gavin is finding so threatening about these people, she thought as she worked on the apron and the men continued to eat and talk in the kitchen. *It's true they have some radical beliefs and ones I don't like. Their attitude toward anyone not white and male is disgusting. Their belief that the world as we know it is about to end is whacky, and their belief that they are God's chosen to repopulate it is whackier still. But how does that hurt anyone?* She turned the apron to continue putting a decorative edge on the body of it, then commenced rocking her foot again to stitch a new seam. *Yes, they have guns. But so far, all I've seen is some target practice and the occasional animal brought back into the compound. It seems like each household just has enough guns for each of the family members. Sheesh—if Gavin saw my collection, he'd go apoplectic!*

Hank suddenly listened closer to what the men in the kitchen were discussing.

"We don't know who he is," Ralph was saying. "He's come up to the gate a couple of times and just sat there for a while. Then he turns around and leaves."

"Maybe he would like to join us," Spud remarked.

"Then why not ask the men at the gate? He never has. Just sits in his Jeep and looks at them."

Hank began to frown. In a whisper, she told Spud over the comm link, "Ask him what this man looks like."

Hearing Ralph describe the man's appearance, Hank hissed, "That's Gavin. What the hell does he think he's doing?"

Spud placatingly told Ralph, "Perhaps he's just curious. I notice this area gets a lot of people in hunting and driving ATVs up and down the trails. At any rate, this isn't getting that tree up there cut. Let's go get it down while we still have decent weather to do it. Never know when we're going to get more snow."

Hank waited until the two men had left the house, then called Voice over the comm link.

"Voice, get in touch with Steve Katz and let's get some shit sliding downhill here. We've got a local agent who's been coming around to the gate into the compound, and he's not exactly being covert about it. News is getting around about him, and he's making the men in here nervous. Tell Katz to get the local office to call off their dog before he gets us killed."

EDGE SAT in the hotel room where the rest of the team had gathered, talking with Katz over the communications link Voice had established through Hal.

"Here's the problem, Steve," Edge explained. "We've got a team embedded with the Shining City group, as you know. They're living there in the compound and gathering intelligence on what's going on there. I can't emphasize this to you strongly enough: *our team looks just like any other Shining City members.* This guy Gavin is going out there and raising suspicions among those in the Shining City group, and it's endangering our team."

"The local office was informed that they weren't to initiate any action unless and until your team was extracted," Katz protested.

"Evidently, this guy doesn't realize this includes staying the hell away from the place," Edge said, his voice bordering on a shout.

Amigo tapped him on his arm. "Take it easy, big guy," he cautioned.

Edge turned and brusquely said, "We're talking about my best friend and his wife. I'll take it easy when I have assurances that this bozo has his ass sitting in a chair somewhere in the local office and isn't out antagonizing these extremists while Spud and Hank are in there."

Everyone had noticed that Edge had devolved into some language he didn't ordinarily use in a rare display of anxiety.

"Tell Katz that," Amigo said.

"Here's the deal, Steve," Edge said, deciding Amigo's suggestion was a good one. "We know that people from Shining City occasionally go into either Logan or Charleston for things they need. Our embedded man has done it himself; it's how we're getting the team's intel reports. We need this local agent to be assigned to a desk until they come back out, and we need all the other local agents to understand that *no one* is to go near that camp. Stick to their local duties, but stay away from Shining City. Can you do that for us?"

"I'll get right on it," Katz said.

"We appreciate that, Steve—we really do."

When the voice communication was severed with Katz, Edge looked around at the rest of the team.

"That's all we need," Amigo remarked. "With mi

compadre in that place, the last thing I wanted to hear about was that the local office has a cowboy in its posse."

A CRASH and the sound of branches snapping startled Hank as she finished up drying and putting away the noontime dishes. Looking out the kitchen window, she noticed the diseased pine was now on the ground and had even landed right where Spud had wanted it to go. *Not bad for a first effort,* she thought, smiling. The men evidently also thought so, as they were congratulating each other with a high five.

Seeing them gather up the tools and start heading down the hill, she set out freshly baked cookies and hot spiced cider for them, then retreated back to her sewing. Hearing the back door open and the men stomp their shoes on the floor while still engaged in animated talk, she just had to smile.

"And look here," Spud said. "My darling wife has made us something to revive ourselves with."

"You have a good woman there," Ralph agreed.

If you knew what I was planning ... Hank thought with a grin.

"We're going to need to get Pastor Benkovic to make us a bit of explosive," Ralph said as they revived themselves with cookies and cider.

"Explosive?" For what?" Spud asked.

"To blow the stump," Ralph said. "He knows how to make it and has all the supplies. Whenever we need to get rid of a stump, he makes up some so we can blow it."

So, Benkovic is the go-to guy for things that go boom. "Is this wise?" Spud asked. "I've heard rumors that a man comes and sits by the gate. What if he's an agent of the ZOG?

Making explosives is illegal according to ZOG law. What if he hears an explosion? He could bring the ZOG down on us!"

Ralph turned to him. "There's truth in what you say. I wonder why Pastor Benkovic doesn't see that this may be poking the sleeping tiger?"

"The ZOG tiger never sleeps," Spud said. "It's prepared to strike at the least provocation." *Probably true in Gavin's case.*

"Then how do we get rid of the stump?" Ralph asked.

"We get a winch and pulley system set up," Spud said, recalling what Hank had shown him when he asked questions about pulling stumps. "It's safer and just as effective as using explosives, and we conserve the wood."

"A good plan," Ralph agreed.

After the men had finished congratulating each other on a job well done and Ralph had made his way back next door, Spud came into the living room and gathered Hank up, sitting her down on the couch with him. Giving a point toward the door, she said, "I didn't quite know what to do with the med kit you had Doc Rich make up."

"I guess it can stay right there," Spud said. "I'm just concerned that Joe and Ellen aren't quite as prepared as they think they are, so having it where it can be grabbed in a hurry is probably best."

Hank grinned. "That was some job you and Ralph did getting that tree cut down."

"You think so?"

"Sure. But just so you know: now you've got to top it, limb it, get all the wood from those cut up and stacked, and take what's left over and make a slash pile with it."

"You're a spoil sport."

She stood up and leaned to kiss him. "And you're my

lumberjack." Pulling her tablet from where she'd wedged it next to the arm of the couch, she set it in front of him and commanded Hal to play a video she'd selected.

Spud sat watching it in amazement. It was an old Monty Python skit, and when it got to the refrain, Hank began to dance around and point at him while actors dressed up as Canadian Mounties sang, "He's a lumberjack, and he's OK ..."

He laughed as he leapt up and grabbed her, stilling her dance. "You will never catch me in high heels and a bra," he said.

Back at the hotel, the team listening in was laughing uproariously.

"There will be no discussing Doc Andy while on this mission," Hank cautioned.

"He's gay, Hank. I don't think he's a transvestite. I don't think I could ever do this with him." He passed a hand up her dress.

"You know, I think that's why Neandertal men like women in dresses," Hank commented.

The rest of the team was now beginning to wonder just what was going on. They would only be able to engage in some conjecture, as Spud quickly said, "Hal, hide Spud," and Hank followed with, "Hal, hide Hank."

"So much for mission first," Crow said, eliciting chuckles from the rest.

"You need to consider, Love, that women can run faster with their skirts up than men with their pants down," Spud said, caressing her naked thigh under her skirt.

"Did cutting that wood up on the hill get you with a bit of wood of your own?" Hank asked.

"As long as you don't cut it down ..."

"We don't have a saw big enough for that," Hank said.

"But if you come with me to the bedroom, I have another way to take care of it."

AFTER MAKING LOVE, showering, and getting back dressed, Hank went out to the kitchen with Spud on her heels to prepare their dinner prior to Spud heading off to the men's Bible study.

"This is one thing I hate," Spud said. "I can't simply skip this thing tonight and spend the rest of the evening cuddled with my wife."

"You could have told them in the morning that you were sick."

"Sick of listening to racist and anti-government diatribe being justified with Bible verses taken out of context," Spud grumbled.

"Then you wouldn't be lying when you told them you were sick," Hank concluded.

"What is this you're feeding me tonight?" he asked, examining what was on his plate. Thus far, he'd been exposed to a number of things he thought he'd never see again unless the team was engaged in another survival exercise.

"Not quite sure," Hank said. "It was in the home-canned goods, and it wasn't labelled."

Oh, this is trouble ... Mystery meat for dinner, and whoever canned it didn't want anyone to know what it is.

Hank skewered a piece on her fork and sniffed it, then popped it into her mouth. Chewing on it thoughtfully, she said, "Tastes like chicken."

"Isn't that what they always say when you're getting fed

something like rat or rattlesnake?" Spud asked, sniffing it himself.

"I'm pretty sure it's chicken. A little tougher than the usual, but I'm still betting it's chicken. Maybe rooster. I understand rooster can be a bit tough, which would explain why it was canned. There's another jar of it down there in the cellar. Maybe I can make a pot pie with it."

"Yes, but what kind of pot pie will it actually be? Chicken pot pie? Or maybe turtle pot pie," Spud said. "There are definitely things I miss about Nebraska."

The team members listening in weren't envious of Spud's situation as they sat eating Chinese takeout.

"Well, I'm off," Spud said as he finished up eating. "Do you have anything planned for the evening?"

"I was going to take the potatoes I got harvested today and see if any of the households could use some," Hank said.

"Bundle up and take an umbrella," Spud advised. "It's a good thing Ralph and I got that tree down while we could. The rain moved in pretty fast."

"Don't worry. I'm in no mood for hypothermia. At least not while I don't have a good source of skin-to-skin warmth to get me out of it immediately available."

With Spud departed, Hank washed the dishes and got them dried and put away, then cleaned up the kitchen. Wrapping her hair in a tichel and her body in a thick, warm shawl, she headed out with her wicker basket of potatoes held in one hand and balanced on her hip, her other hand holding a large umbrella. *Just what a former desert dweller needs: cold and wet.*

She made her rounds, starting first at the Coffin's house next to theirs, chatting for a brief moment with Kathy, then moving on around the oval group of houses until she came to the Frisch's house. Knocking on the back door, she at first got no answer. *That's odd. Ellen should be home.* She knocked again. To her surprise, Joe answered. She immediately lowered her head. *What do I do now? I'm not supposed to be alone with him, nor can I speak without Spud's permission.*

Catching a glance from the corner of her eye, she could see that something wasn't right. Joe looked frazzled, tired, and his face bordered on panic.

"Sister Banyon," he gasped out. "Sister, is your husband with you? I may have need of him."

From within the house, Hank heard a weak cry of pain from Helen. "What's wrong, brother?" she asked.

"Ellen. Ellen has been in labor for the better part of the past twenty-four hours, but the baby isn't coming. I think something might be wrong," Joe said, his voice begging.

Hank's eyes went wide. *Twenty-four hours, and no baby yet?* Dropping the umbrella and her basket of potatoes, she turned and ran for the assembly building as potatoes scattered on the ground under her feet.

"Spencer! Spencer!" she screamed out as she neared the building. Bursting through the door, she ran in to where the men were assembled for their Bible study. Benkovic looked up at her and adopted a disapproving look as the rest of the men turned in her direction. She immediately lowered her face, her sodden hair dripping water onto the floor.

"What is it, wife?" Spud asked, knowing Hank would never have interrupted the men's Bible study unless it was something urgent.

"Ellen. Ellen Frisch. She's in labor. Has been for nearly an entire day, but Joe ... Brother Frisch says the baby isn't coming."

Spud dropped his Bible on his chair and ran out the

door, Hank following him. "I'm going to get the med kit. You go back to the Frisches' house. I'll meet up with you there."

Hank clamored back up the hill to the Frisches' house while Spud ran full tilt for their own. She went into the house without bothering to knock, and made her way into the bedroom. Ellen Frisch was lying on her side with Joe grasping her hand and telling her, "It's alright—Katie went to get her husband. He'll be right here." When he looked up at Hank, his face held none of the assurances he was trying to give his wife.

Spud noticed that other members of the community were heading in the direction of the Frisch house as he ran in that direction himself, the med kit he'd asked Doc Rich to make up in his hand. As he rushed to the house, he called over the comm link: "Medical 2, I need you. There's an emergency in the compound."

"Is it what I think it is?" Doc Rich returned. "Is the pregnant woman having a difficult labor?"

"Patient is in her mid-twenties. This is her first pregnancy. Approximately twenty-four hours into labor with labor not progressing."

Spud rushed into the house and made his way to where Ellen Frisch was still lying in the bed on her side, her anxious husband looking up at him, his face pleading. Hank likewise looked at him, her face similarly etched with concern.

"We need to find out how far along she is and what the position of the baby is," Doc Rich said. "Feel her uterus and tell me what you feel."

"Brother," Spud began to Joe, "I will need to touch your wife in ways another man should not touch her unless it's this sort of circumstance. Do you understand?"

"Do what you need to do," Joe said, his eyes filling with tears.

Spud felt Ellen's pregnant belly. To his relief, he could tell the baby was head down, but to his dismay, not facing as it should be.

"The baby is sunny side up," he relayed to Doc Rich Joe believing Spud was addressing him.

"OK. Do you know how to examine her cervix to see how effaced and dilated she is?"

Oh, boy. "I'll need to examine inside her," he told Joe.

"Do it. Do whatever she needs you to do," Joe replied frantically.

Hank stroked Ellen's forehead, noticing that there now seemed to be a small gathering at the bedroom door. "Relax, Ellen," she said soothingly, then quietly told Joe to get up and close the door. The last thing Ellen and Joe needed at this point was an audience.

In spite of his feeling uncomfortable with what he needed to do, Spud followed Doc Rich's directions, inserting his hand into Ellen's vagina and feeling her cervix.

"She's at seven centimeters, seventy percent effaced, and minus three," Spud told her.

"There's a chance we can turn this baby," Doc Rich said. "Here's what I want you to do: get her on her hands and knees, then have Hank lift up on the baby's bottom while you try to turn the baby's shoulders."

"She's exhausted," Spud said.

"Get pillows, rolled up blankets, whatever then, for her to rest her upper body on."

"Give me a hand, Katie," Spud said. The two of them turned Ellen so that she was on her hands and knees, then propped her up with pillows. Directing Hank to lift the baby, Spud tried to get the baby to turn between contractions as Joe directed Ellen to relax and breathe.

Spud stopped at one point and listened to the baby's heartbeat, relaying to Doc Rich that the baby still had strong heart sounds and a normal heart rate. Then he continued to try and get the baby to turn, having Ellen rock back and forth between contractions.

Hank suddenly looked up at Spud. "Something just happened."

Spud looked back at her and smiled. "The baby just turned to face toward Ellen's spine. That's just what's needed."

In the hotel room, the team watched as Doc Rich pumped her fist. "Were you able to feel if her water has broken?" she asked Spud over the comm link.

"I didn't—" His comment was interrupted by a gush of fluid from Ellen's vagina. "That answers that question," he said. "Her water just broke."

"Now that the baby is in the cephalic presentation and her water has broken, I expect things will move rather quickly," Doc Rich said. Over the comm link, she could hear Ellen let out a cry as a strong contraction hit her. "Have her push with each contraction, then get her to relax and breathe in between. Let's get this baby born."

"Shouldn't she be on her back?" Joe asked anxiously.

"We're going to let her stay just like this," Spud told him. "It will be easier on her and the baby if she just stays in this position."

As the minutes went by, Spud would feel Ellen tense with each contraction, prompting him to gently exhort her to push while Joe and Hank encouraged her to relax once the contraction was over. Only about twenty minutes had passed when Spud tapped Joe and said, "I think you should be at this end of your wife, brother."

Joe came hesitatingly down to where he could see what was happening. "I see the baby's head!" he cried excitedly. "What a head of hair!"

"Push, Ellen," Spud said, then reported to Doc Rich, "Baby's head is crowning."

"A few more good pushes, and hopefully we hear the baby announce how cold it is outside the womb," Doc Rich returned, instinctively crossing her fingers.

Spud had Joe assist with the delivery of his child, but at first, the baby seemed relatively unresponsive. "Rub his back," Spud advised Joe, and as he did so, shortly the baby coughed and then cried, color flushing him.

"You have a little boy," Hank told Ellen, who was now shedding tears of joy. She turned over and watched as Spud took the baby and placed it on her stomach, Joe keeping a protective hand on the child as he continued to cry and squirm. Spud clamped the umbilical cord and tied it off, then offered a pair of surgical scissors to Joe. "The father is usually given the honor of cutting the cord," he said.

Once the cord was cut, the baby cleaned, diapered, and swaddled in a baby blanket, Joe took his child and presented him to Ellen. She beamed at the baby, speaking quietly to him, and then put him to her breast.

Hank watched the scene, feeling both happy for the Frisches and also experiencing a sense of longing. *Will I ever have a child?* she wondered.

Spud tapped her on her arm, and the two of them went to make a quiet departure. Opening the bedroom door, they were greeted by the sight of … Benkovic.

He stood in the doorframe, scowling at Hank. "Woman, where is your tichel?" he demanded.

Hank immediately hung her head.

"What is your explanation?" Spud asked her.

"I don't know, husband," she said. "I was wearing it when I first arrived at the house. It must have fallen from my head when I ran to get you."

"The entire community has been disturbed tonight," Benkovic said accusingly. "They are all standing here and outside on the porch. You shout and scream, you disrupt the Bible study, and you are in public without your tichel. What do you think your chastisement should be?" Benkovic demanded of her.

Hank looked over at Spud. They were both thinking the same thing. *Chastisement?*

In the hotel room, Edge had suddenly sat up straight at Benkovic's pronouncement. "Lord, no," he said.

"What, big guy?" Amigo asked.

"He wants to punish Hank, and we know what kind of punishment he likes to deal out. Everyone grab your gear. You, too, Doc Frank. I'll drive. Crow and Cloud, get into your gear while I head to the airport. The rest of us can gear up when we get in the helicopter. We're going into the compound. We need to get Hank and Spud out of there —*right now!*"

"Oh, this is gonna be a bitch," Crow grumbled as he grabbed his gear and ran for the SUV.

"Why? What's the problem?" Edge asked as they both hopped in for the ride to the airport along with the rest of the team members.

"It's night, and it's raining," Crow said. "When we go into hover, the rotor wash is going to kick up the spray. We'll be in whiteout conditions. And we've got to try and make sure the rope hits the ground before you guys do, or the static on the line is going to knock you cold."

"Helicopters are fun, they said. Try it, you'll like it, they said," Edge reflected. Then he added for Spud and Hank over the comm link, "Hang in there, guys—the cavalry is on the way. Stall 'em till we get there."

As Edge raced for the airport as fast as he dared on the wet and winding roads, Spud stood facing Benkovic, his eyes narrowing. "What do you intend to do?"

"She will be subject to the same punishment any man would deserve for her transgressions," Benkovic declared, making it clear he intended to whip Hank into compliance. He grabbed her by the wrist and turned to haul her with him.

"Get your hand off of my wife," Spud said sternly.

"What did you say?" Benkovic asked, indignant.

"I said, *get your hand off of my wife!*" Spud reiterated more forcefully.

Benkovic glared at him. As he did so, Spud heard Edge say over the comm link, "Husbands ought to love their own wives as their own bodies; he who loves his wife loves himself. For no one ever hated his own flesh, but nourishes and cherishes it, just as the Lord does the church. It's in Ephesians."

Spud was familiar with the passage, and had no problem repeating it for Benkovic. He then added, "I, being the one who has nourished Katie and cherished her am also the one responsible for how she has grown. If she has erred, then I am responsible for the error. Take your hand off my wife! If someone is to be whipped tonight, it will be me— not her."

Hank spun to face him, the horror erupting across her face as she vigorously shook her head no. Spud continued to glare at Benkovic. To put emphasis to his words, he stripped off his shirt and threw it on the floor, standing before the man bare-chested and causing Hank to break down and cry.

"Well?" Spud demanded. "Will you hold the one responsible to face the punishment or not?"

Benkovic released Hank and said in a voice both calm and chill, "Very well. Then face the punishment for her you will."

"He will not!" Joe Frisch spoke up from behind Spud. "If it had not been for him, my son would likely be dead, and my wife along with him. It was my refusal to consider that her labor might not go smoothly that led to all of this. Heathen or not, I should have made sure she was close to a hospital, where a properly-trained doctor could have seen this coming much sooner than I realized what was happening."

"This was no fault of yours, Brother Frisch," Benkovic said. "Brother Banyon is correct when he says he is responsible for his wife's transgressions." He went to leave, Spud taking steps to follow him.

"You are wrong," Frisch said. "A new commandment I give to you, that you love one another; as I have loved you, that you also love one another. By this all will know that you are My disciples, if you have love for one another. This Yeshua HaMashiach has said Himself, and placed it as the greatest commandment. Who, then, are Yeshua's disciples? What Sister Banyon did, she did out of love for my wife. What she did perhaps saved Ellen's life, and certainly saved my son's life. She did it without regard to any other rule we may have and at her own peril. What Brother Banyon claims, he claims because of love for his wife, and so he, too, acts according to Yeshua's greatest commandment. So what I do, I do out of love for Brother Banyon, to spare him a punishment that he would take for the love of his wife, and which I take for the love of the man who put my living son in my arms when I was certain my child was dead in Ellen's womb. Given you feel so *certain* that a punishment should be handed out for Yahweh's goodness in bringing a new life into this community—a life that I and Ellen created, then *I* will take the punishment and take it with a grateful heart. Because had Yahweh not drawn Brother Banyon to be here among us, instead of holding my son in her arms and planning a full life for him, Ellen would be grieving, and I would be building my son a coffin." Frisch stripped off his own shirt and stood defiantly before Benkovic.

Hearing the men make their arguments before the pastor and seeing them both standing naked from the waist up, the rest of the people gathered at the house erupted in chaos, shouting defiantly and jostling Benkovic on every side. As they did so, Spud and Hank heard in their earpieces, "Cavalry's here." Over the din of the shouting Shining City members, 100UN could be heard arriving over the western edge of the hollow formed by the former coal mine.

Everyone suddenly stopped, then screamed when they saw the searchlight hanging below the nose of the helicopter illuminate the ground. *"The ZOG! The agents of the ZOG are here!"* was the universal cry as the people in the compound started to scatter.

"*You* have brought the ZOG upon us!" Benkovic spat, pointing a finger at Spud.

"Not I, *you!*" Spud declared, pointing his finger at Benkovic in return and causing the fleeing people to stop in their tracks. "It was your failure to live by Yeshua's great commandment that caused Yahweh to bring down a punishment of his own!"

"Go get your weapons!" Benkovic screamed at the crowd. "Shoot the helicopter down!"

"Do that, and you will cause every person in this place to be killed," Spud declared, once again getting people to stop. "This is Yahweh's will, that *this* man and *this man alone* be taken by the agents of the ZOG to face the punishment that Yahweh Himself has decreed. They have not come for *any of you*—only Benkovic. Because if there is any apostate that has ever lived in this place, it's the one who set himself up as a god over you."

As Spud addressed the crowd, Hank watched the swirl of mist form under 100UN, then saw the three men of the team emerge from within it and race up the hill dressed in their SWAT gear and with their tactical rifles at the ready. Arriving at the back of the crowd, they calmly walked forward, the people parting on either side. Though their faces remained full of fear, none of the Shining City people made a move to hinder the progress being made by Edge in the lead, followed by Amigo and Voice.

"We're here for Robert Benkovic," Edge announced in his deep voice.

More people parted, leaving Benkovic standing facing Edge and his teammates. Edge walked up to him, seeming to dwarf the man, towering over him with his six-foot-six frame and two hundred and sixty pounds of muscle.

"Robert Benkovic?" Edge asked.

Benkovic puffed his chest and looked defiantly at Edge, nearly causing Edge to laugh when Edge considered how easy it would be to single-handedly bring Benkovic into compliance. *And it won't take a whip*, Edge thought.

"I am," Benkovic said, the tone of his voice sounding as if he believed the people in the compound would come to his rescue at any moment.

Edge pulled credentials from under his tactical vest. "Robert Benkovic, my name is Edgar Gearing. I'm a Special Agent with the Bureau of Alcohol, Tobacco, and Firearms." Folding his credentials holder, Edge continued with, "Mr. Benkovic, you are under arrest for the illegal manufacture of explosives and false imprisonment. You may also be held for malicious assault, which is a felony charge under the laws of the State of West Virginia. Authorities in West Virginia will be informed of the evidence against you on that charge." He took out a small card from his credentials folder and began to read it aloud. "You have the right to remain silent. Anything you say can and will be used against you in a court of law. You have the right to an attorney. If you cannot afford an attorney, one will be provided for you. Do you understand the rights I have just read to you?"

"I don't recognize the ZOG's laws—only Yahweh's laws," Benkovic declared haughtily.

Edge cut him a steel-edged look as sharp as the knife he wore in a scabbard on his belt. "I didn't ask if you abided by the laws of the State of West Virginia nor those of the federal government," he said coolly. "I asked if you understood your rights."

"I understand them," Benkovic conceded.

"Understanding them, are you willing to talk to me?"

"You have no evidence," Benkovic declared. "Your arrest is based on falsehood and lies."

"Do you think *I* will lie?" Katherine Coffin asked him, walking up to look him in the eye.

*What is **this**?* Hank thought.

"Don't make yourself an apostate, woman," Benkovic cautioned, glaring at her. "*Again.*"

"Maybe you can explain," Ralph Coffin began, "why you

declared her an apostate and put the whip to her when she, too, did what she did out of love for a neighbor."

Hank gasped and placed her hand over her mouth. She had no idea that Kathy Coffin had been whipped. "What did you do?" Hank practically whispered to her neighbor.

"Once, when Ralph was sick enough to be bedridden, I took some hot soup and bread to one of the single men who was also sick. The flu, I believe, for both of them. Because Ralph was sick, I entered the man's house without my husband with me."

You've got to be kidding me! Hank thought. *This deserves being whipped?*

"You brought this upon yourself," Spud informed Benkovic. "By subjecting people to scourging, and specifically thirty-nine stripes, you believed it was your place to recreate Yeshua's agony. This was reserved for Yeshua, because He was pure and thus an unstained lamb to be given as a sacrifice to atone for the sins of the likes of us. This isn't appropriate to return someone to true faith as if the penitent should be equal to Yeshua. Yeshua dictated instead that any who would not accept His truth be left to their own devices, and you should shake the dust from your sandals as you cast them out to face Yahweh's wrath." He turned to the gathered people. "This is the reason Yahweh has given Benkovic over to the authority of the ZOG."

Some of the gathered people simply stood silently. Others nodded their agreement as Edge patted Benkovic down, carefully feeling for any hidden escape tools like those Hank had used in their recent training exercise, then placed him in handcuffs to be taken by helicopter to Charleston, where he would be turned over to ATF agents at the airport. Edge gave Hank and Spud a look, and noting them both do a subtle shake 'no' of their head, walked

Benkovic down to where Crow and Cloud had landed, Voice and Amigo walking behind him.

As the people watched the helicopter take off, Ralph Coffin turned to Spud and said, "We no longer have a pastor."

"I'm sure there's one here who can take the role upon himself," Spud said.

"I believe I know him," Ralph said. "Will you, Brother Banyon? I haven't ever heard you utter an untruth, and believe you will be a fit man to shepherd this flock."

Spud looked at him, his Secret Service face engraved in place.

"Not I," he finally said. "But, I believe I know of someone who is good for the job."

20

Hank folded the clothing she and Spud had purchased at garage sales and placed it back into plastic bags as Zena Howell passed her items from the closets and dresser. While the women packed the lighter household goods she and Spud had brought in, the men packed the trailer with the furniture. Hank had insisted that a few things be left behind for the Howells, including the treadle sewing machine for Zena and the crosscut saws for the community's use. She also left a mattress to replace the one on the Frisches' bed after Ellen had given birth in it.

She had felt conflicted when visiting the Frisches during their last days in the compound. Holding their son and seeing his wide-eyed look as he took in the woman he already recognized wasn't his mother, she couldn't help but wonder once again if she and Spud would ever have children. The Frisches had wanted to name the child after Spud and call him "Spencer," but Spud insisted they call him "Jesse" instead, given the name in Hebrew means "a blessing".

When everything was finally loaded, Hank gave Zena a hug, followed by a hug for both Larry Junior and Lois while Spud shook Larry Senior's hand. "Take good care of the people, Pastor Howell," Spud said.

"May Yahweh watch over you on your travels," Larry returned.

Climbing into the Tacoma with the trailer hitched behind it, Spud and Hank gave the Howells and the other gathered community members a wave goodbye and headed out with Spud behind the wheel.

"You're not going to get stuck," Hank admonished him, knowing what he was thinking as the truck began to move on the still rain-slick dirt road. "Just take it nice and easy and everything will be fine."

Spud didn't feel like everything would be fine, however —and his white knuckles showed it. So, once they were away from Sharples, Hank had him stop on the pavement, and getting out, swapped places with him. Turning and giving him a smirk, she got the truck back in gear and soon had them traveling down the road at a bit quicker pace, pulling the tichel from her head as well and tossing it into the back seat.

The rest of the mission contingent had relocated from Logan to Charleston, and Spud had coordinated to have them meet up at a particular address in the city. As Hank arrived with the truck and trailer, she put on a Santa hat, took a bow and stuck it on the hood, then ran up to the front of the house and dropped the keys off with an envelope in the mailbox affixed next to the door, letting the lid drop with a *clank!*

As she made her way at a fast stride to the government SUV that waited for her at the curb, Spud held the door for her. Just as the man of the house opened his front door, he could see her jump into the SUV, Spud sliding in behind her.

Opening his mailbox, the man took out the truck keys, staring at them and then to the curb where he could see the bright red bow fixed to the top of the hood. As the SUV drove off, he tore open the envelope. In it, he found a note along with a vehicle title, the name 'Katie Hank' filled in for the seller and with the buyer field left to be filled in.

Unfolding the note, he read, *Thanks for the lease of your truck. We've returned it undamaged, but with a few more miles on the odometer. It has a nearly full tank of gas. The trailer and contents are also yours to keep. Perhaps you can sell everything on Craigslist; it's all used but in good shape, so you should get a good price for it. Merry Christmas! Katie Hank and Spencer Banyon.*

He walked down and ran his hand over the hood. "Well, I'll be," he muttered. "They gave me my little beast back. And selling all this stuff might give me enough money to keep the mortgage paid on the house until I find out whether I got the job I applied for with UPS." Tears welled in his eyes. "Merry Christmas, you two," he spoke in the direction where the SUV was disappearing around a corner in the distance, then turned to go back into the house to tell his wife and kids what had just happened.

Crow drove the SUV with the team members out to the Yeager Airport just east of the city of Charleston. Being admitted to the ramp when he showed his credentials, he drove the SUV up next to where 100UN stood. With the usual bucket brigade to load the aircraft with gear, followed by the boarding of personnel, he returned the SUV to where it could be picked up by an agent in the local ATF office and boarded the helicopter himself, joining Cloud in getting the helicopter started and ready for flight. Gaining their IFR clearance, Crow lifted off while Cloud announced to the personnel in the back that their flight time would be approximately five and a half hours to York, Nebraska with a fuel stop in Springfield, Illinois.

As they flew westward, Edge noticed that Hank had a couple of items in her lap. "Whatcha got there, Hank?"

Hank looked into her lap and smiled weakly. "Oh ... a couple of souvenirs from the mission."

Edge waited for her to explain. Lifting up a long scarf, she said, "This is my tichel. The headwrap I was required to wear while embedded."

"That the same one that fell off your head right before all hell broke loose?" he asked.

"One and the same," Hank said.

"What's the other thing?"

She held it up. "A new frilly apron," she said. "I thought you might like it."

The other people in the helicopter snickered at that.

"You bought another apron?" Edge asked.

"Nope. I made this one. With a treadle sewing machine. I left the machine with Zena Howell. I thought she could use it."

"I think I'll let Rose stick with wearing the aprons from now on," Edge said. "Sorry to disappoint you."

"Well, I actually did think I'd like to keep it," Hank said.

"What about you, Spud? Did you keep something from the mission?"

"Yeah," Spud said, giving no further explanation.

"Well? What did you keep?" Edge badgered him.

"Not telling."

Hank grinned. "He kept his flannel shirt. Because he's a lumberjack."

The entire group aboard the helicopter roared with laughter.

"You would tell them," Spud complained as everyone else broke out with, "He's a lumberjack and he's OK..."

"He may work all day, but he doesn't exactly sleep all night," Hank revealed, getting them laughing even harder.

Zena Howell refolded and placed clothing back neatly in the drawers of the dresser while Larry Senior got a look at the weather stripping Spud had installed on the doors and windows. When she went to put a pair of folded jeans in the bottom drawer, she noticed the wooden plaque that Hank had left there. She gathered it up, remembering the first day that Larry had tacked it up on the outside of the house by the front door after she had handed it to him. Reflecting that she had never imagined even being back in the house that her husband had so lovingly built, never mind him being accepted as the new head of not just this Shining City community but all of them, she hugged it to her chest.

Putting it atop the dresser, she went to put the jeans in the drawer, noticing for the first time the note that had been hidden underneath it. She took it up and unfolded it, reading it and getting wide-eyed.

Larry walked into the bedroom and stood with his hands on his hips. "Brother Banyon did a good job of weather stripping. The house should stay much warmer. I guess the next thing to do will be to get the tree he and Ralph felled turned into lumber and firewood."

"Read this," Zena said, handing him the note.

Larry took the note from her and looked at it.

Pastor Howell, be cautious. I know you will pray and do what is best to protect the community. Be aware, though, that the agents of the ZOG know where you are, and will be watching constantly. Don't give them any excuse to come here.

"It isn't signed," Larry said.

"Of course not," Zena replied. "Do you believe that it would be wise for the Shining City people who pretend to be ZOG agents to sign a note like this one?"

Larry looked around at the house he had made, sadness filling his heart. "There's only one thing to do," he concluded.

OLIVER GAVIN DROVE out in his Jeep to Sharples. Arriving at the gate to the Shining City compound, he found it sitting open and unattended. Driving inside, he looked around warily. He hadn't agreed with Hank and Spud's report that stated the Shining City community posed no threat now that Robert Benkovic had been taken into custody. He was intent on determining that for himself.

When he came into the opening that was once a coal pit, he noticed something right away: it was eerily quiet. No signs revealed that anyone was there. No vehicles, no people, no children at play—nothing. Going up to one of the houses, he found the door unlocked and went inside. It was stripped bare. Even the basement was empty. The only house that stood intact with its contents was the one they had surrounded with crime scene tape while the local office recovered Robert Benkovic's guns, ammunition, and bomb-making materials.

"Sonuvabitch," he cursed. "They're all gone—lock, stock, and barrel." He was not looking forward to reporting this to Howard back in the Charleston Field Office.

Larry Howell drove into a rest area, the caravan of trucks and trailers pulling in behind him. As he got out and gathered with the other drivers, he said, "It won't be long before we arrive. I've been assured by our brothers who found and obtained this property for us that it shouldn't take a lot of effort to clear it of the trees that weren't hauled away when it was harvested for timber. We can have one detail cut the downed wood for firewood, and another work at reclaiming any timber that can be used for building. The town is much larger than Sharples is; about six hundred people, most of whom are white. In spite of there being some mud people among them, I believe we'll find many whose beliefs are aligned with ours and who will join our number, especially since the town is in Mississippi. The main thing we need be mindful of is to simply remain apart and not draw the attention of the ZOG, and thus assure ourselves as the remnant that Yahweh will once again show his blessings upon us."

"The guys say you've changed," Spud remarked as he and Hank made their way back to their home in the Mole Hole beneath the Hamilton Organics main farm complex.

"I don't think anyone could live through an experience like the one we've just lived through and not be changed," Hank said.

"I think it shocked them when you cussed, though. They haven't heard much of that kind of language from you during the time you were embedded."

"It would have seriously blown our cover."

"So ... what are we going to do with this three-day crash period we have?"

"Doc Andy already got the debrief," Hank said. She shrugged. "Maybe I'll start a new book."

"Will it be one of those racy crotch warmers?" Spud asked.

"What is it with you and erotica?"

"It doesn't much strike me one way or another," Spud said. "It's just that we have three days when we won't even be expected to show up for meals."

Hank chuckled. "I might just want to see you in your white tie tux."

"I might just want to see you in your red dress," Spud countered.

Hank's eyes lit up. "Hold that thought," she said, getting up from the love seat. "Stay there—I'll be right back."

Spud stayed seated on the loveseat while Hank went off to the bedroom. It didn't take long for his curiosity about how she would arrive back to be satisfied. Seeing her swaying her hips while walking back to him clad in the long, blue, sequined and jeweled gown that Mike had made for her before they left for Pennsylvania, he experienced an undeniable and obvious physiological reaction.

"You need your flannel shirt?" Hank asked. "Because it looks like you've got some wood to take care of there."

"Just as long as you realize we left the six-foot, two-man crosscut saw with Larry," Spud said. "The flannel shirt probably won't help this lumberjack get that wood taken care of. But I understand you might have a method?"

He reached up and yanked the curtains closed that faced the front of the house in the reading nook while intoning, "Hal, hide Spud—*quick!*" Then he unzipped his pants and reached for Hank.

"I've heard a woman runs faster with her skirt up than a man with his pants down," Hank recalled as he slid his pants down his thighs. She grinned at him and backed off, hiking the dress up and making a dash for the bedroom.

"*You tease!*" Spud declared. Trying to stuff his engorged member back into his pants, he cursed, "Why the hell did I have to be so big?"

As he went to zip his pants back up, he heard her call out, "Don't be too hasty getting those pants zipped. The last thing we want is a frank and beans incident!"

Considering the truth of this statement, Spud opted instead to simply drop his pants on the floor.

"That solves *that* problem!" he said to himself as he dashed after her.

POSTSCRIPT

You are no doubt, especially after reading the Author's Note at the beginning of this novel, wondering why the entire Shining City group wasn't rounded up and arrested. To answer this, one need only take a look at the First Amendment to the United States Constitution. In it is both a guarantee for freedom of expression and a guarantee for freedom of religion.

The First Amendment has met many constitutional challenges and has stood firm. Perhaps one you may know about is the case against the Westboro Baptist Church for their disruptive displays associated with the funerals of service members. Yes, this went all the way to the Supreme Court of the United States who found *for* —let me repeat— *FOR* Westboro Baptist Church. Why? Because they had broken no laws, including trespass, and their actions were protected speech under the First Amendment.

In a day and age when many take offense at all kinds of things, we must remember two things: as far as the law is concerned, it's just a disagreement until your fist hits my face. Then it's assault and battery. The old retort of "sticks and stones may break my bones, but names will never hurt me" needs to be kept in mind, with the exception of something patently false and damaging of a person's reputation, whether spoken (slander) or in print (libel).

And thus, it is that only Robert Benkovic was arrested, and not any of the others. Only he took actions that were unlawful. The others, whether you may find their portrayed beliefs reprehensible or not (and I tried to make them so to make this point), never let their fist touch anyone's face.

But keep in mind, also, that just because a person holds such beliefs doesn't mean *you* must—and you have every right to disagree and voice your disagreement (or not), also without your fist touching anyone's face, of course. It is both the glory and the pitfall of a free society that people are free to express all sorts of ideas spanning from one extreme to another, as long as they do so peacefully. Perhaps Spud's statements about the biblical admonition to simply leave the company of those who don't accept what we have to say while shaking the dust from our sandals is in order.

Find the next book in The Unit series, *Cold Justice* here on Amazon in both print and Kindle editions.

ANNE FOX
THE
UNIT
COLD JUSTICE

PLEASE LEAVE A REVIEW!

If you enjoyed this book, please leave a favorable review where you purchased it, and also at goodreads.com. It's reviews from readers like you that help others find the books they enjoy. Thank you!

Use this link to go directly to the review page for *Shining City*.

https://www.amazon.com/review/create-review?&asin=B08R2FJRWQ

ABOUT THE AUTHOR

Anne Fox spends her time traveling, writing, and spending time with her three cats in El Paso, Texas. An avid firearms enthusiast, instructor, and competitive marksman, as well as an FAA-certified commercial pilot, *The Unit* series marries her love for marksmanship and flying via an overly-active imagination to answer the question "What if?"

CONNECT WITH ANNE

Connect with Anne Fox at

https://www.facebook.com/Anne-Fox-Author-1119777951559223

Twitter: @AnneFox83514907

Goodreads: https://www.goodreads.com/author/show/18917324.Anne_Fox

Bookbub: https://www.bookbub.com/search/authors?search=Anne%20Fox

Instagram: https://www.instagram.com/annefoxauthor/

Interact with Anne Fox on Facebook on the Anne Fox – Author Group, and also find Anne on MeWe.

Made in the USA
Coppell, TX
06 April 2022

76099724R00208